*"Don't be afraid,"* he murmured, sending a rumbling thrill racing down her spine.

"I'm not," Abigail whispered, her voice throaty.

He seemed to consider that a long moment, never once loosing his hold on her, for which she was thankful.

Licking her lips, she realized that she stood on a precipice and all she longed to do was to jump. He couldn't see her face any more than she could see his. The anonymity gave her a boldness she didn't know she harbored. Still, she needed a little push. A small test of the waters, just to be sure.

With her heart racing, she licked her lips. She'd never done this, had never been so . . . wicked. Abigail shifted. . .

His sharp intake of breath caused a little thrill to shoot up her middle. His hips moved just barely, and his grip on her tightened.

"What . . . do you . . . want?"

With an audacity that belonged to the woman she was pretending to be, she lifted her chin and murmured, her voice a husky purr, "You."

# SARI ROBINS

# The Governess Wears Scarlet

**AVON**

*An Imprint of HarperCollinsPublishers*

AVON BOOKS
*An Imprint of* HarperCollins*Publishers*
10 East 53rd Street
New York, New York 10022-5299

Copyright © 2008 by Sari Earl
ISBN: 978-0-06-078249-8
www.avonromance.com

First Avon Books paperback printing: February 2008

*For Amy*

# Acknowledgments

**I** am grateful to my husband and children, who make every day more meaningful and more beautiful for me. They give me so much encouragement and joy.

Thank you to all my family and friends, especially my mother, who continue to enthusiastically champion my efforts. Thank you to Susan Grimshaw, Frances Drouin, Dorothy Rece, Bill Eubanks, Laura Goeller, Vladimira Vojta, Willa Cline, Barb at RF Designs, Nancy Yost, Deb Brink, Becky Rose, Jan Epstein, Marilyn and Normie Blumenthal, Esther Levine, and Martha Jo Katz. Special thanks to Jennifer Linowes and Jennifer Hartz.

My gratitude to the incomparable Avon Books team! Thank you to Pam, Buzzy, and Adrienne!!! Tom, Gail, and Patricia—thanks for my gorgeous covers! I appreciate the awesome sales force—Brian, Donna, Judy, and the entire Merch Sales Team; Mike, Carla, and the whole Field Sales Team; International Sales; Foreign Rights/Sub Rights. Special thanks to Lyssa Keusch and May Chen—I adore working with you!

Thank you very much. Your support means the world to me.

# The
# Governess
# Wears
# Scarlet

# Chapter 1

*London, 1812*

The old restlessness was upon him again like a serpent uncoiled from sleep and ready to strike. It did not matter that he was a gentleman with influential friends and important connections. It was of no consequence that he had a shiny new title that he'd finally managed to secure after years of peddling himself like a whore with the rent overdue. Here he was once more, prowling the streets of London in search of the justice he so desperately longed to mete out.

He recognized that he was up to his old tricks again partly in response to the frustrations of his daily profession. Being one of the most powerful barristers in England should have been satisfying enough to quench his thirst for justice. But lately the wheels of justice seemed to turn torturously slow. Endless politics interfered; the administrative bureaucracy prolonged even the simplest of cases. And when he'd tried to speed things along, he'd run into even more hurdles . . .

Here on the streets, things were simpler. Right and wrong could be easily judged and justice meted out with striking efficiency. If thieves robbed a gentleman too deep in his cups, he could chase them down and "convince them" to return the booty. If a gang attacked a woman, he could intervene and stop the assault, making sure that the men saw the error of their ways. If knaves plotted to kill the Prince of Wales, he could track them to their lair, gather the evidence, and gain confessions, all without undue complications.

After that particular intervention, he couldn't tell whether the prince had been happier that the plot had been upset or that it had been thwarted without public notice. The Prince of Wales had very quickly and quietly granted him the title of viscount, making the night-prowling barrister into the first Viscount Steele.

In the swirling darkness of the fog-shrouded night, Steele barely withheld a snort. The irony was not lost on him. After years of striving to become the titled noble his dear Deidre had deserved him to be, he'd achieved his ambition through the vigilante work that he'd given up for her.

The image of Deidre's ethereal beauty rose up in his mind like a specter to haunt him. With her lovely dark curls, brown eyes, and milky white skin, she'd been the epitome of a refined English miss. *Too bloody refined for a rough-edged country bumpkin like me*. But, oh, how he'd loved her from the moment he'd laid eyes on her. He had thanked the gods a thousand times since for that rainy night when her carriage had been attacked by a highwayman. He had always relished being a Sentinel, one of the band of brothers that kept the country safe from outlaws, but until that night it had never felt like his destiny calling.

Yet the very occupation that had led him to Deidre was what he'd given up to claim her hand. And he'd surrender it all a thousand times again if he could have her back beside him.

The familiar grief constricted his chest like a vise. It had been eight years and nine months since her death, and to his utter shame, her features grew hazier with each passing year. The terrible sense of loss was still there, though.

Sighing, he welcomed the ache, knowing that he deserved it since he'd caused the end of her tragically short life. If he'd been the kind of man she'd deserved, they wouldn't have had to hide their love and meet secretly. If only he'd been the man he was today.

"The Viscount Steele." His voice was a rasping whisper even to his own ears. He looked about the empty street of Charing Cross, glad that no one was around to hear him exercise his new title.

This was not his first new identity. He wondered if it would be his last. As a testament of his love for Deidre, he'd changed his name, expunged his past, and cut himself off from his only family, the Sentinels, who had welcomed him as a brother. She hadn't asked him to do it, but she'd been delighted. She'd wanted—hell, had deserved—a better man than he'd been born to be. So he'd become another. For her. He'd become Mr. Dagwood, barrister. If only she'd been alive to see him rise to become Solicitor-General of England.

Now he was the Viscount Steele. He wondered what she'd say.

*A viscount doesn't walk the streets of the worst neighborhood in town, dear.* He could hear Deidre's honey-sweet voice.

As he adjusted the black scarf higher over his mouth to mask his features, he whispered to the darkness, "I'm no bloody viscount and you know it."

*Then who are you?* the shadows taunted.

He had no answer for them.

The moonlight barely bathed London's rooftops in an eerie gray glow as Miss Abigail West entered the alleyway to meet the woman who was supposed to have information about her wayward brother.

The fog was thick and the air damp enough to permeate her veil. She was thankful for the anonymity the widow's costume gave her, knowing that if anyone in society knew that she traveled the streets of London at night, she'd never secure a position, and she was in desperate need of a job. Moreover, no one could know that she was related to a fugitive from the law.

Despite those initial reasons for donning her widow's attire, she couldn't deny that pretending to be someone else gave her added courage. In Abigail's mind, widows seemed freer from the constraints of society and tended to have a confidence that she longed to possess.

Abigail's footsteps were muffled by the soft kid lining the bottom of her boots as she approached the woman the street urchin had assured her could be of help. She was a barmaid, the urchin had said, and knew many of the goings-on in this part of London.

The woman waited, as promised, outside the rear door to the tavern where she worked. She was about Abigail's age of three-and-twenty, with brown matted hair and pale pockmarked skin. She wore a blue shawl that she clutched before her.

"Willy sent ya?" the woman demanded, her voice harried.

Abigail nodded. "Yes. I have the money—"

"Not 'ere." Looking over her shoulder, the barmaid motioned for Abigail to follow her.

As they moved away from the rear of the tavern, male muted voices could be heard through the wooden door. Abigail followed the woman down the alley and around the corner into an even darker passageway. A sense of foreboding overcame Abigail, but she told herself that she had little choice; she had to find her brother. Still, she fingered the pistol in her pocket and clutched her walking stick tighter in her other hand.

The barmaid turned. "Show me the blunt."

Removing her hand from her pocket, Abigail held out the coin.

The barmaid reached for the money, but Abigail withdrew it. "First the information."

"The fella yer looking for has brown hair and gray-blue eyes?"

"Yes. His eyes are a unique color in that they're very light. He would be twenty years of age."

The barmaid nodded. "Light eyes. I remember 'im because of the scar."

"Scar?" Abigail's heart skipped a beat.

The barmaid motioned to her face. "Across 'is cheek. Now I want my money!"

The scrape of a boot heel drew Abigail's head up.

A shadowy figure separated from the wall, its movements purposefully heading toward her. "An' I want mine!" the man sneered.

Turning, Abigail pulled out her pistol and pointed it at the man.

Suddenly the barmaid slammed into Abigail's arm, knocking the weapon to the ground. "Get 'er, Fred!"

The man lunged, his meaty hands gripping Abigail's arms. Abigail desperately wrestled to break free. But the man was too big and too strong. He shoved her to the ground, pressing his foul-smelling body on top of hers.

"Get the money!" the barmaid shrieked.

"After I've 'ad my fill! I ain't never 'ad a *highbrow* before!"

Abigail kicked and struggled, reaching . . . reaching . . . Her walking stick was stuck partly beneath her thigh. The odors of gin and unwashed male overwhelmed.

"Yer gonna love it!" His foul breath made her stomach twist.

Her fingers clawed for her walking stick . . . grasping . . . reaching . . . Hard metal kissed her fingers, and she grabbed the hilt, pulled out the knife, and rammed it into the man's gut.

The brute howled in pain, rolling off her.

Panting, Abigail jumped to her feet, the knife clutched tightly in her grasp. The barmaid stepped forward, blocking the only escape.

"She cut me!" The brute stared down at his bloodied shirt.

"Stay back!" Abigail cried, holding up her weapon.

Rising to his feet, he growled, "I'll kill ya fer this!" He lunged.

Abigail spun away, her knife cutting air as the man swatted it aside, and it clattered to the ground. Abigail kicked him in the knee. He grunted and stumbled, reaching for her lost blade. She dodged around him, heading toward the mouth of the alley. But the barmaid tripped Abigail, and she tumbled forward on hands and knees. "Snotty bitch!"

Suddenly an unknown man in a whirling dark cloak raced into the alleyway. He knocked the barmaid off Abigail, and the woman crumpled to the ground.

The brute raced forward, wielding the knife. He lunged, but the nimble rescuer slipped out of reach before the man could make contact. The brute attacked, but the rescuer spun and danced, avoiding every blow as if it were anticipated and landing punches with each turn.

Slowly Abigail rose, hypnotized by the struggle. The rescuer was tall, and his features were purposefully concealed. He wore a dark head covering, like a hood, and a black scarf over the bottom half of his face. Only his eyes shone clearly, dark, yet blazing with intention.

The rescuer landed a glancing blow to the brute's shoulder, and the knife clattered to the ground. The brute snarled, swinging his meaty arms and hounding after his assailant.

"Fred!" The barmaid's shout shook Abigail from her trance. Picking up a brick, the barmaid raced toward the rescuer. Abigail tackled her, slamming them both into the far wall and knocking them to the ground. With a groan, the barmaid lurched up and then fled.

The brute endured a hammering round of blows and then staggered back up against the wall. He was breathing heavily, his body hunched.

"You'd best follow your friend," the rescuer commented, his accent crisp and upper class.

Abigail's head whipped around. A gentleman! And he fought like the devil!

Suddenly the brute let out a nasty hiss, tumbled past the rescuer, and stumbled down the alleyway. Soon he was swallowed by the night, gone, save for the clamor of his retreating boot stomps.

The rescuer's panting breath was the only sound in the darkness. He moved with leopardlike grace as he approached Abigail and extended his hand. "Are you all right?"

She hesitated for only a moment, then slipped her hand into his larger one. His grip was strong but gentle as he helped lift her to stand on wobbly knees. "Thank you, sir."

"No need to thank me, but you're welcome just the same." He had an air of distant respectfulness about him that made her feel safe in his company. He released her hand. "Is that knife yours?"

"Yes."

Turning, he moved deeper into the alley, seemingly to retrieve it.

She spied her pistol on the ground, quickly picked it up, and slipped it into her pocket within easy reach. "Are you a police officer of some kind?"

"No, I'm not a police officer."

"Then why did you help me?"

Returning, he offered Abigail her knife and her walking stick. "Cannot one Englishman help another?"

"That's all there is to it?"

"That's all."

After a long moment, she accepted his offerings. He seemed too good to be true, but his actions spoke louder than his words, and she seemed to be in no danger from him. She slipped the knife into the sheath with a snap.

The gentleman nodded. "Ah, the blade doubles as a walking stick. I've seen that before. Smart of you to come prepared. That was an unsavory pair you encountered."

"Quite. And I only have myself to blame," she added ruefully.

"Are you in some kind of trouble?" She was surprised by the lack of censure in his tone. Most men she knew would be quick to ridicule a woman for her seemingly reckless folly. Few would treat her as he did, as if she must have her own good reasons for her actions.

"Trouble?" *Where should I begin? Fugitive brother in trouble again, lack of funds, in need of a job . . .* "No, I'm not in any trouble."

"I'm merely asking since you don't meet many posh widows alone in Charing Cross at this hour."

She stepped away. "I really must be going . . ."

He moved to follow, yet kept a respectful distance. "May I escort you somewhere?"

No matter how handy she was with her knife, the attack had shaken her. And she felt safe with him. But could she trust a man in a mask who fought like the devil? He was a stranger, and a dangerous one at that. "If you could escort me to Wentworth Square . . ." The words spilled from her mouth before she could stop them. "I'll find my way from there."

"Very well then." As he adjusted the folds of his cloak, Abigail spied a tipstaff with a shiny silver head.

She straightened. "You're a Sentinel. I heard about you . . . in the country, men who protect people from outlaws."

"No, I'm not a Sentinel. There are none in London."

"But . . . the silver staff . . . the mask . . . ?"

"It's a good weapon, that's all. And the mask is merely a convenience." He motioned to her veil. "Something I suspect you can understand." His tone made it clear he did not wish to discuss it further.

She nodded, feeling a sense of affinity with this man and not wanting to insult him. "I do. Like you, I don't wish to have my identity known. Nor do I wish to discuss my business."

Tilting his head, he motioned for her to join him, and they fell in step side-by-side leaving the alleyway. "We make quite a pair; neither of us wants to talk about anything."

He was more than a head taller than she, even

with her heeled boots, and yet his powerful stride was as graceful as any lion's. He was so fascinating, and she was driven by a hungering curiosity. "On the contrary, I would be happy to discuss many topics . . . And I submit to you that we are freer than most to engage in conversation. Since you don't know who I am and I don't know you, we are free to discuss anything since there are no judgments, no repercussions . . ."

His voice was tinged with amusement. "No judgments, no repercussions . . . are you certain I'm not in heaven?"

Abigail smiled beneath her veil. "I certainly hope not." She was surprised by the rapport she felt with this man and longed to know more about him. "What if I start?"

"Be my guest."

"What do you think of . . ." She tried to think of something totally random and unrelated to the night's events. "Men's clubs?"

"Honestly . . . I think they're a bother. Forcing a gentleman to align himself with one group of men and pay for the privilege."

"I think that they're merely an excuse for men to feel puffed up and full of themselves. Something they do quite well enough on their own."

"Ouch! You don't think highly of my fellow man, I see."

"I've met very few who are as creditable as they pretend to be. Besides, I dislike exclusivity."

"What do you admire in a man, then?"

Thinking of her dear mentor, Headmaster Dunn, Abigail replied, "Kindness, consideration for others, a sharp mind put to good use, integrity, honorability, a sense of humor—"

"If we're being truly honest, what about a title?"

"I don't believe that one person is of greater merit simply because of birth."

"Blasphemy!" His tone was mocking.

She grinned beneath her veil. "I would never say such a thing in any other company. Or under other circumstances. So what do you think of the peerage?"

He paused so long, she wondered if he would not answer. Then his shoulders shifted within his black cloak. "I believe that each person should be judged on his actions. How he lives. How he behaves toward others. His work . . ."

"Work? Most noblemen would rather be boiled in oil than engage in trade."

"Not all. And it's not just about trade."

She wondered if she'd offended him. "I make no judgments, sir."

"But clearly you do." His tone was mocking. "It seems you are full of them."

Abigail exhaled, enjoying this conversation more than any she'd had in years. "You're right. I am full of judgments. I suppose I'm being so free with them because unlike most of the time, I feel . . . unconstrained."

"*Unconstrained* . . ." He said the word as if tasting it, causing a thrill to race up her middle. "And here we are at Wentworth Square. Pity."

"Oh . . . that was quick." Too quick. She extended her hand. "Well, thank you very much for all of your help. I'm perfectly capable of finding my way from here."

"Are you certain you wish for me to leave you?" The heavy timbre of his voice caused a quiver in her middle. "I'd be happy to escort you *wherever* you want." He grasped her hand. Heat warmed her palm where he touched, and his thumb grazed the top of her fingers in an intimate caress.

Abigail shivered. Her heartbeat quickened and her breath grew heavy. She was suddenly achingly aware of the tall, powerful man standing before her. His vitality stirred her blood in a way that hadn't happened for five long, lonely years.

"I really do wish to go on alone." But she didn't. "Thank you again. Farewell . . ." But she didn't remove her hand from his intimate grasp. They stood facing each other in the moonlight, the only sound the wind brushing through the nearby trees in the square.

"No thanks are necessary, it has been my pleasure." Bowing, he lifted her hand to his mask and laid a soft kiss through the silk. He straightened. "I've never done that with a mask on before, and I must say, it's highly unsatisfying."

*Not for me.* But she seemed to have lost her ability to speak.

"May I try again?" he asked.

Dumbly she nodded.

He lifted the edge of his mask and pulled her hand beneath it. His lips were like moist flower petals caressing her skin. Her eyes fluttered and closed. Her body flamed, her flesh ached. His tongue traced the inner harbor where her thumb joined her hand, and she thought she might faint. The rush of desire pulsing through her was so overpowering . . . so intense that she was actually frightened by it.

She pulled her hand away. "I . . . I . . . really must be going . . ."

He nodded. "It is getting late . . ."

Part of her grieved that she couldn't savor the forbidden fruit he dangled before her, but she knew that she couldn't afford any entanglements. Straightening, she took a step backward. "Good-bye."

"Until we meet again . . ." With a cursory bow, he turned and melted into the fog.

Abigail peered through her veil into the darkness, wondering if she'd imagined the whole episode, for nothing in her wildest fantasies could have conjured up such a magnificent and mysterious man.

# Chapter 2

Rising from the seat where she'd been waiting for almost an hour, Abigail tried not to let her vexation show. "Of course I don't mind waiting." *Even longer.*

"Excellent." The smartly clad butler nodded, knowing full well that Abigail wouldn't dare leave, or else the agency that had sent her would be hearing about it.

The appointment set for three o'clock had extended into a forty-five-minute waiting match, and she wondered how much longer she would play. Abigail knew from experience that nobility liked to try the patience of their *lessers* simply because they could. But whom was she kidding? She wasn't going anywhere; she couldn't afford to leave for a variety of reasons, most especially that her rent was three days overdue. So play she would.

The butler motioned for her to follow him. "His Lordship has asked that I bring you to the study. He should be with you shortly."

Abigail clenched her hands together before her and pasted on a smile. "That would be lovely."

As she followed the butler down the narrow corridor, her footsteps jarred loudly on the polished wooden floors. Classically rendered oil paintings lined the olive-papered walls, but otherwise there wasn't the adornment typical in a nobleman's home. The house had an empty feel to it, and there was little sign of the two children she hoped to instruct.

The elderly man at the agency, Mr. Linder-Myer, had not explained much about the children except to say that they were two boys, ages five and eight. He had been more interested in discussing the viscount's newly acquired title for unspoken services on behalf of the Crown. The man had wondered aloud what Steele, born a commoner, had done to gain such a coveted designation. Abigail had held her tongue, knowing that if she won the position, she'd learn soon enough. Below-stairs servants loved to gossip, especially about their master.

Mr. Linder-Myer had been odd, to say the least, and unlike most agency representatives, didn't seem to be particularly skilled in interviewing, thank the heavens. He hadn't asked Abigail why she did not have a reference from her first position as a governess to the Byrnwyck family or why she didn't have a reference from her most recent post with Lady Kidder.

After the Byrnwyck disaster, Headmaster Dunn had helped Abigail acquire a position with the Landey family, and Mrs. Landey had told her that she was the best governess they'd ever had.

Abigail sighed. She missed Edgar and George Landey terribly, but knew that they were happy at Eton and well on their way to being responsible, good-hearted gentlemen. She felt no small amount of pride that her years with them had been well spent.

Mr. and Mrs. Landey had given Abigail a glowing reference and Lady Kidder had quickly hired her. Abigail had been with the Kidder family for only a few weeks when her brother's distressing letter had arrived begging Abigail to come to London post haste. Lady Kidder hadn't believed that Abigail had a family emergency and had refused to give her any leave. So Abigail had been forced to quit.

Abigail had to hope that the glowing character reference from Headmaster Dunn and the exemplary reference from Mr. and Mrs. Landey would be enough to secure the position with Lord Steele. She knew that given the chance, she could prove her worth. But first she had to make it through the door. If she was really lucky Lord Steele would rely on Mr. Linder-Myer's supposed expertise. But she wasn't about to count her chickens before they'd hatched—it only led to disappointment.

The butler motioned for Abigail to enter the viscount's inner sanctum, and her footsteps fell suddenly silent on the thick Oriental carpet. The servant bowed and left her in the chamber.

The room was designed to impress, with parchment certificates in gilded frames lining the walls and awards with commemorative engravings set on a mantel. Abigail stared at the book-lined shelves, wondering if Lord Steele actually read the many treatises or if he simply used them as trimmings.

Regardless, the comforting scents of books and leather were welcome as she stood in place, waiting.

Time seemed to crawl to a stop. Still, she waited.
A clock chimed another quarter hour.

Sighing with acceptance, Abigail stepped over
to the wall and glanced at the uneven spines of the
books. It was an impressive collection. Headmaster
Dunn would have approved. Her heart squeezed as
she recalled her dear mentor from Andersen Hall
Orphanage.

Since returning to London she'd visited Headmaster Dunn's grave, just to feel that sense of connection
to someone she loved, and to talk about her troubles
to someone who wouldn't judge her or lay blame at
her very deserving feet.

What would Headmaster Dunn think about her
working for the Viscount Steele? Abigail smiled.
Headmaster Dunn would like that Lord Steele took
very good care of his books. Not a speck of dust lined
the shelves, and the volumes were neatly categorized
by subject matter. Abigail wondered if the rest of the
house was so meticulously kept. Lord Steele was un-
married, so all household matters ultimately resided
with him.

Her gaze was drawn to the oil portrait on the wall
behind the large mahogany desk. She assumed that
it was her potential new employer who stared down
at her. His astonishingly dark eyes were filled with
an intelligent gleam that made her question if the
painter had exercised artistic license. In addition to
the formality of the court attire he wore, the artist
had managed to convey a sense of arrogance in Lord
Steele's patrician nose, angled jaw, and the hint of
gray at the temples of his raven hair.

Stepping closer to the painting, she raised a brow.

"From commoner to viscount. With a large painting like that above your head, perhaps you're as impressed with yourself as Mr. Linder-Myer."

Near the desk, the faint scent of cigar lingered.
Abigail scrunched her nose in distaste. The smell
never failed to remind her of Lord Byrnwyck and
his sycophant of a nephew. Swallowing, she realized
once more how desperately she needed this position
and how her lack of references might impede her.

She turned away, her nervousness sparked anew.

In the corner of the room, a glass case sat atop a
wooden table. Stepping over to it, Abigail read some
of the enclosed parchments. One very ornate one
caught her eye, and she read aloud, "We are pleased
to inform you that you have been chosen as the Solicitor-General of England, Law Officer of the Crown,
la, la, la."

"I hope that there's more to my legal career than
'la, la, la.'" A rich baritone filled the chamber.

Abigail jumped, her cheeks warming from being
caught unawares and being less than respectful.

Quickly she lowered her eyes and curtsied, re-
sisting the urge to explain herself because she knew
from experience that it would not be welcome. "My
lord."

"Steele will do."

"Yes, your . . . ah . . . Lord Steele."

Rising from her curtsy, she kept her head lowered and surreptitiously examined her potential new
employer.

The painter had not done the viscount justice. Oh,
the intelligent gleam was clear in his coal black eyes,
but the artist had failed to convey the sheer power

the man emanated. There was an intensity to Steele, a strength of purpose that could not be captured in oils. Yes, his chiseled features were handsome and his body lean and strapping, but it was the powerful way he strode across the room with a forceful energy that riveted her attention.

Abigail's heart began to race and her palms grew damp. She lowered her head even more, feeling as transparent as a chemise drying on a line in the sun. This was not the kind of man to miss her lack of references, or fail to ask why she'd left her last post. This was the kind of man who had earned the designation that so many were born into.

Steele frowned, and she felt that distaste like a tug deep in her middle.

"It smells of cigar. I told Kent to air this room." Steele strode to the window and unlocked the transom. As he lifted the pane, his muscles bulged, stretching and raising his finely cut Weston coat.

Abigail's eyes widened, mesmerized by the unexpected view of molded thighs encased in cream-colored breeches stretched tight.

She swallowed, hard. Her heart began to race, and an unfamiliar heat smoldered in her middle. The heat simmered deliciously, reminding Abigail of what she'd experienced the other night with the masked stranger.

It had been years since she'd felt anything a shade warmer than frost, and now, within two weeks, two different men had kindled her senses! Granted, anyone with eyes could see that Lord Steele was the kind of man to inspire a little heat. But still, it was highly disconcerting.

Halfway up, the window stuck. As Lord Steele fiddled with the window, Abigail tried to avert her eyes from his glorious physique, but for her life, she could not. She soaked in the sight of his molded thighs and the glimpse of his muscular bottom like a needy orphan staring into a sweets-store window at Christmas.

Steele worked the window free and turned. Abigail hastily swung around, raised her fist to her mouth, and coughed to cover her discomfiture.

"Are you all right? Your face is as red as a beet." He was behind her, gently patting her back.

His touch was so disconcerting that she danced away, smiling weakly. "Yes, ah, just a little tickle. I'm fine, my lord."

Those eyes were a tad too sharp for her comfort, and she prayed that he had no idea how he'd affected her. If he got wind of it, along with her blemished past, she'd be out the door for good.

"Very well, then." With a flick of his gaze, Lord Steele's eyes seemed to capture her from hair to shoes. If she didn't know better, she'd swear that he'd appraised her seen-better-days best gown and worn shoes and found her wanting.

Involuntarily she slid her shoe deeper under her skirts and straightened her spine. Clearing her throat, she tried to appear businesslike.

His brow lifted. "Ready to face the inquisition, are you?"

She swallowed, then nodded.

"I was jesting. I'm not nearly as terrible as you've heard."

Somehow she wasn't reassured.

His lips quirked. "Don't believe me, do you?"

Was her face like an open book? She lowered her head.

The hint of amusement in his mien slowly melted. "You're not much for levity are you, Miss West?"

"I take my post very seriously, my lord."

Steele started; he'd said those very same words to his superior, the Attorney-General of England, this morning. Had he sounded just as starched and somber as this young miss?

Steele studied her a long moment. He was overcome by the sudden urge to unclasp her hands and gently loosen her shoulders so that she didn't appear so . . . knotted up. He wondered what her face would look like without the crease between her golden arched brows, or if her luscious lips sloped into a smile. Would the warmth of her smile penetrate those wide, grayish-blue eyes? They reminded him of the color of slate, and the coldness of rock as well. Those eyes gave nothing away. "You're not afraid of me, are you, Miss West?"

"Am I . . . supposed to be, my lord?" she asked quite seriously.

Steele frowned. He, of all people, knew about the walls people built up to protect their hearts, and this girl had ramparts around hers a mile high.

By the square of her shoulders and the tilt of her chin, Miss West seemed strong, resilient, and yet there was a vulnerability about her eyes that elicited compassion and empathy, even. It was as if she'd seen many lows and was valiantly prepared to face more. *Just like me.*

Steele started, surprised by the sneaky thought. He gave himself a mental shake. He was becoming fanciful in his old age. And he could not afford to do so. He was three-and-thirty, a viscount in his own right, and he was responsible for the safety of two small, defenseless human beings.

Dare he entrust his nephews into this woman's care? She seemed slight, and a bit timid. She didn't look hardy enough to manage the boys while keeping them safe and secure.

And her background was littered with holes. Why had she left her last post with the Kidder family so abruptly? Why didn't she have references from Lord and Lady Byrnwyck, her very first position?

Sir Lee Devane, or as Miss West would know him, Mr. Linder-Myer, had insisted that Miss West was the perfect woman for this unique position. Sir Lee, as a former master of spies for the Foreign Office, considered himself an expert regarding character and believed that Miss West had the strength and stamina for the threats they were facing.

In Sir Lee's words, "She's not the kind of woman to run from the kitchen when things get hot."

But that was not consistent with Miss West leaving her last post so abruptly. Or with the missing references.

They needed a steady hand for the children, a reliable person who could give the children some sense of stability after their recent losses.

In a matter of seconds, Steele worked through the familiar push and pull of intellectual debate inside his head and quickly came to a decision. Ultimately, no matter how much he regarded Sir Lee, he couldn't simply trust something so important to another's word.

So Miss Abigail West, no matter how perfectly suited Sir Lee considered her to be, would have to go.

Steele cleared his throat. "I'm sorry to inform you—"

"Stop! Stop this instant! I command you!" a male voice boomed from near the threshold.

Concealing his irritation, Steele glanced toward the door.

A plump, baldheaded gentleman dressed in a fine burgundy coat with shiny brass buttons stood in the doorway. His features were twisted into a look that could sour the milk in a cow's udder.

"You cannot hire that Jezebel!" Benbrook's watery brown eyes glared daggers at Miss West. "I know all about her and I will not have her in my house!"

The young lady stepped backward, closer to Steele as if for protection.

For the thousandth time, Steele questioned if he was mad to have taken up this Herculean task. "It's my house, not yours, Benbrook. But that aside, I have this matter well in hand."

The Viscount Benbrook shook his fat finger at Steele as if he were some school lad up to mischief. "Clearly you're unfit!"

Steele gritted his teeth, the dig poking into the old wound that never seemed to heal. "I handle legal matters for the Crown, Benbrook. I can certainly manage a simple interview."

"Not if you're even considering this . . . common . . . lowly . . ."

"Now see here, Benbrook—" Steele felt for the lady, having faced his father-in-law's hostile snobbery on many occasions himself.

"You will do as I say! She's the worst sort of grasping . . ." Benbrook's face twisted in disgust. ". . . brassy . . ." His lips curled. ". . . presumptuous . . ."

With each word, Miss West seemed to shrink into herself.

Steele scowled. "Enough, Benbrook!"

". . . strumpet!"

Steele stepped in front of Miss West, shielding her from the ranting prig. "Get out!" He pointed toward the door. "I'll not have you insulting my guest in my house!"

Benbrook's brown eyes narrowed, and his lip curled into a sneer. "It's no wonder you defend her! Neither of you knows your place!"

Something shifted inside Steele, and he felt the familiar coldness envelop him like steely armor. No one, and especially not a priggish sod like Benbrook, could tell Steele what to do and with whom to do it.

With a smile, Steele turned to the cowering young lady. "Congratulations, Miss West. The position is yours."

# Chapter 3

Steele grinned while his father-in-law sputtered, "But you cannot!"

Straightening her spine, Miss West quickly recovered. "Ah . . . thank you, Lord Steele. When would you like me to begin?" Questions may have been swirling in her slate blue eyes, but she kept her head about her.

Good. Mayhap Sir Lee was right about her. Still, she'd been pretty mousy when it came to Benbrook's attack. Did she have the necessary backbone to get the job done? Regardless, Steele couldn't look backward now; the deed was done and he would make hay with it.

Steele looked to Benbrook. "I assume you brought the boys with you and that they are here."

Benbrook shrieked, his face molten with fury, "Of course I did! But I'll not stand for this . . . this . . . unsuitable wench . . ."

Steele stepped toward his father-in-law, getting so close as to see the man's enlarged irises. The odor of port wafted around the fat lord like a foul mist. "Don't say one more word, you self-righteous prig.

Or I'll kick you, your grandsons, and your bloody troubles right out my door!"

At the mention of his troubles, Benbrook's eyes widened and he closed his pudgy lips and sulked. "This is not the end of it," he retorted churlishly.

Miss West pointedly ignored Benbrook. "I will start right away, Lord Steele."

Nodding, Steele placed his hand on the small of Miss West's back as he gently steered her around Benbrook and toward the door. His hand fit perfectly there, he was surprised to note, and she responded quickly to his touch. Clearly she was quite willing to leave him to the petulant Lord Benbrook. Smart girl. "Excellent. Speak to my butler, Carlton, about the details."

In the threshold, she paused and looked up at him. Her golden brow furrowed and then cleared, as if she was finding the words difficult. "Your trust has not been misplaced, my lord. I promise, I will not disappoint you."

"Be careful what you promise. My good opinion is hard to come by."

"Then I will earn it, my lord."

The sincerity reflected in her eyes and in her voice gave him a moment's pause. Steele trusted very few people, and one of those had recently disappointed him. Heath Bartlett, the barrister that Steele relied on most in his staff, had gone behind his back and freed a suspected murderess without so much as a by-your-leave. All had turned out well in the end, since the lady in question was innocent. But still, that sense of betrayal lingered like a chill he couldn't shake.

Holding her skirts, Miss West curtsied, and Steele caught a whiff of her clean, sweet scent, reminding him of ling, the low-growing heather with tiny pink bellflowers. "If you will excuse me, my lord."

Exhaling, he nodded.

A fleeting sense of loss overcame him as he closed the door behind her. Her freshness and sincerity were a marked contrast to the fractious, inebriated lord standing behind him.

Girding himself, Steele turned and motioned toward the chair before his desk. "Let us sit and discuss this calmly, shall we?" Although the decision was not up for reconsideration, as Benbrook would soon learn.

Benbrook dropped into the chair with a huff. "She's a grasping harpy."

"You've been drinking."

"I must, to maintain my sanity!"

Steele found it hard to argue; the man had been through a lot, and had much more yet to face. A few drinks were a small consolation under the circumstances.

Benbrook leaned forward and placed his pudgy arm on Steele's desk, straining the seams of his burgundy coat. "Look. I know of what I speak. I have it on good authority that that woman tried to seduce Lord Byrnwyck's son. You know, the grown one from his first marriage to Lady Paige."

"Oh, please," Steele scoffed. The leather creaked as he lowered himself into his chair. "She's a babe in the wood compared to Byrnwyck."

"Not that son. Phineas, the younger, more impressionable one. She was retained to care for Byrnwyck's daughters by his latest wife, but was more interested in playing with the full-grown son, if you know what I mean."

Steele waved his hand in dismissal. "I don't care which of that clan you mean, she's about as predatory as a lamb. Besides"—he raised a brow—"do you really fear for my virtue?"

Shifting in his seat, Benbrook harrumphed. "You're a viscount now . . ."

"Finally worth catching, eh?" Steele experienced the old hurt like a splinter in his flesh.

Benbrook bristled. "You were a ruffian! Hardly worthy of my Deidre! And if it weren't for you . . ." He swallowed, looking away.

"If it weren't for me, she wouldn't be dead," Steele finished the thought.

"She certainly wouldn't have had to sneak around . . ."

"The same could be said if you'd accepted me and our marriage! She was so terrified of upsetting you and was trying to give me the chance to prove myself before breaking the news to you, that we never even had one night under the same roof! Married, but sneaking around as if we'd committed some crime!"

"It was a crime! You were hardly worthy of my daughter!"

Every time Steele and Benbrook got together, it was as if Deidre hung over them like an angry specter. Each man was raw with guilt and shame and grief, and the other man was a glaringly conspicuous target. It was the reason the two men had, by tacit agreement, stayed apart these almost nine years.

Benbrook smacked the desk with his palm. "But enough of that! We're talking about Miss West, not ancient history! She'll be a bad influence on my grandsons."

Exhaling, Steele forced himself to calm down; he had promised Sir Lee to *try* not to harp on the past, and he would keep his word no matter how difficult that charge might be. "Sir Lee believes that Miss West is perfect for the job."

"I wouldn't even have a bloody governess if it weren't for . . ." Benbrook's voice trailed off, his grief for his lost son and daughter-in-law etched on his face.

Lord Benbrook's daughter-in-law, Emily, mother to Felix and Seth, had left a note written in the event of anything ever happening to her. Lord Steele and Sir Lee had determined that it was drafted without fear of a specific threat in mind; it was merely a precaution written out of love for her children.

In the letter, Emily had expressed her desire that if she died, the boys were to have a governess until the age of twelve. She'd explained in the note that she wanted the boys to have a female influence in their lives, separate and apart from their formal education. *A tutor*, she'd written, *will be necessary as well, but a female must be the primary giver of care.*

Wiping a hand across his eyes, Benbrook recovered. "Miss Lorena Farmer is a better choice, I tell you, and you will have more peace in your home if you do as I say!"

"Who's Miss Farmer?"

"She rode along with us from Dorset and was quite useful with the lads. The girl who'd been helping out with the boys since the last governess suddenly became ill and resigned. Luckily for us, our cook had heard that Miss Farmer was headed to London to seek out a post as a governess."

Steele rubbed his chin. "Very lucky indeed."

Ignoring the obvious notion that he'd been played, Benbrook reached into his coat and pulled out a sheet of vellum. "Miss Farmer comes highly recommended and has impeccable references, unlike *your* Miss West."

Steele's eyes narrowed. "Don't bark up that tree, Benbrook. Sir Lee selected Miss West, not me. I don't consort with my staff. I never have and never will."

Benbrook slid the paper across the desk. "I want Miss Farmer."

Steele ignored the vellum. "Well, we don't always get what we want, do we?"

"You are only their guardian temporarily!"

"Thank the heavens."

"You don't know how to handle such things! You've never been a father!"

Steele leaned forward, his anger steeping. "And why is that, Benbrook? Why is it that I never had any children with my lovely wife?"

Benbrook looked away, his face pained.

Steele smile was cold. "Thanks to you—"

"And to you!"

"Yes, and to me, I have no children and never will. I know how it feels to know with certainty that there will be no heirs in my line. Do you want to start gambling with yours now?"

Benbrook swallowed.

Now was as good a place as any to draw his line in the sand. Benbrook had best get used to the new arrangement, for Steele wasn't about to be bullied. "You agreed to follow my judgment and accept my decisions in all things in exchange for my help. That price starts coming due now."

Benbrook stood. "This is preposterous! I agreed to accept your help as it regarded the investigation and finding the villain who killed my son! I never agreed to accept your decisions as it regards raising my grandchildren!"

"So I'm good enough to place myself in the line of fire, yet not good enough to decide who wipes your grandchildren's noses?"

"You're hardly fit!"

"You're the one who asked for my help!"

"I had little enough choice! My children are dead! Dead! First Deidre and now Robert and Emily . . ." Benbrook shook like a wet dog, and then suddenly his face fell and he collapsed into the chair like a deflated balloon. "They're all dead!" Wiping his meaty hand across his eyes, he sobbed. "Dead . . ."

Exhaling, Steele stood and walked over to the open window, giving Benbrook the pretense of privacy. With his back to his father-in-law, he found that he had no words of comfort for this man. But Steele felt for him nonetheless. Steele knew a thing or two about loss. He understood the overwhelming grief that shattered your soul and made waking each day a nightmare. Benbrook was living in his, and only the grandchildren in need of his help were keeping him going at the moment.

As if called forth, a shout reverberated from the garden below.

Steele leaned out, catching the heady scent of roses. His garden was an untamed mess, as he'd given it little care since acquiring this house two years ago. This was the first time that he'd noticed that he seemed to have an abundance of rose blossoms.

The younger son, Seth was his name, was five years old. He sat with his legs spread out before him in a V as he dug into the dirt with a stick.

The older lad, Felix, stood nearby, chucking stones at an orange cat racing along the far wall. The boy was tall for his age and had a strong arm. A stone just barely missed the feline, cracking loudly against the brick wall. The cat shrieked and changed direction.

Steele was about to shout out the window for the lad to stop, but suddenly a lady in navy skirts and golden hair came into view. She moved with graceful alacrity toward the boys. Felix would be as tall as she within a few years, Steele realized, and he wondered how Miss West was going to handle her first situation as governess.

Miss West spoke to the boys for a moment, and neither of them seemed to respond.

Steele frowned. These lads needed a strong hand. Was Miss West too meek to be effective? What had Sir Lee been thinking?

Miss West turned and moved with purpose toward a bramble pile. Reaching down, she lifted a long stick from the heap, swung around, and pointed it toward Felix. She raised her other hand behind her and cried, "En garde!"

Felix started and turned.

Seth looked up, smiled, and then stood, shaking the dirt out of his breeches.

"En garde!" Miss West pranced forward, slashing her stick through the air like a sword.

Benbrook came up next to Steele, his face blotchy and swollen. "Felix! He'll be hurt! We must stop this at once!"

Steele held up his hand. "No, wait and see."

Squaring his shoulders, Felix stepped over to the bramble pile and selected his own stick.

Seth hopped about like an excited bunny.

Felix squatted, and with one arm held high behind him and the branch pointed directly at Miss West's heart, he lunged.

Miss West smacked his branch with hers and then skipped out of harm's way.

Felix charged after her, his stick thrust forward and swinging.

She neatly swept aside his stick and swirled, like a dancer at a ball with her skirts twirling around her.

Seth squeaked with delight, waving his own little stick in the air.

Thwarted, Felix stomped his foot in frustration. But to his credit, instead of throwing a tantrum, he raised his sword once more. "En garde!"

With a mischievous grin, Miss West raised her sword.

The combatants circled each other.

Felix's face was twisted with determination.

Miss West's cheeks glowed pink, and she was beaming with delight. Steele realized that he'd been right; when she wasn't so starched, she was lovely to behold.

Felix charged.

Miss West brilliantly swept him aside. "Ha!"

The clank of the combatants' skirmishing sticks echoed through the garden. They parried and pranced like dancers at a soirée, meeting then receding so neatly as if in harmony.

Felix was panting; Miss West looked as if she could go at it all day.

The sticks locked and Miss West gave a push that sent Felix falling backward. The lad regained his balance and glared daggers at Miss West.

Steele wondered where Miss West had learned to fence so well.

Her sword arm was still extended when, with her other hand, she motioned for Felix to advance. The challenge in her movement was clear even from the window.

Raising his sword, Felix lunged once more.

Miss West knocked his stick aside and spun around him, landing a loud thwack to the boy's behind.

"Ow!" Felix yelped, grabbing his rear and scowling.

"Saucy," Steele murmured with admiration.

"Impertinent!" Benbrook huffed. "How dare she?"

Smiling, Steele pointed. "Look."

Miss West had lowered her sword and spoke quietly to the boys. They listened with rapt attention. Then each boy nodded vigorously.

With great solemnity, Miss West stepped backward and raised her stick to her forehead.

Straightening, the two boys did the same.

She bowed.

The boys followed suit.

Miss West tossed aside her stick and turned, with her hand extended. Seth bounced forward, grasped her hand, and the two headed toward the house.

After a moment, Felix tossed aside his stick and followed quickly at her heels.

Scratching his chin, Steele nodded. "Now that's a governess." Mayhap this crazy scheme would work out.

Now if only he could keep the boys alive until their next birthdays.

# Chapter 4

Abigail shook her head, wondering if she'd heard right. "What do you mean, I'm going to be sleeping here?" Her eyes traveled the expansive room decorated in Chippendale furnishings and gilded splendor. "These chambers are for the mistress of the house!"

Carlton, Lord Steele's butler, stood in the doorway rubbing a cloth over the four silver spoons in his hand. Each spoon was given meticulous attention before he moved on to the next. "Cursed first footman," he muttered to himself. "Doesn't he know I'm too busy for him to break his arm? This isn't a charity hospital. Everyone must carry his weight."

Carlton studied a silver spoon, holding it this way and that in the light. "And now I've a dratted governess to deal with," he muttered. "Had to hire a porter with a horse and cart to haul her trunk from her lodgings . . ."

Sure enough, Abigail spied her trunk in the corner by the window. The old brown luggage was scratched and shoddy, with a long strip of leather holding it together since the lock had broken. It was hardly worthy of the elegant furnishings of the chamber. "I cannot stay here. These rooms are not appropriate for a governess."

"It's your duty to do as you're told, Miss West. The sooner you grasp that, the easier this will be on you."

Abigail straightened. *What the blazes does he mean by that?* "I don't understand."

Stabbing a spoon at her, Carlton glared. "It's quite simple. Don't expect that what you signed on for won't change. Additional duties can be tacked onto whatever you thought you'd be doing no matter how . . . unpleasant or . . . *unorthodox*."

"Unorthodox?"

A look of distaste washed over Carlton's thin face as he resumed his polishing once more. "We live at the whim of the master. Lord Steele gets what Lord Steele wants." Peering at her from the corner of his eye, his contemptuous gaze traveled from Abigail's face down to her breasts. "And you are subject to his *every* desire."

A terrible taste soiled her mouth. Abigail swallowed. Could Steele know about Phineas and somehow fancy that he'd gotten himself a plaything along with a governess? Lord Steele had seemed so nice, but clearly he expected a level of compliance beyond anything she'd ever encountered before.

Abigail bit her lip. Mayhap she was reaching unwarranted conclusions.

"Where does Lord Steele sleep?" she asked.

Carlton waved a spoon toward the large double doors at the side of the room. "In the master's suite next door, of course. His Lordship was quite explicit that he wants you *within arm's reach.*"

Abigail felt ill. Pressing her hand to her aching belly, she turned away, trying to sort out what to do. She already owed the moneylender the thirty shillings she'd used to pay off her rent. If she quit this job she'd be in the duns for sure! And what about Reggie? She needed to stay in London to find him.

And the boys . . . in the few hours they'd spent together, Seth and Felix had managed to worm their way into her resistant little heart. Her charges were the only people that she truly allowed herself to love. And these two boys desperately needed the love she longed to give. This was the first time she'd ever had charges who were orphans, like her. And the boys' grief was so painfully apparent that her heart ached in harmony with theirs.

Could she desert them?

Finishing the last spoon, Carlton adjusted the sleeve of his black swallow-tailed coat. "I don't have the time for this. I have many pressing matters to attend to and have little patience for your discontent."

"Discontent . . . ?" Gritting her teeth, Abigail held up her hand. "Just give me a moment."

She exhaled. If she left now, the boys were well off and Steele would certainly find another governess soon enough. Perhaps a woman willing to put up with the additional requirements of the job that Abigail had been blind to. She couldn't quite believe that "servicing" the master was part and parcel of the duties. Steele had to know about her past and have selected her specifically because of it.

She straightened. Did Mr. Linder-Myer know about this arrangement? Was that why he'd ignored her missing references? Had all this been a ploy? That meant that if she left now, she'd never gain a post through that agency, or probably any other agency in the city of London! Where did that leave her?

Abigail looked up and caught a glimpse of her haunted face in the gilded mirror above the dressing table. She was so tired of playing the victim, so tired of being on her own.

Suddenly Headmaster Dunn's face swarmed her vision. *Never compromise your principles,* he spoke in her mind. *For at the end of the day, they'll stand by you as staunchly as any friend.*

Swallowing, Abigail turned back to Carlton. "There's been some mistake. I thank you for your time, but I will not be taking this post."

Quickly she lifted her skirts and sprinted down the hall. She swept down the servants' stairs and into the kitchen. The hustle and clamor of preparations for the evening meal were under way, and the odor of fish made Abigail even sicker. She barely avoided toppling a tray of liver and onions as she raced toward the door. "Sorry!"

Once outside in the darkening evening, Abigail sucked in the fresh air and closed her eyes, hoping to block out the painful truth of it. She was on her own and in trouble; she was without employment, a place to live, food to eat . . .

Angrily she wiped away a tear. She'd considered herself lucky, secure for a time, at least. She'd been such a fool not to have noticed that something was amiss, that Lord Steele was not as he'd appeared. She wondered what additional consequences she'd have to face; a peer wouldn't take kindly to not getting what he wanted.

"Oh, dear Lord," she groaned, recalling her words to Steele about not disappointing him. Pressing her hand to her forehead, she desperately tried to think of what to do. If only Headmaster Dunn were alive! He'd always helped her out in the past. If only she had a friend to talk to! Someone to help her think through her options. She glared up at the house, spying movements in the windows. What would Carlton say to Lord Steele? How would he react? Should she try to explain herself? How could she face the man, knowing what he wanted of her?

With her heart racing and bile rising in her throat, she forced herself to straighten. "I'll not let them get to me. I can't. I won't."

Before she could question her actions, she turned and marched down the alley at the side of the house and out to the street. Spotting the park across the way, she dashed across the cobblestone street and made her way onto the pebbled lane. Her feet crunched loudly as she strode along, but she made it only about thirty paces before the energy drained from her legs like sap bleeding from a tree.

Spying a bench, she collapsed into it, slouching in a manner that would have had any governess worth her salt smacking her shoulders to straighten.

Dusk was falling, and she welcomed the veil of darkness. She wanted to hide, wanted to crawl away and cry. She knew she was being pathetic, but she spared herself a few moments of self-pity before she'd have to be the businesslike adult she'd been pretending to be ever since her parents had died ten years earlier.

The leaves rustling in the tress calmed her, and she inhaled a deep breath, smelling pine. "I'm alive," she muttered to the shadows. "I have my limbs. I have my sanity, what more do I need?"

She straightened. *Oh no, I have to somehow retrieve my things!*

As she pressed her hand to her mouth, Abigail's eyes widened in horror. What if they searched her trunk and found the secret compartment? Her pistol! And her widow's costume! What would they think of her then?

She bit her lip, trying to decide what to do. She'd always consoled herself with the fact that the pistol was not loaded and was secure inside a locked box inside the secret compartment with the widow's costume, but still . . .

"What the blazes is wrong with you?" a smooth, cultured voice demanded.

Abigail blinked, only then realizing that it was full dark. Moonlight speared through the trees, encircling Abigail's little bench in a whitish glow.

Pebbles crunched under Steele's leather boots as he made his way toward her like a commanding general leading an army. Carlton was at his heels, his black coattails flying. Mrs. Pitts, the housekeeper, padded behind, her keys jangling with every huffing step.

Slowly Abigail stood, her knees wobbling only slightly.

"Are you ill?" Steele demanded.

Abigail stepped backward, bumping her knees up against the wooden bench. She didn't know what to say. She knew she should answer, but she had no words for this man who'd presumed so much.

"She looks fit ta me." Mrs. Pitts sniffed. "Mayhap she's flighty."

"Why did you leave like that?" Lord Steele demanded. The moonlight shone on his raven hair, and his eyes pierced into her like beacons in the night. His chiseled features were locked into a hard glare, and his body thrummed with barely contained irritation.

She felt the power emanating from his brawny physique like a siren's call and cursed the power he so negligently exercised on others. The man was breathtakingly handsome, and distantly she wondered if in the past his servants had seen bedding him as some sort of additional recompense.

*Well, not me!* From deep inside her, anger sparked, and she welcomed it, fanning the tiny flame with every slight and insult she'd suffered at the hands of nobility over the last five years.

Crossing his arms, Steele challenged, "I have no time or patience for games. Answer me!"

Games? Here stood a man demanding that she play along in a role of his design and he said *she* was the one playing games? Her anger warped and turned toward this big, brawny target. "You're the one with the twisted games, not me!"

"What the hell are you talking about?"

"Don't you curse at me!"

The muscle in his jaw worked. "Then explain yourself so that a reasonably intelligent person can understand you."

Abigail met that dark, gleaming gaze with

narrowed eyes. "Let me be perfectly clear so a *reasonably intelligent* person can understand one simple thing: I cannot work for you."

"Cannot or will not?"

Abigail lifted her chin. "Will not. Not for the likes of you."

"Why, you impertinent wench!" Carlton hissed.

Two more sets of feet came scrambling down the lane, sending pebbles flying.

Seth raced toward her. "Miss Abigail! Miss Abigail! They say you're leaving!"

Felix charged after his brother. "Seth! Come back here!"

Seth slammed into Abigail's skirts. "Tell him it ain't true!"

Without thought Abigail corrected, "It's *not* true."

Turning toward his brother, Seth jeered, "See! I told you she wouldn't leave!"

Abigail's heart dropped. "Oh no, that's not what I meant."

Lord Steele turned and looked down the path. "Where are the footmen that are supposed to be keeping an eye on you? You're never supposed to be left unattended!" Fury interlaced his voice, causing Seth to clutch at Abigail's skirts.

"Unruly lads!" Carlton's eyes were filled with aggravation, and his lips curled in distaste. "This is house business, and the two of you don't belong here!" Carlton grabbed Seth by the shoulder and yanked him away from Abigail.

Seth shrieked, swinging his arms in defense. A fist landed on Carlton's middle.

"Why, you disobedient pup!" Carlton shook Seth, hard.

"Ow!" Seth cried in obvious pain.

Fury engulfed Abigail. "Unhand him!" Stepping over, she wrenched Carlton's hand off Seth's shoulder and twisted his wrist around so that the man's whole body was forced to follow. The butler collapsed on his knees with a yelp of pain.

Leaning forward, Abigail hissed in Carlton's ear, "If you ever lay a hand on him again, you'll be the finest one-handed butler in all of London!"

"You're hurting me!" Carlton cried.

Disgusted, Abigail shoved him away, and he collapsed on the ground whimpering and clutching his wrist.

Silence filled the park as everyone's eyes landed on Abigail.

Lord Steele exhaled softly. "You are definitely not what I expected."

"I can say the same for you," Abigail retorted, shocked by the fury, now lit, that blazed within her. It filled her with a fire that made her want to scorch the earth with righteous vengeance.

Two burly footmen came racing up the path. "Sorry, m'lord. We told the lads not to leave the house."

Looking down at Seth, Steele declared, "You cannot leave the house unattended. Do you understand me?"

"He wasn't unattended." Felix stepped up beside his brother. "He was with me."

Steele furrowed his brow. After a moment, he nodded. "You're absolutely right. I wasn't being fair."

Abigail blinked, surprised.

Lord Steele squatted down and spoke to Seth. "The *new* rule in my house is that neither of you leaves without being attended by at least two adults. Do you agree?"

Abigail could hardly conceal her astonishment that Steele would ask the boys to agree and not simply make his edict and expect it to be followed without question.

"Can Miss Abigail be one of the adults?" Felix asked, his eyes seeking hers.

Her heart twisted with the agony of deserting these two children.

Steele nodded. "Yes." His gaze met hers, and she was shocked to see a hint of admiration shining in his dark eyes. "I believe she's proven herself handy in a pinch."

Seth preened. "Then I agree!"

"Me, too," Felix declared.

"Then we have a deal." Extending his hand, he shook hands with each boy with dramatic solemnity. "Now please go back to the house with Foster and Claude before your grandfather worries."

"But we want to be with Miss Abigail!" Seth wailed.

Steele rose. "Miss Abigail will be joining you for dinner in a moment. You must dress first, though. She would be most disappointed if you showed up for dinner in your shirtsleeves."

The lads looked to her for confirmation, and she hadn't the heart to tell them the truth. They'd learn soon enough. "Go along, boys."

Steele's smile was tight. "See. Now please return to the house."

"Yes, Lord Steele." The lads nodded glumly.

To the two footmen, Steele added, "Never again."

"Yes, Your Lordship!"

The two footmen led the boys away, the sounds of crunching pebbles dwindling with their departure.

Carlton rose and moved before Lord Steele. Adjusting his coat and clutching his wrist, he sniffed. "I demand a reckoning."

Mrs. Pitts nodded, her keys jangling loudly in the moonlit park.

"Oh, there'll be one, don't you worry." Lord Steele scratched his chin, a thoughtful look on his face.

"Now!" Carlton demanded.

Steele's head lifted. "Pardon me?"

The butler swallowed, but raised his chin high in the air. "After all I've been put through, anything less is unacceptable!"

A hint of iron seeped into Steele's tone. "Go back to the house, Carlton. Wait for me in your rooms, and we'll discuss this matter later, once you've calmed down."

"She must be punished! The children must be punished!"

Lord Steele straightened to his full height, towering over the butler. "Have you ever known me not to be fair? I will do what's necessary and what's right."

"What's right?" A note of hysteria permeated Carlton's voice. "I didn't sign on for this! None of it! Up at all hours! Unreasonable footmen! Unruly children! Violent governesses! Heaven help me!"

"Ah, Carlton, ah . . . perhaps we should go . . . ?" Mrs. Pitts stepped back as if hoping to separate herself from his outburst.

Turning on her, Carlton sneered. "Don't pretend you weren't complaining just as loudly as me in the quiet of your rooms!"

Mrs. Pitts's face blanched white in the moonlight. "I don't know what yer talkin' about."

Steele turned to the housekeeper. "Help him get back to the house, Mrs. Pitts, and calm him down. I'll deal with you both later."

Then he grasped Abigail's elbow and drew her to walk beside him deeper into the park, deeper into the shadows, where they would be alone.

# Chapter 5

A bigail tried not to be unsettled by the tall, powerful man grasping her arm and leading her farther down the dark lane. The crunch of the pebbles beneath their shoes echoed loudly in the empty park. "Where are we going?"

"To speak privately." Steele's voice was hard.

"That would be improper—"

"I'm your employer and propriety is not exactly an issue—"

"But you're *not* my employer." Abigail dug in her heels. "And I'm not going anywhere with the likes of you." She'd halted in a pool of moonlight, and was satisfied to note the frustration locking his chiseled jaw into place.

Steele towered over her, his stare drilling into her. After a long moment, he turned away, running his hand through his already mussed hair in frustration. She suddenly realized that he wore no cravat and that his coat was unbuttoned, as if it had been donned in great haste. He'd probably been dressing when Carlton had informed him of Abigail's departure.

An odd little thrill raced up her middle that he would be so bothered as to immediately chase after her. Strangely, that thrill felt nothing like the gut-wrenching panic she usually experienced when dealing with unhappy employers, but felt much more like . . . *anticipation*.

Crossing his arms, Steele shrugged. "Is it because I was born a commoner, not as a peer?"

Stunned, she furrowed her brow in confusion. "No, of course not. That has nothing to do with it."

"Then is it because I actually work for a living?"

"That's the most ridiculous thing I've ever heard!"

He laughed, but the sound contained no mirth. "Oh, you'd be amazed how many people expect me to step down as solicitor-general now that I'm a peer of the realm. As if all I've ever worked for is summed up in a fancy title."

Abigail was astonished by the hint of hurt interlacing his tone. "If you stop working, how would you pay your bills?"

He laughed once more, but this time with real amusement. "Excellent point. But few peers have experienced a hollow belly to make that connection. Obviously you have."

Abigail straightened, pushing away any sense of affinity with this man. "Is that some kind of threat?"

He stiffened. "What sort of man do you think I am?"

Raising her hands to the heavens in frustration, she cried, "I've hardly a clue! One moment you're kind and considerate of the boys and the next you're insulting me beyond the pale!"

"Insulting you? You're the one who refuses to work for 'the likes' of me!"

Curling her fingers into fists, Abigail tried to rein in this unfamiliar fury. "Look. This obviously was a mistake. Let us simply part ways and be done with it."

"You can do that? You can simply desert those two boys? Orphans who've already lost so much?"

Abigail swallowed. "You can find another governess—"

"They've grown attached to you."

"Yes, but—"

"The boys trust you. You know how hard it can be to win over young boys. You've already done it and you can't let them down."

"Well—"

"They need you."

"I don't think—"

"You agreed."

"Yes, I know. But—"

"What is it, then? Are you positioning for more money?"

Abigail straightened. "I would never!"

He stepped forward, toe to toe with her, like duelists at dawn. "Then what the blazes are you about?" His breath washed over her in a pleasant, clove-scented breeze. "You flounce in and—"

"I don't flounce!" she cried, glaring up into that chiseled, unnervingly handsome face.

"Fine, you fence your way into those children's hearts and then, after they've grown attached to you, you forsake them?"

"I don't *want* to leave them!"

"Then don't!"

Abigail was quaking, her face was hot, and her heart was racing. She flushed with an unfamiliar fire surging through her.

Steele stood so close, she could feel the waves of heat and frustration he emitted. It was mesmerizing, intoxicating, and the way her body hungered for more of him was frightening. The man had to be a sorcerer of some kind to have such an effect on her.

Swallowing, Abigail forced herself to take a shaky step back. She stared down at Steele's boots, which caught a gleam of moonlight on their polished surface.

"Don't do that." His voice was a teasing whisper as he stepped to follow her, keeping less than an inch separating them.

She felt the heat of his flesh and the force he emanated with every fiber of her being. "Do what?" she murmured.

"Back down. Become that gray mouse once more."

She blinked, and her anger flared like a goddess incensed. "You, don't do that!"

"What?"

"Charm me and insult me all in one breath!" She began to pace, sending pebbles flying from under her heels. "What is wrong with you? You're handsome as sin, and despite your odd notions of propriety, you can be amiable—"

He straightened. "You think I'm handsome?" Then he shook his head as if to clear it. "What do you mean, odd notions of propriety?"

Abigail kept pacing, her mind lost to the puzzle

of it. "You shouldn't have difficulty finding women willing enough to bed you. It boggles the mind that you would feel the need to force your attentions—"

"Now hold on one moment!" Steele grabbed her arm and pulled her to face him. "I've never forced my attentions on a woman in my life!"

She glared at his hand on her arm. "The same way you've never manhandled a woman in your life!"

"Fine." He released her. "But it's not the same. I swear on everything I hold dear that I have never been with a woman who didn't, quite clearly, want to be with me."

"I suppose that I'm the first one who's ever made a fuss about it! And given your appeal, I can understand why, but still!"

"Can you please explain yourself in a way I can understand? You're being nonsensical!"

Abigail met those blazing eyes, glare for glare. "Let me be perfectly clear: I will not lie with you!"

Steele's jaw worked. "What? I never asked you to!"

"You made it abundantly clear!"

"How? When?"

"When you set me up to sleep in the mistress's rooms!"

Steele blinked. "You think . . . You think that your job requires . . . that you . . . service me?" His face was incredulous.

Abigail lifted her chin. "When I challenged Carlton about the sleeping arrangements, he said . . . that it was my *duty* to sleep in the mistress's chamber and that my duties weren't necessarily what I'd signed on for. No matter how odd or *unorthodox*."

Steele stilled. "Did he say that you are supposed to sleep with me?" Anger so cold infused his face that Abigail realized he'd barely been vexed before.

Straightening, Abigail opened her mouth and then closed it as doubt slithered across her mind. "Well, no. But he did say that I was subject to your whims and that you specifically wanted me within arm's reach."

"That's very different from a demand that you bed me."

Even though it was starting to sound a little ridiculous even to her ears, Abigail protested, "But he also said that I had better learn to accept that what you want you get. And that . . . and that you wanted me to sleep near you."

His features relaxed. Shaking his head, he chuckled. "No wonder you're so upset."

"So you didn't want me to sleep in the mistress's chambers?"

Laughing, he waved a hand. "Oh no, I do want you to. But not for the reasons you think. Certainly not to . . . 'service your liege lord.'" He shook his head.

Crossing her arms, Abigail was starting to feel more than a bit foolish. But Carlton had made it seem so . . .

Carlton clearly hated children, and his duties had changed because his employer had said so. And with the first footman ill, he'd been forced to take on those duties as well. Carlton was talking about himself, not Abigail sleeping with her employer! Abigail slapped her hand over her mouth as mortification washed over her.

"Bedding me as a job requirement!" Pressing his palm to his middle, Steele chuckled.

"It's not that funny," Abigail muttered, embarrassed.

"I know, I know," Laughing, he shook his head. "I just can't . . . seem to stop . . . laughing!"

Abigail realized she was having difficulty keeping a straight face. His hilarity was so joyful and sincere that she was finding it hard not to join in.

A little chuckle escaped her lips. She pressed her hand to her mouth to catch it.

Their eyes met, and amusement sparked between them.

Grinning sheepishly, she shook her head. "I'm a dolt."

"No, no, anyone . . ." He waved a hand, trying to keep his face sincere. "Anyone might think that . . . there's a reason I . . . pay . . . so well . . . for *active* duty!" He laughed out loud.

Something wild loosened inside her and she giggled.

"What do you suppose I'd give for a Christmas bonus?" He chortled.

Laying her hand on his arm, she cried, "Or for my pension!"

Abigail's cheeks ached, as they'd been unused to smiling for so long. She blinked, realizing that her eyes were teary, for the first time in ages with joy, not sorrow.

His eyes met hers, his look piercing through the protective armor she used to shield herself from the world, and warming her in a place that had known only cold for a very long time. It felt good. Warm, happy. Yet at the same time, disconcerting.

Suddenly she realized that her hand was on his arm. Quickly she removed it, hoping that he had not noticed.

Abigail inhaled a shaky breath and looked around. They stood in the quiet, moonlit park, alone, save for the owl hooting in the trees. Looking down, she adjusted her gown and peered at Steele through her lashes. She was glaringly conscious of how handsome and appealing the man was. And how boldly she'd just spoken about bedding him.

Abigail's cheeks flamed with heat, her blush spreading from her hairline to her toes.

"Ahhh," Steele sighed, rubbing his eyes. "That was . . . that was . . . most unexpected."

Abigail licked her lips and tried not to be too embarrassed. "I can't believe that I was so mistaken . . ." The man probably had women lining up at his bedchamber door.

"Carlton . . ." Stroking his hand across his chiseled jaw, Steele exhaled. "To be fair, when I hired Carlton, I had no intention of ever having children in my house. I never anticipated such a change in his duties. Or my circumstances."

Abigail could barely contain her relief that Steele was moving on to a safer topic than her faux pas or the notion of copulation. She coughed into her fist. "You, ah . . . never expected to have children?"

"Are you asking because you believe that everyone should have children or because you think that all peers yearn to continue their line?"

This topic was much easier for a governess, and she jumped on it like a fish to a hook. "Not everyone is made to be a parent. Certainly not someone like

Carlton, who so obviously despises anyone under four feet high."

"I didn't realize that he disliked children so much. Had I known . . ." He shook his head.

"What would you have done differently? Not taken Seth and Felix in?"

"No, but it looks as if I need to find Carlton another position and find myself another butler."

Her brow furrowed. "If I may, I would like to know why Seth and Felix are coming to live with you."

Steele looked down at the lovely lady, enjoying how the moon lit her blond hair, reminding him of golden gossamer. He knew that he couldn't tell this woman the truth; she'd leave for sure. And suddenly he couldn't imagine letting her go.

Sighing, he stared up at the stars sprinkling the dark sky. "It's so beautiful out tonight." He couldn't recall the last time he'd noticed.

As if suddenly uncomfortable, she bit her lip. "It's getting late. The boys are probably waiting . . ."

Steele wasn't ready to go back to the house, to his responsibilities and everything relying on him there. He knew that he should be working; he had three legal briefs to review and a contract negotiation to plan. But he didn't want the intimacy between him and this unique young lady to end. He couldn't remember the last time he'd laughed so freely or connected so easily with another human being. "We have a few things left to discuss. Why don't we take the path the long way around to get back to the house?"

Uncertainty filled her gaze.

Extending his arm, he smiled. "I promise, I won't bite. No matter how odd my notions of propriety."

Even in the moonlight, he could tell that her cheeks tinged deliciously pink.

He couldn't quite believe that she'd thought him so depraved.

Or that if she had been willing, he would've been sorely tempted.

# Chapter 6

Sounds of the creatures of the night reverberated through the moonlit park as Steele led the mystifying Miss West down the pebbled lane. The woman was a conundrum, a shrinking mouse one moment and a fiery goddess the next. He realized he longed to unlock the puzzle she presented and reveal the secrets inside.

Inhaling the rich scent of pine traveling on the evening breeze, Steele recalled Sir Lee's words, *Not the kind of woman to run from the kitchen when things get hot.* Based on how she'd handled Carlton, she seemed to be one to rush inside and put out the flames. Still, she'd cowered before Benbrook, shrinking into herself like a snail.

And what was the story with Lord Byrnwyck's son Phineas?

Peering sideways at the lady, he noticed once more how pretty she was when she wasn't trying to be a schoolmarm. Her profile was particularly pleasing to the eye, with her slightly upturned nose, pronounced cheekbones, and bowed lips. Had something truly transpired between her and Phineas Byrnwyck?

Phineas was a lanky young man, Steele recalled, with blond curling locks, pale blue eyes, and milky white skin that any debutante would envy. Impartially, Steele could see that he might be appealing in a Byronesque sort of way. Had Miss West fallen for the young greenhorn? An unfamiliar feeling twisted in his gut, but he ignored it and forced himself to focus on the lady beside him.

Steele shortened his stride to match her smaller tread, and again was amazed at how she'd managed to fell Carlton, a much larger man. "Where did you learn that move that you used on Carlton?"

"You won't believe me if I told you." Her voice had a breathy quality to it that at first he'd labeled as trepidation. Now he knew it to be more of a reluctance to speak. *As if words might somehow betray her*, he thought.

As a barrister, Steele had learned to listen for those hidden meanings beneath people's words, and he never dismissed the idle thoughts that whispered in his mind. *As if words might betray her.*

He wondered what it would take for her to open up and speak freely. Somehow he suspected that she might have some very interesting things to say; thus far she'd been a constant surprise. "Try me. I believe I can maintain an open mind."

The moonlight blanketed the trees, giving some sense that they were alone in the world.

"Very well. I learned it from a book."

He felt his brows rise. "A book taught you how to bring a man to his knees?"

Miss West nodded.

"I must read this volume," Steele murmured, fascinated. "Where can I find it?"

"At Andersen Hall Orphanage, in Headmaster Dunn's library." Turning slightly away so that her features were masked by darkness, she murmured, "I went to live there after my parents passed."

"I serve on the board of trustees at Andersen Hall."

She looked up. "You do?"

"Yes. Even though I'm new to the board, I am very impressed with how the institution is managed and the progressive principles upon which it's founded."

"Andersen Hall reflects the man who shaped it. Headmaster Dunn was brilliant and caring and loved all the children as if they were his own . . ." Her voice caught.

Steele had to resist the urge to squeeze the small hand resting on his arm. "I'm so sorry for his loss. His death must have been a terrible blow for you."

She nodded. "Headmaster Dunn was . . . very dear to me."

"He was a good man. Principled. Much more so than many of the men I've encountered. And canny. Very canny." Steele's lips almost lifted as he recalled his first encounter with Uriah Dunn and how handily the man had manipulated him. He remembered this meeting without rancor. Yet it was the compromise Steele had made with Uriah Dunn that allowed Sir Lee to blackmail him into helping Benbrook. Sir Lee was one of three people in the world who knew that Steele had knowingly allowed the Thief of Robinson Square to escape justice. If anyone learned that secret, Steele's reputation would be in tatters.

Steele exhaled. "Headmaster Dunn had a way of making one see things his way, without being a bully about it. I wish I had that gift."

Miss West peered up at him. "Why? So you can convince Carlton that he likes children? I don't believe that even Headmaster Dunn would be able to do that. Mrs. Pitts, on the other hand, seems quite biddable."

Sir Lee had been right; she was perceptive. Then it hit him: She'd quite neatly deflected him from the subject of Headmaster Dunn and her grief. She seemed unwilling to allow anyone to breach the mighty walls that surrounded her heart. If he managed it, he wondered what he'd find. He filed away that notion for later consideration.

"Pray tell me the name of this book," he asked.

"It's called *Defensive Arts of the Eastern Civilizations*, by J. Imperatori. It's filled with defensive exercises."

"They must be very good exercises."

"Only if one remembers to use them," she muttered under her breath. "Sometimes I wonder if I've forgotten more than I've learned."

"When you grabbed Carlton, you weren't thinking. You acted instinctively. Often it's that way with certain moves; you can't overthink."

She stared up at him, wide-eyed and curious.

He added quickly, "Or so I've heard from some of the Bow Street Runners." He changed the topic.

"Did you simply happen upon this book or did you seek it out?"

Peering up at him from the corner of her eye, she replied, "That's a very astute question. You must be a very good barrister. Do you like it?"

She was trying to deflect him once again. Very interesting. But he wasn't an Officer of the Crown for nothing. "Were you being bullied? Is that why you sought out the book?"

Looking away, she stared off into the darkness. "It was a long time ago, I can hardly remember."

"How old were you when you went to Andersen Hall?"

"Thirteen."

Steele scratched his chin. "I wonder that Headmaster Dunn didn't do a better job of protecting his charges."

Her head whipped around. "Headmaster Dunn couldn't be everywhere at every turn. He did the best anyone could have ever done under the circumstances. No, he did better!"

"So you took it upon yourself to stop the harassment."

She gritted her teeth as if admitting to anything went against the grain. "Are all barristers this curious?"

His lips lifted into a smile. "No, I seem to be one of the more inquiring variety." Especially as it pertained to Miss West.

"For the record, Headmaster Dunn ran the orphanage better than any navy ship."

"I know. He was a singular character in every way."

That seemed to mollify her. "Exactly so. I owe him a great deal and count my lucky stars to have landed at Andersen Hall."

"So if you didn't worry over yourself, you sought out the book to protect someone else."

She missed a step, and he slipped his arm around her tiny waist to keep her from falling. He caught a whiff of her clean, heathery scent, far more pleasant than the cloying, flowery perfumes most ladies of fashion wore. Still, this young miss was as mannerly as any of them. Again he realized that it was only a quirk of fate as to who was a penniless orphan and who a titled heiress.

Swallowing, she straightened and stepped away, as if uncomfortable with his touch. "Uh, thank you, I'm fine."

Tilting his head, he removed his arm and they continued walking side by side.

Miss West offered, "Some people . . . some people can handle more than others."

"And you were helping someone who wasn't quite as . . . resilient."

"Yes." The word was offered grudgingly, as if she were uncomfortable laying claim to this remarkable conduct.

Staring up at the star-speckled night, Steele realized that Miss West had a sense of justice that paralleled his. She'd seen someone being unduly harassed, saw that no one was doing anything to stop it, and took matters into her own hands. "I'm impressed." Steele scratched his chin. "I imagine the bully had to be a good bit older than you and likely a few stone heavier as well. I'll bet when he crossed you, he didn't know what hit him!"

Her brow furrowed. "How do you know so much?"

"It's my job to try to read between the lines. Although, I confess, I haven't been very good at it of late." His heart skipped a beat. He hadn't admitted that to anyone!

He swallowed as the terrible fear of the politically astute pricked at his heart. No one in office confessed to failure. Not in his world. It was political and social suicide.

He forced himself to consider the ramifications. Miss West was a governess—and one with a frayed shawl, scrappy shoes, and spotty references, no less. He comforted himself with the thought that there was little harm to be wrought. Still, he never should've spoken so freely.

*What's wrong with me these days?* he wondered. Heath Bartlett's betrayal had shaken him, that was true, but he'd begun making mistakes long before then. And he was taking chances and accepting tasks that no man in his right mind would undertake. He'd taken in two young lads he had hardly even known existed before last week and had accepted guardianship of their lives. Additionally, he was assisting Lord Benbrook, a man who'd never wanted to be his relation and who had wrought turmoil in his life from the very moment they'd met.

Objectively, Steele accepted that the reemergence of his recalcitrant father-in-law in his life had raised thorny emotions better off unfelt. And that it was his love for Deidre and sense of duty to her memory and to her nephews that had inspired his actions. That, and Sir Lee Devane's blackmail, of course.

He shook his head, realizing that he was under strain from Benbrook, the lads, the investigation, and his recent failings at work. He wasn't operating at his best and needed to dig his way out of the rut he was in.

And crafting fantasies about pretty young governesses wasn't going to help him one bit.

He needed to gain Miss West's trust, get her to agree to work for him, and get on with his investigation. He had enough to do to unearth the truth behind Benbrook's claims and stop a killer on the loose. There was no room in his life for anything else, particularly not for pesky emotions and moonlight confessions.

Nodding, Steele exhaled, feeling more in command now that he had his priorities in order.

Miss West bit her lip. "Headmaster Dunn called blunders 'opportunities' and taught us that it is only through mistakes that we learn."

Her lack of censure reassured him even more, but he felt the need to add, "I can't afford to make mistakes. Not in my position."

"What is a solicitor-general?"

Feeling on safe ground, he replied, "I represent the Crown on legal matters. In the courts, I provide legal advice, questions involving public welfare. I'm consulted for legal matters involving debts to the Crown, thefts from the Crown . . . and the like."

"So you wouldn't handle the petty things . . . like ordinary pilfering or disorderly conduct and such?"

"Not usually, no."

Nodding, she seemed to relax.

"Why?"

She shrugged. "I'm simply trying to understand."

They had just reached the corner nearing his house. Feeling an urgency to settle matters, he stopped and faced her. "So what do I have to do to convince you to come work for me, Miss West?"

She bit her bottom lip. "Why do you want me to sleep in the mistress's chambers?"

"Truth be told . . ." Steele mentally kicked himself, for he never trusted a word someone said when he prefaced a comment with "truth be told." He was going to have to learn to lie better to maintain the façade. "The fact of the matter is that the upstairs is under construction."

"Oh."

He couldn't tell if that was an "Oh, I believe you," or an "Oh, that doesn't seem quite plausible." The light from the adjacent house glowed on her fair hair and washed her pale face in a golden radiance. Still, he could not read her features and realized that this lady had learned to hide her feelings well.

Steele added, "As I said before, I didn't expect the children." That much was true. "And so when I purchased the house I paid little attention to the nurseries. Regrettably, they are in disrepair, and I'm taking steps to remedy that situation. In the interim, I would like you and the lads to take advantage of the unused rooms on my floor, and that happens to include the mistress's chambers."

"If I may ask, how did you come to be the

guardian of Seth and Felix? Lord Benbrook seems quite . . . attached."

"That's a very polite way of saying officious and demanding."

He was pleased to see her lips lift into a little smile. "I did not say that, so don't ever try to quote me."

"Lord Benbrook is attached to the boys, certainly. They are his grandchildren."

"Then why is he giving you guardianship?"

Steele considered his options and decided on a variation of the truth. "Lord Benbrook is my father-in-law. I was married to his daughter." They were only words, he told himself, as he pushed away the familiar grief.

"Was?"

"She died."

"I'm so sorry." Her luminous eyes were filled with compassion.

"Thank you. It was a long time ago."

"My parents died a long time ago, but that doesn't diminish the loss or the fact that I miss them still."

Surprisingly, her empathy somehow allowed him both to feel the pain, but not to experience its ache quite as acutely. "Yes, well, I'm the only family that Benbrook trusts with the safety of his grandchildren, and he fears that he's . . . not long for this world."

Raising her hand to her mouth, Miss West cried, "Those poor boys! First their parents and now this!"

Steele felt a tad guilty about working on Miss West's sympathies, but he would do whatever necessary to get the job done. "Yes, well, Felix and Seth are certainly in need of kindness. And you leaving right now . . ."

Abigail swallowed as a fresh wave of mortification swept over her. "I suppose this whole misunderstanding is really my fault." Her cheeks warmed, and she couldn't meet Lord Steele's eyes. "I jumped to some very unfair conclusions about you . . . I mean, you wishing to be with me . . . how absurd!"

"Yes, well . . . Carlton certainly complicated things." His face was unreadable. Abigail probably should be counting her lucky stars that the man wasn't insulted.

She cleared her throat, trying to move past the embarrassing faux pas. "Ah, Carlton . . . he may not be so pleased to have me stay on."

"As I mentioned, I think I'm going to find him another post. But that is my concern. You just worry about keeping those boys safe."

"Safe?"

"Their parents' deaths have left them shaken, and I've promised Benbrook that I won't let anything happen to them. So I'm going to take extra pains where they're concerned."

"That rule about the two adults accompanying them when they leave the house?"

"Exactly. I want them watched and attended at all times by at least two adults. For the first few months that we're together, I want to ensure that not a scratch touches them."

"But they're boys . . ."

"I know, but I insist on this arrangement." He extended his hand. "So do we have an agreement? You help me with the boys and I take care of everything else."

She stared at the graceful masculine fingers stretching toward her, appreciating how kind he was being about the whole misunderstanding business.

Yet there was something that made her hesitate, a tiny ring of alarm. It wasn't fear, more like . . . agitation. Lord Steele made her belly tingle. If that wasn't bad enough, he seemed to further incite the passions the masked rescuer had recently ignited in her. She didn't quite trust him, either. He was disarming, far too handsome for her peace of mind, and there was something unsettling about him that she couldn't quite put her finger on.

But that was ridiculous. She desperately needed this job and was fond of Seth and Felix already. What was there to possibly be concerned about? She dismissed the warnings in her mind as the silly remnants of her appalling embarrassment.

Nodding, she slipped her small hand into his.

His fingers held her firmly, yet were gentler than she'd imagined. And his skin was surprisingly smooth and very, very warm. Heat seeped from his palm to hers with such intensity that she felt a tingle race up her arm and rush into her chest. Looking down, she stared at their joined hands, realizing that she could hardly tell where his flesh ended and hers began.

Their eyes met. A strange panic licked at her middle, and she quickly slipped her hand from his and stepped back. "Agreed." She hoped he didn't notice how breathless she sounded.

He shook himself, as if startled. "Yes, well. I'm glad that's settled." Distractedly he motioned toward the house. "If you will. I'm sure the boys must be ready for dinner."

She stepped alongside him. "Ah, will you be joining us?"

"Regrettably, no. Lord Benbrook and I have some matters to discuss."

"Of course." Somehow she felt rejected. But that was ludicrous.

At the foot of the stairs to his house, he stopped and turned to her, as if wanting to say something. His mouth opened and then closed.

She stared up at him, realizing once more how elegantly handsome he was and how insane she'd been to have thought that he might want to bed her.

The footman opened the door, spilling light down the steps like a golden path.

Still Lord Steele hesitated, and she waited expectantly for his words.

"I . . . well . . . I suppose you've never quite had a first day like this one."

"No." Ruefully she shook her head. "Today certainly was unique. I'm sure that none of us will be quick to forget it, although I'd certainly like to try."

"Not me. I found it quite . . . refreshing."

*Refreshing.* An unexpected little thrill flashed inside her chest, but she dampened it, not understanding why it would matter.

Together they walked inside.

# Chapter 7

For the next week Abigail tried not to think about how intimately her and Lord Steele's hands had fit together after their stroll in the park. She attempted not to recall the astonishing thrill that had rocketed up her arm and into her chest when they'd touched. She tried exceedingly hard not to analyze the exhilarating flash in her middle when their eyes had met. She did her best not to dwell on Steele's stonily handsome features and how they softened when he'd laughed. But most importantly, she'd done *everything in her power* not to think about the mortifying fact that she'd boldly declared that she would not sleep with him.

As if bedding him were even an option!

But this afternoon as she sat idly watching the boys as they attempted to fly a kite across the grassy knoll of Coleridge Square Park, it was very hard not to think upon such things.

Lord Steele had been quite nice about the whole bedding misunderstanding, actually. He hadn't mentioned it once, since. He hadn't said much of anything else, either. Abigail tried to pretend that she wasn't disappointed.

He'd been closeted in his study for much of those seven days, and she'd hardly had a glimpse of him. The man seemed to live for work, not the other way around. He certainly wasn't like the other gentlemen she'd known. But then again, he'd climbed so high because of his work. Now that he'd achieved so much, shouldn't he enjoy the fruits of his labor?

Abigail sighed, chiding herself to count her lucky stars that she had an employer who knew how to leave her alone to do her job. Still, he should at least be spending some time with the lads. They needed to know him and love him—he was to be their closest family.

A familiar longing speared her gut. She sighed. "Where are you, Reggie?" she whispered to her wayward brother.

Was he involved with brigands? Deeply in debt? His letter had been so vague. Yet alarming in the extreme, begging her to come to London and bring any money she might have.

"If you ask me to come to London, you could at least have told me where you were," she muttered, frustration and anger soothing her fears. Her brother was so inconsiderate at times. He'd told her to ask around Charing Cross, *covertly*, no less, to find him.

"Who does he think I am, a Bow Street Runner?"

But the day was too lovely to focus on such a frustrating state of affairs, she told herself. Abigail pushed it all from her mind, trying to force herself to enjoy the beauty around her and not allow herself to be haunted by fears that could not be assuaged.

Even though it was only spring, the afternoon air was thick with a heat that seemed to come down from the sun and swell up from the earth in a shimmer of humidity. Many of the governesses sitting on the benches lining the outskirts of the grasses fanned themselves with vigor. Abigail had given up on any attempt to waft the steamy air around her and had settled for simply sitting as still as possible. Sweat moistened her face, and her underarms had a very unladylike feeling of dampness. Still, the tree above her was heavy with green leaves and provided a welcome shade to relieve the worst of the heat.

The boys didn't seem to mind the high temperature one bit as they raced and pranced. They were fully occupied with their new kite and wouldn't have known if it was hotter than Hades. Felix was in the lead, holding the wooden spool, with Seth following after him whining for a turn.

The yellow kite had been a gift from Lord Steele, left for the lads to find after their studies. Lord Benbrook had departed that morning, and Abigail supposed that Steele had wanted to give the boys a distraction. It was a good thought, although he couldn't have counted on such breezeless weather.

"Let go!" Felix screamed, yanking on the kite in Seth's hands.

Seth gripped it harder. "I want to fly it!"

Abigail straightened, lifting her head.

Felix raised his hand as if to strike.

"No!" Abigail leaped from her seat and charged forward.

Felix looked up, his face twisted in anger. "He's being an idiot!" But he lowered his hand.

"You're the idiot!" Seth screamed, tears spilling out his red-rimmed eyes.

Abigail watched Felix carefully, but the taunt didn't seem to trouble him.

Pointing a finger at Felix, Abigail charged, "Don't you *ever* raise a hand to your brother! Do you hear me?"

"I wouldn't have hit him." Felix pouted, crossing his arms.

"Have you ever struck him?"

"Yes!" Seth cried. "He punched me!"

"When?"

Seth puffed out his chest in justified resentment. "On my birthday. He punched me in the arm for each year I was born."

"That doesn't count!" Felix exclaimed, flinging his arms in the air. "It's a tradition."

"One you relish hardily, I'm sure," Abigail muttered with relief. It seemed that Felix might get irritated with his brother, but the anger didn't propel him to real violence.

Abigail turned to Seth. "Do you get to punch Felix on his birthday?"

"Well . . . yes."

"Then since he's older, it would seem that you get to punch him three more times than he punches you."

Seth blinked. "I . . . hadn't ever thought of that." He smirked, mollified.

"Now, about this kite." Abigail crossed her arms. "Please don't make me have to inform Lord Steele that you must return his gift."

Both boys started. "What?"

"I'll be forced to do so if you two can't figure out a way to play together." Unwinding her arms, Abigail held open her hands. "Do you want to fly the kite?"

"Yes!" the boys cried in unison.

"Then you must find a way to work together." She looked each boy in the eye. "Agreed?"

Sighing, Felix nodded. "Agreed."

"Yes." Seth rubbed his eyes.

Abigail waved them off. "Go on now."

The boys traipsed off.

"Here, let me show you the best way to hold it." Felix leaned toward his brother.

"Thanks," Seth replied.

A new air of camaraderie enveloped their play.

Satisfied, Abigail returned to her seat in the shade and sighed. But she could not seem to quiet the thread of anxiety woven in her heart. The altercation between the boys had brought her fears about how so many conflicts seemed to come to blows. She'd certainly had enough experience with lightning tempers. Her brother had been the worst offender.

It had happened again and again when he was a child. Reggie was easily affronted, and no matter how much Abigail had worked with him on trying not to take life too seriously, he always seemed to wind up in nasty confrontations. If a boy had pushed him in jest, he'd slammed him back at full force. If a girl had teased him, he'd barked out the nastiest retort. Heaven forbid someone said a cross word to Abigail, Reggie would make him pay, usually in resourceful ways that struck far deeper than any slight Abigail might have suffered.

Reggie used to say that he was the only one allowed to be cross with Abigail. And when he was feeling anxious, she bore the brunt of that favored treatment. His tongue-lashings could be quite scathing, but Abigail had never taken them to heart. Not the times he'd told her that if only she'd been born a boy, they could have earned a decent wage and not been homeless for a time before they'd made it to Andersen Hall Orphanage.

Abigail had ignored the instances when he'd retorted that if she'd only been smarter, they wouldn't have lost their home when their parents had died. Or her favorite, the times he'd charged that if only she'd have been kinder to the neighbor, Mr. Wormier, they would've had a home and never would have had to leave Bury St. Edmunds.

Abigail bit her tongue at those times, having given up on reminding Reggie that she couldn't help being born a girl, she'd done as well as she could as a grieving thirteen-year-old child, and marriage to Mr. Wormier wasn't ever an option. Not that she could have stomached such a lecherous husband.

After each tirade had lost its steam, Reggie would be completely repentant and good sense would reassert itself. And it was hard for Abigail to hold her anger for him. Reggie was such a lost soul, and she couldn't bear the pain of his knowing that she was angry with him. When it came to his sister, Reggie always made peace. With others, he wasn't quite so redeemable.

When Abigail had lost her position in the Byrnwyck household, she'd intended to keep the information from her brother. What sane woman would want her little brother knowing that she'd lost her heart, her good sense, and her virtue in one feel swoop?

But events conspired to intensify her ruin.

Since she'd been tossed from the house with a swiftness that had left her reeling, Abigail had had to rely on her friendship with Warren and Jan, the innkeeper and his wife, to keep a roof over her head. For almost three weeks Abigail had hardly left her small room at the top of the rickety stairs. She'd been in a state, barely eating or drinking. All she could do was cry until she passed out in a fit of exhaustion, then wake up and cry some more. Her heart had ached so sorely, she'd thought she might die from heartbreak. But that was clearly an escape Abigail was not meant to have.

Instead, her dear friend Jan had thought that Abigail needed family support and hence wrote to Reggie, seeking his help.

Reggie had found Abigail suffering in her tiny room and kicked up a riot. He'd demanded the whole sordid tale, dragging it out of Abigail one shameful detail after the next. He'd ruthlessly questioned her on Phineas's part, Lord Byrnwyck's role, and the interference of Lord Byrnwyck's nasty nephew, Silas.

Abigail had attempted to paint the picture a little sunnier, but Reggie would have none of it. Ranting and raving, he'd screamed about beating Phineas, skewering Byrnwyck, and trampling Silas beneath his horse's hooves.

Abigail had tried to calm him down, but her heart hadn't been in it. Secretly she'd longed for such revenge, although she'd never truly wished them ill.

Not without them recovering . . . *ultimately* . . . after a long and painful convalescence.

That rainy night, Reggie had stormed from the inn intent on avenging his sister. He'd taken rocks and smashed the prized hundred-year-old stained glass windows adorning Byrnwyck Manor's library. Then when chased, he'd run into the barn and set all the horses free from their stalls. When confusion had overcome the manor, he'd sneaked into Byrnwyck's private study and stolen the Byrnwyck family crest.

It was silver inlaid with mother-of-pearl and the family motto etched in gold. It was worth a few pounds for its weight alone, but it was even more valuable since it was Lord Byrnwyck's most prized possession.

If there was one thing about Reggie, he knew how to strike someone where it hurt.

When Abigail realized what her brother had done, she'd begged him to return the crest and make away, fearful of what Lord Byrnwyck would do to him. She knew that if it weren't for her foolish mistake with Phineas, Reggie would never have gotten so angry and dug himself a hole so deep. She needed to get Reggie out of trouble.

But Reggie wasn't ready to make amends. Instead he'd drawn a picture of the crest burning in a raging fire and had it delivered to Byrnwyck Manor, signature and all.

In that single irrational act of revenge, Reggie had become a fugitive from the law. And he'd been one ever since.

Lord Byrnwyck had had a warrant issued for Reggie's arrest and had set the constable on him.

Reggie ran off in the middle of the night, leaving Abigail frantic with anxiety.

Thwarted, Lord Byrnwyck had set a price on Reggie's head. He'd hired Bow Street Runners to track Reggie down. He even tried to throw Abigail in jail as an accomplice. It was only Jan and Warren's staunch intervention, swearing oaths that Abigail had been with them all along and had no notion of her brother's activities, that had saved her. That, and the fact that they'd told the magistrate that they'd never serve him dinner at their inn again if he didn't do what was right.

Throughout this whole ordeal, Abigail never heard a word from Phineas. She'd wondered what he knew, but like so many other questions in life, that one would have to go unanswered.

Still, Phineas's betrayal haunted her. How could she have loved someone so unworthy? How could she have been such a fool? How could she trust a man not to dupe her or hurt her when her judgment of character was so clearly wrong?

So she'd allowed her girlhood dreams of love and marriage and a family to dissolve into mist, to reside with the unicorns and dragons and fairy godmothers that she no longer believed in. And so her heart had grown harder, and her nights lonelier.

Images of the masked rescuer rose in her mind's eye.

Could he be a kindred spirit? Lonely, searching for . . . what? What could drive a man to roam the streets of London at night in a mask?

"Where are you?" she whispered, wondering if he had a home, a wife . . .

Nay, something about the man screamed *solitude*. Besides, he made for a much more appealing hero if he was tormented and lonely and . . .

Abigail straightened. Perhaps he was disfigured and that's why he covered his face. Was he burned in a fire? Wounded by some terrible tragedy? Born with a horrible birthmark?

Her heart went out to him. The poor man! No wonder he refused to show his face. He probably had a fascinating story of pain and redemption. Her imagination painted a dark and brooding picture. Very romantic.

She would never know, though. He certainly wasn't about to share his life. She'd probably never see him again. So where was the harm in thinking about him? In dreaming about him? In having a little fun to pass the time?

Leaning back into the bench, Abigail allowed her mind to drift, creating a hero from the masked rescuer, one who won her love through his bravery, integrity, and selfless sacrifice in the protection of others. Woven in with those traits, he had to have the most important quality of all—he had to love her unconditionally and forever.

She sighed, watching the boys. "I swear if a man like this exists I'll eat my own stockings with nary any salt or pepper." She chuckled to herself, knowing that that day would never come.

For men like her hero existed only in the world of fantasy and imagination. None was flesh and bone. And even if such a man existed, he wouldn't want the likes of her.

Her mind drifted back to the masked rescuer.

Would they meet again? If so, how? Even though she knew it was based in fantasy, her heart warmed toward him.

*If I can get closer, what will I find?* she wondered. Suddenly she very much wanted to find out.

# Chapter 8

Sighing, Abigail pushed away all thoughts of the masked hero from her mind as she watched Seth and Felix struggle with the kite. Nary a breath of wind could be felt, and the boys were having a difficult time of it.

The yellow kite sputtered to the grass.

"It's my turn!" Seth squealed.

Running toward the kite, Felix twirled the string around the wooden spool. "You gave it a go and failed. It's too hard. If I can't get it up, you certainly can't."

"Lord Steele said it would fly! I wanna try again!"

Lord Steele hadn't actually said it, he'd written it on the note that he'd left with the kite. It would have been nice if he'd joined the boys in trying out their new toy, but Abigail supposed he was busy with the demands of his very important position. He'd certainly been too occupied to take meals with the boys, something she hoped would change now that Benbrook was gone.

Working the string, Felix snarled. "This is a stupid waste of time!"

Seth grabbed at the kite.

Felix shoved it at his brother. "Fine, take it!"

Noting that the two footmen standing near the boys were staying out of the situation, Abigail straightened. "Why don't we try a new strategy?"

Felix turned her way. "It's broken. It won't work."

"Lord Steele wouldn't give us a broken kite!" Seth cried, his lower lip quaking perilously. "He wouldn't do that!"

"No, he certainly wouldn't." Abigail rose and approached the boys. The sun was so bright, she had to squint beneath the shade of her bonnet. "In this weather you need to work together. You need a really fast runner to get the string far forward, and you need someone to hold the kite off the ground and give it a good shove into the air."

"I can do that!" Seth exclaimed, brightening. "I can shove, I can shove!"

Felix raised a brow as if trying to decide if this was some sort of ploy.

"Give it a try and you'll see," Abigail urged.

Felix adjusted the string. "Fine. But you'll have to keep up, Seth, otherwise you need to let go so as not to tear the kite."

Seth nodded. "I'll keep up. I'll keep up."

The boys gave it another try, this time with Felix running forward with a swath of uncoiled string and Seth following far behind holding the kite high above his little head. Miraculously, a slight breeze gusted just at that moment and the yellow kite swung aloft in an unsteady arc.

Seth shouted with glee, racing behind the struggling kite. Felix's face was locked in concentration, but a smile played on his lips as he swung and angled the spool. The kite labored to gain loft, dropping suddenly, then sweeping up high into the air.

"Well done!" Abigail cried, clapping her hands. She had never actually flown a kite herself, but she'd had a notion of how it was supposed to work and had guessed that coordination might be a good idea. Thank heavens she'd been right! Her heart warmed with joy for the boys.

Seth and Felix raced off, intent on maintaining their success. The two footmen followed close behind. Abigail relaxed back into the bench, a feeling of contentment sweeping over her.

Felix and Seth moved back and forth on the grass, the breeze now blowing more steadily, making the boys and everyone in the park breathe more easily.

After a time Seth grew bored, his eyes veering away from the kite toward the flock of ducks congesting the shores of the pond.

"Would you like to feed the ducks?" Abigail called to Seth.

Nodding excitedly, the young lad raced over. "Yes!"

Abigail reached under her bench to the bag of old bread she'd taken from the kitchen. Seth and the burly footman Claude approached.

"I like your bonnet," Seth commented, reaching up and touching one of the round pale yellow beads adorning the brown cotton.

"Thank you, Seth." It had been an expensive indulgence at the time, but Abigail had been at a low point, alone for Christmas Eve and feeling a bit pitiful. She loved wearing the bonnet. It made her feel fashionable, if only slightly.

"I'll take him to the ducks," Claude offered. "Why don't you keep an eye on Felix in case he needs help with the kite, Miss West?"

Abigail nodded. "Very well. Please don't let Seth too near the water."

"No, Miss West, I wouldn't allow that." Claude passed the bag of bread to Seth and pointed. "We'll go to that bridge over there."

Abigail looked to where he motioned. A stone bridge arched over a tributary leading to the pond. A group of ducks swarmed beneath the bridge as a cluster of children stood at the top of the bridge tossing down crumbs. "Very well."

Claude took Seth's hand, and together they walked toward the stone bridge. Abigail watched them until they were situated near the ducks, then she turned her attention to Felix once more.

Abigail enjoyed watching Felix master the kite, but worried about him being out in the sun for so long. Reaching beneath her bench, she grasped the flask of water she'd brought and stood.

It took only a little bit of negotiating to get Felix to drink while Abigail held the spool. The kite fluttered and pulled, and Abigail watched it, nervous that she might ruin Felix's hard work. Yet she managed quite ably and was a bit sad to hand the spool back to Felix once more.

It had been great fun, if only for a moment, and Abigail regretted that she had been so worried that she hadn't enjoyed it more.

After ensuring that Foster would stay with Felix,

Abigail walked toward the stone bridge, trying to pick out Seth in the small crowd of adults and children clustered on top of it.

Suddenly a small cry rang out and a child fell from the bridge into the water with a great splash. Abigail dropped her flask, lifted her skirts, and jumped into the stream. The water clutched at her gown as she trudged deeper into the stream, the water rising to her waist, to her shoulders, to her chin. The child in the water struggled and screamed, his flailing arms the only thing visible among the splashes.

Abigail stopped wading and dropped to float, pulling the water past her with large swings of her arms. Her entire being was focused on that child and getting his head above water.

Just as Abigail made it to the child, another splash rang out beside her. She grabbed the child by his brown coat and lifted him up with both arms, while kicking frantically with her legs. *It was Seth!*

Seth kicked and screamed madly.

"I've got you!" Abigail cried, her chest laboring and her kicks frantic but tiring.

Seth thrashed, landing a glancing blow to her eye.

"Seth!" Abigail cried. "Stop struggling. You're all right! I've got you."

Her words must have reached him, for Seth suddenly clutched her around the neck so tight, she sank deep into the water. Kicking madly to stay afloat, Abigail wondered how she was going to manage to get him to the shore.

"Here, let me help you," a breathless male voice came from behind.

Large hands encircled Abigail's waist, lifting her

up and helping her stay above water. The hands propelled her toward the shore. She clutched at Seth, her feet grasping for purchase. Grabbing at firm ground with her feet, she yanked herself and her precious bundle through the water. She collapsed on her rear as soon as she could, clutching Seth to her chest and hugging him close.

Her breath pierced her chest with every inhalation and her muscles burned with effort, but she was so thankful she wanted to sing.

Shoving aside her flopping bonnet, Abigail lowered her face to Seth's. "Are you all right?"

Seth's lips were quivering, his face washed white.

A quack resounded to her left, and Abigail almost groaned as a flock of ducks swarmed over begging for food.

"Tell me, Seth, are you hurt?"

He looked so pitiful, her heart ached for him.

A duck nipped at Abigail's arm. *Quack!*

Abigail jerked her arm away. "Leave off!"

Seth's eyes veered toward the ducks.

"Please answer me, Seth!" she cried. "Does anything hurt?"

Something yanked at her sodden bonnet, wrenching her head to one side. "Ow!"

*Quack!*

A giggle burst from Seth's throat.

Another jerk on her bonnet. *Quack! Quack!*

The ducks thought her stylish pale yellow beads were pieces of bread!

*Quack!* Another pluck at her bonnet, yanking her head to the left.

"Ow!"

Seth laughed. His eyes were bright and no longer frightened. Another duck yanked at a button on her bonnet, but she hardly cared.

Abigail wiped tears of relief from her eyes. She was perfectly content to sit for an hour or two while the ducks decimated her prized bonnet. It was worth every bead.

"Spoiled rotten little beggars!" The man standing above waved his arms to scare them away. He was of medium height and medium build, but his face was . . . well . . . the word that came to Abigail's mind was . . . gorgeous. He had bright, pale blue eyes, a sloping nose, and a cleft chin that combined into an undeniable boyish handsomeness. His wet blond hair was spiked around his head, making him appear like a boy from the wild. And at the moment he was madly flapping his arms. "Shoo! Shoo!"

Abigail was too tired to tell him not to bother.

"Shoo!" The man pranced as he flapped. "Shoo!" Seth giggled.

Abigail had to agree; the man looked ridiculous.

Suddenly Felix and Foster, the other footman, came running up.

"I want to go swimming, too!" Felix cried.

Seth preened. "I got to go swimming! I got to go swimming!"

"Let me help you." The blond-haired man grabbed her beneath the arms and pulled her to stand.

Abigail was forced to rise or he would have pulled her arms from their sockets. "Ah, I appreciate your help . . ."

"Yes, well, you probably want to make yourself presentable."

Abigail suddenly became aware of the crowd of onlookers gathered at the edge of the water.

Embarrassed, she realized that she must look a fright. She busily helped Seth stand and handed him over to Foster's care.

Foster mussed Seth's hair. "Got a little hot, did you? Needed a dip?"

Seth beamed. "I went for a swim!"

Foster looked around. "Where's Claude?"

Straightening her ruined walking dress, Abigail scanned the crowd. "Good question." She was going to have to have a word with the wayward footman. Seth could have drowned.

"That was quite courageous of you, miss," the blond-haired man declared. "Jumping in after your charge like that."

"I didn't even know it was Seth," Abigail admitted.

"Even more worthy!"

"Your help was quite opportune and greatly appreciated . . . ah . . ."

He bowed. "Nigel Littlethom at your service!" The man seemed a little excitable, and his every sentence was stated with great aplomb.

"Yes, well, Mr. Littlethom, I am Miss Abigail West, and the boy you saved is Lord Benbrook's grandson."

"You saved the lad, not I!" Littlethom declared with a flourish of his hand. "I simply assisted you to the shore."

"Well, I am indebted to you just the same." She looked up into his bright blue eyes, realizing that his hair was drying into a bit of a peak above his forehead, reminding Abigail of a rooster's comb. Yet the man still managed to look gorgeous. A gorgeous, strutting rooster. She smiled at her own silliness.

"It is my pleasure to be of service!" Mr. Littlethom declared, giving her a boyish smile that was so bright, she had to blink.

She peeled her eyes away from his handsome face, noticing the rest of him. "Oh dear! Your coat!"

His gray coat was soaked through and torn at the shoulders; his breeches were so sodden as to be like paste on his legs.

Gallantly he pulled off his coat and draped it on her shoulders. It must have weighed a stone and smelled unappealingly of sweaty male. Abigail tried not to show her distaste. "Ah, thank you, but it's quite warm out today and I hardly need it."

"No, I insist!"

"We should get the lads home," Foster commented, eyeing the crowd.

"I will escort you!" Littlethom declared.

"Thank you so much. We are greatly in your debt. But there is no need for us to put you out any further." Abigail handed the man back his coat, which he grudgingly accepted. "In fact, you must give me your address and I will pay for your cleaning and repairs."

"There is no need, but if I may ask a boon of you?"

"Of course."

"Please allow me to stop by the residence and inquire after the boy. And you, of course."

"That would be most kind of you, sir."

"Until then!" Turning, the man padded off, his shoes making a funny squeaking sound with every step.

Watching him go, Seth giggled.

"He was odd," Felix commented.

"He was courageous," Abigail countered. "He helped your brother out from the water." She drew them along beside her down the path. "Now come along. Let us go back to the house to change clothing."

"I can't believe that you jumped in." Felix swatted his brother's shoulder as they meandered down the walkway.

"I didn't mean to . . . but there were a lot of people trying to get to the ducks . . ." Seth preened. "And I got to go swimming!"

"Wait until Lord Steele hears. He won't be pleased."

Rubbing his head, Foster muttered, "No he won't be. Especially not with Claude."

"Nor me," Abigail muttered. *Keep them safe*, Steele had asked.

Abigail grimaced. Almost drowning did not exactly fit into that category.

Looking down at Seth, she rationalized that little enough harm was done. Yet somehow she doubted that Steele would see it that way. A tiny thrill of anticipation licked up her spine as they neared the house. Lord Steele would have to come out of his study to confront her. Instead of slowing, her steps quickened.

# Chapter 9

"What do you mean, no harm was done?" Steele demanded from the young governess. "The boy could have drowned!"

"But he didn't," Miss West replied with vigor. "In fact, he's quite elated about the whole thing; he thinks that he got to go swimming when his brother didn't."

Despite her dreadful bonnet clenched in her hands before her and those soulful gray eyes looking up at him, Miss West still didn't look nearly as contrite as she should. Instead, somehow she managed to look too delectable for her own good. It couldn't be the damp golden hair sticking up around her head like hay. But it might've had something to do with the fact that her soggy clothing clung to her shapely body tighter than any opera dancer's costume.

Steele did his best to keep his eyes locked with hers and not allow them to veer down to the luscious swell of her bosom. "That's a five-year-old's version. Not reality."

"But that's the only one that counts in the end. Since all is well."

All wasn't well, since Steele's jaw had been clenched ever since he'd learned of the incident. The boys had been in his care for only a week and Seth almost drowned? If anything happened to them . . . "Where was Claude?"

"He was with Seth, but then after the fall and all, I lost track . . ."

"Did he leave his post?"

Her teeth clenched and her eyes flashed with anger. "I don't want to lay blame until we hear his side of what happened . . ."

"But he's nowhere to be found."

"Yes."

"Something smells fishy to me."

She looked up hopefully as her cheeks flushed pink. "I can go and change . . ."

"You're not getting away that easily." He hadn't been referring to her clothing and, in truth, she smelled quite nicely of heather and woman. Aside from the fact that he knew that she could hardly catch cold in this mild weather, he wasn't quite ready to have her turn tail and run, or change clothing and ruin his lovely view.

Miss West gritted her teeth, and a decidedly defiant gleam lit her gaze. "I know that things didn't go well today—"

"You think?" His tone was sardonic. He tried to feel guilty over how much he was enjoying this little interview, but couldn't muster the remorse. Despite the fact that he'd hardly seen more than a glimpse of Miss West the last seven days, she'd been on his mind far too much for his good. Whenever he thought about their little encounter in the park and how she'd boldly declared that she wouldn't sleep with him, his lips would lift into a little smile. Whenever he considered how she'd protected Seth with that audacious move that had brought Carlton to his knees, he couldn't quite help the swell of admiration from blooming inside him. And when he reflected on how nice it was to speak with an interesting woman with a brain in her head, he would find himself nodding with appreciation.

The danger, however, came when he dwelled on how the air had crackled with sensual awareness between them, how deliciously warm her smooth skin had felt touching his. And how her gossamer golden hair had seemed to beg for his caress, and how tempted he was to taste those lush bowed lips.

Miss West might as well have been wearing a sign that spelled *Danger*. And Steele was too astute and too cautious a man not to heed the warning. So he'd stayed away. He'd stopped himself from going to the schoolroom to check on the boys. He'd made sure not to dine with the lads or interrupt their play. He told himself that it was good for the boys as well, since they were settling in and he didn't want to disrupt their routine.

But now Steele had no choice but to engage the intriguing Miss West. And he wasn't fool enough not to enjoy it.

Raising her brow, she crossed her arms, causing her bosom to swell quite deliciously. "Are we done, my lord?"

He frowned, keeping his eyes locked with hers. "I'll inform you when I am finished with you, Miss West."

The energy surging through him reminded him of the feeling when he was in court examining a witness. The unpredictability of the encounter was exhilarating, and he loved the challenge. "Tell me again why you weren't watching Seth."

"I was with Felix. And the kite. I couldn't be in two places at once." Her eyes narrowed slightly.

"Why are you looking at me that way?"

"What way?"

"As if somehow this is my fault."

Her chin lifted a notch.

"Well?" he demanded. "Spit it out."

She lanced him with a searing gaze of gray-blue fire. "Perhaps if you'd come along . . ."

He straightened. "I have work to do."

"Every moment of every day?"

"For your information, being Solicitor-General of England requires some of my time." Distantly he was amazed that he was even engaging in this conversation with a member of his staff. Yet somehow he found himself annoyingly irritated that she didn't think well of him.

Her lip lifted into a funny little curl.

"You don't believe me?" he asked, shocked.

"I've been here one week, and in that time you've barely spared the boys more than a word or two."

He didn't like the course of this conversation, yet somehow found himself going deeper down its path. "So?"

"So, you're to be their closest family and they hardly know you!"

Steele pursed his lips, telling himself that it

could be easily justified by the fact that he was just temporarily the boys' guardian.

"You've been avoiding them," she declared, which was close enough to the truth to make him shift uncomfortably.

Turning, he stepped away from her and moved to stare out the window.

Miss West stepped behind him. He could feel her presence like a burning stove emanating a heat that warmed his skin in a decidedly unsettling way.

Furtively he inhaled her womanly scent, wondering why Miss West had been sent to vex him when instead there had to be hundreds of snippety, repulsive, know-their-place governesses in England.

She asked gently, "Is it because they remind you of your wife?"

He started. "No. Of course not."

"It wouldn't be so unnatural," she replied. "They look like her."

He turned, surprised. "How do you know?"

"I saw a portrait of her up in the attics."

"What were you doing in the attics?"

Her cheeks flushed pink, and he realized that she'd been checking to make sure that he hadn't been lying about the repairs to the nurseries.

"You don't trust anyone's word, do you?"

She looked away guiltily. "I just wanted to see for myself."

He chuckled. "I would've done the same."

She looked up, and their eyes met. Connection flashed between them, spearing his gut with the familiar lust that had been plaguing his nights these last seven days.

He'd felt a similar kind of awareness between himself and women before. Yet this was the first time the intensity of this sensual spark burning between them was enough to steal the breath from his throat.

Certainly having her sleeping in the next room didn't help matters. He could hear her fumbling around at all hours of the night and wondered what she was up to.

"You don't sleep much, do you?" he asked suddenly.

Blinking, she started. "Pardon?"

"At night. I hear you . . ."

Her brow furrowed, and then she looked away, seemingly embarrassed. "I'm sorry. Did I disturb you?"

"No," he lied. "I was awake anyway."

Her cheeks flushed pink. "I'm so sorry. It's just that I seem to have difficulty sleeping when there's so much to do."

"So much to do?" He wondered if he was over-working her.

"You know . . . arrange things . . . organize . . . make lists."

He crossed his arms. "What kind of organizing? Are you uncomfortable in your quarters?"

"Oh no! The room is lovely! Nicer than I've ever had, even before my parents died. Comfort is certainly not the issue . . ." Her voice trailed off.

"Then what is?"

Shaking her head, she exhaled and then yawned, as if thinking about sleep made her tired. She was very odd, and yet somehow so very endearing. "Well, I just . . . someone once told me that I'm . . . a nester."

He suddenly wondered if that friend who knew of her nocturnal habits was male or female. "A nester?"

"I need to . . . nest."

"Like a bird?"

"Yes. I suppose when it comes right down to it, I . . . it's hard for me to settle in to a new place."

"I understand."

"You do?"

*More than you will ever know.* "You exhaust yourself with tasks until your head crashes onto the pillow in unconsciousness."

Her brow furrowed and then she smiled. "I suppose so."

He found his lips yearning to lift and match hers. But he quelled the desire, realizing that he was feeling far too much affinity for this woman. Brusquely he motioned to her hat. "Your bonnet is a disaster."

Staring down at it, she smiled fondly and sighed. "I know."

"I daresay the water killed it."

"It was a mighty sacrifice," she teased. "But well worth it. You should've seen Seth's face when the ducks thought the beads were bread crumbs. He was positively delighted." Her eyes flashed with humor and her cheeks glowed to a lovely hue. She was really quite pretty; no wonder he'd felt the need to keep his distance.

He reminded himself that it had been quite a good idea, since spending time with the woman only seemed to heighten his desire. Yet for his life, he was unwilling to end this interview just yet.

The new butler, Dudley, swept into the room and stood sergeant-stiff by the door.

Trying not to be annoyed by the interruption, Steele looked up. "Yes, Dudley?"

"Mr. Linder-Myer, here to see you, my lord."

The smile dropped from Miss West's face faster than a cutpurse could escape. She stiffened and clutched that hideous bonnet as if it were a lifeline.

Steele hid his frown. This could be a simple matter of Sir Lee checking in now that Benbrook was gone. But knowing Sir Lee, he'd probably gotten wind of the incident at the park already. The man seemed to have eyes and ears everywhere. "Yes, show him in."

Straightening her worn, waterlogged skirts, Miss West gritted her teeth and muttered, "How could you?"

"How could I what?"

Skepticism flashed in her gaze. "I can't believe that you contacted Mr. Linder-Myer over this."

"Who says that I did?"

"Then why is he here?"

Steele had no answer, so he fell back on a reflexive technique he used in court, striking the offense. "I can't believe that you dare to question me."

He regretted the words immediately.

It was as if he'd just painted a thick unbreakable line segregating himself from her—powerful employer to powerless servant, eminent lord to lowly commoner. Any sense of intimacy that had grown between them evaporated into mist.

She stiffened, and the very air around her chilled a few degrees. "Forgive me, my lord. I forgot my place. It will not happen again."

Her slate blue eyes shuttered and her face looked carved from stone, reminding him of a marble statue he'd seen among the Elgin Marbles, beautiful yet as remote as the years past when it was carved.

He frowned. "I . . . It's all right. I didn't mean . . ."

"Mr. Linder-Myer," Dudley declared near the door, and Sir Lee Devane swept into the room.

# Chapter 10

Sir Lee ambled into the study flourishing his gold-topped cane. By his craggy face and hunched stature, one might have supposed that the elderly man was harmless. Especially given his usually cheerful mien and relaxed pose.

But Sir Lee was about as harmless as a scythe.

The knighted gentleman might have retired as a master of spies, but the man who'd been in charge of intelligence on every suspicious foreigner in England for years still kept his hands in the pot. Hence, Sir Lee was the man that Lord Benbrook had approached when he'd needed help but didn't want to involve the authorities or have any publicity of any kind. At the time, Benbrook had explained that the Devonshire family had suffered a great scandal years before, and since then his family's personal affairs were of the utmost confidentiality.

Sir Lee had drafted Steele to their cause. And, to Steele's irritation, Sir Lee was the one who'd been calling the tunes of late to which Steele had been dancing.

Although one might have supposed that Sir Lee

wore the old-fashioned dove gray coat and knee breeches with white stockings to bolster his assumed role as agency representative, in truth, this was his preferred attire. The man seemed to have chosen a fashion he admired a number of years back and had stuck with it since.

With a twinkle in his green eyes, Sir Lee bowed. "Good day to you, Lord Steele. Miss West."

Steele nodded. "Linder-Myer."

Pasting on a wooden smile, Miss West dipped into a slight curtsy. "Good day, Mr. Linder-Myer. What a surprise to see you so soon." Each word was laced with just a hint of scorn directed solely at Steele.

Steele pursed his lips, distracted and annoyed that she would think him so trite as to call the agency representative with the merest cause. Then again, the incident had placed Seth's life in danger. But he was certainly capable enough of handling things without calling in for reinforcements, and from an agency interviewer, no less.

"Why, you're soaked to the bone!" Sir Lee cried. "You should change into dry clothing immediately! You'll catch your death!"

Miss West bowed her head. "How considerate of you to think of my health, Mr. Linder-Myer."

"She's hardier than she looks," Steele defended, feeling just a little bit guilty for keeping her standing there in her wet clothing.

Sir Lee tsked. "But it would be a terrible thing if Miss West caught cold. Especially where there's certain to be a pot of hot tea in the house. Tea is always welcome, if there's some about." Sir Lee rubbed his middle distractedly. "And cakes, too, always welcome, and always refreshing."

Withholding a grimace that he was once again dancing to Sir Lee's tunes, Steele nodded. "May I invite you to stay for tea, Mr. Linder-Myer?"

"Oh, how kind of you, Lord Steele! But I wouldn't want to impose."

Steele smiled. "Oh no, it's no imposition." Stepping over to the pull, he yanked on the cord.

Dudley appeared in seconds.

"Tea and cakes, please, Dudley."

Dudley's eyes leaped to Miss West.

Tilting his head, Steele exhaled. "Miss West will be joining us, *after* she's had an opportunity to change her attire."

Sir Lee beamed. "Excellent! And when you return, I want to hear all the details of the incident at the park this morning."

Miss West's eyes snapped to Steele's and her lips pursed in obvious irritation. "Certainly. If you will excuse me, my lord?" Each word was laced with frost.

"Of course."

She left the room, her back as stiff as whalebone, her unspoken rebuke chilling the air.

Steele closed the door a bit harder than he'd meant to behind her. "Why are you here, Sir Lee?"

The old gent's mask of innocence fell away. "I heard that you'd had an incident and I wanted to check up on things."

Stepping behind his desk, Steele sat down, the leather of his chair creaking beneath him. "Everything's fine. No harm was done." The irony that he was repeating Miss West's proclamation was not lost on him, but he hardly cared. He hated being checked up on as if he weren't capable of handling matters.

"Has the footman Claude turned up?"

"No."

"I'll get some men on it. I'll let you know as soon as we find him." Sir Lee lowered himself into the chair opposite Steele and rested both hands on his gold-topped cane. "I understand that Miss West dove into the water and saved the lad. Were it not for her . . ."

Rubbing his hands over his eyes, Steele tried not to let the fear gnawing at his guts affect him. "I wasn't quite clear on that part. I was more focused on how Seth fell in, in the first instance."

Sir Lee's craggy face broke into a smile. "That's what I always liked about you, Steele; you keep your eyes on the true issue."

"Don't butter me up, Sir Lee. This could have been a disaster."

Sir Lee shrugged. "I know. But it wasn't. And I didn't call on you today only because of the incident in the park. I have news." The old gent leaned forward. "Until now, I wasn't one hundred percent certain that Benbrook's son and daughter-in-law's carriage accident involved foul play."

"But Benbrook is so certain, and there's the threatening letter against Benbrook's life—"

Sir Lee held up his hand. "I like to be sure of my facts, that's all."

"And?"

"And I've interviewed the witnesses, and the carriage accident that killed Seth and Felix's parents last month was indeed staged."

Steele's hands clenched on the desk. "Do you think that Seth and Felix are in danger?"

Sir Lee pursed his lips. "The threatening letter Benbrook received recently was focused only on him. Maybe the killer thought that Benbrook was in that carriage instead of his son?"

"Still, we don't know the killer's motive . . ." Steele hated the idea of anyone intent on harming Seth and Felix. "A lot of people have cause to hate Benbrook . . ."

Sir Lee leaned forward. "Yourself included."

"The man's a pompous ass."

Sir Lee waved a hand. "Still, the motive could be revenge, a debt, inheritance . . . we won't know until we find the perpetrator."

"What is the story with his relatives? Who's in line to inherit?"

"In order after Benbrook dies are . . ." Sir Lee ticked off his fingers. "Felix, Seth, then Benbrook's brother in India, Gordon Devonshire."

"What do we know about this Gordon Devonshire?"

"There was a scandal. Benbrook is more secretive than any agent I know—"

"Which is why he brought you in, instead of a Bow Street Runner or the authorities," Steele interjected.

"Exactly. But I was able to get him to admit that the scandal years ago involved Gordon Devonshire sleeping with Benbrook's then fiancée."

Steele cringed. "Ouch. That means bad blood between the brothers."

"Yes. Apparently Benbrook broke it off with the girl and banished his brother to distant shores."

"Gordon certainly has motive."

"Yes, but no one's heard from the man in years. And I've done some checking around. The people who knew him in England say that he's not the kind of man to take bold steps."

"Maybe India changed him."

Sir Lee shook his head. "They describe him as . . . weak-willed, not very bright, and incapable of managing a long-distance murder plot. Besides, the rift happened over twenty years ago. Why wait until now to take revenge? And the man must be well over sixty—"

"Age doesn't stop you," Steele interjected.

Sir Lee's eyes twinkled. "But I'm unique," he teased.

"I noticed." Steele leaned back in his chair, and it creaked stridently. He knew that he should get it fixed, but he liked the noise when he was working alone in his study. It was his nest, he supposed, and he liked it that way. "Did Gordon Devonshire have any children?"

"A son. Patrick Devonshire. He would be about twenty-one."

"So Gordon was married when he had the affair?"

Sir Lee scowled. "Yes. And I'm checking up on Gordon and the son, Patrick. But it'll take some time."

Tapping his finger to his lips, Steele sighed. "I wish

Benbrook had taken my advice; then we'd have a better shot at knowing if inheritance is the motive."

"I don't disagree. But Benbrook doesn't want to make you his heir, and the transfers must be very complicated."

Steele looked away. "I can manage it and it's legal."

"With the help of a certain prince?" Sir Lee asked.

Ignoring the lure, Steele leaned forward, and the chair squeaked loudly. "All you need to know is that if I'm Benbrook's heir, then we can know the motive and likely suspect."

"Don't you worry for your safety?"

"I can take care of myself."

Sir Lee's lips pursed and his eyes narrowed. Steele kept his face fixed; there was no way the old gent could know that Steele had been a Sentinel or about his midnight excursions. The man *might* know that Steele had saved the prince's life, but Steele wasn't about to say anything that would breach his promise to the prince.

"It's not a bad idea," Sir Lee admitted after a moment. "If anyone tries anything against you, then we know for certain that inheritance is the motive and that Gordon is likely the killer."

"Exactly! And it would only be temporary. Once the killer is found I return guardianship of the boys and all rights back to Benbrook."

Scratching his chin, Sir Lee pursed his lips. "You still have the papers?"

Steele opened the desk drawer, selected the parchment, and laid it on the desk. "Right here. Do you think that once Benbrook learns of today's mishap he may change his mind?"

"Doubtful. I think he'd be much more likely to make you his heir if you considered getting married."

"As I told you before, Sir Lee, I'm not in the market to find a wife," Steele bit out.

The old gent shook his head. "If you can show Benbrook that you have established a fine home in which to be able to raise his two grandchildren, then I think he will be more disposed to place his signature across those pages. And not just for the short term."

"I am giving them a home."

"Temporarily. You're a bachelor. You live for your work and spend more time at your offices than in your house. It doesn't recommend you as a father."

Despite himself, Steele was affronted. "I'd make a blasted good father."

Sir Lee lifted a shoulder in a negligent shrug. "Perhaps. But speaking as someone who failed miserably as a parent, no matter how well intentioned, we often do more harm than good."

"Everyone makes mistakes."

"Disowning your daughter for marrying the man she loves is not exactly an everyday mistake. She died penniless and alone in an institution for the poor." His voice was laced with condemnation and sorrow.

Steele was uncomfortable with such bare grief. "But you found your grandson . . ."

"Only through a score of amazing good luck." Sir Lee swallowed.

"He seems to have forgiven you . . ."

"Thank God he doesn't hate me . . . but I cannot forgive myself for all I've done . . ." His craggy face was pained. "All I can do is try to make it up to him." Suddenly Sir Lee looked up and his eyes narrowed. "It takes a rare statesman to get me so off topic . . . We're talking about you getting married, not my family affairs."

Steele crossed his arms. "I don't believe that marrying will convince Benbrook to make me his heir. Why, I'd be replacing Deidre. He wouldn't want that."

"I think that Benbrook is more concerned about the future than the past." Sir Lee's green eyes took on a distant cast filled with sadness. "Losing one's child will do that to a man."

Steele shifted. "Did he say for certain that he would make me his heir if I married?"

"Oh, he made it quite clear. He hates his brother and has little use for his wife's side of the family. I think if you proved yourself worthy then he'd consider giving you all of it . . . to go to the boys eventually of course."

"He's never found me worthy before." Steele couldn't disguise the bitterness in his tone.

"He's never felt his mortality so strongly before. Nor was he without a son to raise his grandchildren." Sir Lee toyed with his gold-topped cane. "Mark my words, marry well and Benbrook will make you his heir. Then you are the target, the children are safer, and your future is lined with gold."

"Marry well, meaning . . ."

"Simple enough, she's got to be of noble blood, good connections, good character. I know what it'll take to satisfy Benbrook that the children will be raised in a manner befitting their station. I can guide you."

"Having certain connections does not make a lady a good mother."

"What attributes do you think make a good mother?"

"How am I supposed to know?" Steele scoffed, irritated by the conversation.

Scratching his ear, Sir Lee sighed. "I suppose we need to ask someone who actually *has* experience with children. But even with those additional requirements, you should have plenty of choices given that you're a viscount now."

Steele shifted. "I'm not a prize pig up for market."

"Of course not. But you're not a young man any longer."

"I'm not so far from thirty!"

Sir Lee sniffed. "Many men have six children by now."

"Six?" Steele swallowed.

"Still, you've just received a very coveted designation. By the by, you never did tell me what you did to gain your title . . ."

"I thought you had eyes and ears everywhere, Sir Lee."

The old gent's craggy face grimaced. "Are you going to tell me or not?"

"No."

"Fine. Then let's get back to business."

Steele knew that Sir Lee wasn't finished digging, but he had to admire a man who never became dejected, just delayed.

Sir Lee went on, "I still think you need a wife for Benbrook to cooperate."

"Fine. I'll think about it."

Sir Lee reached for the parchment and slipped it into his pocket. "Then I'll start working on Benbrook."

A knock resounded at the door.

"Come." Steele called.

Two servants entered and set up the tea service by the sofa and chairs across the room.

Eyeing the cakes, Sir Lee stood and ambled over to the sofa. Steele noticed that he kept his cane within easy reach of his right hand. That cane would make a nice weapon, if necessary, Steele noted, having no doubt that Sir Lee knew how to use it. Suddenly the black-shrouded lady came to mind. She'd carried a similar cane. Could Sir Lee's cane hide a blade, too? Somehow Steele knew that it did.

He rose, filing away that useful piece of information.

The footman Jonathan asked, "Will there be anything else, Your Lordship?"

"No. Thank you."

The footman left just as Miss West breezed into the room. "I'll be happy to pour, if you wish, my lord." Her demeanor was smoothly professional, yet her tone was still cool as ice, and she would not meet his eyes.

Steele frowned, feeling as if he'd lost ground with her and not liking it one bit. "Thank you."

She nodded and moved to the tea set and poured. She'd changed into a pale blue gown with short white ruffled sleeves and a white band woven neatly below her lovely bosom. The gown looked as if it had once been a darker hue, but had faded over time. For some reason this bothered Steele. It wasn't that he expected her to be in silks and lace, but still, she needn't look so . . . dowdy.

The thought surprised him, as he'd never once looked at the attire of his servants with anything less than an eye toward functionality. He supposed when it came right down to it, he'd never quite looked at one of his servants through the eyes of an appreciative male.

The thought rankled, since he knew that he shouldn't be looking at Miss West in any such way. But he was a healthy male of barely over thirty, hardly dead, and not yet done appreciating a lovely female form.

*Maybe I should marry*, he realized. There certainly were some benefits. But the real issue was: Could he find a respectable young lady with excellent connections who wouldn't bore him to tears?

# Chapter 11

Except for the anxiety and anger lacing her tongue, Abigail tasted nothing. The fine Oriental tea was wasted on her, as was the fresh raspberry scone sitting untouched on the plate before her.

She kept waiting for the gentlemen to broach the subject of the incident in the park or the topic of her dismissal. Or at least give her a hearty tongue-lashing. Instead, Mr. Linder-Myer and Lord Steele seemed content discussing the weather, the latest news in the broadsheets, and not much of anything of import.

Abigail wished that they'd get to it already instead of making her twist in the wind.

After a while, Abigail realized that if she listened carefully, there was an undercurrent to the gentlemen's conversation that she did not understand.

Lord Steele certainty paid a good deal of deference to the agency representative. Even if Mr. Linder-Myer was a gentleman, Lord Steele was paying an inordinate amount of respect to the man. Mayhap it was the old gent's age, or his cheery demeanor, but somehow Lord Steele seemed to have a great deal of patience for someone so very far beneath him in station.

Did it come from Lord Steele's past? Or was there something more to this relationship?

Mr. Linder-Myer turned to Abigail. "So, Miss West. How do you think the boys are adjusting to their new home?"

She focused her attention on the older gentleman. "As well as can be expected, I suppose. They're resilient, certainly. Else they'd hardly be as well as they are." She shifted in her seat. "Yet it is quite a difficult transition, Mr. Linder-Myer. Felix feels tremendous responsibility for being the elder, and Seth, well, he doesn't understand Felix's need for privacy with his grief. Seth misses his mother terribly. They both do. Everything is so new, everyone is so different . . ." Her voice trailed off as the enormity of the boys' pain squeezed at her heart.

Scratching his chin, Mr. Linder-Myer looked troubled. "Is there nothing that can be done?"

Biting her lip, Abigail kept her eyes trained on the tips of Steele's shiny black boots, as she dared not meet his eyes. "Well, perhaps if they got to know everyone in the house a bit better . . ."

Abigail felt the force of Steele's scowl like a windstorm pressing against her skin.

Steele uncrossed and recrossed his long legs. "They've hardly been here a week. Give it some time."

Tapping his finger to his lips, Mr. Linder-Myer's eyes narrowed and fixed on Abigail with an intensity she found unnerving. "So you think that the boys miss their mother?"

"Terribly."

"Do you believe that a child needs a mother?"

The familiar grief splintered her heart. "Yes. Unequivocally, yes."

"And a governess is no replacement for a mother?"

She shook her head, confused by the direction of this conversation. "No . . ."

"Even though a special bond can develop between a governess and her charges, it cannot compare to one's mother."

"No. Of course not . . . but . . ." The seed of a bad feeling planted itself deep in her middle.

"Governesses come and go, but a mother is forever."

That bad little seed in her middle blossomed into a full-blown feeling of awfulness. "Well, yes . . ."

Mr. Linder-Myer lifted his gray bushy brows and glared pointedly at Lord Steele.

Lord Steele grimaced and busied himself with his tea.

Anxiously Abigail clutched her hands, trying to hide her grip inside her skirts. She peeked through her lashes at Lord Steele, but he wouldn't meet her eye.

*Oh no! Don't sack me! Please don't sack me!*

Leaning forward, the old gent cleared his throat. "Is it not true that you've been a governess in a number of different homes, Miss West?"

"Ah, pardon?" A familiar burning feeling itched at the backs of her eyes, as she braced herself for the worst.

Mr. Linder-Myer frowned, as if she were being obtuse. Well, she was. And she wasn't about to make it any easier for him to dismiss her. He'd made it quite clear that she was dispensable. Not a very nice thing to do by her way of thinking.

Mr. Linder-Myer jabbed his cane on the floor, his craggy features fixed, his green eyes intent. "Yes or no, young lady. You have served in many homes and been with many families."

Lord Steele straightened, and his gaze fixed on Abigail. She felt the force of his attention like a warming stove that had been opened, and all she wanted to do was slam it closed and get out of the kitchen.

Her fingernails bit into her palms but she couldn't care, not when Lord Steele was looking at her as if she were the source of a terrible disease and Mr. Linder-Myer seemed intent on seeing her shunned.

Exhaling, she prepared herself for the guillotine blade that was about to drop. "Yes. I've been with a few different families."

Seemingly pleased, Mr. Linder-Myer nodded. "You see, my point exactly!"

Abigail didn't see at all and she wouldn't meet his eyes. Instead she busied herself by reaching for a scone and taking a bite. It was like eating sawdust.

Her throat closed, and a dry cough erupted from her mouth.

"Are you all right?" Steele asked, rising.

She tried to motion that she was all right, but she was coughing too hard. Her cheeks flamed with embarrassment.

Steele came over to her and patted her back.

"I'm . . . I'm . . ." Her were eyes tearing, her throat aching, and mortification made her squirm.

"Here, drink some tea." He handed her the teacup and cupped his hand over hers as she drank.

She sipped gratefully, the tea soothing her scratchy throat. Steele's touch warmed her in a way that was far too affecting for an employer. Maybe it was a good thing she was being sacked. Being around Steele was becoming harder and harder, or in truth, delicious-er and delicious-er. His effect on her was scrumptiously intoxicating enough to be dangerous, certainly for her as his employee.

But oh, how she'd miss the astonishing thrill deep in her middle whenever their eyes met, and the rare but wonderful touch of his silky smooth skin. It was easier to think of that than the children. No, she couldn't bear to dwell on losing them.

After a moment, she lifted her head. "Ah . . . thank you."

"Would you like some more?" Steele asked. He was so close, she could see the hint of black stubble that was trying to break through his skin.

Inhaling a shaky breath, she smiled. "No, I'm fine." The pleasing scents of male and the gingery spiced cologne he wore blanketed her.

He removed his hand from hers. She felt bereft by the loss of that caring contact and knew that it would be a long time before she forgot the touch of his hand. Her fingers still felt warm where he'd held her. "Let me know if you want any more."

Breathless, she smiled. "I . . . ah . . . thank you. . . ."

Nodding, he moved back to sit in the chair opposite.

Mr. Linder-Myer adjusted his leg, wincing as if in

pain. "So as I was saying, you've had a variety of employers."

Abigail sighed, knowing that it did no good to argue with an employer who'd decided that you were no longer needed. "Yes."

"What attributes do you feel make a good mother?"

Abigail started. "Ah . . . what . . . beg pardon?"

Mr. Linder-Myer waved a hand. "You had to have noticed that some mothers are good and some are dreadful."

Abigail shifted in her chair, confused as to what this had to do with sacking her. "I wouldn't call any mother I've ever worked for 'dreadful' . . ."

The old gent's eyes twinkled. "You can share the tittle-tattle; we won't tell."

Pressing her hand to her chest, Abigail straightened. "So this isn't about me?"

"You? I'm not helping Lord Steele here retain a second governess. I don't think it's necessary for two boys. Do you?"

A *second* governess. So they weren't replacing her. "Ah, no."

Mr. Linder-Myer continued, "Although we might consider retaining a tutor at some point, that's not the topic. And while I know what qualities are important in a member of staff, I'm a little less clear on good traits to be found in a mother. You know, for children."

Abigail relaxed, starting to accept that she wasn't being sacked. "Well . . . patience is important. And a good heart, certainly. Compassion. Sympathy."

"What about education?"

Abigail lifted her shoulder in a shrug. "One hardly needs to be a scholar to make a good mother."

"Can it make any difference whatsoever?"

"Well, if you're thinking about an education for the children, then it does help to have a parent who believes in the importance of learning and instruction."

"Not just having tutors around."

Abigail nodded. "I think so. If the children see education as something valued by the parents, valued in the household, then it can be a good influence."

Mr. Linder-Myer nodded. "Interesting. Anything else?"

"Ah, well, I suppose a sense of humor helps . . ."

"How so?"

"Children can be trying at times, and it's easier if one doesn't take herself too seriously."

"Excellent point." Winking at Abigail, Mr. Linder-Myer beamed. "Especially if the father is a stick-in-the-mud."

Steele scowled. "I'm not a stick-in-the-mud."

Abigail turned to him, surprised.

"A little levity wouldn't kill you," Mr. Linder-Myer countered. Leaning forward conspiratorially, he waved his cane toward Steele. "He's in the market for a new wife, you see."

Abigail felt her middle drop to somewhere below her knees. "Ah, I . . . didn't know that . . ." Why did she feel so disappointed? It wasn't as if he were interested in her. And a viscount certainly wouldn't look twice at a mousy employee with faded gowns, frayed shawls, and dog-eared shoes.

She suddenly realized how stupid she'd been, dwelling on the touch of his hand or the look in his eye. There had been no connection between them when their eyes had met. It had all been the creation of the overly active mind of a desperately lonely woman.

"Have no fear, whatever happens won't affect your job," Steele murmured, not meeting her eye.

She bowed her head, feeling dejected and pitiful. She was even more the fool for feeling so awful about the whole thing. She was three-and-twenty and felt older than the great English oak that had been standing at Andersen Hall Orphanage for three hundred years.

She needed to find Reggie. He was her only family, the only living person in the world with whom she could truly claim a connection. She couldn't rely on anything or anyone else.

Clearing her throat, she looked up. "I have a friend. She's ill." Her words were stilted, but all plans for a smoother introduction of the topic fell away in light of the hole she was feeling in her heart.

Steele looked more diverted than concerned, as if he were anxious to change the topic. "Oh? I'm sorry to hear that."

"She's an orphan, like me, and has no one." Knowing that the lists of Andersen Hall residents went back only a few years and didn't include her or her brother, Abigail added, "We were at Andersen Hall Orphanage together."

Mr. Linder-Myer's cat green eyes were curious. "What's wrong with her?"

"Cancer. Dreadful business. She's in terrible pain . . ."

Steele frowned. "Is there anything that can be done?"

Abigail exhaled with relief at the opening he'd given her. "Yes. I want to see her. See to her comfort."

Steele's face looked pained. "I can't afford to have you leave the boys . . ."

"Of course I wouldn't leave the boys. I would never neglect my duties. But after they're abed . . . you don't need me then, do you?"

Surprisingly, Steele looked to Mr. Linder-Myer, and some unknown message passed between them.

She rushed on as the lies gushed forth, "I can't imagine that she's long for this world . . . it would mean a lot to me to be able to comfort her in her final days . . ."

Steele nodded. "So long as it's after the boys are abed and it doesn't otherwise interfere with your duties . . ."

"Never."

"Then it should be fine."

Abigail felt her shoulders drop with relief.

Steele added, "Please be sure to have Cook provide you with some soup and breads for her. We always make extra for such occasions. And I'm sure Mrs. Pitts has some blankets, too."

Abigail felt a tad guilty as she nodded. "I'm so very grateful. Thank you so much, my lord."

He waved a hand as if it were nothing. "It's the least we can do."

"Well, I appreciate it."

"I'm sure the lads are missing you. Why don't you go check on them while I see Mr. Linder-Myer out?"

Mr. Linder-Myer started. "Oh yes, I do have a business to run and governesses to place." He stood. "Thank you so much, Lord Steele, for your gracious hospitality." He turned to Abigail, his green eyes twinkling. "It was such a pleasure to encounter you again, my dear. I know we'll have the opportunity to see each other quite soon."

Abigail frowned, wondering why Mr. Linder-Myer thought that they would be seeing each other soon.

At the look on her face, the old gent explained, "Oh, haven't I told you? I'm helping Lord Steele find his new wife."

Lord Steele looked as if he were about to argue but then closed his mouth.

Mr. Linder-Myer beamed. "He's in quite the hurry. And if I have anything to do with it, which I do, we're to make short work of it. I'll bet ten shillings he'll be wed within the month."

# Chapter 12

Abigail trudged through the streets, her mood blacker than the mourning skirts she wore. The shadows seemed to reach out for her from the nearby alleyways, and the capricious moon had withdrawn behind a veil of clouds. Her every attempt at finding Reggie was hitting a brick wall. But she wasn't fool enough not to realize that her foul mood had more to do with Lord Steele than anything else. She'd been aggravated ever since Mr. Linder-Myer had informed her that Lord Steele was soon to marry.

It was about her position in the household, of course. No matter what assurances Steele gave her about keeping her job, once a new mistress of the house asserted her position, everyone was up for replacement. It was the nature of things for ladies to want to surround themselves with familiar faces. It wasn't a bad occurrence, unless one relied on wages and was subject to termination.

Abigail grimaced beneath her veil. She felt angry, reckless even. She knew that she needed to head back to the house, it was well past midnight, but she'd made little headway in her efforts to find Reggie, and she'd be damned if she didn't try her utmost.

It was astonishing how different she felt when she was in her widow's costume. More assured, less awkward; even the pitch of her voice changed once she donned the black veil. Lost was that breathy, nervous intonation, replaced instead by the confident voice of the worldly woman she was pretending to be.

When she was dressed in her mourning garb, she walked a little straighter, her step a little firmer. That might have had something to do with the three-inch heels on her black boots, a height endowed by the shoemaker, not naturally by God. She even smelled different, since she kept her costume hidden in a special cedar box in a secret compartment of her trunk. As soon as Abigail smelled the cedar, she fell under the spell of her widow's persona. In that guise, she spoke to people she'd never dare address in the light of day and confronted scoundrels who would have otherwise had her running for her life.

One of those scoundrels had been particularly helpful this evening, a cutpurse named Slippery Milo who was so undersized, he could slip through crowds with the ease of a cat. The man was often mistaken for a young lad, and he used that "gift," as he called it, to his favor. Abigail had to admire a man who played the cards he was given, even if she didn't agree with the moral choices he made.

Abigail turned a corner just as Slippery Milo had described. It was so blasted dark, she could hardly see. But the cutpurse had been right on target thus far with his instructions, and they seemed to take into account the lack of light. Slippery Milo's keen intelligence had struck her, and she'd had to wonder how different his life would have turned out if he'd been provided a sound education.

Unbidden, Headmaster Dunn flashed in her mind. She was so lucky to have found a friend and mentor in him, someone who took the time to nurture her hunger for learning. He'd recognized her acumen and had nourished her intelligence as a wet nurse fed a babe.

No doubt Headmaster Dunn wouldn't deem her too intelligent for prowling the streets in one of the worst parts of London. He would chide her foolishness at being so heedless of her safety. He would consider her imprudent to chase her wayward brother in this manner. But the most deeply mortifying fact was that if Headmaster Dunn knew of it, he'd be horrified that she'd crafted a ridiculous, baseless fantasy about her employer.

A guilty, stupid feeling sank like a stone in her belly, fueling her ill temper. She wanted to expunge it, destroy it so there were no vestiges remaining as proof to the world what an idiotic, nonsensical chit she was. She shrugged her cloak more securely on her shoulders, welcoming the guise of the worldly widow, becoming the woman that she preferred to be. Strong, defiant, wild even. *The widow moved undaunted, fought for what she needed, took what she wanted.* Reckless energy spurred Abigail's steps, and she clenched her hands, ready as the sophisticated widow for whatever would greet her.

Soon she would come upon the man the cutpurse had called Jumper. Jumper supposedly ran messages back and forth between thieves in this part of town, and he was said to know who was where and when. It was a small thread of possibility that he would know Reggie, but it was all Abigail had to work with, and she would spin it for all it was worth.

One more left turn and she would be at the small square Jumper used as a rendezvous point. Abigail clutched the walking stick that hid her blade. The hard metal bolstered her confidence and firmed her resolve to do whatever necessary to find her little brother. She also carried a pistol in a specially woven pocket of her cloak, just in case. Her instincts warned her that tonight she might need extra protection. She was loath to use the firearm, finding it unreliable and unwieldy, but she believed in being prepared.

She did not intend to use either weapon on Jumper, however; they were simply a precaution. Instead she had coin in her purse, ready to pay for the information she needed. It had taken Abigail only a few days in London to realize that no one would help her out of the goodness of his heart, and that currency was her surest means to securing information. Hence her deeper debt to the moneylender.

Inwardly she shivered, thinking of the pair who'd attacked her . . . that barmaid, if that's what she was, and Fred. She'd walked into a trap, and only the masked gentleman's help had prevented terrible results.

Again that exciting curiosity enveloped her when she considered the masked rescuer. Why had he saved her? What business brought him to Charing Cross in an alley in the middle of the night? How did he learn to fight like the devil? Would she ever meet him again? If she did, would he want her the way he'd wanted her the other night, arousing wickedly delicious sensations? And if he did, would she stop him? Just thinking about how his lips had felt on her skin and how his tongue . . . She shivered.

After that night, Abigail had surreptitiously scanned the newspapers looking for any hint of the masked vigilante. But it was as if the man didn't exist, or perhaps he truly was a figment of her imagination.

The way she romanticized the masked stranger and fantasized about meeting him again made her realize how desperately lonely she really was. His touch had been like an elixir, expunging all worry about Reggie and obliterating all thought from her mind. There had been no room in her head for anything . . . she could only *feel*. It had been one of the most sinfully indulgent moments in her life.

Never before had Abigail dwelled on such base notions of body and flesh . . . but the man inspired such an exciting rush of . . . *curiosity* in her. She was insatiably, hungrily *curious* about the man. She couldn't deny the kinship she'd felt with him. And when they'd spoken so freely, she'd been impressed with his progressive notions. She had no doubt that if she knew him better, they would have even more in common.

In all her many fantasies about the man, that kinship was always present. And often she added the moving notion that he might be disfigured in some way. Hence the mask. Could he have been burned in a fire? Born with a disfiguring mark? Silly romantic that she was, she felt a compassion for the man that she'd rarely felt for any other.

Abigail wondered if she'd meet him again while she looked for Reggie. A small thrill raced up her middle. But she quashed it, knowing that real life could never hold up to the fantasy. Mayhap she was better off never encountering him again, keeping her secret dreams safe from shattering disappointment.

As Abigail neared the turn she was to make, loud voices could be heard. Her steps faltered, but she refused to stop. She couldn't go back empty-handed, not now when she'd risked so much. She would face this Jumper fellow and learn anything he knew. Then she'd find Reggie and bail him out of the mess he was in and . . . well, at least they'd be together. Family, once and for all.

Boots scuffling on the cobblestones reached her ears from around the bend. Jumper wasn't alone. A trickle of fear crawled up her spine. But she told herself that if Jumper didn't know anything, perhaps his companions would. The cutpurse had assured her that Jumper wasn't a dangerous fellow, more "a man o' commerce," Slippery Milo had said.

Suddenly a large arm wrapped around her waist and pulled her down the side alley. Before she could cry out, a gloved hand covered her mouth. She tasted leather and fear.

She fought and kicked, desperately trying to reach for her blade. But the man was too big and had her wrapped in arms of granite. "Shh! It's me. From the other night." His voice was muffled, but she knew immediately that it was her masked rescuer.

Still, she tried to push him off. "What are you doing here?"

His stonelike grip only tightened. "Following someone—"

"Who?"

"Pray, keep quiet!" he hissed, his breath warming her ear. "Danger's afoot!"

Abigail stilled, trusting the man enough to listen to him. For the moment.

Her rescuer eased the grip of his gloved hand over her mouth to give her more air, but still he clutched her more compactly than the pages of a closed book.

She swallowed as excitement thrilled through her. Her body was flaming, her heart racing, her mind in a whirl. What was the danger? Why was he holding her as if afraid she'd run? Did he want something of her? Why did his embrace feel so blasted good?

His burly arms held her in an intimate manner more appropriate to the bedchamber than an alleyway. Her breasts were squashed up against his rock-hard chest. Her legs pressed into his thick, muscular thighs. His broad shoulders and his imposing stature made her feel protected and secure in an extraordinarily unfamiliar way.

Strangely, the most overwhelming feeling coursing through her had little to do with fear and more to do with fascination at how this masked man made her feel. It was as if he were a bonfire and she longed to dance in his flames.

"I don't know, I swear!" A man's whiny voice could be heard from around the bend.

Abigail stiffened, forcing herself to discard her fantasies and remember that danger truly might be afoot.

A muffled thud was followed by a low groan.

Abigail swallowed. Thank heavens the masked gentleman had stopped her from walking into that melee! Peering up, she tried to get a glimpse of her rescuer's face, but even in the darkness, she could discern that he still wore his mask.

Boot heels scuffled on the cobblestones nearby. They seemed to be coming closer.

Quietly but firmly, the gentleman savior pulled her deeper into the alley and pressed her into a crevice where two walls joined, covering her body with his own, as if to protect her. His black cloak should conceal them. But if they were discovered, Abigail had no doubt that the man would place himself between her and danger.

Gratitude washed through her for this masked man. He'd proven himself twice now. Distantly she wondered why he'd bother, why he'd care. But she thanked the good Lord for that caring, regardless of its source, and the man in which it had manifested.

As she stood fixed in the darkness, Abigail tried to force herself to think about the danger and about their scandalously pleasurable pose. Her body thrummed with excitement and awareness of every inch of his tall, broad-shouldered form. He was acting like a flesh-and-blood shield, and she'd never felt more deliciously safe.

"You'll tell me what ya know or I'll cut yer bloody heart out!"

A terrified cry rang out.

Involuntarily her breath seized and she clutched

his arm. Thank heavens he'd stopped her! Gratitude warmed her heart. At the moment she would willingly give this man anything he wanted of her. She only prayed that he would *want* to stake his claim.

Shock and guilt flashed through her. She was a proper young lady. What she'd just thought was scandalous and beyond the pale. Bedding a stranger? A masked stranger, no less, and she didn't even know his name. She had to protect her integrity! She needed to maintain her moral fiber! She should be ashamed of her degenerate thoughts!

But her body couldn't seem to drum up an ounce of shame or care one fig about her moral fiber. It ached for the feel of flesh on flesh, hungered for a taste of forbidden passion, and longed for the feel of a man deep inside her.

Her cheeks burned at the wicked thought, but as she licked her lips, she tasted passion, and deep inside her core, she felt the tug of desire.

Distantly she knew that she shouldn't be thinking about passion with danger only steps away. But the peril seemed to heighten her desire and fuel her hunger.

Her flesh was flaming so that she had to wonder if he felt it, too. She shifted restlessly against him.

He seemed to stiffen.

Her legs parted slightly, welcoming him closer.

His body grew harder, if that was possible. He moved deeper into the juncture between her thighs.

She shivered, tilting her head and arching her back.

His hot breath seemed to be coming faster, warming her neck.

Abigail closed her eyes, feeling every inch of his body and wallowing in the delicious flames that were licking at her flesh, enticing her to do wicked things that no decent lady would ever consider.

He seemed to want her, too.

She ached to *be* that worldly widow. To take what she wanted, *consequences be damned*.

"I don't know a thing!" the whiny voice cried.

Muffled cries and many boot steps followed.

Silence fell.

As the long, tense moments passed, doubt slithered through Abigail's mind, poisoning the delicious desire pulsing through her. He wasn't making any moves to take her. Was she doing it again? Reading too much into a man's actions, creating a fantasy, concocting a connection where none existed? Suddenly she knew that she'd been wrong. This man was a stranger, who no doubt had legions of women yearning for the pleasures of his arms. She, on the other hand, was a pitiful spinster whose loneliness made her jump to imaginary conclusions.

She'd done it with Lord Steele, and she was making that same mistake with this Good Samaritan.

Swallowing, Abigail tensed, prepared to move if the man was ready to release her.

But her rescuer held her tight. "They're still around," he whispered, his heavy breath heating her ear.

After an awkward moment, he muttered, "Why do you continue to prowl these neighborhoods? It's not safe, especially for a woman alone. What are you seeking?"

*You*, the secret thought flashed in her mind, shocking her. She suddenly realized that even though Reggie was at the forefront of her concerns, secretly she'd been longing for another exciting encounter with this man. Abruptly she recognized that the unquenchable *curiosity* that she'd been feeling, up close felt much more like . . . blazing *desire*. She positively *ached* with a longing she'd never felt in all her three-and-twenty years.

Involuntarily she shivered.

"Don't be afraid," he murmured, sending a rumbling thrill racing down her spine.

"I'm not," she whispered, her voice throaty.

He seemed to consider that a long moment, never once loosening his hold on her, for which she was thankful.

Passion licked at her belly and warmed her deepest places. Her body flamed, burning, yearning . . . The outrageous thought penetrated her consciousness: *No one would ever know.* Temptation fanned her desire until she felt singed by a yearning so intense, she quaked.

Licking her lips, she realized that she stood on a precipice, and all she longed to do was to jump. He couldn't see her face any more than she could see his. The anonymity gave her a boldness she didn't know she harbored. Still, she needed a little push. A small test of the waters, just to be sure.

With her heart racing, she bit her lip. She'd never done this, had never been so . . . wicked. Abigail shifted, pushing his thigh deeper into the crevice of her parted legs.

His sharp intake of breath caused a little thrill to shoot up her middle. His hips moved, just barely, and something long and hard pressed into her belly.

She gasped.

His grip on her tightened. "What . . . do you . . . want?"

With an audacity that belonged to the woman she was pretending to be, she lifted her chin. "You."

# Chapter 13

Steele couldn't quite believe it, but the proof was in his arms. The mysterious widow wanted him. And he was desperate to have her.

Still, he hesitated. What kind of deranged lady prowled the worst streets of London well after dark?

A woman who felt soft and warm and luscious in his arms, that's who.

What lady carried a blade and fought with thugs?

A woman who had lush breasts and shapely curves that he longed to explore.

What kind of lady kept her face veiled and her identity concealed?

A woman who smelled like desire and welcomed his touch.

She shifted against him, her legs widening, welcoming him into her softness.

Who was he to question her actions or motives when he prowled these very same streets concealing his features, too?

How mad must he be to be holding a complete stranger in his arms? Yet he wanted to take her up on her clear and tempting offer.

He needed this. Badly. He'd realized when he'd first kissed her hand that he had been too long without female company. That was why he'd been so attracted to the pretty young governess. That was why he'd been so distracted of late. That was why he'd been so restless, so anxious for confrontation. He'd ignored his manly needs for too long and was well overdue. *It would be completely anonymous*, he told himself.

The fact that the lady wanted him, simply for himself, was like an aphrodisiac, heightening his fierce desire until he barely kept a rein on his control. The widow didn't know he was a viscount or solicitor-general. She couldn't want anything from him except what he could give her as a *flesh-and-blood man*. And that flesh was on fire, aching with a need that drove all vestiges of gentility from his mind.

His arms gripped her tighter; her body clung to his like moss on a rock. A hard, long rock, aching with need.

Arching her back, she pressed her breasts against his chest. His hands naturally slid downward, easing into the curve of her buttocks. He pressed his face into her neck, smelling a scent that reminded him of cedar, of all things. He was almost glad she wore no perfume, nothing to remind him of anyone else.

She groaned, and he felt its rumble where it mattered most.

Her body's sinuous movements against his frame were the salvos that crumbled his final resistance.

Leaning his face into her neck, he flowed with her, their bodies joining through the thin fabric of their civilized clothes. It was a dance of sorts to a rhythm that intoxicated to the point of blotting out the world. They moved and pressed and rubbed and explored, until they were panting with lust and the need between them was so great, they were enveloped in a pulsing heat of desire.

Gripped by his need, Steele seized her hem and lifted her skirts, his hands raking up her leg and seeking the one place that would sate his hunger. She was hot and moist, ready for him. His passion peaked, and he knew he could not make it much longer—the beast inside him roared, demanding satisfaction.

Making quick work of his breeches and smalls, he reached his arms around her, grabbed her buttocks, and lifted her up. Her legs parted completely, wrapping around him, clutching him close.

Pressing her up against the wall, he braced his legs and their dance continued, but at a much faster pace. His member pressed into the juncture of her thighs, seeking that heat, yearning to plunge into her wetness. Finally he found his way and thrust deep inside.

Sight and sound were lost. He was overcome by the urgency pulsing inside of him, the thundering need that demanded to be met. She felt fantastic. Tight, hot and wet. He plunged deep inside of her again and again. Suddenly, her body tensed, a muffled cry rang out and her hands gripped his shoulders. Deep inside, her muscles clenched, convulsing around him.

It was too much. He pounded into her, his heart galloping, his breath shuddering, and his world shattering as he poured his seed deep within her.

Their panting breaths mingled even through their coverings. The air smelled of woman and desire. The darkness was enveloping, and all Steele wanted to do was let his legs collapse, lie down, and sleep. But he was in an alleyway in one of the worst neighborhoods in London, and this was not to be.

Slowly he braced himself and gently let her slip off him until her feet were planted on the ground. Still she leaned heavily against him, as if she, too, was not ready yet to stand on her own. So they leaned into each other, buttressing themselves until the moment reality was fully restored.

"Wha' 'ave we 'ere?" a female voice cried.

A tall, rail-thin woman in a dirty, low-cut gown stood with her hand on her bony hip, glaring at them. "This is my alley an' none but me gets ta work 'ere!"

The widow stiffened, as if realizing that she'd just been mistaken for a prostitute.

"Off wit' ya, ya little twat!" The whore shook her fist. "Or I'll pound ya bloody!"

Pushing away from Steele, the widow slipped her hand inside her cloak and pulled out a pistol. She aimed it at the prostitute.

The woman's pale face turned ashen. "'Old yer 'orses there! 'Old yer 'orses!"

"You're the one who needs to be off." The widow's voice was as firm as any sergeant's.

Despite himself, Steele was impressed with the way the widow handled herself. And, he realized, he'd missed the pistol completely when he'd been busy with the widow's clothing. A failing that could be deadly in other circumstances, and a mistake he would not make again.

With a flick of the firearm, the widow motioned

for the prostitute to depart back the way she'd come. "Now."

The whore flailed her bony arms. "Fine! Ya can 'ave it fer tonight!" She turned, muttering, "But it's my alley an' I'll be back tamarra, an' I'd betta not catch ya 'ere again or there'll be 'ell ta pay!" Her clomping footsteps echoed down the alley.

An awkward silence descended.

Slipping the firearm back inside the folds of her cloak, the widow exhaled. "She was right about one thing, I'd better go."

Steele started. "Yes, of course." He was a little startled by how quickly she was ready to be free of him. Granted, he didn't need any entanglements, yet the abruptness of it stung. And it struck him that she had to get back to her life—the one he knew nothing about.

*Who am I to look a gift horse in the mouth?* he admonished in his mind. *I need to get back to my life, too. And it's a busy life, one filled with important purpose and achievements.*

He forced himself to accept that this little interlude was over. "May I . . . may I escort you . . . somewhere?"

"No," she barked. Then, as if realizing her tone, she amended, "Thank you. But no. I'm fine."

"Well, then . . ."

"Yes, well, I suppose . . . I suppose . . . This is farewell."

He told his feet to move, but they didn't budge. Shaking his head, he shrugged. "Ah . . . I confess, I feel odd parting company with you after . . . well, and leaving you here . . ." He squared his shoulders.

Even if she wanted it this way, he was willing to play the cad only so much. "I can't in good conscience leave you here alone."

She nodded as if considering it. "Then escort me to Pryor Street. I can hail a hackney there." She was decisive. Strong-minded. And didn't mind telling him what she wanted quite directly. She was unlike any lady he'd ever encountered before. Well, he amended, at least not like any under sixty. He couldn't help but think of Sir Lee's friend Lady Blankett, who took speaking directly to a higher art form.

"To Pryor Street, then." He extended his arm, and silently she accepted it.

It was an odd stroll through the dark, winding streets. Rats scurried; muttered voices could be heard from inside some of the buildings. The sound of horse hooves echoed in the distance.

She wasn't one for talking much, he realized. Unlike most women he knew. But then again, most of the ladies he knew wouldn't copulate in an alleyway, either.

At Pryor Street, she turned to face him. "Thank you. I'm fine now."

"I'll call for a hackney." Sticking his hand beneath his bandana, he whistled. The jingle of a rig and the clatter of horses' hooves neared.

A hackney came around the bend and rolled to a stop before them.

Reaching up, Steele opened the door.

Accepting his hand, she moved to step up inside the carriage, but she hesitated. "I want you to know something."

"Yes?"

"I've never . . . I don't . . ." She seemed at a loss, but then her shoulders squared and she looked up at him through her veil. "I've never done anything like this before."

Part of him didn't believe her and considered it a ploy. But he couldn't discount the ring of truth to her voice. Years of interrogating witnesses had taught him its resonant hum. She wasn't lying—or at least she didn't believe that she was lying. The two could be very different.

He tilted his head. "If it makes any difference, neither have I."

She nodded as if it did make a difference to her. Again he had to wonder at this woman, her motives, and her life. But his desire to remain anonymous squelched his natural curiosity.

She climbed inside the hackney and sat. With her dark clothing, she blended into the carriage's interior. "Good-bye."

"Good-bye."

"Where to?" the driver called.

Steele supposed that the widow would not let him hear the address, but she surprised him by replying, "St. Lanyard's Square."

He closed the door and smacked it with his palm. The driver cried out to the horse, and the carriage moved off.

As Steele watched the black hackney melt into the night, he wondered if he would ever see the wicked widow again.

When the coach was almost out of sight, a cry rang out. "Whoa!"

The hackney suddenly stopped. The driver turned as if speaking to his passenger.

Steele stepped forward, wondering if something was wrong. Then the driver cried out and the horse took off once more. The hackney turned at the corner, going in the opposite direction from St. Lanyard's Square.

Steele chuckled. The wicked widow was no fool. The only question was, would he be fool enough to try to find her again?

# Chapter 14

"**U**nbelievable," Abigail breathed as she peered over her shoulder to examine her back in the tall gilded mirror. She was completely naked, the glow of the single candle near her feet casting her body in golden shadows. A basin sat on the table by her side as she held soapy wet cloths in each hand, and the scent of heather filled the air in a comforting bouquet.

A nasty red mark stained the pale skin between her shoulder blades, and others dotted her back like raisins in a scone.

"I coupled against a wall," she breathed, fascinated by the evidence of her conduct. "Against a blasted wall."

Her lips lifted in a secret smile. "And it was bloody fantastic."

Although she'd certainly been exposed to such language in her years at Andersen Hall Orphanage, she made it her business never to curse just in case she might accidentally use it in front of the children. But tonight she made an exception. Because tonight had been an *exceptional* night.

Her eyes traveled down to the white rounded mounds of her derrière, reminding her of the feel of the mysterious stranger's hands clutching her flesh in fiery passion.

She shifted her bare feet, her skin hot, her body agitated. It was as if once roused, her desire had no wish to slumber once more. She should be exhausted, yet instead she felt vital, her every sense awake, her mind filled with wonder.

Her perception of her body and what it was capable of feeling had immeasurably changed. She'd never understood why certain women longed for coupling. She'd never comprehended that special secret that they'd already known—that at the hands of a skilled lover, breathtaking, mind-spinning sensations were achievable.

She'd never known that her body was capable of such an amazing symphony of passion. With the mysterious rescuer conducting every canto with a master's hand, every part of her body had sung in a harmony of pleasure.

Phineas Byrnwyck had taken her virginity, yet he'd never shown her the satisfaction possible for a woman when bedding a man. Her stomach churned with mortification as she recalled what an innocent fool she'd been. Willing enough, certainly, to try to please the man she loved—but she hadn't truly understood what he'd been about. She'd gone along without truly grasping the consequences of her actions.

And Phineas hadn't appreciated the fact that she was wholly without understanding of what went on between man and woman. He'd taken advantage of her ignorance and had pressed her to show her affection physically before she'd been ready.

He should have been more chivalrous.

"Chivalry is for poems and fairy tales," she murmured as she gently rubbed the soapy cloth down her back. "Not twenty-year-old bucks who've had everything they've ever wanted handed to them on a silver platter." She winced in pain as the rough cloth swept over the raw spot above her buttocks.

She couldn't think back on her relationship with Phineas or that time without being angry at herself for playing such a fool. Stupidly she'd assumed that his sweet words of adoration would last her a lifetime. She'd trusted his assurances that he'd cherish her and never do anything to harm her. She'd believed him when he'd sworn that he would move mountains to marry her.

But those declarations had disintegrated to dust the moment he'd had to face his wretched father and cousin. For Phineas, a mountain might have been easier to move. Lord Byrnwyck and his foul nephew Silas had made sure that Abigail was without a job, without references, and definitely without a husband.

So she'd been ruined. Her heart broken. Her life in disrepair. And for what? Now she realized Phineas had been incapable of the kind of love she'd longed for. He'd been too cowardly to stake a real claim for her heart. And stupidly she'd given him the one gift that could never be returned.

Now, to add insult to injury, she realized that he'd been a lousy lover, too!

Compared to what Abigail had felt with her rescuer tonight—well, being with Phineas would be like comparing days-old milk to fine champagne. And her rescuer was definitely the fine tipple.

Exhaling, she turned to face the mirror and rubbed the cloth up the column of her neck. She was decent-looking enough, certainly no diamond of the first water. Her eyes were the same as her father's had been, rounded and a pale blue that sometimes appeared gray in certain light. Her nose was upturned and uninspiring, but certainly not ugly. Her skin was fair, a good complement to her blond hair just like her mother's. Nodding, she decided that she was adequately pretty.

She tilted her head, examining her body in the candlelight with a critical eye. Rounded high breasts, each about the size of a grapefruit; a small curved waist that flared into reasonably sized hips. They weren't quite what Mrs. Nagel, the marm at Andersen Hall Orphanage, would have called "birthing hips," but they were enough to balance out her hourglass shape. All in all, she wasn't bad off in the physical way of things.

Wistfully she wondered, if she hadn't met Phineas, if she hadn't been ruined, would she have ever married? Would she have ever found true love?

The soapy cloth had grown cold in her hand, she realized with a start. She dipped it in the tepid water and squeezed, the scent of heather soap filling the air.

Purposefully she pushed all foolish thoughts of a different future, a family of her own, from her mind. She couldn't repair the past. She could only trudge onward, playing the hand of cards she'd been dealt.

As she rubbed the wet cloth over her breasts, her mind drifted back to the mysterious rescuer. It was dangerous, what she'd done. Trusting her body to a total stranger, throwing caution so far to the wind.

Of its own accord, her hand grazed her belly. What if she became with child? Slowly she shook her head. Somehow she just knew it would not be. Part of her longed to know the feeling of a babe inside of her, part of her knew that it would be the end of her job, of her career. And some deep inner instinct told her that it was not meant to be. She'd been with Phineas many times and nothing had come of it.

Had she been with child, would he have married her? Somehow she doubted it. Part of her wondered if she was barren, and that idea had a certain ironic ring to it. Maybe the good Lord was watching out for her in some odd way, and the thing many women found to be a curse, for her could be a blessing?

Still, her conduct tonight had been reckless in the extreme. But coupling with that stranger had been one of the most astonishing experiences of her life-time. She couldn't regret it. Couldn't imagine want-ing to live her life without *knowing*. It would have been a tragedy to die without experiencing the pas-sion that her body was capable of feeling. The fiery sensations inspired by the masked rescuer's hands on her burning flesh, the feel of his fingers driving her to madness, the force of his member filling her deep inside her core.

In her reflection, Abigail watched in wonder as her skin flushed pink, her nipples hardened to high pebbles, and her womb pitched with warmth.

Slowly she ran the cloth over her breast, raising

bumps across her warming skin. Stirring images flashed in her mind—the masked man touching her, pressing against her, thrusting inside her . . .

A bird cried out in the distance announcing a prelude to the dawn. Abigail knew that she hadn't much time. Understood that soon she would be called upon to perform her duties.

*But not yet . . .*

She wasn't ready for this exploration to end. She wanted to know more, wanted to relive those feelings.

The sound of movement echoed in the silent house, coming from behind the closed door connected to the master's chambers. Lord Steele must be rising. The day beginning.

Quickly she dropped the cloths into the basin and reached for her dressing gown, fear and guilt making her movements jerky.

No one could know about her sinful conduct! No one could ever guess at her wicked thoughts! Thank the heavens that the masked man did not know her identity!

If anyone found out, she'd lose her position, her income, her future. She didn't think she could face being ruined again.

Tying the sash of her dressing gown so tightly that it pinched, she rushed to the wardrobe to dress. She'd be the perfect governess. An exemplary employee.

Yanking open the wardrobe door, Abigail selected her most sober gown of gray wool, with long sleeves and a high collar. Then, in contrast to her high-heeled black boots of last night, she selected flat, worn slippers of faded brown.

Exhaling, she tried to calm her apprehensive heart.

No one would ever know that underneath this prim costume she was a scarlet woman, even more so because she couldn't wait to sin again.

# Chapter 15

**H**ours later, Abigail eyed the bright afternoon sun through the open window, calculating how long it might be until dark. The boys went to bed about eight, and she would be freed from her duties by nine. She had Lord Steele's permission to visit her ill friend, so no one would question her if she went out.

Anticipation coursed through her, which she quickly tried to hide by burying her nose in the pages of the book she was reading, so the boys wouldn't notice.

Seth sat on the window seat, the sun shining gold in his hair while he read a leather volume of poems. His brother reclined on a sofa across the sitting room, an irritated frown on his face, as he obviously didn't like his reading selection.

Seth suddenly looked up from his book and shot her a sweet smile.

Instinctively she smiled in response, her heart warming.

Guilt twisted in her middle; did her nocturnal activities make her unworthy of teaching these sweet lads? She bit her lip, objectively pondering the question without merely trying to justify her behavior. She was a good governess. She understood and cared for Seth and Felix. She was capable and smart and more than a bit competent. What she did at night was her own business. *So long as no one knew.*

She recognized that she'd never intended to be so wicked; she'd simply been trying to find her brother. Still, she wasn't deluded enough not to realize that if she went out again tonight she wouldn't be able to help but look for *him*, and not just Reggie.

Thinking of the masked man, she chided herself mentally, *He's a distraction you do not need.*

She might not need the diversion, but she certainly yearned for it. Again. And again and again. She was like a slave to her longings, her good sense and usual caution dissipating faster than steam from boiling water.

"Why do you keep checking your watch, Miss West?" Seth asked. "Are we going somewhere?"

Tucking her timepiece back into the folds of her skirt, Abigail forced herself to look at the open pages of the book in her lap. "I'm simply checking to see how long we've been reading."

"Is it long enough?" Felix asked, his tone irritated. "I hate poems. They're for girls and softies."

Seth pouted. "I like rhyming."

"My point exactly." Felix sneered. "Softies."

Standing, Seth stomped his foot. "I am not a softy!" He turned to Abigail. "Felix called me a softy!"

Abigail frowned at her elder charge, disappointed that he would use the derogatory play yard term toward his brother. At Andersen Hall Orphanage.

calling another boy a softy usually ended up in an exchange of blows. "Apologize to your brother, Felix. There shall be no name calling."

"I didn't call him a softy," Felix defended with his chin in the air. "It was a statement of a general sort, not necessarily directed at him."

"What a fine legalistic argument." Lord Steele moved into the salon, his masculine vitality filling the small space with an energy that charged the air. He was dressed in a coat of the finest Weston cut, of a flattering royal blue that made his ebony hair and dark eyes shine in great contrast. He wore tight ivory breeches that matched his high-collared ivory shirt, and tall black boots that squeaked slightly as he crossed the chamber and settled on the window bench beside Seth.

Abigail couldn't quite contain the sudden racing of her heart and the warmth that seeped into her cheeks. She had hoped that her late night excursion would have cured her of these sudden rushes of heat when she encountered her employer, but she supposed that was too much to count on.

In fact, the awareness Abigail felt for Lord Steele was suddenly much more discomforting because Abigail worried that he might somehow, through some magical ability, be able to detect her newly sinful state.

She looked down, adjusting her somber gray skirts and praying that she didn't have some sort of sign on her forehead branding her a strumpet.

Just remembering that the savior was unknown to her and that her identity was unknown to him made her feel a little bit better. But still, she coughed into her fist and made a business of settling a ribbon to hold her place in her book before meeting Lord Steele's eye.

Felix sneered. "See, even Lord Steele says I didn't call you a softy."

Lord Steele shook his head. "On the contrary, I said that it was a fine legalistic argument, but your message was quite clear. You insulted your brother. Quite plainly, and quite intentionally."

"I did not!"

Lord Steele fixed Felix with a look that begged no contradiction. "Apologize to your brother."

Felix's eyes narrowed.

"Apologize." Steele's gaze was commanding enough that Abigail had to bite her tongue to keep from apologizing herself.

Felix looked away, muttering, "Fine, I'm sorry."

"For what?" Steele asked, his tone exacting.

"Fine. For calling him a softy." Felix scowled.

"Don't tell me." Lord Steele jerked his chin toward Seth. "Tell him."

Seth looked up at his brother expectantly.

Felix's scowl deepened. "Fine. I'm sorry."

Steele nodded. "Good. You should know I have little patience for bullies."

Abigail frowned. "As I was just telling the boys, we don't engage in name-calling. Besides, Felix is not a bully."

Steele raised one of his dark winged brows at her questioningly.

She lifted her shoulder in a faint shrug. "It was a bullying moment. Every boy has them."

His brow lifted higher, and Steele's gaze was filled with amusement. "How would you know? Have you ever been a boy?"

"No, but—" Abigail bit her lip, stopping herself from blurting out that she'd had firsthand knowledge from having a brother.

"I am not a bully!" Felix crossed his arms, his face contorted and his eyes shiny with unshed tears. Clearly his feelings were hurt. Abigail was reminded once more that he was only eight years old.

Sighing, Abigail set aside her book, stood, and walked over to Felix. Wrapping her arm around his shoulders, she was glad that he didn't shrug her off. Another year or two and he'd hardly have patience for her contact. "I know that you're not a bully, Felix. We all do. But what you said was hurtful to your brother. You do recognize that, don't you?"

His small shoulders lifted slightly. "Maybe."

Abigail licked her lips, speaking softly. "Sometimes I know you feel like lashing out, and the desire is sometimes too great to resist. But you have to understand that the injury you inflict with words cannot be healed with a simple 'I'm sorry.' Once the insult is out there, it can never be taken back. So you must think carefully before you lash out."

Felix pouted.

Lord Steele tilted his head. "Felix, how would you feel if I called you a softy?"

Sniffing, Felix muttered, "I wouldn't care."

Seth jumped up, his small fist raised in anger. "You take that back! My brother's not a softy!"

Lord Steele's lips lifted, but he worked hard to conceal his smile. "Are you defending his honor?"

"Yes!"

Lord Steele nodded to Seth. "Defending your brother from insult is quite admirable."

Abigail gave Lord Steele credit for not poking fun at Seth. A few of the fathers she'd known would have taken no care to save a boy's feelings when he was making such a display. With some men, the drive to compete sometimes reared its ugly head even with children. Abigail was glad that Lord Steele seemed above that.

Seth shook his fist. "I said, you take that back! Felix's not a softy!"

Felix's eyes fixed on his brother, and warmth and confusion and guilt washed over his face in a flash. Abigail's heart went out to him. It wasn't easy being the older sibling.

Lord Steele's dark gaze flitted to Abigail, and when their eyes met, her belly flipped. "Since I know you've been taking lessons in swordplay from Miss West, I have no desire to meet you at dawn." The amusement and admiration in his eyes warmed her in places that her employer had no right even knowing existed. "I sincerely take back my insult and apologize."

Swallowing, Abigail ripped her gaze from his, her heart pounding and her mouth dry as a bone.

With his eyes fixed on Seth, Felix repeated, "I am sorry, little brother."

"I know you didn't mean it, Felix," his brother replied with an air of worldliness.

"How?"

Seth shrugged. "Lord Byron likes poetry, and so does the Prince Regent. So I know you wouldn't call them softies."

Felix turned to Lord Steele, his face inquiring. "Do you like poetry?"

Steele scratched his chin. "I suppose it depends on the poem. Some poetry is inspiring, some thought provoking . . . Some is simply . . . insipid."

With a serious expression on his small face, Seth turned to Abigail. "And you, Miss West? How do you find poems?"

"I find that poetry is best appreciated when one has a full stomach and a good night's sleep."

Lord Steele smiled. "I can heartily agree."

"Why?" Seth asked.

"I venture I'm easily distracted. When I'm supposed to be thinking of rustling leaves and busy byways, I think of my rumbling belly and buttered biscuits."

Both boys smiled, and the mood in the room lightened.

The new butler, Dudley, stepped into the room. Thank the heavens Lord Steele had seen fit to find Carlton another position in a household sans children.

Lord Steele stood. "Yes?"

"A Mr. Nigel Littlethom is calling."

Lord Steele's dark brow furrowed.

Dudley turned to Abigail. "For Miss West."

Steele could not quite contain the flash of displeasure in his gut. Miss West had a gentleman caller. He told himself that it was because she was in his employ and her time was spoken for—for the boys, of course.

He turned to the pretty young governess, realizing that his plan to lessen his attraction for her was failing miserably. Despite the amazing encounter the night before, his appetite had not been sated. In fact, he felt particularly susceptible to the swell of her breasts, the curve of her slender waist, and the slope of her shapely hips. No matter how much she tried to hide them beneath her astonishingly dull attire. Except for her face and her hands, every bit of her skin was covered in cloth.

And still he couldn't help but feel his blood stirring.

This was wholly unacceptable! He couldn't go around half-cocked all day. Something had to be done. And for all his intelligence, he could think of only one thing: a trip to the stews to meet the wicked widow. He needed to sate these unholy appetites, satisfy his lustful hungers.

It would be to the benefit of this innocent governess, he rationalized, and would keep his house in better order.

Abigail blinked. "Oh. Mr. Littlethom!"

"You know him?" Lord Steele inquired, enjoying a bit too much how her gray-blue eyes sparkled.

"He's the man who helped Seth from the water. At the park. When he fell in."

Lord Steele moved toward the door. "Then I must meet this man and thank him myself."

Miss West did not follow, but instead chewed her thumb in a fashion quite unmannerly for a governess. But when she did it she looked adorable.

Steele waited. "Is something amiss?"

"No. It's just . . . I would not want to take up your time. I can pass along your thanks."

She wanted to greet the man privately. Steele wondered if she had a *tendre* for him. Steele was surprised by the disappointment he felt at this insignificant fact.

Seth grabbed Steele's coattail. "Can you read to us, please, Lord Steele?"

Stepping forward, Miss West shook her head. "Don't bother Lord Steele right now. He's very busy."

Astonishingly, Seth had managed to soften Steele's sense of rejection. Steele held up his hand. "You go along, Miss West, and see to your visitor. The lads and I have some poetry to read."

He was glad to see the surprise in her eyes. She shouldn't assume that she knew everything there was to know about everyone in the house.

Turning, he led Seth back to the bench by the window.

Miss West stood in the doorway, uncertain. "Are you sure?"

Ignoring her, Steele motioned for Felix to join them. "Bring that book you were reading, and we'll see what sort of poetry you have there."

Felix grinned. "Insipid or inspiring."

"Insipid or inspiring."

Abigail watched the three of them a long moment, knowing she'd been dismissed and trying not to feel unwanted. She should be glad that Lord Steele had finally taken an interest in his nephews. Yet for some odd reason, she felt as if she'd disappointed him somehow.

"Mr. Littlethom is waiting in the front drawing room," Dudley reminded.

"Ah, yes, of course." Turning, Abigail tried to be excited at the opportunity to thank Seth's rescuer from the park. But a rescuer of a different sort was the only one she longed to see.

# Chapter 16

Abigail felt churlish. No matter how boyishly handsome the man was to look at, he was driving her to the edges of her patience. She'd sat with Mr. Littlethom for three quarters of an hour, and the entire time she'd wished to be elsewhere. Reading with the boys. Taking a nap. Reorganizing her stocking drawer. Anywhere but with the man who seemed completely infatuated with her.

Or, correct that, infatuated with her position with the Viscount Steele. Mr. Littlethom thought that her role in the household was somehow a great credit to her as a person. He'd gone on and on about her status and asked questions about how the household functioned. He certainly was very curious, to the point of rudeness. And she'd started to get suspicious of his motives.

Then the man had confessed. He hoped to gain employ in the viscount's household as a tutor. The poor man had been dismissed when his last students had gone off to Eton. He'd been heartbroken, he'd assured her, since he'd been with the family for more than three years. He'd been so upset about it that he'd taken himself off to London in hopes of starting afresh, with a family that had young lads, where he could help anew.

It was on his first day in London that he'd arrived at the park and come upon young Seth in the water. He considered it a sign.

Abigail didn't believe in signs. But after much cajoling, Abigail had promised to have a word with Lord Steele about the matter. She didn't know how she felt about it. On the one hand, Mr. Littlethom had helped haul them from the water at the park. And he wasn't a bad sort if he didn't open his mouth too much. Moreover, he specialized in languages, a topic in which she was particularly weak and the boys would need to know well.

On the other hand, he was maddeningly annoying.

She thought about it a long moment, realizing that any new tutor would change the balance of power in the household just when the boys were getting settled. And what if the new tutor wound up being a cruel taskmaster? She'd certainly seen her share of martinetlike educators. She wouldn't be able to abide someone who was too quick with punishments or too harsh with criticism. Mr. Littlethom did seem quite officious. Mayhap he'd be a gentle teacher?

Abigail sighed. At the end of the day, perhaps one was better off with the devil one knew . . .

*Devil* . . .

Abigail's mind veered once more toward that evening. Would she go out? Would she seek Jumper once more in hopes of finding a clue to her brother's whereabouts?

Whom was she trying to fool? She was watching the clock like a usurer watching a calendar in anticipation of the money coming due.

She wanted to see her rescuer—well, not see him. But feel him and touch him and . . .

"Are you unwell, Miss West?" Lord Steele interrupted her wicked thoughts. He'd come upon her where she stood daydreaming in the hallway. She hadn't heard his footfalls because of the thick carpeting, or perhaps it was the fact that her mind was elsewhere—in the sewers.

"Ah yes, fine." She coughed into her hand, her cheeks burning with mortification.

"How is your visit with *your* Mr. Littlethom?"

Abigail tried not to bristle at the second "your" and instead pasted on a smile. "Fine. Thank you."

"Good." He moved past.

Abigail licked her lips. "Ah, my lord?"

Steele turned, his broad shoulders filling the small hallway, making Abigail feel practically elfin. "Yes, Miss West?"

"Mr. Littlethom, it turns out, is a tutor."

"You don't say."

"I did not know that when he came to Seth's aid in the park."

"I thought you were the one who rescued Seth."

"Well, Mr. Littlethom helped us out of the water. He was quite brave."

"How admirable of him." Steele's gaze was shuttered and his chiseled features noncommittal. "And here I thought chivalry was dead."

Abigail blinked, agreeing completely but unwilling to miss the opening Steele presented. "It was quite gallant of him, I agree. And he ruined a coat in the process." She held open her hands in offering. "Even when I offered, he wouldn't think of letting me pay his repair bill."

Steele rubbed the hard line of his jaw. "Are you asking me to pay his tailor's bill?"

"Oh no! Of course not!"

"You're simply trying to tell me what a wonderful man Mr. Littlethom is."

"Well, no. But now that you mention it . . ."

"Please get to the point, Miss West. I have a pressing matter to attend to this evening and I'm going out."

Even though Abigail didn't believe in signs, she'd take this fact as an indicator that she was meant to go out, too. With Lord Steele away, no one would question her comings and goings, since Lord Steele had made it known that Abigail might be visiting her sick friend. Funny, the guilt over that little white lie was growing fainter and fainter with each passing moment.

Abigail could hardly contain the thrill of excitement skating across her skin as she considered the evening ahead. "Well, I shouldn't keep you . . ."

"But what were you saying about Mr. Littlethom?"

She shook her head. "Oh yes. Well, I was wondering . . . if you might be open to interviewing Mr. Littlethom. As a tutor for the boys."

Was it Abigail's imagination, or did the air in the hallway suddenly grow chilly?

"You want me to find a position for Mr. Littlethom in this household?"

"Well, if it suits your plans, of course."

"My plans?"

"For the boys' education."

Lord Steele frowned as if this were a novel notion to him. Strange.

Abigail stepped forward. "You do have plans for their instruction, don't you?"

Scratching his temple exactly where the flecks of gray mixed with his ebony hair, Steele seemed to consider it a long moment. "Do governesses normally insert themselves into the decisions of their employers?"

Abigail straightened. "That's not my intention—"

"Why don't you focus on your area of expertise, the physical care of Seth and Felix, and I will worry about their *intellectual* needs."

Abigail felt her jaw clench. It took brains to be a good governess. Anyone who'd ever known a stupid one knew that.

Gritting her teeth, Abigail curtsied. "I apologize if I offended you, my lord. I realize now that I need to remember my position in the household. I won't detain you any further."

Turning, she swept down the hallway, telling herself that she had something wonderful to look forward to. Her rescuer didn't care about her status in the household, her usefulness as a governess, or her intellect or supposed lack thereof. All he wanted was her body. Nice and simple. No complications. No idiotic assumptions or expectations. Just hot, salacious coupling, plain and simple. And she was ready to give it to him.

\* \* \*

As Steele watched Miss West's lush hips sway down the hallway, he cursed himself for being so abrupt. But he had no patience for her *tendre* for Mr. Littlethom. The thought of having two people in his household stealing glances, sneaking a quick graze of the fingertips, sharing secret dreams . . . well, it made him want to kick up a row.

Didn't staff these days know that such associations were forbidden in a household? He supposed that they were too infatuated to care. He was filled with disgust. Lovers had no consideration for others.

Why couldn't people find a way to satisfy their primal hungers without infringing on the daily life of others? As he was going to do. *Tonight*. He was going to find his wicked widow and sate his appetite once and for all. Then he wouldn't notice how shapely his governess's hips were, or how nicely her bosom swelled when she sighed, or how sweetly she smelled of heather when she swept past. He definitely wouldn't marvel at how golden her hair looked as the sun shone in through the salon window or wonder if her mane felt as soft as it looked. And he *certainly* wouldn't care that she had a *tendre* for a chivalrous tutor who'd come to her aid.

Rubbing his chin, Steele nodded. Sating primal needs. That was the order of the day, and he was primed and ready. Now if only he could find his wicked widow and convince her to have another run at it.

He smiled. He could be really convincing when he wanted to be. And somehow he doubted that his wicked widow would protest. She was too fiery a woman to say no to a little *innocent* pleasure.

"Devil take me," he muttered to himself, when he realized that his member was swelling at the thought. He was the blasted Solicitor-General of England; he should certainly know how to control his wayward body.

He'd grown bloody good at controlling his every emotion and his every action over the last eight years. So good at it, in fact, that what he'd done last night, tossing control to the wind . . . well, it was about the most reckless thing he'd ever done.

The scary thought intervened—could he possibly get her with child? Slowly he shook his head. The lady probably took precautions. Or mayhap she was too old to carry a babe?

He pushed the thought aside—if the widow wasn't worried, then neither would he be. He was a stranger to her, and she didn't seem to be concerned about future entanglements. In fact, she was quite quick to see him gone.

His curiosity was aroused, as was another part of him.

And he couldn't wait to see her again, and sate both passions.

# Chapter 17

"**G**ood night, Miss West," Seth murmured, as he lay tucked under his covers, his eyes bright in the candlelight, his cheeks flushed pink.

Sitting beside him on the bed, Abigail laid her hand on his sleepy brow and was surprised by the heat of his skin. Concern flashed through her. "Sit up, Seth."

He lifted himself halfway out of the covers to sit.

Reaching behind him, Abigail stuck her hand down the loose collar of his nightshirt to feel his back. His skin burned to the touch.

"How do you feel?" she asked, trying to keep the anxiety from her voice.

"Oh, all right," he murmured. "My head hurts a little."

Her gaze searched his features, hoping for any hint as to why he had such a fever. "Anything else?"

His hand rested on his stomach. "My tummy feels funny."

Abigail recalled that Seth had hardly touched his dinner. Felix had been talking about a new story that he'd read in a book, and she'd been so diverted that she'd assumed Seth had been similarly distracted from his food. But now she wasn't so sure.

Abigail stood. "I'll be right back."

She raced down the corridor and informed a footman that Seth had a fever, so the staff should be at the ready if she required anything. Then she went to the kitchen and asked for some water with lemons and sugar to be brought to Seth's room, and fetched some clean rags and a basin filled with cool water.

Upon returning to the boys' rooms, she was disappointed not to have been wrong about Seth's condition. Seth's eyes were shadowed and his lids heavy, and he looked so positively miserable, Abigail wanted to cry. But instead she got busy, peeling off his clothing and wiping down his skin with cool cloths, trying to lower his fever.

Felix looked up from the pages of the book he was reading, seemingly surprised by the goings-on. "What's wrong?"

"Seth has a fever," Abigail replied calmly.

"A fever!" Seth's half-closed eyes flew open.

"Not to worry, we'll get it down," she assured herself as much as the boys. "I've been trained by Dr. Michael Winner, the greatest children's doctor in London. I know what I'm doing."

After bathing Seth with cool water and cajoling him to drink water mixed with lemons and sugar, Abigail was relieved when Seth fell into a restless sleep. Felix, thank the heavens, slept like the dead, and none of the business going on in their rooms bothered him a bit.

That evening each minute seeped into an hour,

each hour bled into the next, and all thought of nighttime excursions flew from Abigail's mind.

For the next two days, the entire focus of Abigail's existence was centered on Seth's comfort. It was easy not to think about the masked rescuer, easy not to dwell on the things she'd done. *Later*, she promised herself. Later she'd go out. Later she'd search for Reggie. Then her eyes would close, she'd hug Seth close and feel the innocence of living one moment until the next, as she hoped for his fever to break.

"Please just let him not get worse," she prayed, knowing that there was only so much she could do.

Abigail was suddenly glad that because of the repairs to the nurseries, Lord Steele had given the boys a room on the same floor as she. She would pop into her room now and again for a quick nap, but was always close in case she was needed.

During those two days, Felix would visit Lord Steele in his study and they would read together. Then the boy would go out in the company of two footmen, Foster and Zachariah, while Abigail stayed with Seth. There was still no word on the missing footman Claude, and although Abigail found it strange, she was too busy to give it much thought.

During the day she would read to Seth, bathe him, and sing him songs. Seth was surprisingly good-spirited through it all, his mood seeming to lighten with the rise of the sun each day and darken with the beginning of night. He sorely missed his mother, and Abigail's heart bled with agony as he cried in her arms.

On the third day, Abigail and Seth lay together on the window seat in the parlor, the golden sun blanketing them in its warm embrace.

"And so the knight jumped on his trusted steed," Abigail read, her eyelids heavy, her breath deep and head fairly swimming with the desire for slumber.

A small snore erupted from Seth's open mouth.

Lowering the book, Abigail looked down at him. His pallor was better, his cheeks less pink, and his face not quite so pale. His breathing was even, his body relaxed. Gently she cupped his forehead in her hand. Relief swept through her; his skin felt cool to the touch. The fever had broken.

She allowed her eyes to close, her body to relax, and welcomed the sleep of thankfulness.

Steele strode down the carpeted hallway, nearing the parlor where he knew Miss West and Seth were reading. He'd had trouble working the last two days, ever since Seth had come down with a fever. He attributed some of his restlessness to his inability to find the wicked widow three nights ago, but recently he'd felt compelled to stay home, wanting to be near in case he was needed.

Not that Miss West required his help. Her efficient caring left little room for him to do anything but check in on Seth now and again. The lad was good-natured, Steele had to admit, weathering the baths and lemon drinks and broths with stalwart amicability. The boy was calm, too, as if knowing that he was in good hands.

Again Steele had to credit Sir Lee for selecting

Miss West as the boys' governess. Her every act was wrapped in genuine caring, her every word soft to the ear. When a challenge arose, she met it with aplomb. But Steele could tell, for all her competence, she was worried. Her eyes were shadowed, anxiety pinched her brow, and her voice had that breathless quality that belied her apprehension.

She hid it from the boys, but when they weren't looking, she would gaze at them with the kind of glance that spoke of loved ones lost and the fear that it might happen again. Miss West had known grief, and in every swipe of the wet cloth to Seth's fevered skin, in every spoonful of liquid she made him drink, she was clearly striving to keep the ill fates at bay.

As Steele approached the doorway, his steps slowed and he listened. Silence greeted him. Quietly he strode inside.

Steele's heart skipped a beat. He couldn't think of anything more beautiful than the sight before him, reminding him suddenly of a Madonna and child.

Miss West lay in the window seat, her body curled protectively around Seth, his small body nestled into hers. Her hand cupped the boy's forehead; a book lay beside them as if negligently dropped. The golden glow of midday sun washed over them, coating them in honeyed warmth. Miss West's unkempt hair glistened like strands of gold, her lashes splaying long shadows across her dewy pink cheeks. A contented smile played on her rosy lips. Her breast rose and fell evenly, her body perfectly relaxed in repose.

*That woman is meant to be a mother*, the thought whispered in his mind, surprising him. He suddenly wondered if she wanted children of her own. Did she long for marriage, motherhood? What did Miss West yearn for? Of what did she dream? He unexpectedly found that he wanted to know.

Was that why she was interested in Mr. Littlethom? Was a family of her own what she secretly hoped to gain?

He shifted, suddenly hating the idea of her leaving. His gut clenched just thinking about her not being here with her sunny hair and overly serious face and flashes of unpredictability. His house was happier since her arrival, and he didn't want that effect to end. But it would once the boys left. He certainly didn't need a governess if he didn't have the children. He scowled, not liking the course of his musings.

*I need to get back to work*, he chided. *I'm becoming maudlin in my old age, and productivity is the only answer.* A draft of a contract was waiting for his review, a brief needed a reply, a letter of inquiry required a response. He had important responsibilities.

But still, he couldn't get his feet to turn as he soaked in the purity and beauty of the slumbering pair.

Steele liked the way Miss West's hair swooped around her face like a framework of gold.

Seth was snoring quietly and evenly, his color healthier; his cheeks no longer had a feverish flush.

Suddenly Seth let out a little snort and shifted slightly. With his eyes still closed and clearly still in slumber, he grasped Miss West's free hand and clutched it tightly into his own. Seth sighed soundly, then burrowed deeper into the protective circle of Miss West's arm.

With her eyes still closed, Miss West hugged him tenderly and exhaled.

Feeling like an interloper, Steele turned to go. The boards beneath his feet creaked in protest.

Miss West's eyes flew open.

Her eyes were lighter, more blue than gray today, and it took but a second for the haziness to clear and for them to focus. On him. She did not move, obviously not wanting to disturb Seth.

Steele inquired, "How is he?"

"Better," she whispered. "The fever broke."

"Good."

She swallowed, speaking quietly, "I was beginning to worry that we'd have to call for the doctor."

"No." Steele hated doctors, dreaded their solemn faces and empty cures. Calling for the doctor signaled defeat, the death knell for sure. His mother had lasted less than a day after the doctor had come with his fatal pronouncements. His father had made it less than three days after the doctor's ineffective potions. The thought of Seth . . .

"No, what?" Miss West asked, her brow furrowing.

Steele blinked. "Ah, no doctors."

"Dr. Winner, from Andersen Hall, is a friend. He's really good, especially with children."

"You said his fever broke; we don't need him."

She pursed her lips. "You don't believe in the medical profession."

"I think the medical profession is quite advantageous . . . if you're a money-grubbing doctor."

Her eyes filled with sympathy. "Whom did you lose?"

Looking down at his hands, he was surprised at the knot suddenly choking his throat. "My mother, then my . . . father." He hadn't spoken of them in years and was surprised by the grief lashing through him.

"I'm so sorry."

"The doctor was useless," Steele choked out. "It was almost like . . . the doctor was a precursor to death."

"They can be sometimes. I think it's the nature of things."

"I understand that there's only so much a doctor can do . . . but every time I've called for one"—he looked up—"someone I love dies."

Her eyes glanced at Seth. But the lad slept on, his breath even, his slumber deep.

She motioned to the chair. "Please sit beside me. The talking soothes Seth, and I want to hear what happened."

To his own great shock, Steele lifted the chair and set it next to the sleeping boy and his governess. "I don't know that there's much to tell."

"Then tell me about your parents. What were they like?"

Steele realized that he wanted to talk to Miss West, wanted to be near her. There was something about her mien that inspired trust, and the knowledge that she had a sympathetic ear.

For the next hour Steele recounted the tale he'd never spoken of to a soul. How his mother had come down with a terrible cough that made him wince with agony simply hearing it. How her labored breath whistled with torturous struggle. How her body had burned with fever and her mind had been lost to non-sensical ranting.

Miss West would ask a question now and again, but mostly she listened, her compassion clear, yet she did not pity him, just the situation.

His father's passing had been a bit easier, mostly because the man had hardly complained. The master carpenter was finishing up a new mantel at the local vicar's house when his apprentice accidentally cut him with a blade. The fever had set in the next night and burned him to a cinder. When Steele's aunt was at a loss for what else she could do, they'd gathered their last money and called for the doctor.

"It was a waste of our money," Steele explained, bitterness lacing his tongue. "I hate doctors, they're useless."

"Not all of them," Miss West countered. Then she told him of Dr. Michael Winner, the man who treated all the children at Andersen Hall Orphanage and never took a penny for it. She told him about the times the man had sat all night with a sick child, mixed hundreds of liniments, set countless bones, and stitched innumerable gashes. All with good humor, a caring spirit, and for no fee.

She sighed. "Doctors are merely human, and they come in all shapes and sizes, good and bad. But mostly they aim to do well, to relieve suffering."

"You believe that?" Steele asked.

"I do. It takes a certain kind of man to commit to helping others. And as far as the money, he deserves to be able to put bread on his table as much as the next person. Don't condemn him for it." Her brow furrowed. "How old were you when your father died?"

"Twelve." He suddenly realized that she knew exactly what it mean to be an orphan. "You were thirteen when you went to Andersen Hall Orphanage?"

"Yes."

He nodded, his heart aching for her. They were a pair in their loss.

"And I count myself lucky for having made it there," she added.

"I was lucky, too. I was taken in by a group of brothers in my village." The Cutler brothers had welcomed him into their fold. They had given him a place beside them, as one of them. They had given him a reason to be, instead of wallowing in grief and loneliness. "I'll be forever grateful to them," he murmured.

"Do you ever get to see them?"

He shook his head. For Deidre he'd cut all ties with his old life. Then after she'd died, grief had overwhelmed, and he hadn't had the energy to reconnect. Thereafter he'd been so busy building his career and becoming a man Deidre could be proud of.

One year had bled into the next, and soon he was too ashamed to contact the Cutlers.

"Do you miss them?" she asked.

His brow furrowed. "I do." He realized that he missed the camaraderie, having a place.

"Then why don't you contact them? Write them a letter, invite them to come see you?"

He shook his head. "I'm a different man now. I don't know if they would welcome word from me after so long. I don't know if they'd even like me."

"Of course they'd like you. You're eminently good-natured."

"Ahhh." He made a face. "You have not heard of my stellar reputation?"

She looked away.

"So you have." He scratched his chin. "Which of the fine descriptions have you heard about me? Was it the 'Filled with more ambition than the House of Commons when a vote is tight?' Or, my personal favorite, 'As sharp as a scythe and leaves you just as bloody.'"

"Ouch!" She made a face. "You don't seem bothered by these statements. Instead . . . you seem proud."

"I'm not ashamed of my ambition; it's gotten me where I am today. I made a goal for myself, and then did everything in my power to attain it. Some may call it ruthless, striving, grasping." He shrugged. "I needed to become the man my wife deserved." He looked away, as if shocked that he'd shared that information.

Shifting on the seat, he added quickly, "The other sentiment, about being like a scythe . . . well, I suppose I am proud of that since it's been said as it applies to me in court." He nodded. "And I do take it as a compliment. When I can cross-examine a hostile witness and distill the facts from the rubbish he tries to pawn off as truth."

Abigail couldn't quite forget his comment about being the man his wife had deserved, but clearly he did not wish to discuss it. "It must be gratifying to do a job so well."

"It is. And to feel like I am serving my country."

She shook her head. "I can't help but venture that your friends would be glad to hear from you. And not just because of your position. There's great integrity to all you do."

His brow furrowed as if this were a new concept to him.

Abigail continued, "I know it would be gratifying to me if one of my charges grew up to be a man like you."

He crossed his legs, seemingly uncomfortable.

"Did I embarrass you?" she asked.

"No . . . well . . . I'm sincerely flattered that you think so well of me. But you haven't known me for long—"

"If you have any doubts about your character, children are the best judges, and both Seth and Felix adore you."

"Well, I don't feel as if I've done a very good job getting to know them," he confessed.

"Felix has been crowing about the stories you read together. He's quite taken with you, and I have to tell you that boys don't lie about such things. They either like you or they don't. Very simple. Write to your friends. They'd be delighted to hear from you."

Scratching his chin, he realized that he was tempted by the notion of writing to the Cutler brothers. The oldest, Johnny, must be forty by now. Gabriel, thirty-five. The twins, Kincaid and Peter, would be about his age. "It's been so long since I left them. I wonder if they're angry."

"When was the last time you met a man angry that another man didn't keep in touch?"

The way she presented it, it did sound silly. "Never."

"I think men don't care or fuss about such things as much as women do."

He nodded, a feeling of lightness in his chest. "I'll do it."

"Good. Please let me know how they respond."

Seth snorted, stirred, and sat up. Blinking, he rubbed his eyes. "Lord Steele?"

"How are you, Seth?" Steele asked, leaning forward and catching a whiff of Miss West's heather scent.

"Better. Hungry. When's breakfast?"

Steele smiled, exchanging a glance with Miss West. She was beaming. "I think buttered biscuits are in order."

Seth's eyes brightened. "With raspberry jam?"

Lord Steele stood. "With whatever you want!"

"Yippee!" Seth jumped up and raced out the door.

"Not so fast!" Miss West chided, but the boy was gone.

"I think he's feeling better," Steele commented.

"Most definitely." Slowly Miss West rose from the seat.

Steele grasped her arm. "Here, let me help you."

"Ah, thank you. I got a bit stiff sitting for so long."

Awkward silence encased them as he released her arm.

Miss West looked up. "I'd better be off to the kitchen, before Seth turns everyone on his head."

"Yes."

She smiled shyly. "Thanks for keeping me company."

He looked away, chagrined. "Ah, you're welcome."

Her skirts swooshed as she walked out the door.

The parlor felt empty, and quiet, and Steele suddenly did not mind. He felt better, as if a burden that had been weighing on his heart had lightened. The internal acrimony that had plagued him for so many years had been replaced with a feeling of . . . acceptance. It wasn't quite forgiveness, but more akin to understanding.

Exhaling, Steele tried to recall what he'd intended to do with the rest of his day.

Work.

He checked his watch. Where had the day gone?

He had papers that needed reviewing and a letter to draft.

But he couldn't seem to garner the desire to go to his study. Instead, he found his footsteps leading him down toward the kitchens.

# Chapter 18

Three nights later, Abigail slowly crept along in the dark alleyway, her senses honed to pick up any hint of her masked savior. But there was nothing. No well-balanced footfalls, no deliciously masculine scent, no tingling awareness racing across her skin. Nothing.

She swallowed her disappointment, telling herself that he'd probably forgotten her. It had been a week since they'd met. A week since he'd woken her slumbering desires.

She pushed aside the disenchantment; she needed to focus her energies on finding Reggie. Guilt pricked at her gut for allowing herself to be diverted from her task, but it was a tiny pinch overshadowed by desperate longing. She yearned for that fantastic heat, the intoxicating pleasure, the astonishing sensations in her most private places. Just remembering the passion she'd experienced made her skin warm all over.

"Stop it!" she whispered to herself, clenching her hands so that her nails bit her palms. She welcomed the pain, needing to regain control over herself and not get distracted from the important mission of finding her brother. He was in deep trouble and in need of her help. And if she didn't start paying attention to her surroundings, she might find herself in deep trouble, too.

A rat scurried along the nearby wall. A cry rang out in the distance. The odor of refuse and the Thames hung over the streets, pungent and cloying, like a whore's perfume. She'd certainly been exposed to enough of such scents, having interviewed more streetwalkers than she could count in hopes that someone had seen her brother.

Images of some of the women seemed to stay with her long after the interviews were over and they'd parted ways. There was Betty, with the haunted, hollow eyes. Jane, with consumption, who had clothing that hung on her willowy frame in rags. Mallory, who had a cough that rattled and a baby just eleven months old that her sister kept while she worked to pay for food.

Swallowing, Abigail squeezed her eyes closed and pushed away the images from her mind. She knew that when she encountered these women she was a bit too free with her money, even when the information was negligible. But she had to do something . . . Clenching the small pouch in her pocket, she weighed the little coin she had left. Still, she was so much better off than these women, so much better off . . .

She tried not to dwell on the fact that if not for Andersen Hall Orphanage, she might have been just a few steps behind these women. She thanked her good fortune for landing at the orphanage. She thanked God for introducing her to Headmaster Dunn. She was grateful for the chance she'd had to succeed.

But what of Reggie? He hadn't really used that opportunity to best advantage. He'd dashed all her hopes for him, and she hated to admit it, but she was disappointed. He was smart, literate, and had the kindest heart a man could have. But that kind heart accompanied a temper that lit in a flash. When he was angry, rational thought flew out the window, and Reggie usually wound up in boiling water.

A harsh cough echoed in the alleyway, and Abigail's footsteps froze. About ten paces away on the ground, a man rolled over, his open mouth emitting a small snore. Examining the sky, Abigail was glad to see that few clouds blocked the moon, so rain shouldn't be imminent. She knew what it was like to sleep in the open, and rain was no one's favored bedfellow.

Abigail recalled the nights she and Reggie had slept in haylofts and leaf piles until they'd found their way to London and only by happenstance to Andersen Hall Orphanage. Shivering, she rubbed her hand up her arm, wondering where Reggie slept now.

Reggie was a nomad, making do with one odd job and another, and avoiding the law at every turn. Now he was in trouble again, and was scared enough to contact his sister. It was a frightening thought, and a responsibility that Abigail didn't take lightly.

Abigail quickened her pace, ready to finally meet the infamous Jumper and find out what he knew.

She turned the corner and spied a slim figure leaning on a doorframe. A lantern rested on a hook to his right, spilling a hazy greenish-golden glow around the man's legs.

He was a lanky fellow with matted blond hair, a

hooked nose, and an Adam's apple that was as big as a child's fist. He had gangly arms that hung loosely at his sides and stuck out of the sleeves of his worn brown coat. His legs seemed a mile long, an effect enhanced by the fact that his black breeches were a hand's-width shorter than his brown, calf-length scuffed boots.

He matched the cutpurse's description to a T.

*Thank you, Slippery Milo*, Abigail mouthed the words to herself and proceeded into the square.

Ignoring the familiar knot in her middle, she forced her tone to be forceful yet friendly. "Are you Jumper?"

The man grimaced at her, his face a mask of insolent disregard that would do an earl proud. "Who a' you?"

"You're Jumper?"

"Who's askin'?"

Abigail moved into the pool of lantern light. "Slippery Milo sent me."

"Who?"

"The cutpurse."

Jumper sniffed, rubbing his lanky hand across his hooked nose. "I don't associate with such folk."

"Then why did he know that you'd be here?"

Jumper shrugged a bony shoulder. "So I'm a popular fella, well known in these parts."

"Look, Mr. Jumper, I'm looking for a man named Reg or Reggie. With light blue eyes and blond hair."

"Don't know 'im."

"I will pay you for information . . ."

"I'm 'appy to take your money."

". . . if the information is accurate, of course."

Wincing, Jumper stuck a finger in his ear and dug as if intent on a find. "What's 'is name again?"

"Reggie. He may have a scar on his cheek." Abigail didn't know if the barmaid had been lying or not, but figured it was worth mentioning.

Looking away, Jumper pulled out a flask and swallowed, his Adam's apple bobbing. The odor of gin wafted around him like a halo. "I may 'ave seen 'im . . ."

"May have or have actually seen him?"

"Actually."

Abigail released the breath she'd been holding. Reaching into her purse, she pulled out three coins, praying that the man was telling the truth. She held them in her extended hand.

He eyed the coins. "Check by Juniper Street. There's a flower stall near the market."

"He's running a flower stall?"

"'E's soft on the chit that's running it."

Could it be? Could she truly be on the brink of finding Reggie? "What does she look like?"

Jumper frowned.

"Please . . ."

His gaze traveled toward her slowly, almost as if against his will. "Red-'aired. With bosom enough to nurse three 'ealthy babes."

Abigail's heart leaped. Reggie always preferred crimson-haired women! "Thank you! Thank you, Mr. Jumper!" She handed him the coins, which he accepted, quickly slipping them into a hidden pocket in his coat.

She moved to go, but suddenly turned. "When I

was young, we lived in the country, and there was a harvest fair every autumn."

Silently he listened, studying her as if she'd gone mad.

"There were always great contests. Games of sport. Archery, horsemanship, carving . . ." She felt her lips lift as she remembered the welcome heat of the autumn sun, the tantalizing smells of cooked meats and pastries, the colorful banners flying about and the sounds of the vendors crying out, advertising their wares. "And the leaping contest was my favorite. I'll never forget the man who jumped over a horse."

Jumper straightened, going to his full height, his head a full foot above the lantern hanging on the wall.

Nodding, Abigail bit her lower lip. "I'd venture you would have done well at that." She turned to go. "Thank you, again."

"Wait!"

Surprised, Abigail stopped.

Peering to the left and to the right, Jumper stepped closer. He covered his mouth with the back of his hand, whispering, "Ya didna 'ear it from me, but Lucifer Laverty's lookin' for 'im, too."

"Lucifer Laverty?" What was it with these odd names?

"Shh!"

"Who's Lucifer Laverty?"

"'E's one a' the meanest sons a' bitches you'll ever want ta meet. I 'eard there was a row, about a job. But ya didna 'ear it from me."

"A job?"

"Ya know, a job. Laverty runs the circuit."

"The circuit?"

He looked at her as if she was daft.

She shook her head, flummoxed. "I'm sorry, Mr. Jumper, but I don't understand."

"The circuit from Medford Place to Gillingham Square is Laverty's. 'E runs all the trade."

She nodded, an uneasy feeling twisting in her gut. "Trade" was often used on the street to mean the business of thievery. In some quarters stealing was as well organized as some of the tradesmen's leagues. "Thank you for telling me, Jumper."

"I warn ya, Lucifer Laverty's bad news, and anyone who crosses 'im might as well be signing 'is own death warrant!"

# Chapter 19

**H**earing distant voices, Steele stepped back into the shadows, careful not to make a sound. A woman's well-cultured inflection! His heart skipped a beat. The wicked widow! He forced his excitement to calm; he wasn't a pimple-cheeked youngling seeking his blushing bride. He was a mature adult seeking companionship—that was all. It was a matter of sating passion, mutually, of course, and he didn't want to appear the overeager stallion. Still, his feet inched forward of their own accord.

A man's voice drifted toward him. Steele froze mid-inch.

The male voice, then the woman's—too indistinct to hear the words, but Steele was certain that it was the widow.

So she wasn't alone! Did she have another lover? Was she so quick to drop him for someone new? It had been only a week since their tryst!

Anger flashed in his gut, but he suppressed it, quietly stepping forward so that he could hear better.

Steele melted against the wall behind him, years of practice making his movements instinctive. He dared not approach closer, but now at least he could catch some of the exchange.

"A job?" she asked, her words barely discernible. Blast that stupid veil!

"Ya know, a job. Laverty runs the circuit." The man's voice was louder than hers, even though he clearly was trying to whisper.

Her response was muffled, lost to him.

The man spoke, "The circuit from Medford Place to Gillingham Square is Laverty's. 'E runs all the trade."

"Thank you . . ." Her words were indecipherable. ". . . Jumper."

Jumper was a message runner in this area, Steele knew. Why was the widow speaking to him?

Jumper spoke, "I warn ya, Lucifer Laverty's bad news, and anyone who crosses 'im might as well be signing 'is own death warrant!"

What was the lady up to? Messing with the circuit? Involved with Lucifer Laverty?

Steele had to learn more. Carefully he moved around the bend. The faint golden-green glow of a lantern could be seen in the distance.

Jumper and the widow stood in a courtyard at the junction of six interconnecting alleyways. One of those alleyways was where he and the widow had been the other night.

So she'd been on her way here. Possibly to meet Jumper.

Steele had never met the man, but he'd heard a snippet or two. Jumper was too far away and it was too dark to discern his features. But Steele could tell that he was tall, a full head-span above Steele, and lanky, with long arms and legs. By his stance and his demeanor, the fellow seemed fit enough. Still, Steele knew he could take him, if it came to that.

The dark-garbed widow stood near Jumper, her head well below his shoulders. There was no sense of intimacy between the two. No heads leaning forward, no hand on an arm, no touching at all.

So they weren't lovers. Steele exhaled. Once he'd realized it was Jumper, he should have known. He didn't know why he expected the widow to be discerning, his vanity perhaps, but he did.

Still, what was she doing in one of London's worst neighborhoods conversing with riffraff about Lucifer Laverty and the circuit?

Steele felt his usual caution cool his ardor. He was Solicitor-General of England, and his reputation, his position, and his hard-won status in society would ill afford him to mix with anyone involved with Lucifer Laverty.

The two people parted, neither making a move to embrace. Jumper quickly turned the corner and was gone.

The widow took the alleyway to the left.

Steele had little doubt whom he wanted to follow. It was probably because he knew that if he retraced his steps and crossed Piper Lane, he'd intersect with the lady behind the market square. That row was filled with vendors' stalls and cubbies, vacant at this time of night.

His heart began to race at the thought of encountering her alone on such a deserted avenue.

But the widow could be very bad news for him, and he knew he should stay away. Lucifer Laverty, the circuit . . . Clearly she was playing with fire, and he had no intention of getting burned.

But what if she was in over her head? What if she didn't appreciate the danger? What if she was an innocent embroiled in something far more complex than she understood?

As these thoughts raced through his mind, Steele's legs began to move, retracing his steps and heading toward that intersection. It was as if his body had a will of its own, heedless of any concerns.

He would ask her, that's what he'd do. He'd learn more about her activities before moving forward with anything physical.

At least that's what he told himself. His body, on the other hand, seemed without precondition.

His legs ate up the distance, hurrying toward the market square and the widow he intended to confront.

The row behind the market square was just as empty as he'd known it would be. The stalls were boarded and shuttered for the night, the vendors long gone. The air carried the faint scent of mildew and wood and anise, of all things. The shadows hung long, and the silence was hushed expectantly.

He heard her long before he could discern her dark-cloaked figure moving through the darkness. Her shoes had wooden heels padded with a thin layer of leather. If she wanted to be perfectly silent, she'd have to wear purely leather-soled shoes just like his.

Steele moved into the center of the lane, blocking her exit. Silently he waited for her to see him.

Her skirts whispered slightly in the night, reminding him of what lay underneath them. His heartbeat quickened.

Her steps slowed; she seemed to tense, reaching into the folds of her cloak.

"It's me," he called out. "From the other night."

She cautiously continued her steps forward as if unafraid, yet wary, her hand remaining out of sight in the folds of her cloak.

Well, what did he expect—her to jump into his arms? They were perfect strangers. Just so long as she hadn't hoped never to see him again . . .

The thought made him frown beneath his mask.

She stopped well outside arm's reach, as if hesitant of the next move. "Hello."

"Hello."

A heavy silence descended as each assessed the other.

"I didn't know"—her voice was less sure than the other night—"if I'd ever see you again . . ."

Did that mean that she'd hoped to avoid him?

"Nor I, you." He tilted his head. "Yet here we are."

"Yet here we are," she echoed quietly. Looking around, she seemed to evaluate her surroundings. The moonlight bathed the rows of stalls with a whitish glow couched in shadows. "This is the market row."

"Yes. Have you been here before?" he couldn't help but ask, trying to imagine who she was in her daily life.

"It's so quiet."

"It won't be in a few hours."

"No, I suppose not. What time do you think it is?"

"Close to three."

"Three!" Her arms tensed and she seemed alarmed.

"Why are you so concerned? Do you have an appointment?"

"It's just . . . later than I thought. Well, I must be going." She stepped sideways, as if to go around him.

It took every ounce of willpower not to cry out, *No!* Quickly he realized that maybe she was simply waiting for him to make the first move. If he wanted anything to do with her, he'd better stop acting so disinterested and make an overture.

"So soon?" he asked, stepping in front of her. "I confess, I'm glad to see you again."

Her steps faltered. "You are?"

"Yes. Of all people I might come across . . . well, I'm glad to run into you most."

"Really." After a moment she nodded. "Me, too."

Anticipation bubbled inside him, along with a rush of confidence. "In fact, I'd hoped to meet you again. Tonight."

"Why?" Her voice had taken on a firmer quality, reminding him of the bold woman he'd encountered the other night.

"Well, I wanted to see you again . . . and . . . to . . . touch you."

Her hand lifted to her bosom as she inhaled a deep, shuddering breath that made her breasts swell. Desire flashed deep in his belly, hungry and insistent.

He licked his lips. "Would that . . . suit you?"

"Perhaps." Her voice was throaty with need.

He took a step forward.

She stepped closer, less than a foot away.

His senses tingled with awareness at every rise and fall of that lush chest, every sway of those rounded hips. He longed to lay his hands on her, but recognized the slight hesitation in her manner. For all her worldliness, she seemed cautious. Smart woman.

He smiled, teasing, "Perhaps? Did I not please you the other night?"

His strategy worked, for she seemed to relax slightly. Playfully she set her hand on hip, replying, "Are you trolling for a compliment, sir? For I assure you, it takes a lot to please me."

"A lot? How much is that?" He held out his hands, palms facing each other about eight inches apart. "This much?" He widened the space between his hands. "Or this much?"

She moved her gloved hands to mimic his, palms parallel to each other—but hers were about two feet apart. "Don't be stingy. I want at least this much." Her voice was tantalizing with mischievous expectation.

"I'm not a horse," he grumbled teasingly.

Moving closer, she reached up and laid each hand on the round of his shoulders. "You see? Perfect match."

He grabbed her waist, pulling her against him. She gasped, then melted into him like butter on a hot bun.

His arms wrapped around her, his hands roamed, exploring the breadth of her back, the curving arch and the delicious mounds of flesh of her derrière that fit so perfectly in his hands. He squeezed and kneaded, eliciting a heady groan from deep inside her that was music to his ears.

She thrust her hands deep beneath his coat, teasing his chest, his waist, his back. Then, reaching around him, her hands drifted downward to his buttocks, pulling him even closer against her.

He swallowed as desire flashed through him like lightning. He was harder than granite and desperate to have her.

His hard member pressed into her belly. Her legs were parted, his thigh deep in that amazing juncture that he longed to claim.

She was panting, her body quaking. Her desire seemed to match his.

Swallowing, he looked around for where he could take her.

He grabbed her hand. "Come!"

She followed along willingly, her presence beside him like a hot wind from the south, insistently warming him, reminding him of the heat possible with her.

He kicked open a wooden door to one of the vendors' stalls, and a loud *thwack* resounded through the night.

He froze a moment, yet the only sounds in the darkness were their panting breaths and the beat of his racing heart.

He peered inside the stall, at the same time continuing to listen to see if he'd drawn any attention. It was small, a rectangular closet, really, that smelled of wool and dust. It was filled with stacks of bowls and cups, and in the corner—a pile of rugs!

Steele pulled her inside, stepping through the various stacks of crockery and closing the door. A plate toppled over, cracking loudly.

With his heart racing, he paused, listening for any activity, but by this point he was pretty certain that such sounds didn't seem to cry alarm to anyone in particular.

"Shh!" he whispered, leaning down to the plate. "Be quiet!"

She giggled.

Drawing her along, he tried to be more careful as he danced through the various piles in exaggerated motions, mimicking a dancer at a ball. "After you, my lady," he spoke to a pile of bowls. "Good to see you, sir," he offered to some cups as he twisted out of the way.

Giggling, she playfully parodied him through the crockery maze. "I must agree that it is a fine evening for a reel, m'lady."

Finally arriving at the corner, he drew the widow past him, spun her around, and pushed her down onto the mound of rugs. Reaching up, she wrapped her arms around his neck and pulled him down on top of her.

Her legs parted; her body was soft and welcoming. Pressing his face into her neck, he inhaled deeply, smelling that woody scent once more. He was so glad that she wore no perfume and had such a unique scent, realizing that he didn't want to meet anyone socially who might remind him of her.

The sudden thought flashed in his mind, *I may know her! I may have even danced with her at a ball or shared dinner with her at someone's home!*

The thought shook him to the core.

Curiosity overwhelmed him, and instinctively he reached for the hem of her veil.

She grabbed that hand and placed it full on her lush, soft breast, then slipped her hands beneath his coat, and her hands roamed, eliciting a shudder from him.

Diverted, for the moment, he kneaded her, enjoying the way her breath quickened and her nipple pebbled beneath his fingers. She let out a little moan, and for his life, he couldn't help but think that he might recognize that voice.

His natural inquisitiveness reared.

Raising his other hand, he reached for the veil.

She caught his wrist, holding it tight. "There's only one way this is going to happen tonight." Her tone brooked no argument, and he had no doubt that she would make good on her threat to walk away.

*What kind of an idiot am I to press my luck when I'm being handed this most glorious gift on a silver platter?*

*It was foolish to think that I'd recognized her voice when I've spoken to virtually thousands of women in London through my job and my social connections.*

*And what if she'd asked me to reveal myself in return?*

*You're the Viscount Steele, Solicitor-General of England, for bloody sakes! This is the only way for you, too!*

*Don't be a blasted fool!*

He moved to lower his hand, but she held it fast. "I want your word!"

It seemed as important to her as to him to remain

anonymous, he realized. He wondered what she feared. But given that he had much to fear himself, he could understand.

"I want your word that you will not try to learn my identity. And I will grant you the same promise."

"I give you my word. I will not try to discover who you are." Not tonight anyway.

"Not now, not ever!" she demanded.

Gritting his teeth, he realized once more that this lady was no fool. He understood that it was do or die, and there was no way he could walk away from this encounter. Not now when his body was thrumming with need and he knew that his obstinacy was the only thing standing between him and bedding this fiery woman.

"I promise that I will not try to learn your identity . . . ever."

Slowly she released his hand, but her body was still tense, her breath tight. She shook her head, her body still locked as if trying to decide if she should remain with him.

*I should never have tried to change the rules of the game, especially in mid-play.*

"I'm sorry," he offered. Odd, normally he had a terrible time admitting when he'd done something wrong. Yet the apology came easily to his tongue. He supposed it was the very personal stakes that drove his act of contrition. "I shouldn't have, and I won't do it again. It was wrong of me." It was astonishingly easy, in fact.

She let out a long breath as if relenting.

"All right if we . . . continue?" he asked.

She paused. "Yes."

Worried she might change her mind, he caressed her curves, relishing the soft contours that made her a flesh-and-blood woman.

Slowly her hand inside his coat roved down his back, continuing her exploration.

Greedily he reached for the hem of her gown. Drawing up her skirts, his fingers raced across the warm flesh of her calves. Her legs were curved, smooth, fantastic to the touch.

She let out a breathy sigh of anticipation.

His hand reached higher.

He caressed her thighs, and her hips began to move to a rhythm he longed to dance. With his fingers sliding higher, he sought that incredible place he yearned to touch.

The scent of woman and desire overwhelmed.

His fingers found their prize.

She gasped, her flesh hot and moist.

He parted her flesh, opening her to his eager exploration. She moaned, clutching his shoulders as if to never let him go.

With each of her moans, his desire spiked, and he didn't know how long he could wait to take her. Her body's writhing called to him, but he wanted to please her, in part, he understood, to make up for challenging her trust.

He didn't want her to have any regrets.

Suddenly she gasped, her back arched, and her hands gripped at the rug beneath her.

He smiled beneath his mask, satisfied with his efforts, and pleased that she responded so well.

After a long, shuddering breath, her body went slack.

Rising, Steele yanked at his breeches, impatient with the clothing and desperate to feed his hunger.

She opened herself to him, wet and ready.

Thrusting deep inside her, he heard a thunderous moan and knew it belonged to him. Nothing in this world felt as fantastic as the fiery woman gripping him deep into her womb.

They moved as one, clutching, grinding, panting. He was enthralled. Time was lost. There was only the rhythm, the feeling, the urge to mate.

He pounded into her and she groaned with pleasure at every deep thrust. Suddenly she tensed, gripping his shoulders and holding her breath tight. He increased his pace, aching for her. She shuddered deep within.

He couldn't wait much longer. "Hold me!"

She hugged his shoulders, holding him tight.

He exploded deep inside the widow, the perfect stranger.

# Chapter 20

Abigail felt as if she'd been brought back from the dead. Her chest ached with the piercing need for air, and stars danced before her closed eyes. Her body pulsed beneath the masked stranger's, every spot of exposed skin burning with his touch.

The moist juncture between her thighs throbbed, feeling full and stretched with his member still deep inside of her. She felt his every intake of breath as a reminder of the passion they'd just shared.

Swallowing, she tried to gather her wits, while at the same time she yearned for this experience never to end. When she was with the masked gentleman, every worry escaped from her mind and she did nothing but *feel*.

A little voice inside her head chided her to respect the fact that she shouldn't be here with this man. That any proper young lady wouldn't stoop to such damnation. But if this was what being damned felt like, she'd be hell-bent for sure—and not worry overmuch about it. For the moment at least.

She sighed.

"Hmm," he hummed, sending vibrations streaming through her. "You feel incredible," he mumbled, his voice muffled by the mask and the fact that his mouth was pressed into her neck.

A sense of euphoria swept over her, along with feelings of goodwill toward the man lying on top of her.

"You do, too," she murmured. "Better than . . ." Her voice trailed off.

He moved away an inch, his face so close to hers, yet concealed by his mask and the darkness. "Better than what?"

"Actually, better than I've ever felt before."

He made a small, satisfied grunt.

She added, "Not that I have so much experience. I've only been with one man in my life." Beneath her veil she made a face. "And that wasn't too many times, either."

"I am not a raging stallion, by any means," he confessed. "I prefer . . . solitude to . . . complications."

She smiled. "Women can be very complicating, I know."

"I don't mean to insult—"

"Oh, you haven't. I was simply speaking the truth; women tend to make things quite thorny."

"But not you."

"No, I have no interest in making things any more complicated than they are." The costs were too high. Her reputation, her job . . . Guilt stabbed her middle, but she pushed it away.

The masked rescuer was breathing heavily, his body relaxed on top of hers. He made her feel good. Secure. Yet at the same time he inspired an astonishing excitement within her. The sensations reminded her of Lord Steele.

She blinked, shocked. Thinking of Lord Steele with this bold masked stranger deep inside her felt like an abomination. The two men had absolutely *nothing* in common, and just the idea of Lord Steele even knowing what she was doing was enough to make her stomach twist with anxiety and guilt.

"Are you all right?" he inquired.

"Why do you ask?"

"You tensed. Am I hurting you?"

She realized that she was no longer comfortable, her euphoria replaced by the notion that she'd better get home before her employer started asking questions. And she had to find time for a quick bath, too. Between the odor of passion and the wetness between her thighs, she knew that she couldn't make it through an entire day without bathing.

Abigail put her hand on his shoulder. "Actually, I need you to get up. I have to go." He didn't move.

"Please?"

She couldn't see his face, but could tell that he was displeased.

Removing himself from her, he adjusted his clothing. "Where are you off to in such a hurry?"

She could hardly see in the darkness of the small stall, not much larger than her usual governess's chamber. As opposed to her current rooms, which were far too grand.

Under her veil she frowned. Why did she keep thinking about Lord Steele and the house? Probably, she supposed, because she knew that she needed to be back to her duties, posthaste.

Straightening, she lowered her skirts and fixed her clothing as best as she could.

"I asked where you are off to in such a hurry?" he demanded, an edge having entered his voice.

Recalling how the fear had clutched her heart when he'd tried to raise her veil, she frowned. "I thought we'd been over this ground already."

"I didn't ask to see your face, just where you're off to."

"A fine legalistic distinction, don't you think?"

His fists curled as if she'd insulted him. "I think we need to talk."

"I don't have time for talking. I must go." She stood, and he rose as well, adjusting his clothing in the small space. Their bodies were so close, it was hard not to grab on to each other for balance, but somehow they managed, an invisible wall having been erected between them within the last two minutes.

His tone was crisp. "I confess it's rare for the lady to be so cavalier."

"Cavalier? Hardly. Just late."

"For what? Or should I say for whom?"

"Tenacious, aren't you?"

"Perhaps if you'd answer my question . . ."

"I already gave you my answer—faces, names, and lives do not fit into this . . ." She waved her hand, at a loss for words.

"*Affaire*?" Steele couldn't believe that he'd said the word. The man who wanted no complications, no engagements, and certainly no mistress had just voiced the notion that he and this woman were engaged in an *affaire*. It didn't surprise him that he couldn't shake his natural curiosity about her identity. He'd never been able to pass up a puzzle or a mystery.

She straightened. "*Affaire*? I wouldn't call it that."

"Then what is it?"

Adjusting her veil as if to make certain that nothing showed, she replied, "Anonymous."

"Anonymous?"

"Yes. You go your way and I go mine. There is no 'thing' between us."

Despite himself, he couldn't quite let it go at that.

Twisting around, Steele sat on the pile of rugs where they'd just been. What made this woman tick? Why was she so different from any woman he'd encountered before? And why did she stir his blood in a way he hadn't felt in years? He knew that he'd given his word about her identity, but this woman inflamed his already robust curiosity to overpowering proportions.

Then there was the matter of her safety. Somehow she was involved with Lucifer Laverty and the circuit. He feared that she might not grasp the danger, and he couldn't in good conscience simply walk away.

He stood. "Why were you meeting with Jumper?"

She stiffened. "What?"

"Why were you meeting Jumper?"

"I have no idea what you're talking about." She turned away curtly.

He leaned forward. "I saw you speaking with Jumper. What is your business with him?"

Lifting her skirts, she wove her way through the various piles, knocking over two stacks in a clatter of crockery. "I must go."

He jumped up and followed her, grabbing her arm just as she made it outside the door. "Don't you walk away from me!"

She stopped, her body tense with irritation. "Look, we had a fine time. Now I must go."

"I asked you a question! Answer me!"

"No."

"No?" The answer struck him dumb. No one ever refused to answer him. He frowned. "What's your business with the circuit?"

Shrugging off his arm, she turned and strode down the alleyway, heading in the wrong direction, back toward where she'd met Jumper.

"I'm talking to you!" He was right at her heels.

"And I'm ignoring you," she retorted over her shoulder.

He grabbed her, swung her around.

"Unhand me!"

"Not until you answer me!"

"Let me go!" She yanked at her arm, hard.

He wrapped his arms around her in a hug quite dissimilar from the embrace they'd shared moments before. "I want answers!"

She was stiff as whalebone, nothing like the softly sensual woman a short while ago. "Then ask someone else!"

"What do you want with Lucifer Laverty? Tell me!"

Suddenly a hard object was pressed into his gut.

"If you don't unhand me, I'll be forced to shoot." Her voice was cool, with just a hint of a tremor.

"I don't believe you," he scoffed. It would take a coldhearted woman to bed him one minute and shoot him the next. A small voice in his head warned that he didn't know that this woman wasn't deranged; he had no idea what drove her. But his instincts told him that she wouldn't shoot him. When he'd spoken with her, he'd felt a natural affinity. Yes, she met in alleyways with less-than-noble characters, but he sensed that she had some kind of reason. His gut feeling was that she was in trouble but unwilling to ask for help.

"Let me go," she bit out, her voice harsh with anger.

"What's your business with Lucifer Laverty?"

"Do you want to die?" she demanded. "For I'll give you your wish."

"Go ahead."

A loud boom resounded.

*I can't believe she did it*, Steele thought.

Then all went black.

# Chapter 21

Wincing, Abigail caught the masked man, trying to break his fall as he sagged to the ground like a rag doll. He was so heavy that she wound up partially on the ground herself. She looked over at Jumper. "Please tell me that you didn't kill him."

Jumper leaned on the post he'd just used to knock out the masked man, looking very proud of himself. "Naw. Not even close."

"He'll be all right?"

"Oh, 'e'll have a blazing good 'eadache in the morning. I'll tell ya that. But 'e'll be fine."

Wanting desperately to believe him, Abigail extricated herself from the arms that felt like the weighty lines on a ship, and stood. But she immediately crouched down, checking the man's pulse at the base of his neck. She counted the steady beats of his heart and exhaled, reassured. She hadn't wanted to hurt him. But he'd been so insistent, so demandingly belligerent, and Jumper had come along. She could have stopped it. She had one moment when she could have called out a warning and stopped Jumper from dropping that post upon his head. But she'd wanted to escape, hadn't wanted to give any answers, and she knew that she never would have shot the masked rescuer. She'd just given herself to the man; she could hardly pull the trigger and end his life.

But they'd *agreed* and he'd tried to maneuver around that agreement. Staring down at his still form, she realized that she felt vulnerable, raw, and uncertain of her feelings about herself, how she'd responded to this stranger, and the astonishing effect he seemed to have on her.

"So who is 'e?" Jumper asked, leaning forward.

Shaking her head, she wished the masked man could have let things be. Jumper's interference was opportune, she told herself. Then why did she suddenly wish that it was the masked man standing conscious beside her?

"So who is 'e?" Jumper repeated, pulling her from her guilty musings.

She blinked. "Pardon?"

"Aren't ya gonna pull off 'is mask?"

"Ah . . ." Her hand hovered near the bottom of the cloth masking his features. It was so tempting. He was unconscious; he'd never know. Recalling the exchange of promises between them, she tried to tell herself that he'd broken their agreement with his questions, and now she was free of any obligations. But it was an argument based on web-thin premises. *She'd* made a promise and *she* would keep it. He might not know, but she would. "No. I will not unmask him."

"Then I will." Jumper reached down.

"No!" She grabbed his wrist.

"Why the 'ell not? 'E was attacking you! What the 'ell do you owe 'im?"

"He saved my life." Besides, she'd made a promise, and the man was vulnerable. She couldn't allow him to be exploited that way.

Jumper snorted; she could tell his features were dubious even in the dim light.

"Really." She rose. "I fell into a trap. I was being attacked . . . If it weren't for him . . ." Her mind veered away from memory. "I owe him my life; I will not take advantage of him when he's down. And I can't let you, either. It's not right."

Frowning, Jumper blew out a loud gust of air. "Bloody 'ell."

"Promise me you won't try to learn his identity, Jumper."

"'E couldna lent ya blunt or something. 'E 'ad to 'ave saved yer life. That's the one favor ya gotta respect."

"Will you respect it?"

Grimacing, he waved a hand. "Fine. Fine. I promise I won't peek."

"Or have anyone else peek."

"Or 'ave anyone else peek." Jumper jerked a thumb. "Ya best be off now, Leo the Butcher comes round early, and soon everyone else'll be about, too."

Abigail's eyes moved to the man, guilt twisting like a maggot in her heart. "We can't leave him here."

Scratching his head, Jumper sniffed. "I know a good place."

"He'll be safe?"

"Safe as a babe in a bed."

"Show me."

*　*　*

Light pierced Steele's eyelids, but he refused to wake. The pain in his head was excruciating, like a nail being driven through his crown.

He must have gotten riotously soused last night. But his mouth wasn't dry as sand, as it usually was after a night of revelry. And instead of the smell of brandy, the scent greeting his nose was . . . dung.

Dung?

He sat up. Sharp pain sliced through his head like a scythe. He groaned, raising his fingers to a lump the size of a plum. "What the . . . ?"

Bright golden light hurt his eyes as he blinked them open.

Golden. No, not golden, but straw bathed in sunlight.

Hay. He was surrounded by mounds of hay. And the odor of dung was so powerful, he almost gagged.

A pig squealed. A cow mooed.

A barn. He was in a bloody barn.

Swallowing back his bile, Steele looked around. The loft of a barn, he corrected, eyeing the wooden beams overhead. Golden wisps of light broke through the cracks in the wood, hailing the dawn.

The sounds of animals moving below. A door creaking open, footsteps shuffling around.

*How the blazes did I get here?*

He forced his mind to remember.

The widow! They were arguing . . . and then she shot him!

With his heart racing, Steele planted his hands all over his torso, feeling for blood, or pain. But all he felt were the buttons of his coat, the wool of his cloak. No pain, no blood, no injury of any kind. Relief flooded through him. He wasn't shot.

But the sound. And all had gone black.

His head.

He must have been hit from behind.

He didn't know if he was pleased that he hadn't been felled by the widow's hand or frightened that someone else had come upon them.

But wait a minute. She was facing his attacker. She must have seen the person, must have known it was going to happen.

And she hadn't warned him.

His fingers curled and his teeth clenched with impotent rage. Did she have a collaborator? Had he been played?

His fury was quick and hot as he recalled her moans and how she'd led him along like a dog in heat. *Had her partner been waiting in the shadows and* —his gut twisted—*watching?*

Slowly he shook his head. Somehow he knew that they hadn't been watched. After all his training, all his years of vigilance, he knew the feel of eyes upon him. He would have known. And even more compelling, the widow had not behaved like a woman acting a part or performing for another. There had been no awareness to her actions. No sense that another had been witnessing their act.

Rubbing his temple, he forced his aching mind to *work*.

So the other person had come after.

But that person and the widow clearly had been in league together. Or else she would have warned him.

Why was he assuming that she was rational? Why was he presuming that she wasn't deranged?

Because every encounter, everything he'd witnessed told him that she was sane, yet driven to a purpose that he did not understand.

Peering over the side of the loft and noting the many rungs on the ladder leading down, he doubted she'd have been able to get him up to the loft by herself.

No, it had likely been a man, and a strong one, to carry him up that ladder.

The first time he'd encountered her, she'd been cornered by that nasty pair. Then the next she'd been with Jumper, talking about Lucifer Laverty. The circuit.

Jumper!

He had been nearby. And although they hadn't been acting like lovers, they'd certainly exchanged words on some pretty clandestine topics.

The logic of the idea settled upon him, and he suspected that Jumper was the man who had struck him.

Exhaling, he scowled, anger and frustration making his belly roil.

Jumper was going to have a few questions to answer tonight.

Suddenly Steele's heart lurched. Jumper's currency was information! The man's every act was predicated on knowing everything he could about everyone around him.

His hand flew to his mask. It was secure. But had Jumper looked? Did Jumper know who he was?

But Jumper wouldn't recognize his face. The man

didn't run in his circles, even as solicitor-general. And Steele's likeness had never appeared in the broadsheets, since in every criminal case it had been the defendant's picture that had been displayed. For once he appreciated that anonymity.

But what of the widow? Had she broken the very promise she'd demanded of him? Could she know his face? Could they have met before at a ball or musicale or society event?

The agony of the betrayal, his humiliation and anger were too great. He ran his hand over his eyes, feeling ill. What had he done? Had he well and truly been compromised?

A strangled laugh broke through his lips.

Compromised. Like a lily white miss at the hands of a lecherous rake. In all his thirty-odd years, he never would have considered the possibility of being compromised.

But in truth, she might not know him. And even if she did recognize him, whom would she tell without first explaining how she knew of his nocturnal activities? She could not let his secret be known without conceding her own behavior. But more importantly, who in his right mind would believe that the Viscount Steele roamed the streets of London at night in a mask? He felt reassured.

The bigger question that begged to be answered was whether he could now seek out her identity if she'd breached her vow. The barrister in him cried out that all obligations toward her were dissolved by her actions. The gentleman in him knew that no matter what she'd done, he'd given his word and he could not break his vow.

"So you're safe for the moment, my little witch," he muttered.

"Who's there?" a voice cried in alarm from below. It was male, and young.

Rising on unsteady legs, Steele called out, "Have no fear. I mean no harm. I was just sleeping off a wild night."

"Who are you?" the voice demanded with a quiver of indignation.

Steele brushed off the stray sticks of hay clinging to his breeches. "Never fear, there's coin in it for your hospitality." Adjusting his mask, he exhaled and moved toward the ladder. He would find out if anyone had been seen bringing him here. "And extra coin for some information."

# Chapter 22

Later that day, Steele strode down the lane as the cries of children and the reprimands of their nannies greeted his ears. The air was warm, and spring had burst upon the park in a splendor of thick green bushes filled with tiny white flowers whose name he'd forgotten long ago. The flowers carried a light honeyed scent that had bees buzzing and hovering among the petals.

Steele wondered what the blazes he was doing here.

After a bracing bath of icy cold water, he'd gone to his study to work. But for the first time in as long as he could recall, work gave him no escape. Usually searching through the maze of words in legal documents and decoding the finer implications gave him great satisfaction. Not today. Today his mind was pricked by anger, nipped by anxiety, clouded with hidden doubt that he would not acknowledge.

So he'd left the study that usually gave him comfort and instead prowled around the house looking for a purpose to distract him.

And when he didn't find *them*, he'd had to ask

the butler where his charges and their governess
might be.

"At the park," he'd been told. "Perhaps to meet a
Mr. Littlethom."

So here he was, searching for his charges on a
sunny late morning, hoping that they, at least, would
take his mind off the mistakes he'd made the night
before.

As he approached the open lawns, he noted the
group of governesses clustered like hens in a barn-
yard while a gaggle of children screamed and played
nearby. The nannies gathered around a set of benches
tucked beneath lush green trees as if strategically
placed for that very purpose.

Whereas most of the governesses clucked among
themselves with little thought to the world around
them, Miss West listened to the others with only one
ear, her attention and her eyes never once leaving her
charges.

Steele felt his steps slow as he watched her watching the boys. She was prettier than any of the women
around her, with her wide-set, grayish-blue eyes, her
upturned nose, and those lush lips that budded into
a perfect bow.

Her blue gown and white bonnet were both
prim and unbecoming, yet she had an air about
her of freshness, of youthful vitality that frumpish
clothing could not hide. He could only imagine how
breathtaking she'd be if she was able to wear the
fashionable gowns he'd seen the debutantes wearing
this season.

Again, he had to wonder what had happened
between her and Phineas Byrnwyck. She was

tempting, to be sure. He veered his mind away from that thought; this woman was in his employ and thus beyond his reach.

And as an employer, he had to admire how she'd nod now and again, respond to the other women with a word, but keep her keen gaze fixed on the children at play.

Seth sat a few feet away, his usual pose of legs spread in a V as he dug in the dirt. Yet he was not alone, as three pretty little girls with golden curls hovered nearby.

One girl in a short green gown stepped over to show Seth something in her hand. He inspected it, commented, and she smiled, as if she'd somehow pleased him. Leaning over, she added it to a pile of rocks near his leg. Another girl came over to show him another stone. He shook his head and she walked away, disappointment on her apple-cheeked face. Then she leaned over and picked up another stone and showed it to Seth. He must have accepted it, for it, too, went into the pile. The apple-cheeked girl spun away, pleased.

Felix stood in a grassy area nearby, his head leaning toward a carrot-topped boy's as the two of them seemed engrossed in discussion. Then they ran off, joining a cluster of boys playing tag the tiger.

Suddenly Miss West stood, her bearing reflecting heightened awareness that reminded him of a hunting dog that caught a scent.

Steele's gaze followed hers. Felix and a dark-haired boy were nose to nose, a heated argument in full swing.

Miss West called out, "The tag was fair."

The lads argued on.

Miss West raised her voice to be heard above the women clucking around her who seemed oblivious to the conflict, "The tag was fair!"

The boys looked over at her, query in their gazes.

"It was fair. I saw it."

Felix nodded. The other boy shrugged. They spun on their heels, resuming the game again as if nothing had transpired.

Miss West lowered herself onto the bench once more, the women around her not missing a beat in their conversation.

An older nanny with a wide white bonnet noted Steele's presence and muttered a word to the women nearest to her. A sudden hush descended over the group and all eyes turned to him, except for Miss West's, which were still fixed on her charges.

A slim, sandy-haired governess tugged on Miss West's sleeve, whispering something his ears did not catch.

Miss West started and her gaze moved to him.

Their eyes met across the grassy patch. He felt sucked into those blue-gray depths, experiencing that stirring charge that he had hoped might have been expunged with his late night activities. He'd wanted the wicked widow to sate his desires and negate the attraction for his pretty governess. But he supposed that desirability was an elemental thing that could not be deleted, only ignored.

He suddenly realized that the other governesses were studying him with the keen scrutiny of farmers assessing a pig for market. Aware of his audience, he pulled his gaze from Miss West's and assumed the mien of cool indifference worn by so many members of the *ton*.

Scanning the area, he noted that there were no gentlemen in this grassy knoll, just nannies and their charges, making him feel the intruder. At least Mr. Littlethom wasn't about. Steele ignored the shaft of jealousy in his gut as he wondered about Miss West's supposed meeting with the tutor.

Miss West motioned to the two footmen standing aside under a tree, gesturing that they were in charge of watching the boys while she would speak with Steele. Zachariah and Foster nodded their understanding, their sudden alertness evidencing their awareness that Steele was nearby.

Miss West approached and stopped just a few feet before him. He noted that she was shorter than his widow and carried herself with a humble demeanor, whereas the widow had an air of purposeful authority about her.

*Why the blazes am I comparing the two women? They are worlds apart!*

Angrily he pushed all thoughts of the widow from his mind. "Good morning, Miss West."

She looked up at him expectantly, questions swirling in those gray-blue eyes. "Good morning, Lord Steele."

He scanned the area once more, irritation making his words clipped. "I was told that you were with Mr. Littlethom. Where is he?"

"I was wondering the very same thing myself, my lord. He did not arrive as he'd told me he would."

Steele ignored the small swell of satisfaction that Mr. Littlethom was proving that he was unworthy of Miss West.

Miss West waved a hand. "I suppose he must have a good reason for not being here."

Pressing his lips together, Steele sniffed. "You are too forgiving. If someone doesn't keep an appointment, it means that he does not value your time."

"Oh, I don't know. Perhaps he was delayed." Her eyes lit up. "Maybe he even secured a new position!"

He raised a brow. "You seem inordinately involved in his dealings, Miss West."

Looking away, she shrugged. "He did us a service; it's only natural that I wish him well." Watching the boys, she smiled. "But I'll venture that the boys will be much happier to see you than a tutor."

The boys. Not her.

"How are Seth and Felix doing?" he asked, following her gaze.

Motioning to where the children played, she explained, "Felix has made fast friends with Lord Wentworth's son, Lucas, and Seth has found some playmates who like collecting rocks almost as much as he does." She turned back to face him, her gaze expectant. "I'm sure, like me, they will be curious as to what we owe the great pleasure of you joining us today."

Steele suddenly realized that he'd had no true intention in coming here. "I, ah . . . I was wondering if the lads might be interested in"—he looked over at the governesses and noted that one was peeling an orange—"eating."

Miss West's lips lifted into a half smile. "The boys do love to eat. I think that they would enjoy that every much."

His brow furrowed, as he felt the need for it to be more special for him to have come all the way here. He smiled, suddenly inspired. "Ices."

He was gratified to see her eyes widen. "Ices? Why, the boys will be above the moon!" She turned. "Felix! Seth!"

The lads looked over.

"Lord Steele is taking you for ices!"

Seth squealed. Felix cried, "Yippee!" Both boys dashed toward them.

The governesses sitting on the benches buzzed and twittered, some clearly impressed, others flashing Miss West covetous glances.

Steele's eyes narrowed. "You did that on purpose."

Miss West raised her brows, her face a mask of innocence. "Did what, my lord?"

"Shouting about the ices."

A small half smile lifted those lush lips. "Well, yes. Lucas Worthington has been crowing to Felix how he's had Gunter's ices twice already. And now everyone knows that I have the best employer in London."

"As if there was any doubt before," he teased.

Her smile widened. "As if there was any doubt before."

Exhaling, Steele realized that coming to the park was a good idea. He was feeling better already. "Foster, please run ahead and call for the carriage to be brought around."

"Yes, Your Lordship." Foster nodded and moved ahead.

"Can I go with Foster?" Seth whined. "I want to run, too!"

"Me, too!" Felix cried.

Steele considered the dangers, and then nodded. "Very well. So long as you stay with both Foster and Zachariah."

The boys squealed with delight, and all four raced ahead.

"Oh don't let me hold you, back, my lord." Miss West waved a hand.

"No," he decided. "I'll walk with you." He rubbed the spot on his temple where it felt like a spike piercing his skull. "I'm not up for a race right now."

"Are you ill?" she asked with concern.

"No. Not at all. It was simply . . . the remains of an overindulgent night."

"Ah."

Ah. What did that mean? Steele pursed his lips. "You don't seem surprised."

She shrugged.

Despite the fact that he knew he shouldn't care, he suddenly felt inclined to explore her opinion. It was as her employer, of course, to help maintain their working relationship. "I wonder, Miss West, is your lack of surprise because you believe that as a viscount I am supposed to be a wastrel?"

"No . . ."

"What it is then? That all nobility overindulge?" Somehow he hated to have her think that he was like so many others in his newly achieved class.

"No . . . it's just . . . well, you work very hard; it makes sense that you would . . . balance that effort."

"Oh." That was the last answer he'd expected from her.

Peering up at him from the corner of her eye, she asked, "Any regrets?"

Thinking about the night in its entirety, the widow's passionate cries in the vendor's stall, the incredible coupling, the information he'd learned, he shook his head. "No."

Silently she nodded as if considering it mightily. "Then you got off lightly."

He hadn't quite thought of it in that way. "I suppose you're right." Steele inhaled a deep breath, smelling pine and grass and feeling the warmth of the sun on his back. "I don't get outside enough to enjoy the sunshine in the daytime."

"We come to the park every day, my lord. The boys would love it if you joined us—any time you can give them."

He hadn't realized that he'd spoken aloud. And it was true, he spent many hours locked in his study, at his office, in court, in meetings; he rarely ventured to a park like this in the daytime. He felt uncomfortable with the admission. "My work does not allow for much . . . play."

"Weather permitting, mine does. On the other hand, your position allows for a much greater impact."

"What do you mean?"

"You put prisoners behind bars, help maintain a system of justice, help protect the Crown. You affect many people; there's greatness to what you do. I simply watch children play."

He was flattered by her depiction, and gratified that she saw his work as significant, since it was so important to him. Still, she shouldn't diminish the importance of her own position. "Felix and Seth adore you. You have a tremendous impact on them."

Her dainty shoulder lifted in a shrug. "Pray don't think that I am seeking a compliment, my lord. I am simply stating the facts as they are."

Steele frowned. "This is a difficult time for Seth and Felix, and they seem to have adjusted to all of it well—I suspect mostly due to you."

Miss West waved a hand behind her. "If you hadn't noticed the sea of nannies back there, I am but one of many. Any of the women sitting there could have done just as well."

Miss West seemed down, as if something weighed on her mind. "Is something bothering you, Miss West?"

She blinked, as if taken aback. "No . . . of course not . . ."

He could tell she was lying. He remembered the serious look on her face as she asked about regrets and wondered if she was plagued by them. He offered gently, "You're very forgiving of others; perhaps you should forgive yourself for your foibles? We all have them." He, more than a few these days.

Her brow furrowed, and she seemed troubled. "This is hardly the kind of conversation I should be having with the man who pays my wages."

Despite her words, Abigail was fairly crumbling under the yoke of all her anxieties and was desperate to share at least a pinch of that burden.

She was overwhelmed by fear for her brother, fretfulness about his involvement with Lucifer Laverty, and full of trepidation about how to proceed.

She was by turns mortified, elated, titillated, and

shamed by how she'd behaved and what she'd done with the masked gentleman.

No matter Jumper's assurances or that she'd feared someone noticing her absence at the house, she shouldn't have left the masked gentleman in that loft. "I shouldn't have done it," she muttered.

Lord Steele's eyes softened. "We all make mistakes."

She looked up, surprised she'd spoken, and even more surprised by the sympathy in his gaze. The man seemed to *really* understand. But how could he?

She decided it was too painful to continue that vein of conversation, so she made light. "You, the impeccable solicitor-general, making mistakes? I think not."

A pained look crossed his handsome features. "Oh, I've had more than my share. Much more."

He looked so distressed, and lost. There was an isolated quality to him, she suddenly realized. For all his title and wealth, the man seemed . . . *lonely.*

The man worked all the time. He seemed to keep to himself. He'd lost his wife. He had no children of his own. She suspected that he wouldn't be fully accepted in the ranks he'd joined, yet he no longer had a place in the ranks he'd left.

*The man is an island*, the thought whispered in her mind.

*Just like me.*

# Chapter 23

Steele and Miss West walked side by side in silence, the cries of the playing children fading in the distance. The sun was warm on their backs, a fragrant breeze of pine and grass kissing their faces.

Her pale hair peeked out from under her bonnet, shining golden in the sunlight. "Do you . . ." He wondered why he was asking, but felt compelled. "Do you have many regrets?"

"My share." Her tone was noncommittal, but he'd seen the softening in her gaze toward him. She had her guard up, but seemed to be sharing a bit of herself with him, and he was eager to learn more.

He wondered, if he pushed would she become tongue-tied or fight back? She tended to be quiet and timid, yet he'd seen her react strongly when she was angry and hadn't the time to question herself. Then she was a lioness protecting those she cared for.

Defending Seth the way she'd done against Carlton showed a hidden pool of courage that he suspected went very deep.

Seth and Felix were fortunate to have her in their lives. Any man would be fortunate to be cared for by such a woman. The idea unsettled him, reminding him of the lack of such caring in his own life.

He immediately pushed away the sneaky longing that threatened his carefully controlled existence.

He didn't *need* anyone. Need meant vulnerability, something he avoided at all costs.

Two ginger-haired, fashionably dressed ladies walked by, arm in arm with their heads tilted together in deep conversation. The taller one was heard to say, "And then he dared to complain about the expense! As if he hadn't agreed to the whole party in the first instance!"

The smaller lady rolled her eyes. "Pray don't tell me he tried the old 'if I'd only known how much it would cost' excuse."

"He did! And when I explained, with great patience I might add, that one must have the essentials—"

"Of course!" The smaller lady waved her fan as if it were a sword. "One can't appear without means."

"Well, he began to question what I considered essential!"

Steele was suddenly reminded that any lady entering his home as his wife would turn his carefully controlled existence on its head. The idea made his stomach sour.

As she listened to the ladies, Miss West's eyes sparkled with contained amusement. He realized that *she* had changed the rhythms of his house, yet he didn't seem to mind. But Miss West was staff, answerable to him. He had little doubt that a lady assuming the role of mistress of the house would be far more disruptive.

The smaller lady's lip curled. "Husbands—it's a wonder we put up with them at all."

The tetchy ladies moved on.

After a few moments had passed, Steele realized that Miss West's mien had become anxious. Her hands were clutched tightly before her; a frown creased her golden brow. She opened her mouth as if to speak and then closed it once more, as if afraid of what she might say or how it would be heard.

He hated when she acted so apprehensive about how she might be received. Again he had to wonder if she'd always been like this, or had the incident with Phineas Byrnwyck scarred her? Anger flashed in his gut, hot and quick. How any man could take advantage of such a wholesome girl was beyond him. His curiosity sparked, and he wondered if she wanted to discuss what had happened.

"We were talking about regrets," he offered, hoping she would open up to him. "And we all have them, Miss West."

The governess licked her lips, venturing, "Yes, well, sometimes . . . things . . . happen . . . not quite as one expects." She seemed to be struggling for words. "And the way one reacts . . ." Her voice trailed off.

"Like one's head only catches up after the fact?" he finished for her, knowing the feeling better than she could imagine.

She blinked. "Well, yes."

Peering up at the elegantly handsome man walking beside her, Abigail had to wonder at the complex person her employer was turning out to be. He'd earned his name, worked to protect Seth and Felix, but there was a hardness to him, a severity that made her think of the hammer of the law.

Yet whenever she'd decided that he was cold, distant, and unreadable, a noble barrister through and through, he'd say something that gave her a glimpse into a softer side of him, one that he kept hidden from the world. He had a sensible self-awareness that some probably deemed weakness. And she found it utterly charming.

"We're human, I suppose," he offered. "It's in our nature to . . . get carried away."

Well, she'd certainly gotten carried away last night. "I believe I'm more human than anyone I've ever met," she muttered, shaking her head.

"Oh please don't be so hard on yourself. It'll force me to retally my offenses."

They shared an awkward smile.

Something deep inside Abigail's heart melted just a bit and the feeling shocked her; she'd hadn't had this sense of affinity with anyone save her brother.

Steele looked off into the trees. "In my experience, the world can be a very unforgiving place."

"My experience, too," she agreed, that warmth spreading to her whole body, like a blanket of understanding.

"Perhaps we should absolve each other?" he offered.

"But we didn't do each other the harm." She peered up at him, teasing gently, "Unless of course you have something to tell me?"

His lips lifted. Those astonishingly dark-as-coal eyes warmed and crinkled at the corners. It was nice to see him smile in such an unguarded manner.

She felt as if he was a closed book and rarely allowed anyone to peek within. She was getting a rare glimpse, she realized, and she wanted to swing open that cover and garner a better look inside.

"Confessions? From the solicitor-general? Are you taking notes for the broadsheets?"

She looked away. "I'm just jesting. You needn't tell me anything."

"But I'd like to."

Abigail's eyes met his and her breath seized in her chest. A fire burned in his eyes, and for the moment its heat was focused on her. She felt it, deep in her bones and in her chest and in places that had no business feeling anything as far as her employer was concerned.

Alarm bells rang in her ears. She shouldn't be looking at Lord Steele this way, and he should certainly not be looking at her as if he wanted to *know* her as a person, not just an employee.

But she couldn't help the heat glowing inside her; her traitorous body longed to know him . . . as a *man*.

She swallowed, her mouth suddenly dry. Inwardly she cursed the fires that had been lit by the masked stranger. This had to be his fault! She felt like a warming stove, once lit, unable to burn out.

This had to be her imagination. Lord Steele was way beyond her measure. And he was not the kind of man to become overly familiar with members of his household.

And the looks he was giving her—well, there was no *lechery* about them. They didn't make her feel uncomfortable or dirty, the way some men made her feel when they looked at her as if they wanted to consume her.

Nay, his glances warmed her the way hot cocoa teased her tongue and then fired her all the way down to her belly.

*I'm turning into a dramatic ninny*, she told herself. *And I'd better stop it right now before I make a complete and utter fool of myself! He's my employer and too principled a man to ever look in my direction.*

The man was simply being amiable. And she was the one who was indecent! This taint of the scarlet woman was bleeding into her daily life, and she had to make it stop!

If only Lord Steele weren't so very breathtakingly handsome. What woman wouldn't want to kiss that chiseled jawline or run her fingers through those raven tresses? What woman with blood in her veins wouldn't want to feel his broad chest against her or have her body crushed beneath his?

And those eyes, they drew one in with sorcererlike compulsion. A woman could lose herself to such a man . . .

Rubbing his hand over his eyes, Lord Steele swallowed. "I confess—"

"Miss West! Miss West!" a voice called.

"Confess what?" Abigail asked breathlessly.

"Miss West! Oh, yoohoo!"

With great reluctance, Abigail tore her gaze from Lord Steele's and turned toward that voice.

# Chapter 24

Mr. Littlethom was striding toward Abigail and Lord Steele, waving a white handkerchief in the air and puffing as if winded from a long sprint. "Miss West!"

He huffed, the pink in his cheeks from exertion only adding to his Adonis-like handsomeness. A sparkle lit his pale blue eyes, and his teeth glistened white with his wide, boyish smile, setting off a dimple Abigail hadn't noticed before. Holding his hand atop his tall black hat that tilted precariously, he rushed forward to greet her. He wore old-fashioned knee breeches in olive green with a gray coat that had seen better days. "Ah, I finally caught you!"

A lock of blond hair had fallen into his eyes, and he negligently shoved it aside. Abigail realized that the two men were like opposite bookends, one sharp as a razor and darkly attractive, and the other blond, boyishly handsome, and not quite the quickest wit in the land.

Swallowing her irritation, Abigail waved to Mr. Littlethom. "Lord Steele, may I introduce Mr. Nigel Littlethom, the tutor I mentioned."

Lord Steele's face had closed and his eyes had shuttered as if any softening at all had been a specter of her imagination. He was the elegant viscount once more.

"Oh, my lord!" Littlethom gushed. "It is my great privilege to meet you finally!"

Lord Steele tilted his head.

Littlethom's face reddened as he squinted up at Steele in a servile manner. "I congratulate myself on being able to be of service to you, my lord."

Steele raised a black-winged brow.

Abigail jumped in, "At the park, Mr. Littlethom helped rescue Seth from the water."

Wiping the handkerchief across his sweaty brow, Mr. Littlethom gushed, "Although I am quite modest by nature, I have been known, on occasion, to show just an inkling of valor."

"Well, you were very brave," Abigail added gamely.

Lord Steele tilted his head. "I extend my thanks to you, Mr. Littlethom. Pray, how did you find yourself to be in such an opportune place at that time?"

The blond tutor preened. "I was meeting a friend at the park, my lord. A governess with whom I used to work. I am a tutor, you see. Latin, French, and Greek languages are my specialty. Although I do not like to boast, I have been told that my teaching skills are"—looking up at the sky, Littlethom pressed his finger to his brow—"profound. That was the very word used by the very discerning Countess Delinsky. Profound."

Mr. Littlethom licked his lips. "Lately, however, I am indeed sorely untested in that regard. My skills, my abundant skills, have fallen into disuse."

"That is a shame," Steele commented noncommittally.

Abigail felt pressed to speak up on Littlethom's behalf. "Mr. Littlethom was telling me that he is without a position at the moment."

Mr. Littlethom clapped his hands together. "Yes, and I hunger for the opportunity to be of service."

"Hmm." Lord Steele looked off into the distance. "Send your references to my man Mr. Linder-Myer at the Excelsior Agency. He will be expecting your application."

"Thank you, my lord! Thank you!" Mr. Littlethom gushed, leaning forward and looking up at Lord Steele as an adoring dog might at its master. "I am grateful! Grateful!"

Abigail thought he was overdoing it a bit, but she could sympathize with being out of work and sorely in need of a position. She resolved to do what she could for the unemployed tutor.

Lord Steele stepped backward. "I make no promises, Mr. Littlethom."

"But still! The opportunity alone!" Tapping his finger to his temple, Mr. Littlethom prattled, "I have a mind like a steel trap, my lord! Mr. Lyner-Minder! At the Excellence Agency!"

"That's Mr. Linder-Myer at the Excelsior Agency," Abigail corrected quickly.

Lord Steele turned away. "Yes, well, good day to you, then."

"Thank you! Thank you, my lord! And thank you, Miss West!"

She smiled. "I didn't do anything. It was nice seeing you, Mr. Littlethom."

"But where are you going?" the tutor cried.

Abigail frowned.

"What of our appointment?"

"Appointment?"

Mr. Littlethom grinned. "Yes, here at the park. Eleven-thirty, you'd said."

They were supposed to meet at ten-thirty, and to Abigail's mind, that opportunity was well and gone. Yet, not wanting to make the man feel foolish, Abigail pursed her lips. "I'm sorry, Mr. Littlethom, but I must cancel our appointment."

The man looked positively crestfallen. "Cancel? But why?"

"Because she must remain with the children," Lord Steele interjected tightly.

Abigail tried to soften the blow. "Lord Steele surprised the boys with a special treat. Gunter's ices."

"Gunter's. Hmm." Mr. Littlethom licked his lips. "I've heard such wonderful things and would dearly love to try them . . ."

Noting the irritated light in Lord Steele's eyes, Abigail interrupted, "Perhaps another time."

Laying his hand on Abigail's arm, Mr. Littlethom brightened. "Oh, you are so good to me, Miss West. I shall not forget your kindness."

Abigail didn't like the man's hand on her arm, nor did she like his obsequious behavior. Still, he might not have enough bread to eat at night, and she could hardly fault him for wanting to work.

And besides, everyone in London wanted Gunter's ices, and she could easily forgive him for begging for an invitation.

"Let us be on our way, Miss West." Lord Steele

was glaring at Mr. Littlethom's hand as a mongoose eyes a snake.

"Yes, of course." She quickly moved away from the tutor, and the man's hand slid off her arm.

Mr. Littlethom pulled off his hat with a flourish. "Until we meet again!"

Smiling faintly, Miss West walked alongside her employer, who had gone from shockingly amicable to downright taciturn.

She sighed.

"You do understand, don't you?" Lord Steele asked.

"What?"

"Why I cannot retain him without making a proper review."

"Who? Ah . . . Mr. Littlethom."

Steele eyed her strangely. "I can't simply hire someone because you wish it to be so."

Abigail's brow furrowed. "No, of course not." She bit her lip. "I just want you to give him a chance."

Steele nodded curtly.

They walked along in silence, the birds twittering overhead and the breeze pressing against her face.

A sharp pain pieced Abigail's eye and she immediately stopped walking, pressing her fingers to her eye.

"Are you all right?" Lord Steele asked.

"Yes, fine. Just a piece of dust blew in my eye."

"Here, let me have a look."

He set his fingers gently beneath her chin and tilted her face up at him.

The breath seized in her chest. His handsome face was so close that through her rapidly blinking eyes she could almost see the shadow of fuzz of his whiskers.

His breath warmed her cheek, and she felt that astonishing charge that he exuded, sending a thrill racing up her spine and raising delicious bumps all over her skin. She forced herself to *breathe* and was overwhelmed by the gingery spice scent he wore.

"I don't see it," he murmured, his gaze traveling from her eyes to her mouth and lingering there.

Her lips parted as her breath suddenly became heavy and her heart hammered.

"I think it's gone," he declared suddenly, and removed himself as if singed by her touch.

"Thank you," she sputtered. Quickly she looked down, smoothing her skirts and collecting herself. She had to stop reacting to her employer this way. For the thousandth time, she cursed the masked man. Never in all her life had she had such difficulty containing her passions; not even Phineas could arouse her senses so.

They walked as uncomfortable silence stretched long.

Staring off into the trees, Lord Steele waved a hand. "You do understand that my household has certain rules about fraternization . . ."

Oh my heavens! Lord Steele had noticed her reaction to him!

*I can't help it! You're wretchedly gorgeous and I'm simply a flesh-and-blood woman!*

But instead of voicing her defenses, she bit her tongue and her cheeks burned with mortification. How could she tell him that she was not interested in bedding her employer? No matter how damningly handsome he was.

She decided to jump in head first. "I'm the first to admit I've made some mistakes." She stared off at the white-blossomed pear tree, unable to meet his eyes. "I know that your father-in-law mentioned what happened with the Byrnwycks . . . I want you to know that I will not make that mistake again."

*Bloody hell!* Steele thought. *She suspects I'm not indifferent to her appeal! I shouldn't have gotten so close, I shouldn't have touched her. But it was innocent enough! She couldn't read my thoughts—if she had she would have run screaming.*

He shook his head, disgusted with himself. *I've never been so affected by my passions. It must be that blasted widow. If I ever get my hands on her again . . .*

But the very idea had the opposite effect of settling his wayward lust.

Miss West pushed a golden tendril of hair deeper into her bonnet, as if aware that it was lovely to behold and not wishing it to be so. "I know you did not ask about what happened with the Byrnwycks, and I appreciate it. But I want you to know that I realize now what wretchedly poor judgment I had . . . and I would never under any circumstances do the same today."

Now he felt really awful; she was blaming herself for the whole Byrnwyck affair when he knew full well that it wasn't her fault. Miss West might be lovely to behold and have the kind of heavenly figure that made men long for transparent gowns. But she was no seductress. She didn't have a designing bone in her well-shaped body.

*I have to convince her that she'll not be subject to any attentions in my regard. How can I reassure her?*

Steele pursed his lips. "I am a principled man, Miss West."

"I didn't mean to imply—"

He held up his hand. "If I may finish?"

She closed her mouth.

"I want you to know that I see the people in my household as under my protection. I believe that certain lines cannot be crossed."

A look of relief washed over her features, as if she'd just been saved from a horrible fate. "I agree!"

"I think that you and I started off on the wrong foot."

Her cheeks tinged pink. "My fault entirely."

"As I recall, Carlton had something to do with it."

She shrugged sheepishly.

He continued, "But now you and I seem on surer footing."

She nodded. "Absolutely."

"I would say that matters are well settled as far as you and I are concerned."

"I agree."

"Then let us be sure to keep things exactly as they are."

The relief in her voice was unmistakable as she breathed, "Wonderful."

"Very well then, let us consider this topic settled."

She nodded. "I do."

The "marriage vow" words didn't sound as awful on her lips as he might have imagined they would, and he wondered if she'd ever say them standing before a vicar. He adjusted his coat, as if something itched between his shoulder blades. Mr. Littlethom didn't deserve her, no matter how handsome he was. Steele had to admit that the man was too attractive for anyone *not* to notice, but he wasn't smart enough for Miss West. She was bright and articulate, and Mr. Littlethom came across as less than her match.

And Steele certainly didn't want to find a governess just to have her go off and get married.

No, Miss West couldn't get married. It just wouldn't do. The very thought was unacceptable.

He made a mental note *never* to consider it again.

# Chapter 25

"Look! There it is!" Felix shouted. "There it is!"

Felix leaned his head out of the carriage window, and Abigail bit back the reprimand on the edge of her tongue. He could hardly fall out of the latched door to the coach.

Partly Abigail hated the way she always thought of the bad things that might occur. But partly she was glad that she was so vigilant, knowing that terrible things did indeed happen, and she should do all she could to help her innocent charges avoid them.

Seth's young face was filled with delight, his nose and cheeks having blossomed freckles from his play in the sun. He bounced up and down on the seat. "I want ices! Lemon or muscadine! I want ices! I want ices!"

Felix pulled his head back into the coach and sat beside his bouncing brother. He was trying to be more contained, but the lad was grinning from ear to ear. "I hear that pistachio is the grandiest flavor."

"Grandiest?" Abigail smiled, their excitement contagious. She was delighted that Lord Steele had allowed her to join in the fun, knowing many governesses who'd never have the chance. "I think you mean *grandest*."

Lord Steele's chiseled features were filled with amusement, as if unable to resist the delight reflecting onto him from his nephews. "*Grandiest* does have a certain ring to it. Quite a superlative."

"Pistachio?" Seth's face twisted in consternation. "Now I can't decide whether to get pistachio or lemon or muscadine . . . I heard my friends talking about the best flavors but don't know which to choose!"

Lord Steele's teeth flashed white with a devilish smile. "I say we try them all!"

Felix's eyes went wide. "All?"

Steele struck his cane down on the carriage floor. "Why the blazes not? Then we can choose which one we like best, so the next time we return we can know what to order."

"Next time?" Seth squealed, bouncing around so energetically, he crashed into his older brother, who for once didn't seem to be bothered in the least.

Felix looked up at Lord Steele, his eyes filled with wonder, as if Steele were a conquering hero. "You really meant it? We can come again?"

"Why not?" Steele's broad shoulders lifted into a shrug.

"Hurrah!" Seth cried, jumping so high his head hit the ceiling of the carriage. "Ouch!"

"Are you all right?" Abigail asked, leaning forward.

Rubbing his head, Seth beamed. "Right as rain!"

"Or ices!" Felix added. "Right as ices!"

"Right as ices!" Seth echoed. "Right as ices!"

Abigail smiled, looking out the window, relishing their joy, and soaking in the elegant Mayfair neighborhood.

"You don't effuse much, do you?" Steele asked.

Abigail blinked.

Scratching the hard line of his jaw, he offered, "You're allowed your share of fun, too."

Abigail scrunched her face, teasing, "I don't recall reading that in my position posting."

"I'll be sure to write that in." Steele smiled, warming her deep inside her middle.

She smiled shyly back, containing her response. She didn't want her employer to think her too caught up, and she had to be careful after their recent conversation. She *never* wanted to give him the impression that she would presume to invoke his attentions.

And he was correct; things were right just as they were. He was being so amiable and even going so far as to allow her to join them on the excursion to Gunter's. He was also being so kind to the boys at a time when they needed his attentions.

They had no one else, and Abigail believed deep in her heart that if Lord Steele allowed himself, he would be a wonderful father to Seth and Felix. The thought warmed her and gave her new hope for the lads' recovery from their recent loss. They would never have their parents back, but given time and love and a family to call their own, they would grow into the finest of men.

Abigail only prayed that Lord Steele chose a wife wisely, selecting a lady who would embrace Seth and Felix as her own and give them the love they deserved.

As the carriage pulled onto the east side of the square, Abigail could make out the sign bearing a pineapple, which was the emblem used by Gunter's Tea Shop at Nos. 7–8 Berkeley Square. Delightful anticipation made her heart race, and a smile teased her lips. She felt as if she were nine years old again, when the happiest times were concentrated into little bursts of joyful moments, like blowing bubbles in the wind or running through tall grasses or skipping rocks on a lake.

This *felt* like one of those moments, and it brought tears to her eyes. Bittersweet joy at the memories, grief over innocence lost, and joy for Seth and Felix that those times were still possible for them.

"Are you sad?" Lord Steele leaned forward, concern in his dark gaze.

"Nay." She shook her head and wiped the corner of her eye. "I'm just so very glad that you came to the park today." Meeting his eyes, she smiled, and it was so heartfelt that she sighed.

His face relaxed and his lips lifted. "I am, too."

"Look! There it is!" Felix cried.

Seth pressed his nose against the glass of the window. "Where? Where?"

Fashionable coaches were lined up on the avenue. Waiters ran back and forth taking orders and carrying sweets. Small parties of gentlemen leaned against the nearby railings enjoying the sun and the establishment's offerings. Other waiters scampered back and forth across the avenue, serving the people clustered under the maple trees in the square's lush garden.

Ten minutes later, Lord Steele's party sat on a bench under one of those very maple trees, waiting for Gunter's ices and sorbets while the two burly footmen perched against a tree nearly. The wooden bench was fairly full, with the boys in the middle and Abigail and Lord Steele acting as bookends.

Excited anticipation hung heavily in the air as a spirited breeze carried the scent of butterscotch to tease their senses.

"My tummy's rumbling," Seth complained, rubbing his middle.

"They must be cooking candies," Abigail surmised. "And I confess the scent alone makes me feel as if I haven't eaten in a week."

Felix looked up at her, clearly trying to distract himself with a new topic. "Have you ever gone a week without food?"

Seth clutched his belly. "A week without food! That sounds dreadful!"

Ignoring the memories of the terrible times she and her brother had shared, Abigail mussed Seth's hair. "I suppose that depends on who's cooking."

Lord Steele watched her with a keen gaze, and she could swear that he'd noticed the way she'd not given an answer.

Abigail looked away, noting that he must be a gifted prosecutor. She hoped to one day watch him at work, but never as the one sitting in the witness chair.

She rubbed her arm, thinking about her fugitive brother. She wondered if Lord Steele might be able to help her in some way. But he was sworn to uphold the law and worked on behalf of the Crown. And her brother might very well be engaged in illegal activities. Moreover, why should he stick his neck out for her? No, the idea was too tenuous to consider, so she pushed it away.

Felix rubbed his hands together while Seth licked his lips again and again until a line of spit encircled his mouth. They all watched the other visitors in the park, eagerly eyeing the ices already served.

"Oooh, I hope that's one of my flavors," Felix muttered, eyeing a green-colored scoop of ice being eaten by a raven-haired girl. "It's gotta be."

A wiry, blond-haired waiter carrying a silver salver brought the ices, each person's serving in a small clear glass. A hush descended over the group as they were being served. Once each spoon was handed out, they all dug in, utensils clattering against the glasses.

After sampling all three of his flavors, Felix turned to Lord Steele. "Pistachio is my favorite. What's yours?"

"Burnt filbert."

Seth shoved a spoon full of cream-colored ice cream into his mouth. "Bewwer than royal ice cweam?"

Abigail knew she should chide the lad for speaking with food in his mouth, but she was too busy licking the last drop of chocolate off the back of her spoon to care.

Lord Steele held up his finger. "Wait, I must try another bite to be sure." Abigail tried not to watch as his spoon slipped between his smooth lips, but she was mesmerized by the look of pure rapture on his handsome features. He sighed and closed his eyes.

"Well, which one?" Felix demanded.

Steele opened his eyes and nodded. "Definitely burnt filbert. I like the nutty flavor."

She pulled her gaze from her employer, wondering why instead of chilled she felt positively heated. Quickly she took another helping of chocolate, flipping the spoon so that the smooth, creamy coldness was pressed flat against her tongue.

Pure heaven.

Her face relaxed, her eyes grew heavy, and she wondered at the last time she'd tasted anything this good. Probably never.

"An' wha' abou' you, Miss West?" Seth asked with a long line of cream running down the side of his chin.

She sighed. "Dark chocolate mixed with burnt filbert."

Lord Steele raised a brow. "Oh, you get to pick two favorites? I didn't know that was allowed."

"It's two ice creams making one flavor," she replied cheekily.

"Are you sure you're not the attorney in this party?" Steele asked.

"Most assuredly," said she.

For all their enjoyment of the ices, the lads were done in short order, dropping their spoons with a clatter into the glasses.

Felix looked longingly at the other children sprinting around the clusters of trees. "Can we . . . ?"

Lord Steele motioned to the two footmen, who quickly swallowed the last of their ices, set down the empty glasses, and jumped forward.

Lord Steele's gaze was measured. "Never out of sight and always within ten paces."

"Yes, Your Lordship!" Foster and Zachariah spoke as one.

Steele turned to the boys. "The same goes for you;

always keep us in sight and never be more than ten paces from one of our party."

"Woo-hoo!" Seth and Felix scampered off.

Sighing with contentment, Abigail leaned back into the wooden bench. For a moment she could pretend that she wasn't there by her employer's leave and that she was with the boys out of pure love, not just the threat of starvation.

Although at the moment she could hardly consider hunger when her belly was pleasantly full with a hearty supplement of delicious cream.

"I can't recall a finer day in my memory," Abigail breathed, collecting the lads' leftover glasses and spoons.

"Oh, I'll do that, miss." A blond-haired waiter with sparkling blue eyes and a ready grin jumped to help. The waiter reached for her glass.

"No, not mine!" She realized that she was speaking loudly and lowered her voice. "I'm not quite finished yet." There had to be at least two spoonfuls of chocolate left.

The man nodded knowingly and removed his hand. "Of course."

Lord Steele eyed the last bit of his ice cream. "That was pretty blazingly delightful."

Abigail smiled. "I'm forced to agree."

Lord Steele handed his empty glass to the waiter and exhaled noisily, stretching his long legs before him.

Abigail suddenly realized that they were virtually alone in the shadow of a maple, as the two footmen had gone off to follow the boys and no other patrons sat nearby. She knew that she should be wary of appearing too informal with her employer, but she felt so sleepily content, she couldn't summon the wherewithal.

"It was most kind of you to buy ices for me and Foster and Zachariah," Abigail commented. "Thank you again—"

"Please stop thanking me, although I must say it was worth every penny to see you roll your eyes as if you'd died and gone to heaven."

Abigail's cheeks heated. "I swear I think I may have."

His eyes crinkled at the corners. "Close enough."

# Chapter 26

Accompanionable silence blanketed Abigail and Lord Steele as they watched the boys scrambling about with their newfound friends. Many families came to enjoy Gunter's in the square's maple tree–lined park.

A storklike matron with graying blond curls and greenish-blue eyes strolled into the glade. She was eating from a clear glass filled with cocoa-colored ices. Her eyes fixed on Lord Steele and narrowed in distaste.

Lord Steele's lips tightened as he nodded slightly.

The matron sniffed, raised her nose in the air, and turned so quickly, the hem of her hunter green promenade dress flounced. The feathers of her extravagant peacock bonnet bounced with each rapid step in the opposite direction.

Lord Steele's face hardened, but Abigail couldn't help but notice that he wasn't as impervious as he wanted to appear. A sadness had entered his dark gaze, and his shoulders seemed to drop as if weighted down.

"Who was that?" Abigail couldn't help but ask.

"Lady Blankett."

"Why does she dislike you so?"

Steele shifted on the bench. "I arrested one of her friends for murder."

"Well, you had to have good reason, didn't you?"

"I thought I did . . ." He looked up at the trees. "I'm coming to the unfortunate conclusion that sometimes I'm a little . . . eager when it comes to seeing justice done."

Abigail shifted slightly, praying that Lord Steele never learned of her brother and his brushes with the law. "Was the friend guilty?"

"No."

"So she's free now?"

His gaze was lost to the memory. "Completely exonerated, thanks to Heath Bartlett."

"Who?"

"A man who works for me."

Abigail lifted a shoulder, feeling inclined to give Lord Steele the benefit of the doubt. "So . . . ultimately you helped her."

Steele's smile was tight. "He did it behind my back, and I probably wouldn't have let him get away with it had I known."

"Why wouldn't you have allowed him to do it?"

"Because the law needs to be respected."

Abigail's heart began to race a bit faster. Blast, if Lord Steele only knew that she'd stabbed a man a few weeks ago! Granted he was trying to rob and rape her, but still . . . Lord Steele was the arm of the law! But what really worried her was Reggie. If he was involved with Lucifer Laverty and the circuit—well, that meant that he and Lord Steele were on opposite sides of the law.

"I took an oath," he continued, almost speaking to himself. "I have to uphold the law. Help the system work its justice . . ." His voice trailed off, and he seemed lost in thought.

She swallowed, vowing never to let her increasing regard for Lord Steele tempt her to confide in him. It would put him in a terrible fix, and heaven only knew how he would deal with her and Reggie. Clearing her throat, she endeavored to change the topic. "Lady Blankett was alone."

Steele started as if pulled from some weighty musings. "Yes."

She prattled on, "I hear that though it's not proper for a lady to be seen alone at many establishments, it's perfectly acceptable for her to be seen at Gunter's."

Steele nodded. "So it is."

"I envy you that."

Steele turned to her. "What?"

"The ability to go where you want when you want. I confess, I often find it quite inconvenient being female."

Instead of making a snide comment or making light, Lord Steele shook his head. "It is a terrible shame." Watching Felix climb a tree, Steele remarked, "I do believe that through our own prejudices, we are leaving waste some of the best talent in our society."

Abigail felt her brows lifting to almost her hairline. "You do?"

"There are some ladies who are so . . . keen-minded, and often have a sense of time and place that surpasses many men. Yet they are stymied by the restraints laid upon them by society and are only relegated to limited roles."

"I had no idea that you were such a progressive-thinking man."

"I have not always held these beliefs and seem to be coming to them late in my life. But certain ladies of my acquaintance are convincing me that the fair sex has much to offer, if we are only willing to accept their talents." Shaking his head, he waved a hand. "Mrs. Catherine Dunn comes to mind. Do you know her from your days at Andersen Hall? She runs the orphanage quite admirably these days."

Abigail swallowed. Since returning to London she'd stayed away from the orphanage, unwilling to face the place without the man who had steered the helm for so many years. Additionally, she didn't want to see anyone who might connect her with Reggie. "Ah . . . I can't recall . . ."

The viscount raised a slender finger. "She's a woman like that. One who can stand on her own two feet against terrible odds."

Abigail was impressed. "Do you know Mrs. Dunn from your work on the board of trustees of the orphanage?"

"Her husband and I . . . well, we've known each other for a long time."

Abigail had heard that Major Dunn was a war hero now. A long way from the mischievous headmaster's son who was the most daring of pranksters.

"Mayhap you and the boys and I will visit there one afternoon," Steele offered. "I'm sure the Dunns would be glad to see you once more."

Abigail swallowed, looking away. "I think it might be painful for the boys to be reminded so explicitly that they are orphans. So soon, anyway."

"You believe so? I thought they might benefit from knowing that they are not alone in their circumstance."

"It may be too soon . . . I don't know when the time is right . . . but I would hate to put them through any more . . ."

"You haven't been back there, have you?"

She shook her head.

Reaching out, Lord Steele grasped her hand in a comforting squeeze. "I'm sure it must be very hard." The compassion in his voice warmed her heart. Staying away from Andersen Hall *had* been hard for her.

His skin was smooth and warm, and she was mesmerized by the long, elegant fingers encircling her own. His hand was so much larger than hers, enveloping hers, making her feel connected and secure. She knew that she shouldn't, but she relished that touch, savoring the sweet contact, knowing that it was only for a moment before he became the aloof, stylish viscount once more and she the frumpish governess.

But for the time, she soaked in the comforting contact, needing it so badly, she yearned for the moment to stretch on forever.

But after a lingering moment, he released her hand, careful to be a few inches away from her.

*He doesn't want me to get any ideas*, she told herself, respecting his efforts.

Raising his fist to his mouth, Lord Steele coughed uncomfortably. "I really should be getting back to work. I have some matters that require my attention." Checking his watch, he stood.

She was reluctant for the intimacy and joy of the afternoon to end. But all good things did. "I'll collect the boys."

One of the footmen, Zachariah, ran off to call for the coach while the remainder of the party clustered near the edge of the park toward the street.

"That was glorious." Felix sighed. "Thank you."

Lord Steele nodded. "You're very welcome."

"When can we come back?" Seth wailed.

Patting his shoulder, Abigail made a stern face. "Let us be grateful we came this once."

Lord Steele leaned down and whispered in Seth's ear. "We may just have to return tomorrow."

"Yippee!" Seth screamed.

Lord Steele smiled, then his gaze was captured by something over Abigail's shoulder. His eyes narrowed and his body stilled, like a fox who had caught a scent.

Abigail turned. A black coach was tearing down the avenue at a breakneck pace.

"There are children about!" Abigail cried, shocked. "He needs to slow down!"

The ground rumbled with the pounding clatter of the horses' hooves as the driver cracked a whip, urging the horses even faster.

Suddenly Lord Steele grabbed Abigail's arm and swung her and the children behind him with his back facing the crazed coach.

"Ow!" Seth complained as they were squeezed in a cocoon of shelter created by her and Steele's bodies.

"What's happening?" Felix demanded. "Why are you hugging us?"

Lord Steele's body jerked. "Ooof!"

"What happened?" Abigail cried, alarmed by the distress in his features.

"Nothing," he bit out, his face a mask of anger and pain.

The carriage wheeled away, followed by the cries of alarm and anger from the people along the avenue.

Abigail anxiously scanned his features, her heart racing, fear tight in her throat. "Are you all right?"

"Is it gone?" Steele asked, his teeth gritted as if he were in pain.

"Yes. Thank the heavens. He was a madman!"

"Are you all right, Your Lordship?" Foster cried, running closer. He'd been about ten paces away, awaiting the carriage.

"Where's my coach?" Steele demanded.

"Right here, Your Lordship!" Zachariah jumped off the carriage as it rolled to a stop by the curb.

"Open the door, man! Now!"

Quickly Zachariah opened the door.

Steele released her arm, opening the shelter she and he had provided for the children. "Get inside the coach, now!"

For once Seth and Felix immediately did as they were told without argument. After ensuring that they were quickly settled, Abigail sat in the coach, anxiety and confusion coursing through her. She hugged the boys close, comforted by her need to protect them.

Looking around, Lord Steele rolled his shoulder and winced as if it pained him.

Zachariah stepped closer. "It was a rock. It hit you hard. How bad are you hurt?"

Steele waved him off, his eyes searching the nearby ground.

Leaning down, he picked up an object the size of a small melon.

A crowd had gathered on this side of the park, their murmurings and anxious faces clearly evidencing that they had witnessed the attack.

A note encased the rock, held together with twine. Steele deftly unwrapped the note and read it silently.

"*Death awaits you!*" a wiry gentleman dandy read aloud over Steele's shoulder.

Steele turned as if surprised by the proximity of the man.

"Who wants to see you dead, Lord Steele?" the dandy asked.

"Dead!" A heavyset matron with a purple turban dropped to the ground like a sack of flour, her turban sliding off her head.

A lady nearby hissed.

Chaos erupted as people gathered to the fallen matron and exclaimed among themselves.

Clutching the note, Steele jumped into the carriage and slammed the door closed behind him. "Make away!"

The driver cracked the whip, and the carriage quickly rolled off.

# Chapter 27

Anfter the incident in the park, Abigail tried to distract the boys, reading stories, playing games, and doing puzzles. It was difficult keeping them inside the house on such a lovely day, but Abigail wanted them near and in a place where she could feel safe.

She knew not to believe anything at face value, but *someone was trying to kill Lord Steele?* Fear gripped her heart every time she even considered the possibility, and her anxiety wasn't calmed by all the comings and goings in the house. Lord Steele was closeted inside his study, and he seemed to be sending footmen to and fro on a host of errands. But she pushed aside her anxiety, instead focusing on the boys.

Finally it was time to help the boys prepare for bed. They complained about it, but she could tell they were as ready as she for the day to near its end. The sun had faded to dusk; the creatures of the night had begun their nighttime chant.

Standing over the boys as they lay in their beds and relaxed into sleep, Abigail envied the easy way their eyes fluttered closed and they released the day into their dreams. She, on the other hand, could not stop thinking about the attack on Lord Steele and all its implications.

Gathering her courage, she decided that she could not rest until she knew more about the events of the day and how Lord Steele was faring.

Her feet invariably took her to his study door, where he was closeted within. But once there, she stood still, her hand poised to knock . . . yet she hesitated.

She didn't want to presume an intimacy in their relationship that allowed her to check up on him. Would her concern be unwelcome?

Meanwhile, inside that very study, Steele stared at the other side of that same closed door, praying that someone would enter and give him a respite from his distress.

His shoulder ached like the dickens. But he was more concerned about the terrible emotions roiling inside his middle than any physical pain.

When he roamed the streets of London at night engaging the lower orders of man, Steele never tasted fear. He never hesitated out of concern for suffering bodily harm. He had an utter confidence of mind, body, and spirit. Ultimately, when it came to protecting himself, he had nothing to lose.

Seth and Felix were a different story completely.

They were mere boys, filled with laughter and mischievousness and innocence . . . They had so much to live for, so much potential. Steele could almost see the men they were to become, and he longed to help them be the best men they could be.

He understood that from this day forth he could no longer hand the boys back to Benbrook with a handshake and a smile. At a very elemental level, he was responsible for them.

Flat and simple: He cared.

Today's attack had sent a shock rippling through his body, reminding him of the impotent terror he'd suffered when he'd lost his wife. He realized that the real reason he'd never gotten close to another woman since Deidre's death was that he couldn't face that terrible loss again. When she'd died, it felt as if his heart had been slashed to ribbons. The pain had been so acute that he'd stayed away from anyone who might make him subject to that agony again.

Yet somehow the boys had managed to change that. When it came to them, it wasn't just about his heart or his hurt . . . He adored them, yet caring for them was wrapped in a cloak of *responsibility*.

Whoever was entrusted with Seth and Felix had to be reliable, smart, and think only of the boys' best interests. That position of influence was sacrosanct. Steele knew that he would never breach that sacred trust, yet he knew enough of his fellow man not to trust just any other to such a critical task.

For the first time, he was humbled that his father-in-law had selected him to protect Seth and Felix. The enormity of Benbrook's faith in him struck him like an arrow, piercing his overblown pride and shattering it into a thousand pieces.

He was ashamed of how quickly he'd relegated the boys to the care of another. He was mortified that he'd considered the investigation as a mental challenge without fully considering the flesh-and-blood children who were at its heart.

Steele's blood ran cold just thinking about what might have happened today.

The rock had struck just below Steele's shoulder. A few inches lower and it might've hit Felix's head.

Rising, Steele walked over to the sideboard and poured himself a hearty portion of brandy. He swallowed it so fast, his throat burned in protest and his eyes blinked with unshed tears. The flames licked all the way down to his hollow belly.

A knock resounded on the door.

"Come," Steele called, squaring his shoulders and wincing with the pain in his back.

Miss West entered, her mien tentative, her golden brow pinched with concern. She dipped quickly into a curtsy, her gaze searching his face as if seeking answers.

Her worry warmed his heart; he couldn't recall the last time a woman had looked at him with real concern in her gaze.

"How are you faring, my lord?" Her tone was slightly breathless, as if fearful of what he might say. Was he so standoffish that she feared rebuff?

He raised the glass. "Just fine now. Thank you for asking."

Biting her lower lip, she seemed unconvinced.

He attempted a smile. "Truly. Matters are well in hand."

Her keen gaze scanned his coat and her eyes narrowed. "You haven't changed clothing since we returned to the house."

"So?"

"Have you had anyone look at your injury?"

Turning away, he poured himself another glass of brandy and swallowed a hearty gulp. He coughed, wincing. "I'm fine."

"Really."

He turned to face her only when he was sure that the pain didn't show in his features. "Yes."

She crossed her arms and a defiant gleam lit her grayish-blue eyes. "Then why do you look like you just swallowed a cat?"

He waved a hand. "I'm sure it's nothing. I've been hurt worse before."

Her golden brow lifted.

"Ahh . . . golf!" he fudged. "It causes the peskiest injuries."

She scowled, her eyes narrowing even further.

"I've seen that look before," he quipped. "On Mrs. Nagel, the housemother at Andersen Hall Orphanage."

"If she were here, she'd have you stripped and bandaged."

Hmm. He sipped his brandy, savoring the smooth smoky flavor. Naked with Miss West wasn't such a bad idea.

He shook his head, reminding himself that she was in his employ and he would never breach her trust in him. "Ah . . . pardon, what did you say?"

"I said, please let me call for a doctor."

"Don't be ridiculous," he scoffed, his instinctive loathing of doctors making his tone sharp. He had little faith that anyone had better knowledge of his body than he. "I don't need a doctor. It's a silly little bump."

He walked over to his chair and sat. The chair squeaked in familiar protest. He leaned back, and sudden pulses of pain radiated from his shoulder in agonizing sharpness. A sweat broke out on his brow and he clenched his teeth, knowing that it would soon pass.

Miss West was staring at him, her tongue stuck out the corner of her lips as if she was concentrating really hard. "Stupid, headstrong . . . *man*," she muttered.

"Pardon?"

"You heard me. I said that you're a stupid, headstrong man." She moved to the bellpull. "I'm calling for a doctor."

"I don't need a doctor!" he bit out, leaning his palms against the desk to ride out the nausea threatening his composure.

"Well, someone has to look at that injury! At least call for your manservant!"

He clenched his teeth. "Lambert is on an errand."

"Someone has to have a look at it!"

She wasn't wrong. And how the blazes was he going to get his coat off? The idea of asking for help made his pride burn. He hated showing weakness; he hated needing others. Yet for some reason, he didn't mind Miss West's presence. In fact, it was quite nice to have someone to grumble to.

Scowling, he asked, "You won't let this pass, will you?"

With her lips set in an insolent glower, she shook her head. "No."

"And I won't call anyone to help. So we're at an impasse."

A staring match ensued. Those blue-gray eyes were filled with defiant purpose, and he had to admire the way she refused to back down. Secretly he prayed she'd win.

"This is ridiculous," she murmured, her eyes locked with his.

"Then leave." Although he sincerely hoped she wouldn't.

"You must have someone look at that injury. Not to do so would be a negligence I couldn't abide."

"Then you come up with an alternative."

"Fine. I'll do it."

"You?" he scoffed, aggravated by a sudden pulse of pain but directing his anger at the pretty little target trying to order him about. "What do you know of such things?"

"I'm a governess, you idiot. I've tended lots of broken bones and scrapes."

"Did you just call me an idiot?"

"Did that rock affect your hearing, too?"

Shockingly, he wasn't remotely offended, but he was quite enjoying sparring with her. "Do you usually call your employer an idiot?"

"Only when he's acting like one."

His lips lifted in a smile, and a rebellious gleam lit her eyes. He was actually quite touched that she'd bully him so. Fancy that, he was enjoying being bullied! And by a woman!

He sniffed. "Fine. So long as you don't call for the doctor."

She nodded, but there was no triumph in her gaze, only steely determination. "I'll go get my salves. I'll be back in a trice."

Spinning on her heel, she danced from the room, her bearing filled with urgent purpose.

He leaned back in his seat, groaning with the sudden pain that pierced his shoulder.

*Bloody, bloody, bloody hell!*

If she bothered to be so wretchedly bossy, she could at least stay and hold his hand or something. Wasn't that what governesses were supposed to do? Why did she have to leave? Couldn't she just look at it while she was here? Didn't she understand that he *hurt?*

He gritted his teeth, wondering why he suddenly had no taste for suffering alone in stoic silence.

He exhaled through the pain, staring at the open door and willing Miss West's speedy return.

Abigail felt as if her feet had wings as she raced up the stairs to her rooms. Quickly she threw open her trunk and yanked out the drawer in which she kept her remedies. Well, not actually *her* remedies, but those taught to her by Dr. Michael Winner, the beloved doctor of the children at Andersen Hall Orphanage.

In the past when she'd gone to this drawer, she'd had a quiet efficiency born of being in service.

But this time, a charge lit her movements. A thrill raced inside her chest, and she marveled at the excitement she felt in aiding Lord Steele.

"I can't believe I called him an idiot!" she breathed to herself. But she'd had such utter conviction that he *was* being an idiot. And he had to be told in no uncertain terms that it would not do.

The man needed someone who would speak to

him plainly, for clearly no one in this household was
going to be straight with him any time soon. They
were all too afraid of him. Well, not afraid, but . . .
intimidated. And he could be quite daunting with his
razor-sharp intelligence, coolly elegant manners, and
no-nonsense mien. But Abigail wasn't intimidated in
the least.

She'd never felt so absolutely, confidently sure of
herself when speaking to someone as she'd just felt
with Lord Steele. It was quite shocking, actually. She
almost felt as if she were another person, one similar
to the black widow she pretended to be, one akin to
the strict governess she often had to be . . . yet wholly
different. It was almost as if she became . . . a new
version of herself. A better, surer, smarter version of
Abigail West.

"I'm thinking nonsense," she muttered as she
dropped her salve and bandages into the dry bowl on
her washstand and lifted the bowl in one hand and
the half-full pitcher in the other.

Abigail shook her head. "The man needs looking
after, pure and simple." For he hadn't enough good
sense in his head when it came to his own precious
health.

With her heart racing and her hands shaking with
urgency, she clutched her supplies to her chest and
raced out of the room and down the stairs.

Nearing the study door, she suddenly feared that
perhaps he'd left out of anger.

Or had asked another for help.

The idea made her stomach lurch.

She knew that she was being selfish, but *she* wanted
to be the one to help Lord Steele. It wasn't enough

that he simply recovered; she wanted to help be part of that cure.

Bracing herself, she swept into the room and almost smiled with relief to see that he was still sitting in his chair behind his desk.

His handsome face was washed in a gray pallor and his eyes were glazed with pain, pinching at her heart. But she forced her features to relax; impervious and professional were the only ways to handle Lord Steele's awkward situation.

Placing the ointment, bandages, and pitcher on the desk, she moved to stand behind him.

"The door," he bit out.

"Yes, of course." Quickly she closed the entry.

"And get me another brandy!"

Her tone was acerbic. "Yes, my lord."

He had the decency to look abashed. "Sorry. But it hurts."

She immediately regretted her rebuke. But there was no point in making an issue of it now. The man needed her help.

Swallowing her last wisps of apprehension, Abigail stepped behind the viscount and reached for his coat.

# Chapter 28

Abigail had never removed a gentleman's coat before and hardly had a notion how snugly the blasted thing fit. Trying to slide one arm out of the sleeve was proving to be quite a challenge. So she yanked on the coat's shoulder. All she got for her efforts was a groan from Steele.

She winced. "Sorry."

"It's fine."

Stepping back, she scratched her chin. "There must be an easier way to do this." Eyeing the garment like a puzzle to be sorted, she narrowed her eyes.

"There is. Step back."

She did as he suggested and waited.

He stood. Then with some hesitancy born from obvious discomfort, he reached his arms backward and downward, as if his hands were stretching toward her.

Quickly she saw her opening, reached around to his chest as if hugging him from behind, and grasped the lapels of his coat. The garment slipped off with much greater ease.

He exhaled heavily, his shoulders sagging.

"That was quite a neat trick," she marveled, laying the coat on the table near the sideboard.

"I've done it a few times before," he quipped.

"You must be feeling better if you're jesting."

He exhaled. "I confess, I'm damned glad to be out of that coat. I hadn't realized how much it was bothering me."

"Do you still want that brandy?"

"Yes, please."

Quietly she poured him another glassful and waited while he drank. The color had returned to his cheeks, and she couldn't help but notice that a shadow of fuzz grazed his chiseled jaw. He was so handsome, she had trouble pulling her eyes from him, but she forced her attraction down, knowing that not only was it improper, but that her attentions were not welcome. "You look better."

He made a face as if pretending to be foxed. "You do, too."

She took a deep breath, not quite knowing how to respond. "Now the shirt."

Nodding, he looked around. "On the sofa."

They walked to the brown leather chaise, where he sat, and she stood in front of him. The heat of his body billowed over her like a warm summer wind and she was suddenly achingly aware of how improper this whole situation was becoming. Her cheeks burned, but she pushed aside all notions of impropriety; the man had almost been murdered today and he needed her help.

Thinking about the thorny issue of the attempt on Lord Steele's life diverted Abigail from focusing on the breadth of Steele's brawny shoulders. Or how the muscles of his chest pressed through his marcella waistcoat. Or how snugly his tan breeches encased his strapping thighs.

He smelled of *male*. Oddly, the masked gentleman came to mind.

Abigail told herself to stop being silly: Many men must have similar scents. Moreover, Lord Steele and the masked gentleman were the only two men she'd been close enough to recently to detect an odor, so the association had to be natural. Her wicked behavior flashed through her mind, making her skin feel singed by the memory.

"Are you all right?" Steele asked. "You suddenly look flushed. I can probably examine it myself if you get me a mirror."

Shaking her head, Abigail pushed away all thought of the masked rescuer. "No, no, of course not. I was thinking of something else. And a mirror will not help you, since the injury is on your back. Besides, I want to help you."

"Are you sure? This really is beyond the call of duty."

Blinking, she met his gaze. His coal black eyes were filled with respect, as if whatever answer she gave was well and good with him.

For all his authoritarian airs, Lord Steele was the most sincerely considerate employer she'd ever had.

"You really are quite nice," she murmured.

"Pray don't tell anyone, or my reputation will be ruined."

They shared a smile, and her heart warmed. When he smiled, his eyes wrinkled at the corners and his whole face softened. He was more breathtakingly handsome than Abigail had ever seen him.

She forced herself to look away, afraid he might notice her attraction. "I really do want to take a look at your injury and make sure that you're all right. I couldn't sleep knowing that you required help but didn't get it."

He nodded. "I can't very well be responsible for an exhausted—"

"And ill-tempered," she interjected.

"—and ill-tempered governess. The lads wouldn't be too pleased with me."

"You must be jesting! After today you couldn't displease them if you tried! You took them to Gunter's, for heaven's sake!"

"That was fun, wasn't it?"

"It was glorious." She sighed, suddenly sad as she thought of the fun that had been shattered and the fright that had followed. "All good things come to an end," she muttered.

"You're right there."

She looked up, not realizing that she'd spoken aloud. Unsettled that she and Lord Steele could be feeling so many of the same sentiments, she moved to stand before him, businesslike once more. "Let us see the damage, now, shall we?"

As she reached for the knot of his cravat, her heart began to hammer and her cheeks to burn. But she forced herself to breathe calmly, not wanting the man to know how deeply he affected her.

He raised a hand. "Let me do it. A mirror would help, but I'm sure I can manage."

"Don't be ridiculous. It'll be faster this way."

Slowly she wrestled with the knot of his cravat. After a few moments, she was exasperated enough to mutter, "It's like a noose."

"For some, the fancier the knot, the more fashionable the wearer." He lifted his hands. "Please allow me."

"No." She gritted her teeth. "I refuse to be bested by a silly piece of cloth. I'll get it."

Steele's coal black eyes were fixed on her face as he lowered his hands. "Very well then."

She could not meet his gaze, instead focusing all her attention on his garments. She prayed that her cheeks weren't as red as they felt.

After some struggle, she managed to loosen the knot and slip off the long winding material.

He exhaled, sending warm, brandy-scented breath wafting over her. "Thank you."

She nodded, satisfied. "You're welcome."

A gap under his collar exposed a patch of clean, smooth skin at his neck. Her hand shook slightly as she reached for the button at his throat. She fumbled with it, then unfastened the clasp.

A line of red rimmed his throat where his shirt collar had been. She frowned. "That was terribly tight."

"You get used to it. I'm sure many of the garments you wear are less than comfortable."

Her eyes flew to his, and a flash of heat seared her belly and warmed her to her core.

"I'm sorry," he muttered, ripping away his gaze and undoing his waistcoat and shirt. "That was inappropriate of me. This is awkward as anything and I'm not helping."

"No, it's fine. It's a strange situation, but I've cared for others before." Granted they usually weren't taller than her shoulders, and none of them had ever inspired the glorious heat that sizzled in her belly and had her longing for this man to be masked and naked . . .

Masked and naked!

*Stop it, you ninny!* she screamed in her head, mortified and furious with herself.

She exhaled shakily, stepping behind him to make sure he couldn't see her face. "Ah . . ." she breathed. "Let us have a look."

Feeling in control of her idiotic musings once more, she told herself, *An injury is an injury. Imagine you're a doctor, like Dr. Michael Winner.* Just thinking of the man who'd helped at Andersen Hall for so many years brought a certain level of calm.

Abigail reached over his broad shoulders for his shirt and pulled it off. The pale golden glory of his muscled shoulders and back were marred by an angry red gash just below his shoulder blade. She couldn't help the gasp that broke from her throat.

"That bad, eh?" he asked.

She swallowed. "You should have told me sooner. This must hurt like the dickens."

Looking over his shoulder at her, he raised a brow. "I should've told you sooner? What would you have done?"

"I don't know . . . tea and sympathy?"

She felt his mirth as if it were a pulse radiating from his skin, and it pleased her more than it should. "I'm so glad I can amuse you at a time like this."

"At a time like what?"

"You were nearly murdered, for heaven's sake!"

His tone was teasing, "Is that like *nearly* being with child? The 'nearly' makes quite a difference to the outcome, I assure you."

Her lips quirked, and she appreciated how he'd lightened the mood. Still, she felt he needed a little scolding, so she boldly chided, "You really must try to be more careful." Moving over to the basin, she dipped the cloth and squeezed it out.

A laugh broke from his throat. "You act as if I had anything to do with it! I certainly didn't invite that rock to hit me."

Stepping behind him, she set the cold cloth on his back. He stiffened, and bumps suddenly rose on his skin, yet he did not make a sound. He was brave and strong-willed. "No, but you're the Solicitor-General of England. You must have known that the job came with certain dangers."

Abigail went over to the desk and opened the stopper on the salve. The familiar scents of olive oil and calendula flowers teased her nose, reminding her of her brother. He'd gotten into so many scrapes as a child that she'd gone to Dr. Michael Winner and asked him to teach her how to make his special liniment.

And now her brother was mixed up with Lucifer Laverty. The name alone caused a terrible lurch in her belly

"What's that salve?" Lord Steele asked.

Abigail pushed away all thought of her wayward brother. She couldn't do anything to aid him right now, and Lord Steele needed her help. "Dr. Michael Winner's secret recipe."

"I smell olive oil and something else . . ."

"Calendula flowers." Exhaling, she moved to stand

behind him and removed the damp cloth. "But that's all you'll get out of me. I've been sworn to secrecy about the rest of the ingredients."

He tensed, the muscles on his back rippling.

She frowned. "It won't hurt. But I'll have to touch you to put it on."

"I don't mind." *Idiot!* Steele couldn't believe he'd said the words aloud and prayed that she wouldn't take them as he'd meant them, unconsciously of course. Being half drunk and half naked in front of the lovely Miss West was loosening his tongue in ways that were less than gentlemanly. Steele chided himself to behave more like the man he was pretending to be, not like the knave he'd been born.

"Ah, sorry, I was only jested . . . jesting," he stammered, trying not to sound as soused as he was feeling. Or mayhap she'd forgive his transgressions if she thought he was foxed? The idea was tempting, but he dismissed it as too immature. He took ownership of his actions, come hell or what may. "I do mind, but your intentions are good. They are, aren't they?"

Peering over his shoulder, he couldn't miss the sympathy in her slate blue eyes, the tiny crease of concern marring her brow.

*I'm wallowing in it*, he realized, *hoarding her caring like a miser stashes his gold*. He loved how she'd scolded him. Cherished how she was cosseting him. He felt like an idiot, but had no inclination to stop—it felt too good.

She nodded. "Of course." Overturning the bottle, she poured the salve into her palm.

Steele inhaled, preparing himself for pain.

Surprisingly, her touch was feather-light, her

circling motions soothing. She rubbed the oil on his injury, but also on the whole of his shoulder. Closing his eyes, he relaxed with a sigh. This was heaven.

It was over too soon for his liking, but all good things were.

Miss West moved over to the desk and collected bandages.

She returned and stood before him. "Ah, I'll bandage it, to keep the ointment in place and protect it from getting bumped."

Reaching around him, she wrapped the cloth across his shoulder like a toga. She was so close, he couldn't help but surreptitiously lean forward and smell her golden hair. Heather and woman. He wondered, *If I dare to touch it, would her hair be as silky soft as it looks?*

He chided himself for being so self-indulgent. She was counting on his integrity; he couldn't breach that trust. He forced his face to be impassive, praying that she couldn't discern his reprehensible thoughts.

She looked into his eyes. "It's not too tight, is it? Your jaw is clenched. Are you unwell?"

"Ah, no. I'm fine." He moved to stand, and she quickly stepped back. He needed to get away from Miss West before he'd do something they'd both regret. Stepping over to the sideboard, he grabbed the bottle of brandy and poured himself a glass.

Turning, he sipped, fortifying himself with the familiar burn. "Ah, yes, well, ah . . . thanks."

Miss West's cheeks were glowing pink, her lush

breasts rising and falling with quick intakes of breath. Clearly she was disconcerted by his rude behavior. "Can I do anything else for you?"

Fantastic images of Miss West doing things for him rose up in his mind. He choked on his brandy.

"Are you all right?" She stepped closer.

"Yes." He coughed, waving her away. He needed to escape, fast! "I should take myself off to bed."

"Do you want me to go with you?"

*Oh, dear Lord in heaven!* It was too much!

To his great shame, he practically sprinted from the room. "Another time perhaps!"

Rushing out the door, he wanted to knock himself over the head for his stupid reply. Another time? Wishful thinking, he knew.

There would be no other time as far as he and Miss West were concerned. In another life perhaps.

Maybe death wouldn't be so bad after all?

# Chapter 29

Mr. Patrick Devonshire was led into a drawing room furnished with expensive Chippendale furniture and the kind of magnificent antiques that would adorn any duke's manor.

But the beefy, ginger-haired man sitting in the luxurious armchair by the crackling fire was no duke. Despite the trappings of civility, the man in the chair was the worst kind of scum that England had to offer. He was the Prince of Darkness in London's crime-ridden streets, and his enemies had aptly named him Lucifer to prove it.

Patrick swallowed, hard. He owed Lucifer Laverty more than one thousand pounds, in addition to a debt no man could easily repay. The only thing keeping him alive at this point was the plan he'd concocted to exact revenge on his uncle and pay back the master criminal, fivefold.

Patrick's armpits were sweating and his breath was tight in his chest. He eyed the dark-skinned, heavy-set thug standing by the window, who had fists as big as mugs. A whooshing sound brought Patrick's attention to the wiry, pasty-faced man perched on the table in the corner. The man flipped a knife in the air, eyeing Patrick as if he'd slice Patrick's throat without blinking. Patrick gulped, knowing that the bastard was just trying to intimidate him, and recognizing that it was working.

The master criminal looked up from the newspaper he was reading in his hand, his icy blue eyes as sharp as any razor. Intelligence and grit blazed from Lucifer Laverty's eyes, and Patrick understood that a mere nod from this man would have him beating at death's door and begging to get in.

"Look who's here," Lucifer Laverty drawled in his thick, working-class accent.

Patrick had heard many rumors about Lucifer's parentage, but the one he most believed accounted Lucifer as born in a brothel and raised by a gaggle of whores. That story gave Patrick an even stronger sense of superiority over the ruffian and was also quite . . . titillating. Since Patrick had been reared by a string of governesses that he'd alternately seduced and then had fired, the notion of working women who had little opportunity to say no was deeply satisfying to him.

The master criminal did not rise from his chair. "It's one of Madame Chantal's pretty ladybirds."

The wiry man sniggered and the muscular thug by the window sneered.

Patrick bit his inner cheek; if being likened to a filthy whore was what he had to suffer to exact his revenge on Viscount Benbrook and claim his due, then so be it.

Smiling, Patrick tilted his head in acknowledgment. "I have been told on occasion that my appearance is more than acceptable to the ladies." He paused. "And those were the ones not being paid."

Lucifer's eyes narrowed, then he smiled. "You do have balls." He smacked the newspaper pages with his hand. "You attacked the Solicitor-General of England in broad daylight."

"I didn't attack him," Patrick corrected. "I gave him a message to pass along to my dear uncle."

Lucifer's face was hard as granite. "If one shred of shit touches me or my circuit, then you'll wish yer ass had never left India."

Patrick shook his head. "As I told you before, nothing leads back to you. No one knows that you were behind the carriage accident that killed my cousin and his wife. You have no motive; there's no connection."

Lucifer's smile was terrifying. "Except you."

Patrick pulled at his suddenly tight neck cloth. "Without me you won't get a pound of the thousand pounds I borrowed."

Lucifer raised a brow. "*Just* the thousand pounds you borrowed?"

"I misspoke. Fivefold of what I borrowed . . . and my eternal gratitude."

Lucifer's eyes glistened with satisfaction. Even after Patrick paid off Lucifer in pounds, Patrick would be forever in the pocket of the Prince of Thieves.

With a calculating look in his eye, Lucifer motioned for Patrick to sit in the chair opposite. "I still don't understand why ya don't just kill the old goat and the boys and be done with it?"

Sitting, Patrick shook his head. "I want Benbrook to suffer the way he made me suffer. He needs to know fear and impotence . . . and that there's not a damned thing he can do to stop me from decimating him."

"I thought you'd never met the man."

"I didn't need to meet him for him to have destroyed my life. And now I'm simply returning the favor."

Patrick's stomach roiled with hatred. "He ostracized my father for no good reason, cut him off from everything and everyone until he felt that he had no choice but to be relegated to that hell pit India. My mother died from one of their filthy diseases in less than a month. After that my father begged for forgiveness, begged to come back. But Benbrook warned him that no money would be ours, no society would accept us, and no place could we call home."

Lucifer tilted his head. "An' now yer father's dead."

"He was too weak to take his due." Patrick clenched his hands. "I won't make that same mistake. Everything that was denied him will be mine!"

Lucifer leaned back in his chair, assessing Patrick. "You really have no trouble killing two innocent boys? Your own flesh and blood?"

"They're Benbrook's kin who are set to inherit what's mine. That's plenty of incentive."

"But you wouldn't let Claude finish the job, and now he can't go back to his position as a footman in Steele's house."

"The fall in the duck pond was to give me entrée with Steele."

Lucifer shifted in his seat, his stony face filled with aggravation. "I grasp the whole part about not being known as Devonshire while in London—"

"No one can know that Patrick Devonshire, heir to the Viscount Benbrook, is in England. That way no suspicion will settle on me when Benbrook and the boys die."

Lucifer scowled at the interruption. "But what I don't understand is this whole tutor business. I got you the fake references—"

"You couldn't pick a name better than Littlethom?" Patrick groused, his pride pricked. "Littlethom?"

The beefy brute by the window sniggered and the wiry fellow jeered, "Wanna show us yer *little* Thom?"

Patrick glared. "I only lower my pants for the women who beg me, sewer scum."

The wiry fellow stepped forward menacingly, but Lucifer held up his hand. "I gave you that name because you need to *remember your place, Littlethom.*"

Patrick realized that the man was a master of manipulation. Every time Patrick used that belittling name, he was reminded of Lucifer and all he owed the knave. He forced his fists to unfurl. "Well, everyone will know who I am when I claim the title of Viscount Benbrook."

"But why the ruse? Why pretend to be a tutor?"

Patrick opened his mouth to interrupt, but Lucifer's eyes glared with warning and Patrick clenched his jaw closed.

"And don't the boys have a governess?" the criminal asked.

The image of Miss West rose in his mind, and Patrick felt his passion stir. She was such a pretty little thing, and reminded him of the first governess he'd ever bedded. Of all the women he'd had, the memory of plowing her was the one he always savored. "A governess is especially helpful when there is no mother." He spoke from experience. "But often tutors are retained as well if they have a specialty. I am presenting myself as a language master."

"But why do you want to be in the house? What good will it do you?"

"I want to know what Benbrook is up to. Get close, but not too close. So being in the house with the boys is ideal. Next, I want to be able to choose the perfect way to inflict the most damage on Benbrook and I want to *witness* his suffering."

"What if someone recognizes you? This is Lord Steele's house! The bloody Solicitor-General of England!"

"I assure you, no one will know that Nigel Littlethorn"—his lips curled in distaste—"is Patrick Devonshire. And if they do, then I'll take care of them."

Lucifer's brow rose, and his face was skeptical. "That's a mighty long tally a' deaths yer startin' ta build."

"After Benbrook and his grandchildren are gone, I will inherit over fifty thousand pounds and the estates. As you well know, money can be quite persuasive." Anticipation swirled in Patrick's middle, and he could almost taste his revenge. "I'm committed to making every effort to see this through."

Lucifer sniffed. "The bloody Solicitor-General of England won't be bribed. *I know.*"

Patrick laughed. "Why do you think I need to get into his house? Money isn't the only way to put someone in your pocket. Being in his house I can find out his weaknesses and his secrets." Rubbing his hands together, Patrick beamed. "Oh, I'll make certain he cooperates . . . don't you worry."

# Chapter 30

Abigail lurched up in her bed, her heart racing from the screams of her nightmare echoing in her mind. Sweat coated her skin; her throat was tight with fear. Scrambling, she kicked off the sheets. She was coated in sweat, her nightgown clinging to her like an extra layer of skin.

Jumping from the bed, she moved to the door connecting her room to Lord Steele's and set her ear to the smooth wood. Straining, she couldn't hear anything except the wind as it whispered through the eaves of the house.

Abigail swallowed, trying to bring her rational mind to the fore. But her dream had been so vivid, the agony of Steele's pain so real. Her skin felt as if pecked by tiny birds, and anxiety pierced her heart.

With her heart in her throat, she raised her fist to knock on the door. *He's your employer, for heaven's sake! You can't disturb him in his bedchamber! And certainly not in the middle of the night! And how will you explain yourself? "I had a nightmare." Don't be a fool!*

She shifted on her bare feet, trying to understand what irrational fear drove her. In her dream, Reggie had been captured by the authorities and had to build his own gallows. But his face kept changing, first becoming Seth's. Then when the job was completed, he turned and suddenly was Lord Steele. Then out of the blue, brigands started throwing stones at Steele. Then they were upon him, savagely attacking. Steele fought and fought, but the thugs were like flies on a corpse, swarming him, *hurting* him.

Crushed by frustration and fear and a terrible sense of impotence, Abigail had screamed, and then she'd woken up.

Dreaming of Reggie was not new to Abigail. In her dreams she was always reaching for him, trying to protect him from terrible danger. Seth changing places with Reggie made a certain kind of sense. Abigail felt responsible for him, too. And she loved them in a similar way—like family.

Dreaming of Lord Steele being struck by stones also made sense after the incident today. But it was the feelings that went along with the dream that had her so shaken. She'd been overcome by fear and caring and a certain sense of . . . connection. As if he were part of her, and if anything happened to him, then she was . . . *lost.* That harming of him was harming her. She'd been overcome by the tragic sense that if he died . . . she'd die. Then it struck her like a bolt of lightning, searing her skin. *I'm in love with Lord Steele.*

The truth of it felt so right, so overwhelmingly in harmony with her feelings and thoughts, that she stood transfixed.

Then her eyes widened with horror.

*Oh no!*

Laying her head in her hands, she curled into a ball and sank to the floor. The one thing she'd sworn never, ever to do again, she'd done. And it was entirely her fault.

*Oh why, oh why did he have to be so strikingly handsome? Or so wretchedly nice? Or so upstanding in character? Or such a kind guardian to Seth and Felix? And considerate and funny . . .*

And he *deserved* to be loved. No one took care of him. He was always the strong one, the stiff-upper-lip gentleman. The island weathering storms. He needed love just as much as anyone—even more so since he was so good to others . . .

*I am well and truly heels over my head in love with him!* She groaned into her hands.

And she knew, without a doubt, that he would never feel the same. She was unworthy of such a man. Unequal to his character. Scarlet woman!

Scrambling up, Abigail slowly backed away from his door. Lord Steele must never learn about her secret excursions as the wicked widow. She couldn't face having him find out that she was such a scarlet woman.

And more importantly, he could never, *ever* learn that she loved him.

The next morning, Steele sat in the breakfast room, his toast and eggs sitting uneaten beside him as he read the *Morning Chronicle.*

The newspaper had written an account of the attack the day before, under the bold, large-type headline, ATTEMPT ON SOLICITOR-GENERAL'S LIFE.

And underneath that headline was a sketch of his likeness.

Looking up from the paper, he scowled. "Blast those journalists!"

So if the widow who'd struck him unconscious the other night had taken a look at his face, if she hadn't recognized him then, she very well could now. Examining the sketch, he noted that the artist had made him appear much older than he was. A smattering of lines encircled his eyes and mouth, and the gray at his temples was far wider than Steele had last seen in his mirror that morning. His pride was slightly affronted, but he took it as a stroke of good luck, maybe keeping his identity safe. But he doubted it. The widow seemed sharp as a whip.

Pointedly ignoring the sketch, he continued reading the article. The piece went on, quite irresponsibly, to conjecture about who might wish to see him dead. His scowl deepened. The list was astonishingly long given the fact that the journalist had decided to include a host of criminals he'd prosecuted in recent years.

He dropped the broadsheets onto the table with a crackle of pages.

At least no one thought that the children might have been the target. That was definitely a good thing.

He picked up the pages once more and continued reading.

"Oh no!" The article before him reported that gossips about town were speculating on his potential search for a wife. He tossed down the paper with a force that scattered the crackling pages. If there was one thing he didn't need, it was the matrons of society sizing him up for market.

Maybe the attack had a benefit? Maybe he would be seen as an unfavorable candidate for marriage? And how did people hear about that anyway? Sir Lee had some answering to do.

As he stared across the table, his eyes fixed on the empty chair opposite him. An unfamiliar longing speared his heart.

The notion of a companion, a true partner, tempted him as never before. He supposed it was Felix and Seth's influence. He was beginning to feel like part of something greater than himself. Benbrook, through Sir Lee, insisted that he marry to provide a mother for the boys. And they deserved a loving home . . .

Yet when he thought about bringing another lady into his house, an intense feeling of rejection cut through him. He did not want to have anyone else in his home, in his bed. He didn't want his carefully controlled existence to change. He liked things as they were . . . with Seth and Felix and Miss West . . .

Steele's breath caught. The shadow of an idea whispered in his mind.

But Lord Benbrook would never approve. And thus Steele would not be made the heir, and he certainly would lose any chance at custody of the boys. The whole scheme would be for naught. For without Felix and Seth, Steele had no need for a wife. Or did he?

Shaking his head, he pushed the idea of marriage

and Miss West from his mind . . . yet they lingered there as if unwilling to let him go.

"Ahem." Dudley stood in the doorway.

Finally pushing the irrational notion from his mind, Steele looked up. "Yes, Dudley?"

"A Mr. Gabriel Cutler and Mr. Andrew Cutler to see you, my lord. They claim an acquaintance and desire an audience with you."

Steele felt his eyes widen. "Here? Now?"

"Yes, my lord." A look of discomfort washed over the butler's face. "I feel I must warn you, it seems that they are under the impression that you invited them to stay here for an extended visit."

Steele jumped up from his seat. Wiping his mouth on his napkin, Steele felt his heart racing. He couldn't recall feeling this kind of nervous anticipation since he was a young greenhorn at the Inns of Court. "Well don't just stand there, show them in!"

Startled, Dudley nodded. "Yes, my lord." He rushed out.

Swallowing, Steele adjusted his coat.

In less than a moment, boot steps pounded in the hallway, drawing near.

Dudley stepped into the room, announcing, "Mr. Gabriel Cutler and Mr. Andrew Cutler."

Brown-haired, olive-skinned Gabriel was just as tall and broad and beefy as Steele remembered him. He resembled a tree trunk as much as anyone Steele had ever known. His green eyes were twinkling as he stepped into the room, his big boots booming on the wooden floors.

Shaking his head, Gabriel grinned. "If I didn't see it with me own eyes I'd hardly have accounted for it! Yer a fancy viscount!" His voice had the familiar cadence of Dorset, reminding Steele of home.

Steele's legs were moving before he'd even realized he stepped forward. "Gabriel!" His extended hand was caught in Gabriel's meaty grasp. Steele exhaled, a feeling of wonder filling him. Gabriel had been like a brother to him and the closest to him. He'd made a place beside him, teaching Steele how to be one of the brothers, being the strongest of friends. He was the one who'd convinced Steele to become a Sentinel.

With his free hand, Steele squeezed the man's arm. "It's so good to see you, my friend!"

"You, too." Gabriel's eyes shone with mirth. "I'd have recognized ya in a room of a thousand men! Although to see ya in the papers, yer gettin' as old as an oak!"

"Ah, you saw the broadsheets."

Gabriel smirked. "Yer always one for gettin' in a fix. Who'd you tiff off now?"

Noting the butler behind Gabriel, Steele murmured, "Later."

Gabriel nodded. "Let me introduce you to my nephew, Andrew."

Steele was shocked. "Johnny's boy?"

"The very same," Gabriel agreed.

Extending his hand, Steele smiled. "Why, you were shorter than a goat when I last saw you!"

Andrew's square chin lifted a notch. "I'm sixteen now, Yer Lordship."

"Steele will do just fine."

"A fancy title and everything." Gabriel shook his head. "Who'd have thought that a raw 'un like you were would make it to be such a fine gentleman. A lord no less!"

Andrew looked at his uncle. "But you were telling me in the coach that you'd have laid bets on him making more of himself."

Gabriel winked. "And so I did." He turned to Steele. "Never did I see a man with such a thirst for justice as ye. When ye left us for London, we thought perhaps ye'd be a Bow Street Runner . . . but then we heard that ye'd become a barrister, well, it made perfect sense. Ye were always smart as a whip."

Steele blinked. "You knew?"

"Oh, we kept an eye on ye, no matter how far off ye thought we were." Gabriel sniffed. "And becoming Solicitor-General of England—well, that was a bit of a shock. Until our neighbor Lord Westerly told us about how the solicitor-general handles special prosecutions. Then it made more sense since we knew you weren't the kind to be spending all yer time behind a desk. No, preserving justice—that's yer calling."

Smiling, Steele shook his head. He'd had no idea that his friends knew about his life. But not only did they know, they approved. Miss West had been right. Contacting them had been a capital idea. A feeling of warmth and fondness swept over him.

Steele turned to Dudley. "Please have Mrs. Pitts prepare some rooms and make my friends welcome."

Nodding, Dudley departed.

Gabriel laid a hand on Steele's arm. "I just want to say, I'm sorry about yer wife."

Steele tilted his head in acknowledgment. "Thank you. I wish you could have known her."

"Me, too."

Steele paused. "But you can meet her nephews, Seth and Felix. They've come to live with me."

Beaming, Gabriel winked. "So that's why the papers say ya need a wife."

Steele's hands clenched. "I don't *need* a wife, I have Miss West."

Gabriel's smile broadened. "Can I have a Miss West, too?"

Pointing his finger, Steele warned, "Don't you dare—"

"Don't get your skirts in a knot." Stepping forward, Gabriel playfully punched Steele in the arm. "I'm just messin' with ya."

Steele realized that he needed to have more of a poker face when it came to Miss West. No one could know about his attraction to her or how fond of her he'd grown. "Miss West is Seth and Felix's governess."

"Ah." Gabriel nodded.

Steele licked his lips. "She's very good with the boys . . . and has proven herself to be . . . resourceful."

Gabriel's eyes narrowed. "Sounds like there's a tale to be told."

Steele realized how happy he was that Gabriel was here. He trusted the man implicitly and didn't have a friend in which to confide.

Turning to Andrew, Gabriel waved a hand. "Go check in the kitchens and see if there's some cakes to be found."

Steele started. "But I want you both to meet the boys and Miss West."

Gabriel smiled. "Oh, we will. But in a few minutes, if that's all right with you?"

Steele nodded.

Motioning to the box on the side table, Gabriel remarked, "For the moment, let's you and I share a smoke and a conversation."

Andrew turned. "I'm off to the kitchens."

After he'd gone, Gabriel sat down in the chair. "He's a good 'un, anxious to see the city and spread his wings a bit. So tell me this tale of yours."

Steele held out a cigar. "It all started when I received a visit from this crafty old bugger named Sir Lee Devane . . ."

# Chapter 31

Yawning, Seth burrowed deeper beneath his covers. "I like your friends."

Sitting beside the boy on the bed, Steele tucked the blanket around Seth's shoulders. "I do, too. I'm glad they came for a visit and you got to meet them."

"So you were an orphan just like us?"

"Yes. But unlike you, I had no brother." Steele looked over his shoulder at the lovely governess who was placing the boys' clothing in the chest of drawers. The candlelight gave her golden hair an added glow. "Nor did I have a nice Miss West to take care of me." She'd been so quiet today. He'd have thought that she'd have given him an "I told you so" for contacting his friends. But she'd stayed away from him, probably to give him and Gabriel time together.

Felix set aside the book he'd been reading. "You were all alone?"

"Yes. I had an aunt who was infirm and unable to take care of me. I was a young lad of twelve, almost a man, yet I was . . . struggling."

"And so you went to live with the Cutler family,"

Felix added, his keen eyes filled with understanding. "Just like we came to live with you."

"Yes." Steele scratched his chin. "Which brings me to what I wanted to discuss with you. I was thinking that maybe it's time for you to call me by a different name other than Lord Steele. It sounds so . . . formal." He noticed Miss West's movements slow as she was clearly listening to every word he said.

"When you went to go live with the Cutler brothers, by what name did you call them?" Felix asked.

"I called them by their Christian names. But I was older and they weren't related to me. You and I are . . . family." A knot formed in his throat. "I need a better name."

Closing the drawer, Miss West turned to him. Her eyes shone brightly in the candlelight, yet her mouth was set in a worried line.

Steele could guess at her concern. "I don't expect you to call me Father. That wouldn't be right."

Miss West's dainty shoulders relaxed so visibly, Steele had to resist the urge to chide her for not giving him more credit. But clearly she had the boys' feelings at heart.

Steele continued, "I was thinking Uncle."

"Uncle what?" Seth asked.

Felix sat up. "Yes, what is your Christian name?"

"I don't use my Christian name. I haven't in years."

"Why not?" Seth asked.

Steele realized that he hadn't gotten close enough to anyone to have him use anything but his last name. Previously his male comrades had called him

Dagwood, and now they referred to him as Steele. His female companions . . . well, he'd never allowed anyone to be that intimate.

He looked at his hands, memories washing over him. "I can't even recall the last time anyone else used it," he lied. It was on the day Deidre had died.

Their secret meeting place had been behind an old chapel near a ravine. Heavy rains had fallen the night before, and Steele had warned Deidre to stick to the longer trail that swept away from the ravine. But always impatient, Deidre had taken the shorter path. When her horse had lost its footing and slipped into the gully, Deidre had cried out his name. He'd run to her, but he'd been too late. She'd slipped from the saddle and broken her neck. He'd cradled her limp body in his arms for hours before he was able to carry her home to her family.

No wonder Benbrook hated him. Steele hated himself sometimes, too.

A warm hand on his shoulder brought him back to the present. Miss West's lovely face was filled with concern. "Perhaps we can discuss it more tomorrow? You seem . . . tired."

Reaching up, he grasped her hand and squeezed.

She held his hand as if it were a precious gift, giving him comfort, giving him strength.

"No, it's time," he decided. Miss West's sympathy and practical kindness had helped him to reach out to the Cutlers and he was so thankful to her. She'd also shown him that grief was a part of life, but that it should not interfere with living. He turned to the boys. "My name is Jason."

"Uncle Jason," Seth made his mouth go round, testing it out. "Uncle Jason."

Felix nodded. "I like it."

"It's a beautiful name," Miss West murmured, looking away, her face filled with emotion.

Without thought Steele kissed her hand.

Her eyes flew up, shock and wonder inside them. "Why . . . why did you do that?"

"I felt like it," he answered truthfully, wondering where he'd gotten the gumption. But he couldn't regret it. Her skin was like velvet against his lips, her heathery scent intoxicating in its sweetness.

Felix snorted. "Oh no! Not kissy stuff!"

Seth giggled.

Removing her hand from his, Miss West stepped backward, not meeting his eye. "It's time for bed. Good night, boys." She blew them each a kiss.

Seth blew her a kiss. "Good night!"

"Good night, Miss West!" Felix cried, making a kiss motion with his lips.

Quickly she backed out of the room.

Steele stood. "Good night, Seth. Good night, Felix." He could not imagine blowing them a kiss, but he rumpled each boy's hair.

"Good night, Uncle Jason," they cried in unison.

Smiling, he left their bedroom in search of Miss West. He had no idea what he'd say to her. Only that he felt so good, so happy, and she seemed at the source.

He found her at the end of the hallway, speaking with Mrs. Pitts.

Mrs. Pitts's back was toward him, and she did not notice him. "Thank you ever so much for that book," the housekeeper said. "When Prince Knightly saved the princess, well, I almost fell out of my chair in a swoon!"

Miss West looked up. "I'm so glad you liked it. Ah, my lord."

Mrs. Pitts turned, her face cherry red with embarrassment. She dipped into a curtsy. "Your Lordship."

"Mrs. Pitts. Miss West, if I may have a word?"

Mrs. Pitts moved off.

Self-consciously Miss West tucked a strand of gossamer golden hair behind her ear. "Yes?"

"I wanted . . . I wanted to thank you. For convincing me to write to the Cutlers."

She folded her arms and then unfolded them as if she didn't quite know what to do with herself. "You wrote to them, not I."

"If not for you, I wouldn't have had the courage to contact them again."

Her cheeks were pink. "I'm glad it turned out well."

Abigail bit her lip, having trouble keeping her resolution to remain aloof from her employer. The way he was treating the boys warmed her in a way that nothing else could. He clearly had opened his heart to them, which to her mind made him the most wonderfully romantic man in the land.

"I appreciate all that you do for the boys," he continued, his words honey-sweet to her ears. "And for . . . me. If there's anything you ever need. Anything I can do . . . please give me the chance to do so."

Abigail's heart skipped a beat. She'd been so alone with her troubles, so worried, so fearful that she was making wrong decisions, imperiling her brother by not doing more. Lord Steele . . . She swallowed . . . He was so smart, knew so much about the law . . . Perhaps it was time to seek some help?

She realized that she was toying with her hands and quickly grasped them together. "I . . . I . . ."

"Yes?"

"I have a brother," she blurted out.

He nodded. "I did not know that."

She tried to think of something more to say, but words did not come.

"Was he with you at Andersen Hall Orphanage?" he asked.

She swallowed. "Yes."

"Where does he live now?"

"London." She knew that she was speaking like an automaton, but she was frozen, filled with fear, yet yearning for Lord Steele's help.

"Ah. Can we expect to meet him, soon?"

"I can't find him."

Steele's eyes softened. "I'm so sorry, that must distress you terribly." Reaching over, he gently grasped her arm. "Would you like for me to help you find him?"

Her eyes burned with unshed tears as she nodded mutely.

Heavy boot steps banged on the nearby staircase. Gabriel Cutler's head appeared, followed by his hulking body. "There ye are!" his voice boomed. "I'm as dry as a bone and in need of a pint! What's holding ye up, man? I've some London beer to drink and some city ladies to woo!"

Looking at Abigail, Steele winced. "I promised I'd take them out."

"Tipton's Tavern, ye said," Gabriel Cutler added. "And the first round's on you!"

A look of apology washed over Steele's handsome face, and he gave her arm a gentle squeeze. "Can we finish this conversation later?"

She was filled with relief; this would give her more time to figure out what she might tell him. "Certainly."

"Tomorrow," he promised.

"Tomorrow. Thank you."

"No need to thank me, I haven't done anything yet."

Cutler tapped his boot, calling out in a singsong voice, "Beer . . . women . . . come on . . ."

"Until tomorrow then," Steele said, turning toward his old friend.

"I hope ye don't plan on waking up too early in the morn," Cutler chided. "For we're going to get bosky!"

"You always were a night owl, Gabriel."

Cutler looked off wistfully. "My favorite time. Cats are out, mischief's afoot . . . ye'll have ta teach me the way of it in London. I'm sure there's some justice to be meted—"

Eyeing Abigail, Lord Steele quickly interjected. "Tipton's Tavern! Pints on me!" Then they were gone.

# Chapter 32

Abigail hammered the spade into the ground and dug up the clump of weeds in the overgrown flower bed. The scent of roses wafted around her in a heady bouquet that made the work all the more enjoyable. The sun warmed her back, and only the rim of her bonnet kept her fair skin protected from being burned. Abigail had made the boys wear caps for that very same reason, despite their protests that it was too hot for such measures.

"Where should I put these, Miss West?" Seth cried, carrying a bundle of brambles in his arms.

Sitting back on her heels, Abigail pointed to the gate at the rear of the untidy garden. "Over there. We'll have Foster haul it to the alley and load it up on a cart."

Felix moved beside his brother, his arms so full of sticks, she could hardly see his face. "Where will the cart go?"

"We'll bring the brambles to Andersen Hall Orphanage to be used for kindling." Looking around, Abigail wiped the sweat from her brow with the back of her hand. "We should bring some clippings, too. These roses are lovely."

Surprisingly, Abigail was looking forward to paying a call on her former residence. Lord Steele's comments about Catherine and Marcus Dunn had inspired her curiosity, and now that Steele knew of her brother, she was eager to visit the place of her youth.

She wondered if Catherine would remember her. Abigail was younger and had kept to herself. Reggie used to tease Abigail calling her Abby the Gale *because* she was so quiet. She understood that his taunt was an attempt to get her to be a bit more gregarious, but it wasn't Abigail's nature. If anyone remembered her, it would be as Reggie's sister. No one could forget Reggie or his outbursts.

Abigail knew that some of her newfound enthusiasm to revisit her past stemmed from the fact that Lord Steele said that he would come with her to Andersen Hall. She wondered what it would be like to walk those musty halls with the compassionate, handsome gentleman by her side.

Her cheeks warmed, but not from the sun. Every time she thought of Lord Steele—which seemed like every other minute—feelings of excitement, anticipation, joy, and wonder would rush through her. Sensations so startlingly intoxicating, she wondered if she might float away on an afternoon cloud. .

But then she'd remind herself that she'd already lived through the terrible fiasco of an affair with her employer's son. This whole matter could end just as badly.

With Phineas she'd seen a man of depth of character where the mere pretense of a gentleman had existed. She'd imagined love when there had been sexual attraction. She'd expected wedding bells and had almost gotten a prison cell.

She'd be a fool to trust these astounding feelings. She'd be mad to read Steele's comments and actions as anything more than simply the considerate acts of a gentleman.

Moreover, acting like a lovesick pup was the last thing that would endear her to her employer.

Embarrassment and mortification would weigh down her joy as effectively as creeling stones.

But he'd looked at her so endearingly last night, his gaze warm, his lips lifted in a sweet smile. Just remembering the glorious feel of his soft lips kissing the back of her hand raised bumps on her skin. She was overwhelmed with gratitude as she recalled how sweetly Steele had spoken to her, wanting to help her find her brother. All those wondrous feelings of joy and excitement would wash over her once more, making her feel giddy.

Feeling as if her emotions were surging up and then down like the ocean's waves, she muttered, "I'll go mad if I keep this up."

Sighing, she went back to work. Tending a garden was such straightforward, enjoyable work, much easier than trying to sort the mixed-up feeling she had about Lord Steele.

*Jason*, the name whispered in her mind. It fit him nicely, reminding her of Jason and the Argonauts. Strong, adventurous, a good leader . . . *Jason* . . . A man of honor and integrity, a man who watched over those he loved . . . *Jason*.

A sudden shadow blocked the sun over Abigail.

Lord Steele stood over her, looking around the garden. He stepped away and the sun shined on her once more. "What are you up to, Miss West?"

She shadowed her eyes with her hand. "Just tidying up a bit, my lord. I hope you don't mind. I thought it would be a good exercise for the boys."

"I'm delighted you've taken an interest in my garden." Scratching his chin, he eyed the overgrown bushes.

"It's somewhat of a mess at the moment, but with a little work, it will be lovely."

"I've been neglectful when it comes to my yard," Steele confessed, as he watched the boys gathering brambles and tossing them onto the pile by the gate. "This was an excellent idea. I think I'll join you."

Abigail's eyes widened. "But what of your injury, my lord?"

"It'll do me good to warm up the old muscles." To her utter shock, Lord Steele shrugged off his coat and then rolled up his sleeves. "I purposefully wore this coat because it's easy to remove," he commented, reminding her of their entanglement the other night. Her cheeks heated at the memory and at the stirring vision before her eyes.

In his white linen shirt and marcella waistcoat, he looked as fit and muscular as any Greek hero. His shoulders were broad and enticing enough to make any woman swoon, so much so that Abigail was glad that she was already on her knees. His trim waist only enhanced his strapping shoulders and back. The memory of the golden glow of his bare back flashed in her mind. Her hands clenched around the spade, recalling the feel of his velvety flesh beneath her fingers.

"Is there a shovel about?" he asked, peering around.

Abigail's gaze fixed on the muscles of his thighs bulging in his tight breeches as he roved about the garden, looking for the tool.

Her mouth went dry as sawdust. She swallowed, hard.

"Ah, there it is." Walking over, he grabbed the shovel from against a nearby tree and came back to stand before Abigail. "Where do you want me?"

"Ah, ah . . ." She blinked.

His brow furrowed. "Are you all right?"

She shook her head to clear it. "Yes, ah . . . how about . . . I was thinking of clearing a path." She pointed to the tree next to where she was working. "Right there. The boys want to put in ropes for a swing. If that's all right with you, of course."

"Excellent notion." Stepping over to the area she'd identified, Steele began to dig out the overgrown brush and toss it over to the side.

Abigail watched, mesmerized by the powerful muscles of his arms. His white shirt stretched tight with every motion, outlining his broad chest and shoulders. She couldn't tear her eyes from his bulging thighs as he leaned to and fro with each dig of the shovel.

She realized that she was ogling, and shook herself awake from the heavenly vision of his thighs. "Are you sure you don't mind, my lord? You must have a lot of important work to do."

"I've come to the conclusion that my work will still be on my desk in an hour's time, so I might as well enjoy the day as much as I can."

Thrusting the blade into the soil, he set his boot upon the shovel and rammed it deeper. "I apologize for leaving so abruptly in the middle of our conversation last night."

Looking down, she swallowed. "Oh, that's all right. You have guests . . ."

"Can you tell me about your brother?" His voice was gentle.

Clearly he'd noticed her difficulty the night before and was trying to make it easier for her. Gratitude washed through her for this considerate man, and her heart warmed.

Biting her lip, she exhaled. "My brother. Well, his name is Reginald. But everyone always called him Reggie. Retiring Reggie, I used to call him, every time he called me Abby the Gale."

Steele rammed the shovel into the soil. "Abby the Gale?"

Smiling shyly, she lifted a shoulder. "My name is Abigail and he used to tease me that I was too quiet. That I needed to get more 'stormy' now and again." She sighed, muttering, "He was stormy enough for the both of us."

"How so?"

Abigail paused, sudden fear pinching her chest. Was confiding in Steele a mistake? He was a man of the law, the most powerful prosecutor in the land. He would have to follow the law; he would have to stand by his oath of office . . .

"There's a warrant out for his arrest," Abigail blurted, then covered her mouth with her hand, shocked that she'd spoken so bluntly.

The shovel stopped mid-swing. "I see." After a moment's pause, he began digging once more. "No wonder he's hard to find. You're not the only one looking for him."

Abigail let out the breath she'd been holding.

Kicking aside a rock, Steele asked, "What's the charge?"

"Theft."

Steele struck the shovel into the ground and leaned his elbow on it. "Did he do it?"

"Yes."

"That could be a problem." Exhaling, he looked around, ensuring that the boys weren't within ear-shot. "Can you tell me what transpired?"

Staring down, she realized that her hands toyed with the spade and she stopped. "It doesn't reflect well on me . . . in fact, I feel like it's my fault . . ."

"Did you break the law?"

She shook her head. "I was simply a reckless fool."

"Regrets?"

A small, mirthless laugh escaped her mouth. "Huge."

"Byrnwyck?"

Looking up, she nodded. "So you'd heard."

He shrugged. "A little. Not much. But I'd prefer to hear it from you."

Biting her lip, she realized that she desperately feared his knowing of her terrible mistakes, yet longed for his help with her brother. The two went hand in hand. Yet her love for her brother overrode any concerns she had for her injured pride or sullied reputation. *I'm a scarlet woman*, she told herself. *I might as well own up to at least some of my misadventures. And perhaps it can help Reggie.*

Slowly the whole sordid tale spilled from her mouth like water pouring from a pitcher. Gradually the words increased, gushing forth; she couldn't seem to stop until the carafe was bone dry.

She spoke of losing her head over Phineas, of stupidly believing Phineas's empty promises . . . She described Lord Byrnwyck and his nephew Silas's outrage, her abrupt dismissal . . . Phineas's betrayal . . . and finally her brother's furious acts of revenge, including stealing the Byrnwyck family crest.

Throughout her tale, she could not meet Steele's eyes, fearful of what she might see there. "Lord Byrnwyck had a warrant issued for Reggie's arrest and set the constable on him. Reggie ran off in the middle of the night. Lord Byrnwyck set a price on Reggie's head and hired Bow Street Runners to track Reggie down. Reggie's been running ever since. That's . . . that's . . . all of it."

When she was done, the silence was deafening. Abigail's heart hammered with instant regret. She'd exposed her stupidity and her impropriety—and to the one man whose good opinion she prized above all others!

He was quiet for so long, fearfully she looked up. Steele's face was hardened in anger.

*Oh no! What have I done?* Her bottom lip began to tremble, and her eyes burned with unshed tears. *Stupid, stupid girl!*

"Did Byrnwyck come after you?" Steele bit out.

"Wh-what?"

"Did Lord Byrnwyck come after you? Did he try to hurt you?"

Abigail rubbed her eye trying to grasp his response. "I . . . well . . . he tried to put me in jail as an accomplice but Jan and her husband saved me."

Steele kicked at the shovel, knocking it over with a clank loud enough that the boys' heads turned in their direction.

Steele waved them off. "It's fine. Go inside and ask Cook to make lemonade."

Quickly the boys tossed their brambles into the pile and ran, happy for the break, but also clearly knowing that something was amiss and not longing to be a part of it.

Abigail couldn't fault them; Steele's anger was like a storm cloud brewing and about to explode.

"Are you going to dismiss me?" she asked, wincing.

Steele's head whipped up. "Pardon?"

"Are you going to let me go?"

"Why? You didn't do anything wrong."

Abigail straightened. "Didn't you just hear what I said? I acted immorally and protected a fugitive of the law!"

His eyes flashed with fury, and the muscle in his jaw worked. "They took advantage of you. Every last one of them! Except your innkeeper friends, of course." He began to pace, his boots crunching in the pebbled brush.

"Phineas never should've laid his filthy hands on you. And Byrnwyck . . . well, he should've done right by you!"

Dropping her head, Abigail stared down at her hands. "It was my own fault. I was a fool to believe that a nobleman would want me for his wife."

Abruptly he stopped pacing, crouched down beside her, and grasped her hand. "Don't ever say that! He doesn't deserve you! The slimy bugger!"

Abigail blinked, shocked by the fervor of his words and the astonishingly wonderful sensation of his warm, large hand cocooning hers.

He squeezed her hand. "You are more worthy than ten thousand Byrnwycks and all of their wretched cousins combined."

His faith in her brought tears to her eyes.

Thinking of the masked rescuer, her joy dimmed. "Don't say that," she whispered. "You don't know the scandalous things I've done."

His face softened, his eyes filling with compassion. "Nothing worse than what I've done." Lifting her hand, he laid a soft kiss on her knuckles. "Nothing worse."

Abigail was swept up in the force of his affectionate gaze, which warmed her deep inside the secret places of her heart, giving her hope . . . "Perhaps we both need a little forgiveness?" she whispered.

"I know I do." His rumbling voice was like a caress.

With her hand still wrapped in his, he lowered his head.

She closed her eyes, her heart hammering, her body yearning . . . She leaned forward . . .

His lips met hers. So smooth, so perfect . . .

A chord struck deep within her soul, one that felt so familiar, so achingly true that all she could think was . . . *I'm home.*

A deep sigh escaped her lips as she melted in his arms. Knowing him, loving him, wanting more of him, as she'd never wanted any man before.

*The masked rescuer cannot compare to this*, she marveled, as his lips caressed hers, teasing, exploring, tasting . . .

Suddenly he pulled back and she was bereft, until he lifted her to stand and pulled her into his arms.

His mouth claimed hers with a passion that stole the breath from her throat and weakened her knees. She clung to him, surrendering to the desire that had been building between them from the moment they'd met.

His mouth lit a fire deep within her, igniting desire so intense, she quivered.

His lips grew more insistent, his tongue more demanding. She met his kisses with a passion that matched his, owning the desire flaming between them.

Ripping off her bonnet, his fingers raked through her hair. He groaned deep in his throat, making her feel like the most desirable woman in the world.

His lips nipped the column of her neck and he murmured, "You smell so good." She moaned. His tongue traced her ear. "You taste so good." She shivered as desire pooled within her. Setting his mouth to her neck, he sucked.

Her head spun. Her mind went blank. She was lost. Her body was engulfed in the flames of his fiery desire.

"Ahem!" A cough. "Ahem!"

Steele looked up, his arms still wrapped around

her. Abigail clung to him, her body flaming, her mind spinning.

"Sorry to interrupt, but I must speak with Lord Steele." Mr. Linder-Myer stood just a few feet away, leaning on his gold-topped cane and peering intently at them.

The world came crashing into Abigail's consciousness. She was wrapped in Steele's arms, ready to give him *everything* . . . and now Mr. Linder-Myer, the man responsible for placing her in this household, knew it, too. Embarrassment flooded her cheeks and she looked down, mortified.

"What is it?" Steele bit out.

"That *family* I was talking to you about." The agency representative sniffed. "The one with the India connections."

Steele straightened. "Progress?"

"Most definitely."

Abigail's heart skipped a beat. *A match! For Steele?*

Steele's gaze sought hers, apologetic. "I'm . . . I'm sorry. But I have to speak with Mr. Linder-Myer."

He wouldn't accept the match? Not when he'd just kissed her with such passion? Or would he? Fear sliced through her as sharp as a blade. Was she falling victim to honeyed words and sweet kisses once more? Was she playing the fool yet again? How could she have imagined that a lord, a viscount no less, would want her?

Perhaps as a mistress.

Never as a wife.

She was not worthy enough to make him a wife.

The pain in her heart was like a wound reopened, aching worse than the original injury.

But she wanted Steele more than she'd ever wanted any man before.

*I love him.*

The knowledge seeped deep into her bones, ensnaring her, owning her. From this day forth, her every action would be predicated on that basic truth.

*How far are you willing to stoop to get him?* a shrill voice whispered in her mind.

Could she bear being the kept woman?

More importantly, could she bear to watch the man she loved wed another?

Steele pulled away, and only then did Abigail realize that she'd been clutching him. "I'm sorry but I have to go."

"Yes, of course." Her voice sounded dull even to her own ears.

Steele noted the dismay on her lovely features, and he hated being the cause of it. He was tempted to tell her about the plot against Benbrook . . .

But she seemed so fragile at the moment, so raw from telling her tale. He hated the idea of putting fear into her heart. And Sir Lee's presence might indicate that the threat could already be gone. So where was the point in upsetting her further without cause?

Part of him realized that he didn't want to tell her because he'd lied to her about his reasons for always keeping the boys with two adults. He also hadn't corrected her when she'd surmised, along with everyone else, that yesterday's attack had been directed at him. She'd had such terrible dealings with nobles and employers, and he was afraid, he realized, that she'd categorize him with the lying bastards who'd abused her trust.

But ultimately it was because of that kiss that he did not tell her the truth and was ready to make his escape.

The kiss had shaken him to the core, and he was still reeling from it. His emotions were whirling, his ideas about himself, the future, Miss West . . . It was a bit too terrifying to consider.

So his mind veered away from having to make any decisions. He would deal with all of it later.

*Later*, he promised himself, as the familiar panic of making himself vulnerable to another reared its ugly head.

"Later," he murmured to her, rising and grabbing his coat. "We'll talk more, later."

Abigail watched the gentlemen go back into the house, her heart aching and her mind whirling. All the while, a familiar voice screamed shrilly inside her head, *What have you done?*

# Chapter 33

Steele entered his study with Sir Lee close at his heels. For a man his age, the old gent was pretty swift on his feet, Steele realized.

Sir Lee's craggy face was not amused. "So you're bedding the governess, now, eh?"

Gritting his teeth, Steele slammed the door. "It was one kiss."

Sir Lee snorted. "Bullocks!"

"It's none of your business." Steele tried to keep his voice calm. He couldn't think of Miss West right now, so mentally he closed the door on her sweet face, barring the feel of her softness in his arms, banning the taste of her honeyed lips from his mind. She'd been on fire, and so had he. But it had been more than mere passion. That kiss had been unlike anything he'd ever experienced before. It had overtaken him, emotionally and physically; he'd been ready to completely relinquish control. He, the man with a carefully ordered existence, had been ready to simply . . . *let go*.

Sir Lee scowled. "Benbrook won't approve of the match. And thus he might not make you his heir."

Steele shook his head, trying to shake off the memory of that kiss. "I'm not marrying her," he murmured.

The former spymaster raised a brow. "Even I did not consider you so low."

Guilt and anger and fear lashed through Steele, stinging like strokes of a whip. "I'm not toying with her!"

Sir Lee's eyes narrowed. "Well, if you're not marrying her and you're not toying with her, then what are your intentions?"

"I . . . don't . . . know," Steele confessed, dropping into his chair. It squeaked noisily in protest as he settled behind his desk. He brushed his hand through his hair, muttering, "I have no earthly idea what I'm doing."

Exhaling, Sir Lee lowered himself into the chair by the desk. "You're thinking with the wrong head, is what you're doing."

"It's not like that!"

"Then what is it like?"

Steele swallowed. "I don't want to talk about it." Adjusting the papers on his desk, he wouldn't meet the man's eyes.

"She has no family, no one to look out for her—"

"You're volunteering for the job?"

The old gent stuck out his chin. "I introduced her to you. I brought her into this house—"

"I swear I won't harm her. I just . . . I just can't . . ." Coward that he was, he justified, "I just can't think about the future right now when the boys are in danger. Why did you come here? What do you know?"

Leaning forward, Sir Lee gripped his gold-topped cane, glaring at Steele as if to see down into his soul.

"Please." Steele hated the note of begging in his voice. "Please tell me what's developed in the plot against Benbrook."

Sir Lee harrumphed. "I'll not let this matter go, you know. You must end this little . . . infatuation. It can only lead to disaster." But then he leaned forward, seemingly relenting. "But you're right, there have been some developments we need to discuss."

*Thank God*, Steele thought, relieved and guilt-ridden. Stupid sod that he was, he hadn't thought this situation through with Miss West. He, the man who planned every step like a perfectly executed play . . . he'd lost his head where she was concerned. She had a way of making him *be* just inside that very moment, and not think past it.

*That kiss.* It had swept him away—to a place where time stopped and there was nothing except *her*. It had been extraordinary . . . and *terrifying*.

Panic about committing to a woman once again lashed through him.

Sir Lee was right about one thing: Benbrook wouldn't approve.

Nor would the match be seen as fortuitous by society's standards. Steele knew what people would say. That he'd risen so high, come so far, but despite the title of viscount, he couldn't escape his birth. The lowly commoner with unrefined tastes would stoop back to his former class to take his wife.

Deidre would be rolling over in her grave. He'd finally become the man she'd deserved . . . and then he'd ruin it over a young miss with fair hair and luminous eyes. Was he out of his mind?

"Are you all right?" Sir Lee asked. "You look a little green about the gills."

"No, ah, I'm fine." Driving away all thoughts of Miss West once and for all, Steele looked up. "I beg of you, please tell me what's developed."

Sir Lee watched him, a funny look in his eye. "Word about town is that you are behind the threat against Benbrook's family."

Steele felt his brows rise to his hairline. "What?"

"Rumor is that you've set the whole thing up as a means of convincing Benbrook to make you his heir. Once you've been made heir and guardian of the children, then you'll have everything that is his. Thus you'll have your revenge against him for not accepting you into his family years ago."

Leaning forward, Steele hammered his fist on the desktop. "You don't believe that claptrap, do you?"

Tilting his head, Sir Lee examined Steele with sharp green eyes. "Is it true?"

"Stuff and nonsense!"

"How did you gain your title?"

Steele's eyes narrowed. "Did you make up that rumor just to get me to tell you how I gained my title?"

"No. The rumor really is being circulated about town among the less reputable elements of society."

Steele straightened. "Are they saying that I'll pay if the boys or Benbrook are eliminated?"

"Yes."

"Bloody, bloody hell!" Steele shoved his hand through his hair, trying to make his brain *work*. "How do I stop the rumors?"

"I don't know that it's possible."

"Bloody, bloody hell!" Standing, Steele began to pace.

Sir Lee watched him with keen eyes. "Why are you so reticent to share how you saved the prince's life?"

He turned away, scraping his brain for a way to keep the boys from danger when every scum-of-the-earth felon saw harming them as a payday. "If you know the story, then why do you keep asking me about it?"

"It's a matter of ownership."

Steele turned on his heel. "What the blazes does that mean?"

"It means you lead separate lives. One of which you will not own up to. It makes for a very unhealthy agent."

Stopping in his tracks, Steele faced the former spymaster. "I'm not your agent! And I'd appreciate you keeping out of my life." He knew that he was talking more about Miss West than about being a Sentinel, but the sentiment was real. "I'm only helping you with Benbrook because you blackmailed me into it. Don't think that gives you leave to dabble in my personal business."

"Like your *affaire* with Miss West?"

"I'm not having an *affaire* with Miss West! I've never even touched her before today! Stay out of my life, Sir Lee!"

"Which life? The solicitor-general's or the viscount's or the Sentinel's?"

Steele scowled. "What are you talking about?"

"Your friends. The Cutlers. At Tipton's Tavern they were quite free about showing off that fancy club you fellows use. After a few pints of brew loosened their tongues, they were happy to explain how the iron-topped tipstaff is a far more reliable weapon than any pistol." Sir Lee leaned back into the chair. "Your secret won't be safe for long if people put together the masked man who's been meting out his own brand of justice about town with the man raised by the Cutlers."

Steele opened his hands in exasperation. "What am I to you? A puzzle to be properly fitted? A man to be set in his place? A scapegoat to be hung out to dry?"

"Until you reconcile who you are, you can never find peace."

"What business is it of yours? What the blazes do you care if I'm at peace or not?"

Rubbing his chin, Sir Lee exhaled. "I suppose I can't help it; when I see a problem I long to fix it."

"I'm not a problem. I don't have any problems besides trying to stop a killer. Which is why you're here. And while we're busy tossing out theories about who is behind this whole plot, you're like a puppet master yanking on everyone's strings, Sir Lee. How do I know you're not behind it?"

"Because Patrick Devonshire is," Sir Lee declared with a flourish.

"Patrick, the nephew? Benbrook's brother's son?"

"Yes."

"He's left India?"

"I assume that he's in England to be able to place a price on Benbrook's head." Sir Lee scratched his craggy cheek. "Although I've yet to be able to connect him to the carriage accident that killed Seth and

Felix's parents." He looked up. "But he's behind it all. I'm sure of it. If he kills Benbrook and then the boys, he inherits it all. It's a simple case of greed."

"But his father would inherit."

"His father is dead. He died about the time this whole nasty business began. If Benbrook and the boys are eliminated, then everything would go to Patrick Devonshire."

"How can you be so sure it's Patrick Devonshire?"

"There was an attempt on Benbrook's life yesterday. We caught the bugger trying to escape Dorset."

Steele's hands clenched. "An 'attempt' . . . Is Benbrook all right?"

"He's fine."

"And did you catch Devonshire?"

"Nay. But we got his hired hand. Now we have a witness who links everything back to Patrick Devonshire. The problem is, the man seems unwilling to point any other fingers. I'd love to know who else is in Patrick's employ. I'd bet ten pounds your former footman Claude would be in the mix."

Steele's hands clenched. "If I ever get my hands on that bugger . . ."

"Which, Devonshire or Claude?"

"Either will do, but both would be ideal."

Exhaling, Sir Lee waved a hand. "My guess is that Patrick Devonshire is circulating the rumor about you being behind the murders to deflect any blame from centering on him. I'm sure his plan was that he be in India or parts abroad when word reached him of the deaths. Your activities as a Sentinel may also play into the mix if he knows of them."

"He doesn't," Steele bit out.

"Does anyone?"

As he thought of the night he'd been unconscious in the barn, Steele's gut clenched. "I don't think so."

"But you're not sure." It was a statement, not a question.

Steele rubbed his hands over his jaw, wondering if he dared ask. He took a chance. "Do you know anything about a widow involved with Lucifer Laverty?"

Sir Lee's eyes widened, then narrowed. "No. Do you think she's in league with Patrick Devonshire?"

"No." Steel shook his head. "Not with Devonshire or the plot. I just . . . it's an unrelated matter."

Sir Lee's gaze glistened with warning. "Lucifer Laverty is as nasty a bloke as they come. Are you sure you want me to dig in that quarter?"

Steele nodded. "Yes. It's just . . . you asked if anyone might know about my nocturnal activities . . ."

"And she might?"

"Yes. But it's more than that. She . . . I think she may be in trouble and I want to try to help her if I can."

The old gent nodded. "I'll look into it. I have some contacts within Lucifer Laverty's organization."

"How come I'm not surprised?"

"Just because they're criminals does not mean that they're not patriotic." Sir Lee leaned forward, his green gaze filled with curiosity. "In your travels about London at night, have you learned anything about Lucifer Laverty that might be helpful?"

"Aside from astonishingly well-organized thievery, Lucifer Laverty's favorite forms of commerce are favors and debt. I don't envy anyone on the debtor's side of the ledger where's he's concerned. The man's a viper." Steele exhaled. "Did the man you caught in Dorset by any chance know Devonshire's whereabouts?"

"Nay."

"So our killer is still on the loose. And he may be in London."

"Yes, and Benbrook will be arriving from Dorset shortly."

Steele straightened. "He doesn't trust me to protect the boys?"

"That's not the issue at all. The attempt on his life really scared him." Sir Lee shifted in his chair. "I think he's feeling . . . mortal, and being with the boys will be a comfort to him. He misses them terribly."

"Benbrook in London means everyone who is a target will be in one city. I don't like it." Stepping over to the window, Steele peered down at the garden. It was empty. Where were the boys and Miss West?

Steele walked over to the entry door and yanked it open. "Dudley!"

The butler scrambled from down the hall. "Yes, my lord?"

"I want you to make sure the boys are with two footmen at all times, even while inside."

"Yes, Your Lordship."

"And I want every room in the house checked. Every floor, every room, closets, the whole house."

"Again, my lord?"

"It's been two days. Have it done."

"Yes, my lord."

Steele gnawed on his lip, tempted to know where Miss West might be. So tempted . . . "By the by, where are the boys?"

"At the park, my lord."

Alarm sliced through him. "The park? When did they go? Who went with them?"

"Miss West and two footmen, Zachariah and Foster, accompanied the boys, my lord." At the look on Steele's face, Dudley asked, "Should they not have gone?"

"No. No. They did what they were supposed to, they told you and were well accompanied." Still, a panicky feeling ate at his guts. He wanted the boys close, Miss West even nearer. He knew that it was completely irrational, but he had the sudden urge to lock them in the house and hold them dear. At least until Patrick Devonshire was no longer a threat. "Which park? The one across the street?"

"No, my lord. Coleridge Square Park is where they went."

Steele knew he was going before the words were out of his mouth. "I'll join them."

"I'll get your hat and gloves, my lord." Bowing, the butler stepped from the room.

Sir Lee's gaze was knowing. "You care for those boys."

"Of course I do."

"They're not just Benbrook's brood?"

Steele shifted his shoulders, feeling the slight ache from where the rock had struck him. "They're . . . my family. If anything happens to those boys, I'll never forgive myself."

Placing his hat on his head, Sir Lee nodded. "Have a care. I'm off to go see about a viper named Lucifer Laverty."

# Chapter 34

Abigail walked with Seth and Felix toward Coleridge Square Park, her mind whirling. Zachariah and Foster trailed behind, their boots shuffling along the sidewalk. The boys rambled on about who they might see at the park and the games they might play, but Abigail hardly heard them.

*I love Lord Steele*, Abigail marveled. *In a way I've never loved anyone before.*

It wasn't the infatuated puppyish adoration she'd felt for Phineas.

It wasn't the fairy-tale dream she'd secretly imagined as a child.

Her feelings for Steele . . . Jason . . . She shivered with delight. Her feelings went beyond anything she'd ever felt before. Her body yearned for his as a flower seeks the sun. Her mind longed to connect with him on every level. Her heart . . . as a swan seeks its lifelong mate, with all her heart she wanted to be his partner, forever.

Abigail swallowed, clutching her hand to her chest. She realized that her feelings for Steele probably weren't reciprocated. He was fond of her, that was clear. He was too much of a true gentleman to toy with her.

*And that kiss!*

It had been beyond her wildest dreams. She'd practically floated away on a cloud.

Yet at this moment the man who'd kissed her as sweetly as she'd ever been kissed was with Mr. Linder-Myer discussing marriage to another.

*Stop being unrealistic*, she told herself. *What did you expect? A proposal on bended knee?*

She was older now, more hardened to the ways of men. She knew that she had to push aside any girlish heartache as the impractical yearnings of a fairy-tale fantasy. She was a scarlet woman, a woman of the world; she should be realistic about her future and any possibility with this man.

*I should offer to become his mistress*, she realized.

But could she continue on as Seth and Felix's governess? No. She couldn't be a proper role model to them; it would be wrong. A child needed someone to look up to, someone to set an example. A child needed . . .

*A child.*

*Steele's child. Nothing in this world would make me happier than to bear his child.* The realization was like a lightning bolt blasting through her, changing . . . *everything.*

She suddenly knew, without question, that she could *not* be Steele's mistress, no matter what justifications she tried to make.

She could become pregnant—and by so doing, condemn that child to a life as the bastard of the

Viscount Steele. *Bastard*. The idea chilled her to the bone. *By-blow, born on the wrong side of the blanket, out-of-wedlock . . .*

Abigail clutched her middle, feeling ill.

She'd always wondered if she was barren. She'd been with Phineas, and nothing had happened. She'd been with the masked man, and nothing had happened. Sick woman that she was, part of her wanted to believe that she truly was barren.

But she couldn't take that chance, not when an innocent child's life lay in the balance. Not when she knew that deep down she yearned to carry Steele's babe.

"Where is everyone?" Felix demanded, kicking a stone.

Abigail looked up, shocked to note that they'd reached the grassy hummock where their friends usually congregated.

The glade was empty.

Birds flitted through the trees, chirping merrily. A squirrel ran up a tree. But no human could be seen.

"Oh my gosh!" Abigail slapped her palm to her forehead. "The fair!" Turning to the boys, she explained, "I'm so sorry. I forgot about the street fair at King's Cross. It's this afternoon."

"Can we go?" Felix asked.

Abigail winced. "I don't think Lord Steele would approve."

"Uncle Jason!" Seth demanded. "You must call him Uncle Jason."

Rubbing his back, Abigail smiled. "He's your Uncle Jason. To me he's Lord Steele."

Felix crossed his arms, his disappointment as clear

as the nose on his face. "I want to go to the street fair!"

Abigail shook her head. "You know the rules: We must inform Dudley of where we are going. I told him Coleridge Square Park. So that is were we must be."

Felix's eyes narrowed, and from the look on his face, his mind was working through ways to get what he wanted. "The rules also require that we are with two adults at all times."

"Yes."

"So why can't Zachariah go back to the house and tell Dudley that we're going to the street fair? That leaves us with you and Foster."

Biting her lip, Abigail considered the suggestion. "How about this? How about Zachariah goes back to the house and *asks* Lord Steele permission for us to go to the street fair? We'll wait here at the park, and if your uncle says yes, then we shall go."

Felix nodded. "Accepted!"

Abigail smiled. "You have the makings of an excellent barrister, Felix."

"What about me?" Seth stomped his foot. "What do I have the makings of?"

"I see you having the making of a tiger." Touching Seth's shoulder, Abigail jumped away. "Tag!"

For the next ten minutes, Seth, Felix, Abigail, and Foster played tag the tiger. Abigail thanked the heavens the lads were entertained while they waited for Zachariah's return.

"Abby," a voice whispered. "Abby the Gale."

Abigail's head whipped around.

She gasped.

Reggie stood in the shade under a nearby oak tree. He was taller than she remembered and had a new scar along his left cheek. Yet she'd know the pale-haired, brawny young man anywhere.

Her heart squeezed with joy at seeing him. Licking her lips, she spoke to the boys, "Felix, Seth!"

The lads looked over at her.

"I'm going to say hello to an acquaintance. I'll be right back."

They waved and continued their game.

Turning, she quickly moved toward her brother, and together they slipped behind the large oak tree.

She threw her arms around him and hugged him close. He smelled of man and beer and felt bigger than Abigail remembered. His muscles had thickened, his shoulders had widened. She hugged him so as never again to let him go.

He squeezed her tightly. "Ah, Abby the Gale. It's been too long."

After long moments, she found her voice, "How did you find me?"

Exhaling, he stared down at her. His light blue eyes glowed with affection. "You look good. You finally have some meat on yer bones."

"Where've you been?" she asked as a million questions rushed through her mind. "Your letter sounded so dire. I was terrified that something terrible had happened to you."

All gladness washed from his features as his face fell and his gaze darkened. He pulled her deeper into the grove, away from where the boys played. The trees shielded them from the sun and any stray eyes.

"What did you do?" she asked, fearfully.

Releasing her, he stepped away. His gray coat was worn at the elbows, his brown breeches torn at the knee, and his brown boots badly scuffed. Still, he was healthy, and that's all that mattered to his sister.

"Do you need money?" she asked. "I can get you some . . ."

He barked a mirthless laugh. "Not enough to cover my debts."

"How much do you need?"

Looking up at her, his gaze was sad beyond his twenty years. "I saw an opportunity and I took it, Abby."

Her heart filled with dread weighing a stone. "What happened?"

"I didn't realize that I was crossing a man you do not cross."

"Lucifer Laverty."

His brow furrowed.

Noting his surprise, she explained, "I've been asking around town for you."

"So you know."

Fear and anger washed through her. "I know nothing beyond the fact that you're involved with some very dangerous people."

"You don't know the half of it," he muttered. Swallowing, he ran his hand through his fair hair. "Look, I found a way out. Lucifer Laverty will forgive my debts and call things square."

"How?"

"I made a deal."

Clenching her hands, she tried to keep the alarm from her voice. Reggie often tried to dig his way out of a hole by digging deeper. "What kind of deal?"

"You come with me . . . to him."

"I don't understand."

"He wants to meet you."

"And do what with me?" she demanded. Swallowing, she lowered her voice, trying to maintain her frayed calm. "For what purpose?"

"He promised me you wouldn't be harmed."

"And you believe him?" Her voice was incredulous.

"I do. No matter that he's a criminal, when he makes a deal, he sticks with it."

Turning away disgusted, Abigail pressed her hand to her aching head. "You have to believe him in order to justify introducing your sister to the most notorious criminal of London. I don't believe him. I can't fathom why he wants anything to do with me." She threw up her hands. "How does he even know that I exist?"

"Will you come?" he begged. "They'll kill me if I don't bring you."

She stilled. "Truly?"

"Yes. It's either bring you or die. That's the deal. Either way, Lucifer Laverty sees the debt as paid."

Exhaling, Abigail peeked through the branches and watched the lads playing with Foster. So innocent, so dear. She swallowed. She'd miss them terribly if anything happened to her.

And Steele . . .

Reggie stepped forward. "They will kill me, Abby. This is my final chance to clear my debt. The only way, they said, or I'll be taking a swim in the Thames, permanently." He held open his hands. "Could you live with that, Abby? Being the cause of my murder?"

Stabbing a finger at him, she growled, "I didn't

cause this! You did!"

"I wouldn't be in this fix if you'd kept your skirts lowered with that Byrnwyck bastard! It's your fault I'm running from the law!"

Gritting her teeth, Abigail felt the unfairness of his charge like a thundercloud inside her, roaring with fury. But the old guilt reared its ugly head, filling her with shame and making her feel responsible. When her parents had died, they charged her with looking after her brother. She'd done a pretty miserable job of it, and if she could help Reggie, she would, come hell or what may.

But he was twenty years old. When would he finally grow up and take responsibility for his own actions? When would he stop blaming her for his stupid choices?

"Abby," Reggie licked his lips. "I'm asking you this as a favor to me. Lucifer promised me he wouldn't hurt you. I don't think that it's too much to ask with my life at stake. Do you?"

"But it makes no sense! What does he want with me?"

"I don't know . . . but if you don't come . . ." He let the threat hang in the air.

"Fine. Let me get the boys home and I'll tell Lord Steele . . ." What? What could she tell the man that would convince him to let her throw herself at the mercy of Lucifer Laverty?

Steele would never allow her to be placed in such danger.

Steele would fight for her, she suddenly knew.

No matter that his feelings did not perfectly match hers, Jason Dagwood, Viscount Steele, was the kind of man who would do battle for his friends and never surrender.

The knowledge warmed her heart and gave her strength.

Hope blossomed within her.

If anyone could see a way out of this mess, it was Steele. "When I bring the boys home—"

"No!" Reggie shook his fist. "The boys come with us!"

Her heart skipped a beat. "What?"

"That's the deal. I bring you and the Devonshire boys and all my debts are paid."

The sky seemed to darken, the breeze suddenly died, and the birds in the trees fell silent. Sudden coldness draped Abigail's heart, and every emotion inside her deadened until she was as icy as a winter's frost. Her brother had just crossed the line between right and wrong so glaringly that every ounce of responsibility and guilt that had ever plagued her evaporated into mist. "Never."

"They'll kill me, Abby!"

"I will not put my children in danger."

"They're not your children!" Reggie shrieked. "You're a hired nanny! To them you're nothing but an interchangeable servant! I'm your flesh and blood!"

"They're children!"

"You're responsible for me! Me!" He slapped his chest. "The one you left without a home! The one you dragged through the streets! The one who tried to save you from the Byrnwycks! This mess is all your fault, and you are *beholden* to me to get me out of it!"

At that second, it was as if a guillotine dropped,

slicing Abigail's life in two. The ghost of who she'd been lay dead on the ground, and a new Abigail emerged from the carnage, freer, bolder, stronger. A feeling of lightness enveloped her, as if it were a new dawn—she had stepped out from the shadow of her brother's troubles, and it was time to start living her own life.

She didn't control her brother and was not accountable for his decisions. He clearly didn't consider her when making his choices; she didn't owe him her life, but she owed it to herself.

She shook her head, her voice low, confident, and laced with sadness. "You have dug yourself into a hole, Reggie, and for that, I am sorry."

Clenching her hands, her voice rose with fervor, "But you are twenty years old. And it is time for you to claim ownership of your own actions. You are the only one responsible for this fix. And I will not allow you to endanger two innocent boys because *you* cast *yourself* into the briars."

"But Abigail—"

"No, Reggie. Leave us alone. I love you but I can't abide by you hurting anyone else. Please go."

# Chapter 35

"**O**h no!" Steele screamed, running forward to the footman lying on the grass. His heart was in his throat and panic thundered through his veins. "Foster! Foster! What happened?"

Squatting beside his footman, Steele grasped his arm and helped Foster sit up. The man's face was battered; blood matted his hair and dripped from his nose. His leg was bent at an odd angle, clearly broken. "I'm sorry, m'lord! I'm so sorry!"

"Are you all right? Where are the boys? Miss West?"

"I'm fine . . ." The man's head swayed as a small sob escaped from his throat. "But the boys! The boys! They stole the boys!"

Swallowing hard, Steele forced his heartbeat to calm. "But they're alive?"

Sniffing, Foster nodded. "Last I saw 'em, the boys were all right. Them and Miss West."

Steele almost sagged with relief. They were alive! *Please, dear God, give me a chance to save them!*

Bowing his head, the footman began to sob.

"Tell me what happened, Foster! Please, tell me!"

"There were too many of them!" The footman wiped his bloody nose with his sleeve. "I fought and fought but then my leg . . ."

"Who?" Steele demanded. "Who were they?"

The footman's eyes cleared, then narrowed, and he spat. "Claude was with them. I thought he came ta help, but he was with the bastards!"

Steele felt his insides go cold. "Claude." The word was an oath; when Steele got his hands on his former servant, he'd kill him. "Tell me everything, Foster. Every last detail."

Wiping his eyes, Foster sniffed. "Miss West went to talk with a young man. She said he was an acquaintance. Then they argued. She told him to go away. Then she told the boys we had to leave. Quickly, she said. But Felix wouldn't budge; he wanted to go to the fair, ya see."

"I know, Zachariah told me," Steele interjected, imagining the young boy demanding that his plan be executed. He was only eight years old; he had not known the danger he was in.

"Miss West demanded they go right away. Seth began ta cry and Felix argued. The men must've been waiting nearby and the ruckus . . . well, the knaves came. Claude and the others."

Steele's heart pounded as fear laced his tongue. "How many?"

The footman frowned. "Five, six? They were big 'uns. And nasty blokes."

Steele swallowed. "What happened then?"

"Claude tried to grab Miss West but she . . . she fought him." Foster's voice was filled with pride. "She was quick, she was—one minute he was grabbing her arm and the next he was on the ground."

*That's my girl!* Steele was shocked at the sudden tears that burned his eyes and the unfamiliar longing that gripped his heart.

Foster continued, "She told us to run. But there were too many."

Steele gripped Foster's arm, fear clenching his heart. "Did they hurt the boys? Miss West?"

Foster's eyes were filled with the terror at the memory. "Felix . . . he ran to a tree and climbed to the top. But Seth . . ." Foster gulped. "One of the buggers grabbed Seth and tossed him over his shoulder!"

Bile rose in Steele's throat. *Please God! Please God! Please God!*

Foster shook his head. "Miss West . . . she went crazy, screaming and . . . she jumped on the man like nothing I've ever seen, tearing at his eyes, yanking on his hair. Screaming and screaming. The man dropped Seth and turned on her."

Steele's heart stopped. Gripping Foster's coat, he cried, "Is she all right? Did they hurt her?"

Foster shook his head, his eyes filled with amazement. "The first fella she'd been talking to jumped in the fray and he wouldn't let anyone touch her. He fought against his own, screaming that Lucifer had promised that she not be hurt."

Steele stilled, his awareness flaring. "Lucifer? Are you sure?"

"Definitely. He said Lucifer. And when the others heard that name, they stopped and let her go."

"They let her go?"

"No, they made the first fella, the one who'd

helped her, hold her arm and keep her from running, not that she would've ever left Felix and Seth. She wouldn't do that."

"No, she wouldn't." Steele wondered about the man who'd helped Miss West, but pushed it aside for later thought. "What happened then?"

"One of the buggers, a hairy fella as big as an ox, he told Felix that he'd break Seth's arm unless Felix came down. Felix was very brave . . . he did as they said. Then they dragged 'em all away . . . Miss West, the boys . . . and the young fella that had helped Miss West . . . they dragged him, too."

Steele swallowed, tasting panic. "But they weren't hurt?"

Foster shook his head. "They were unharmed, last I saw 'em." He looked up, his face filled with fear. "But where have they gone? What are they doing with them? Why did they take them?"

Licking his dry lips, Steele released the footman and stood. His heart thundered, his mind raced, and his breath was coming in hard, fast surges.

"What'll we do?" Foster cried. "What'll we do?"

"First I need to get you medical attention." Exhaling, Steele clenched his hands. "Then I'll bring them home."

# Chapter 36

Abigail paced the small room, her shoes echoing softly on the thin wool drugget covering the floor. The chamber was about twenty paces long and twenty paces wide, with a heavy wooden door to the hallway that was bolted from the other side.

To her left was a side door leading to the small chamber where the boys slept, and to her right a dirty barred window that could not open more than two inches. She'd pushed it open as far as it would go, but the window was secured by a thick chain hammered into the wood. She could not escape that route. But even if she succeeded getting out that window, it was a four-story drop to the ground.

Nor could she try to wave down a Good Samaritan or call for help, since the window looked out over a deserted alleyway and no street was anywhere near. The only good things the window could provide were a hint of fresh air in the musty room and a sense of the hour. The sun had set, darkness had fallen, and by her reckoning it must be about ten o'clock.

The air smelled of burning wood from the smoldering hearth and the single tallow candle that provided the only dim light in the room. Shadows yawned wide, pricking at her nerves and exacerbating her anxiety.

Hugging herself, Abigail exhaled, frustrated, afraid, and wondering what the blazes a criminal like Lucifer Laverty wanted with her and Seth and Felix. The most likely scenario Abigail could scratch up was that they were being held for ransom. And that meant the threat of death. She shuddered. But to cross the Solicitor-General of England?

Then there was the possibility that this was some sort of scheme to exact revenge against Lord Steele. And there had been that attack on him at the park. She did not doubt that it all was related. But how? And if the villain was willing to attack the solicitor-general and kidnap two boys in broad daylight, then what else was he willing to do?

But no, she couldn't think such things or she'd be useless to the boys. They needed her to be calm, to be ready to grab any opportunity that presented itself. She had to be at her very, very best . . .

And she was terrified that she wasn't up to the task.

Clenching her hands, she pushed aside all fears of inadequacy, knowing that she would do whatever necessary to save Seth and Felix from harm . . .

Abigail stepped over to the side door and opened it slightly, checking on them for the thousandth time that night.

A small tallow candle burned on the bedside table, encasing the boys' slumbering faces in a golden glow. They huddled together in sleep, fatigued from the crying and fear that had gripped them since the kidnapping that afternoon.

The tiny room was barely big enough for the bed in which they slept and the bedside table upon which the candle sat. Abigail guessed that it might have been a dressing room or closet at one time. In this instance, however, it was being used by Lucifer Laverty as a prison cell.

The name brought bumps of panic to her skin.

They were at the mercy of one of the most feared and reviled men in London.

And it was Reggie's fault. She still couldn't believe that Reggie had traded her and the boys to save his skin. Her hands clenched. She wanted to strangle him for it.

Her heart pinched as her anger boiled. He was a reckless fool!

Yet he'd fought his own men and paid dearly for it. When they'd arrived at the house, the brutes had been less than gentle with her baby brother as they'd dragged him off to parts unknown.

*Please let the stupid idiot be all right*, she prayed.

Hugging herself, she walked over to the window. Peering through the small opening, Abigail stared at the rooftops, wondering where Steele might be. He'd be terrified, angry, and probably already had an army of Bow Street Runners scouring London for them.

The thought gave her hope . . . If anyone could save them, it was Steele.

She was overwhelmed by the sudden realization that she counted on him and trusted him as she had no other. He shouldered her troubles, accepting them as his own, making her feel as if she were not so very alone in this world. With him, she found a love that went beyond anything she'd ever felt for anyone before, an affinity that was more like a sense of partnership.

The thought that she might never see him again brought harsh tears to her eyes. Brushing them away, she mentally chided herself to be brave, to be a woman worthy of Lord Steele.

"Where are you?" she whispered to the man she loved. "I need you."

At that very moment, Steele stood on the rooftop two stories above Abigail, with Lucifer Laverty's henchman unconscious at his feet. He wore his Sentinel costume like a second skin, truly embracing his former calling so he could be the man he needed to be to save his family.

Every time he thought of Seth or Felix or Abigail, panic would rush through him. But he pushed it down, making sure that his every move was coolly calculated to bring the people he loved home with him safely.

Squatting down, he expertly tied the rope to the chimney joint and yanked it tight. The joint held secure. He uncoiled the rest of the rope and wrapped it around his waist and over his shoulder like a pulley. He stepped over to the edge of the rooftop and looked down six stories into the alley, satisfied to see that it was still deserted.

If Sir Lee's information proved true, Abigail was just twenty or so feet below him. A faint glow of light shone through the small opening of the window where she was supposedly being held. His heart hammered, and his palms were moist inside his gloves.

But he ignored his apprehension, knowing there was a job to do.

Turning, he slowly lowered himself over the edge of the roof and down the side of the house. His feet crept downward as inch by inch he dropped toward that opening. He was careful not to make a sound. According to Sir Lee, there were at least twenty of Lucifer Laverty's men inside the house. Any one of those ruffians would gladly murder him for interfering with Lucifer's plans.

Finally he made it to the opening and exhaled with relief. He peered inside.

His breath caught.

Abigail paced before the mantel, looking whole and hale and more beautiful than any woman he'd ever laid eyes upon in his life.

*I love her*, he realized in that moment. It was like a lightning bolt striking him deep in his soul, searing him with the knowledge that she was his mate.

*I need her*, he realized. *To make me whole.*

He swallowed, overcome.

Never in his life had he experienced such absolute harmony between his heart and his head. Intellectually he knew she was his equal; in his heart he recognized there was no other for him.

He was about to whisper her name, but noticed that she'd suddenly stopped pacing and that her head had swung toward the hallway door expectantly.

Male voices resounded in the hallway, followed by the stomping of booted feet.

Steele went cold.

Quickly Abigail moved before a closed side door, her hands raised into fists before her.

*The boys are in there*, he suddenly knew. Abigail was a lioness, protecting those she loved. Never had he admired a woman more.

The sound of the bolt sliding in the lock met his ears.

Steele tensed, eyeing the thick chain securing the window closed. He would not be able to breach the chain to help Abigail without drawing Lucifer's henchmen. And Gabriel and Andrew Cutler weren't yet in place to execute their plan.

*We need more time!* But they seemingly hadn't harmed Abigail and the boys, and Steele had to pray that they wouldn't just yet.

Leaning forward, he angled away from the opening so he could not be seen but he could see and hear what occurred within. If he needed to, he'd slam through that barred window, come hell or what may.

The door creaked open, splashing a beam of light across the chamber's floor.

He tensed.

The door opened wider and a fist holding a tall, lit candlestick was thrust through the opening, followed by a blond-haired man.

Abigail blinked. "Mr. Littlethom?"

*Son of a bitch! What's he doing here?*

For a moment Littlethom stood in the threshold, eyeing the room, then his gaze landed on Abigail and his face lit into a wide, brilliant smile. "Miss West! I don't know the last time that I was so glad to see someone!"

"I don't . . . I don't understand," she stammered.

Littlethom bowed with a flourish. "I'm here to save you."

# Chapter 37

Littlethom stepped into the room, followed by a heavyset brute with thick fists and quick eyes. Abigail swallowed. The man's curled fists were as big as ham hocks.

Abigail tensed, warily watching the brute as he closed the door behind him.

"Oh, have no fear, Miss West," the handsome tutor chided with a wave of his hand. He was dressed in his old-fashioned gray breeches and an elbow-worn brown coat. His blond hair was slicked back with pomade. Littlethom's mien was relaxed, his smile easy. "William is just here on Mr. Laverty's behalf. So you will know that what I say carries weight and is spoken in seriousness."

*That brute has enough weight to ensure that I definitely will take him seriously*, she thought.

The tutor set the candle down on the small table by the side door, and Abigail stood her ground and would not move away from her position. She caught a whiff of violet cologne as he stepped back, keeping his distance. She could not fathom his purpose here and forced her mind to try to grasp it all.

Stepping back, Littlethom motioned for the brute named William to stand by the barred window. The man stomped across the small chamber, his gaze not once leaving Abigail's face. His eyes reminded Abigail of a hawk, sharp and knowing.

Silently the man peered out the small opening in the window and then spun on his heel. He stood before the window, his shoulders squared, his hands clutched before him.

Littlethom gave an apologetic smile. "I know this is very untoward, but I will endeavor to explain."

"Please do," she bit out.

"This entire situation is the invention of Lord Steele. He placed the children in danger in order to convince Lord Benbrook to make him his heir."

Abigail shook her head. "I don't believe you."

"I applaud your loyalty, Miss West. But I have proof positive of what I speak." Littlethom reached inside his coat pocket, pulling out a roll of vellum.

"What's that?" Abigail asked.

"This is Steele's demand that Benbrook make him his heir, his reasoning being that there is a threat against the children. It is also the document itself, which would declare Steele the heir to everything owned by Benbrook, unsigned, of course. Benbrook has not yet agreed, which is why the boys were kidnapped. Benbrook is on his way to London at this moment, just as Steele had planned."

The man continued, his tone assured, "Steele, you see, is known as the most striving fellow in the kingdom. Everyone knows that he'll do anything to further his ambitions. Even more so, he wants revenge against Benbrook for never accepting him into his family. If Benbrook makes him his heir, then Steele gets the ultimate revenge—money, title . . . everything. He also becomes the man he has always striven to be."

Shaking his head, Littlethom sighed. "It is astonishing the lengths to which a man will go to sate his ambitions."

She shook her head. "I don't believe it."

"Oh, you must, for I have the proof." Littlethom held out the documents. "But there is more. You recall Mr. Lyner-Mider, the agency representative?"

Abigail did not bother to correct him and simply nodded.

"The old gent is not an agency representative at all! He's a nobleman, for heaven's sake! A knight, no less! His name is Sir Lee Devane."

Her suspicions must have shown on her face, because Littlethom's brows rose. "I see you had your own doubts, too. You must have noticed how they interact, all of the secret meetings, messages flying to and fro. Why would an agency representative be so involved in Lord Steele's personal business?"

Littlethom pointed his finger to the ceiling. "You're a smart woman; you must have noticed how strange this all is. But now you must be asking yourself the real questions—why would a knighted gentleman be pretending to work for an employment agency and why would he be so intimately involved with Steele?"

Littlethom was right—she was asking herself those very questions.

Triumphantly he declared, "Because he's in league with Steele! They planned this whole devious plot together!"

In the glow of the candlelight, the tutor's handsome face shone with fervor. "Sir Lee brought Benbrook to London in the first instance. He eliminated any servants who'd known the family before and made sure to bring in people who would be beholden to him for the job. People who had"—he coughed into his fist and gave a rueful smile—"less than stellar references . . . or perhaps were missing letters of reference all together."

He opened his hands. "Not that I am making any judgments on you, Miss West. I made it my business to learn all of the particulars of that terrible Byrnwyck affair . . . The scandalous gossip follows you like a rotten stench that will not go away. You are forever tainted as the grasping governess who tried to snare the lord's son by lifting her skirts . . ."

Inside she cringed. But she kept her face fixed.

Littlethom shook his head. "I assure you I don't believe a word of it. You could never be so cold-blooded. You must have truly believed that he loved you."

At the look on her face, he cried, "You did! You believed that he would marry you!"

She clenched her teeth as her cheeks burned.

Littlethom tsked. "Noblemen . . . they often don't have a noble bone in their bodies. And knowing your disgraceful history, Steele probably thought he'd found himself a little sweetener to go with his plan. I only pray that you didn't fall for his honeyed words and outrageous lies.

"But I stray from the real topic," he went on. "The whole Byrnwyck scandal left you in a terrible coil— forever. You will always be missing that reference and be scandalously tainted. Which is why Sir Lee selected you. He wanted someone who desperately needed the position, someone who would not speak out if things were a bit . . . unusual."

Scratching his temple, he sniffed. "But he underestimated you, Miss West. He did not count on your kindness to others and your inherent goodness. I do, and feel that you deserve to know the truth behind this terrible business."

Stepping forward, he extended the documents toward her. "Go on, see for yourself that all I say is true. You be the judge."

With her heart racing and her mouth dry as dust, Abigail reached out and snatched the vellum from his hands. Quickly she returned to her post before the side door, glaring at the men, making sure that they did not make any moves toward her.

Unrolling the document, she angled it so that she could catch the light of the nearby candle, read the pages, and watch the two men at the same time.

Abigail blinked, shocked that the documents were as he said.

Littlethom winced. "I know it's disappointing when someone you admire turns out to be a scoundrel, but the facts are as I describe them. Steele has placed those sweet, innocent boys in danger purely to further his own ambitions. The man's a lowly crook dressing himself in airs and titles. And recently I learned the most astonishingly shocking thing of all about the *superior* Lord Steele!"

Curling his finger, Littlethom leaned forward with a conspiratorial air. "Those friends of his from Dorset; Cutler, I think their name is . . . Well, they were foxed in a tavern the other night, crowing about how they dress up in black"—he waved a hand at his chin—"wear these masks over their faces, and use fancy iron-topped tipstaffs to prance about at night brawling!"

Abigail felt the color drain from her face and her stomach drop.

Littlethom nodded. "It's true! They went on and on about all of the fighting they do, the blood, the guts, the gore . . . and the worst of it is . . . Steele must be one of them! He was raised by them; they call him brother! And I have it on good authority, from Steele's former butler, Carlton, that Steele is out at all hours of the night, and hardly has any evening attire to repair or clean! The man's a gutter ruffian! No wonder he's so cavalier about killing two boys!"

Abigail felt ill. Her mind was spinning, her insides clenched. She looked up at Littlethom. "So much of what you say bears the color of truth; it cannot be denied."

Littlethom beamed. "You're a smart woman, Miss West, and I applaud you."

"So you are going to let us go?"

Biting his lower lip, Littlethom bridged his hands. "I cannot in good conscience allow the boys to go back to Steele; it's too dangerous. I'm going to take them to a safe place where they will be protected from his evil designs."

"And me?"

"You are free to go. You and your brother."

Her heart skipped a beat. "Lucifer's letting Reggie go?"

"I arranged for it. But I was hoping"—his smile

was self-effacing—"that you would join me . . . to where I take the boys, of course."

"Why would you do so many kind things for me and my brother? I don't understand."

Littlethom's eyes darkened and his voice deepened. "Is it not patently clear, my dear? I admire you. I find you so *deliciously* appealing . . . I cannot get you out of my mind."

Licking his lips, he stepped forward. "I would not protest if you chose to demonstrate your gratitude . . ."

"I'll show you my gratitude," she cried, tossing the papers at his face, grabbing the candlestick from the table, and whipping it around so that the candle flew out and she slammed the metal against his temple.

Nigel Littlethom dropped to the floor with a loud thud.

With her heart racing, Abigail quickly stepped on the wick of the candle, snuffing it out.

The brute by window showed no surprise as he slowly unlocked his hands. His eyes fixed on her, cool, unemotional, and *terrifying*.

She raised the candlestick high over her head. Her arm quaked but her resolve never wavered.

Suddenly the brute's eyes widened. Arching his back, he gasped. He moved forward one booming step, then another, then he collapsed to the floor.

The hilt of a knife stuck out of his back.

Her heart was in her throat as she leaned forward, trying to grasp what had happened.

"Are you all right?" a male voice whispered.

She looked around the room, but it was empty.

At the opening of the window, two eyes appeared.

*Oh my God!*

The masked gentleman hung outside the window.

Grabbing the black fabric at his mouth, he pulled it low, exposing a face so stunningly familiar, Abigail's heart leaped. "It's me, Steele. Tell me you're all right!"

Dumbly she nodded.

"Are the boys all right?"

She nodded.

"Are they in the room behind you?"

"Yes," she whispered.

"With the chain hammered on, I can't open the window from this side. Do you have something that you can use to wedge it open?"

Lowering the candlestick, she walked over to the window and thrust it through the opening. "Get out of the way."

His face disappeared.

Leaning to the left, she wedged the candlestick against the wood, pushing hard. The chain squealed in protest and the candlestick began to bend. Then suddenly one end of the chain broke free from the wood and the window flew open. Steele caught it before it slammed against the outer wall.

Abigail stepped back.

Steele climbed through the opening, black boots, black breeches, black cloak, iron-headed tipstaff, and all. His face was set with determination, his eyes dark with purpose.

Quickly he strode across the room and opened the door to where the boys slept.

He peered inside.

Letting out a deep breath, he leaned against the

doorpost, his face filled with relief. After a moment he looked over at her. Then he closed the door.

Stepping over to her, he grabbed her shoulders and pulled her close. She fell into his embrace, her heart still hammering, her mind still spinning. His brawny arms held her as if he'd never let her go, making her feel cherished, making her feel safe.

Steele pressed his face into her hair. "Why didn't you believe him?"

"I did." Her voice was muffled as he held her close against his muscled chest.

Releasing her slightly, Steele looked down into her eyes, searching for the revulsion and anger and rejection he feared.

"Much of what he said was truth," she explained, her lovely face filled with earnestness. "The parts about Byrnwyck, Mr. Linder-Myer, you asking to be Benbrook's heir . . ."

"Then why—"

"No matter the truth of it all, everything he said was predicated on the notion that you would intentionally harm Seth and Felix." She said it with such utter confidence, his heart swelled. "I may not be a good judge of men when it comes to how they feel about me, but when it comes to my children, I have no doubts."

His brow furrowed as he tried to understand the amazing woman in his arms. All he understood was one basic truth. "I love you."

She blinked, the shock clear in her eyes.

"You don't know that?" he asked with wonder.

Mutely she shook her head.

"You are able to discern the most significant truths

about the people around you but have no idea that I adore you with all my heart?"

Her eyes suddenly shone with unshed tears, but he could still see the doubt lingering within them. He hugged her close. She fit him so perfectly as if made for him. "I swear I love you, Abigail West, more than I've ever loved any woman in all my life."

The door flew open and Gabriel flew into the room in his Sentinel's attire, followed by Andrew at his heels.

"Ah! Things seem to be well under control here," Gabriel cried, lowering his tipstaff.

The man on the floor groaned.

Gabriel stepped forward, peering down. "This is Devonshire?"

Steele nodded. "The bugger himself."

Abigail blinked. "Devonshire? No, that's Mr. Littlethom."

Gabriel laughed. "Little Thom, eh!"

Looking up at Steele, Abigail's gaze was confused.

He laid his hand to her cheek. "Don't worry, darling. I'll explain everything. But first we have to get you and the boys out of here safely." He turned to Gabriel. "How many are there and what's the best exit?"

Gabriel waved his tipstaff. "It was so kind of you to arrange all this fun on our behalf, but the devils have run off like the chickenhearted knaves they are."

"They're gone?" Steele asked.

"We were ready to do our worst. But before things got really merry, some old gent showed up with another man who, turns out, was Lucifer Laverty himself. Lucifer told everybody to pack it up and let you all go. He said something about having made a deal."

Steele nodded. "Sir Lee."

The side door opened and Felix peeked out. Upon seeing Steele, he raced out and threw his arms around Steele's waist, hugging him tight.

Tears stung Steele's eyes as he clutched the boy close.

"Uncle Jason!" Seth cried, racing out of the side room and grabbing Steele's leg.

As he held his family dear, his heart was so filled with relief and joy that it felt as if it might burst. "Let's go home."

# Chapter 38

**H**ours later, Abigail stood before her chamber window watching the dawn spill across the London sky. A honey pink glow blended with purplish-blue, washing the clouds in a symphony of color that surpassed anything man was capable of creating.

Abigail didn't need any more proof of God's existence after tonight's events. But the beauty of the sun-painted sky reminded her that another day eventually arrived, and with it came a new hope, and perhaps the first day of the rest of her life.

Hugging herself, she rubbed her hands up and down her arms, trying to soothe the anxieties that plagued her.

"I'll find your brother, Abigail," Steele had promised as their party had safely entered the vestibule of the house. Laying a hand on her shoulder, he'd leaned close, whispering in her hair, "One way or another, I will find him and bring him back to you."

Mutely she'd nodded, her eyes burning, her heart aching. At that terrible house they'd searched and searched, but Reggie was nowhere to be found.

Then Steele had kissed her sweetly but swiftly on the lips and departed with his comrades.

So Abigail had been left to worry over the two men she loved best in the world, and focus on the two boys who needed her. Seth and Felix were surprisingly upbeat about the whole misadventure, claiming that they'd known all along that Steele would rescue them and rout the evil villains. Still, Abigail made sure to give them lots of love and make them feel as secure as possible as she tucked them into their beds.

After seeing Felix and Seth well settled, she'd bathed and tried to sleep, but rest would not come.

Watching the sky lighten, Abigail marveled for the thousandth time that night, *Jason Dagwood, Viscount Steele, said he loves me! Adores me, even!*

She couldn't quite believe it and feared that perhaps she'd misunderstood, or that he'd merely been overcome by the events of the night. It was too fantastic to imagine that he truly loved her.

*Stop being a ninny! Steele does not lie. Why can't you believe him?*

The idea that his feelings could match hers . . . Her heart leaped as joy and exhilaration swept over her. Hugging herself tight, she spun on her toes, filled with wonder. She loved him so exceedingly, her heart almost ached with happiness.

But her elation was tempered with guilt. She looked over her shoulder at the closet where she kept her cedar chest with its hidden compartment and her widow's costume.

A small voice whispered in her mind, *Let sleeping dogs lie. Pretend that it was another woman. Steele will never know.*

But deep down, she knew that she could not be with Steele without telling him the truth. Otherwise the lie would hang over their heads like a Sword of Damocles waiting to fall. Abigail would be on pins and needles, forever anticipating that he would realize the connection. Or when he made love to her, she would agonize that somehow he'd *know*.

She could not be with him without telling him the truth.

But once he knew what a scarlet woman she really was, would he still want her? The worry gnawed at her like a parasite until she felt ill with anxiety and fear.

Sounds of raised voices came from downstairs. Tightening the tie of her dressing gown, Abigail strode to the door and peered outside.

Lord Benbrook charged up the stairs, his face a dark mask of fury.

Abigail stepped into the carpeted hallway. "Lord Benbrook."

Stampeding toward her, he swept his hand before him, his lips curled in distaste. "Get out of my way!"

"Seth and Felix are whole and hale and not a hair on their heads has been touched."

Benbrook's steps faltered, and for the first time in their acquaintance, his eyes met hers. The terror and anxiety in his brown gaze was countered with a glimmer of hope.

Abigail's heart pinched with compassion for the poor man. He'd lost his children and clearly was petrified that harm had come to Seth and Felix.

"I know you need to see Seth and Felix with your

own eyes," Abigail murmured. "I'll bring you to them immediately."

He blinked as his eyes shone with unshed tears. Pursing his lips, mutely he nodded.

Turning, she led him down the hallway. He followed close behind her, his boots falling silent on the thick carpeting.

She peered over her shoulder. "They're asleep. Do you want me to wake them?"

He shook his head.

Silently Abigail approached the chamber, with Benbrook following close enough for her to catch a whiff of his fear.

As they entered the room, the halo of light from the bedside candle glowed on the boys peacefully asleep in their beds. Seth lay on his back, his mouth slightly open, his eyes closed, his face tranquil. In the next bed, Felix let out a little snore. Still asleep, he grabbed his blanket, slung it over his shoulder, and rolled over, muttering something about a shoe.

Benbrook froze in the threshold, staring at the slumbering boys. He raised a quaking hand to his mouth. His face furrowed and his eyes filled with tears.

Abigail turned away. "I'll leave you."

Slipping past him, she went into the small sitting room next door.

She opened the window, and a breeze carrying the dewy scent of the morning gently kissed her face and lifted her hair off her shoulders.

As the light brightened the sky, birds chirped merrily in the trees, flitting about. They had no notion of the terrifying events of the night past.

A door behind her closed and footsteps neared. Exhaling, she turned.

Benbrook's shoulders were hunched, his face was gaunt, and he moved with a stiffness that betrayed the toll the misadventure had taken on him. Tiredly he moved into the chamber and lowered himself into an overstuffed chair. Closing his eyes, he leaned back with a weary sigh.

Abigail turned back to stare out the window.

They remained silent for a long time.

"I saw Sir Lee . . ." Benbrook broke the silence. "He told me what happened . . ." His voice cracked.

Hugging herself, she turned to face him.

His hands were clenched in his lap; his face looked haggard and pale, as if the life had almost bled out of him. Then his face lit with anger. "I'd like to kill Patrick Devonshire . . . And that bloody footman, too. Mark my words, I'll be front and center for that hanging, and I'll stay there until the very last kick."

Abigail shivered. She didn't want to see any hangings; she'd seen enough violence to last a lifetime.

Swallowing, he rubbed his hand over his eyes. "Sir Lee says that Steele has already set the wheels in motion, and that I'll get to watch those bloody knaves swing before the month's end."

"Not the boys." She shook her head. "They shouldn't be there."

Benbrook looked up, his eyes lighting with understanding. "Nay," he agreed. "Felix and Seth should not witness it."

Benbrook chewed on his bottom lip. "It was a good idea to bring Seth and Felix here. They're

safe . . . because of Steele. I'd had my doubts . . .
but Sir Lee, he knew it was for the best. And he
was right."

Staring down at his hands, Benbrook muttered, "I
never accepted him . . . and you can hardly blame
me . . . Who wants a commoner who tussles with
criminals to marry your daughter? I wanted more for
Deidre. It's my right as a father!"

Pursing her lips, Abigail held her peace.

Benbrook exhaled a shaky sigh. "But if Steele
wasn't a Sentinel, wasn't who he is . . . the man he
is . . . then my little boys . . ." His face furrowed
with anguish. "Then Seth and Felix would be dead.
And I . . . I would be lost."

Looking up, his eyes brimmed with tears that
spilled down the lines of his haggard cheeks. "My
Deidre saved my little boys. She picked the one
man in all of England who could keep them alive
and safe." He sniffed as a weak smile lit his face.
"She was always smarter than me, my Deidre. She
could see what we needed long before I did." Laying
his head in his hands, he sobbed, his shoulders
shaking.

He reached into his coat pocket and pulled out a
handkerchief. Sniffing, he wiped his eyes and face,
slowly recovering his composure. After a few moments, he sighed. "I'll be glad to get the boys back
to Dorset."

Abigail's stomach sank. "What?"

"You don't think I'll leave them here with a man
who works all hours of the day and night?" Benbrook
wiped his nose. "Steele is not cut out to be a father.
I'll grant you that he's a gifted barrister and a man

who fights for his family . . ." His eyes watered; he pursed his lips and swallowed. "But he's no father."

"You're wrong!" Abigail cried. "Any child would be blessed to have a father who loves him as much as Lord Steele loves those boys!"

Benbrook blinked, doubt filling his gaze.

She stepped forward. "He plays with them and reads to them and understands that boys need to be boys. He treats them well but doesn't spoil them. He's a wonderful father!"

Crouching down beside Benbrook, Abigail begged, "Please don't take Seth and Felix away from us!"

"Us?" Benbrook's eyes narrowed, and he stuck out his bottom lip. "So you do have eyes on his title!"

Abigail suddenly laughed.

"What's so funny?" Benbrook demanded.

"In one moment you talk about how Deidre saw things clearly, and yet you can't see the wonderful son-in-law right before your eyes!"

She shook her head, amazed by the man's folly. "Steele's title is the least of his attributes. He's intelligent and honest and honorable and courageous and so sweetly caring that he makes me want to weep with joy for simply knowing him."

"You make me sound like a saint!" Steele strode through the door.

Her breath caught.

Steele's face was shadowed with the hint of a beard, his eyes were weary, and his clothing was filthy and wrinkled. She'd never seen a more handsome man in all her life.

Elation rocketed through her, and before she could think, she jumped up and raced into his arms.

He wrapped his strong arms around her, hugging her close, holding her dear.

"Your brother's fine," Steele murmured in Abigail's hair, inhaling the scent of heather and woman he'd come to adore.

She clutched him tighter. "Thank God!"

"Thank Sir Lee. He made the deal, and Lucifer was forced to let Reggie go."

"What kind of deal?"

"All Sir Lee would say was that Lucifer won't ever bother any of us again."

Abigail shivered.

"Don't worry." Steele hugged her close. "Sir Lee knows what he's about. The man's as crafty as they come. In fact, he's assured me that he'll be able to convince Lord Byrnwyck to drop all the charges against your brother."

She pulled back, questions swirling in her gray-blue eyes.

Steele smiled. "I swear, that crafty old man knows everybody's secrets. I'm just glad he's on our side."

Abigail sagged against him, clearly overcome by relief. "I must repay him! I owe him so much!"

"Sir Lee has his own ideas about repayment. And he wants it from Reggie, not you."

Gently caressing her golden hair, Steele realized that it *was* as soft as gossamer. "Sir Lee thinks that Reggie needs a little structure and discipline in his life."

"The army?"

"The Sentinels. Gabriel and the Cutler brothers will whip him into shape and give him something useful to do with his time."

"And Reggie is all right with this?"

"Your brother's thanking God he's still alive and out of Lucifer's clutches. He's ready to pay any penance he can." Exhaling, Steele winced. "He feels terrible about what he did. He fears you might not be able to forgive him."

Abigail frowned. "I am furious as all sod with him . . . But he didn't mean us any harm. And he did try to help when he realized his mistake . . . and . . . waiting here, not knowing if he was dead or alive . . ." Her lovely face softened. "He's my brother. I *want* to forgive him."

Steele beamed. Rarely had he found a woman whose sense of fairness and integrity so clearly matched his own. "You are amazing. Do you have any idea how much I love you?" He kissed her, her lips so soft and welcoming, he sighed.

"I'll not stand for this!" Benbrook rose from his chair. "I'll not allow you to dally with this . . . this . . ."

Steele looked up, his tone edged in iron. "If you say one word to insult my future wife, I'll have you barred from this house forever."

"Wife?" Benbrook yelped.

"Yes." Steele patted his coat pocket where the special license was folded neatly inside. "There are certain benefits to being the solicitor-general, and getting legal documents signed quickly is one of them. I have the special license right here."

Steele released Abigail, setting his hands on her shoulders. He searched her gaze, still amazed that her feelings could truly match his. He'd had no doubts, but her words as she'd defended him to Benbrook . . . Never before had he experienced such devotion.

Never had he felt so loved and appreciated in all his life.

"My little lioness," he marveled.

Benbrook stepped forward. "Ah, Steele . . ."

Steele glanced at his father-in-law. "Leave."

"I will not make you my heir," Benbrook warned.

"I don't need you bloody money and I don't want it!"

Benbrook huffed. "And I told you from the beginning that you were only temporarily the boys' guardian."

Steele gripped Abigail's shoulders, needing her strength. Her gaze was filled with love and encouragement, and her faith in him as a father gave him the fortitude to turn to his father-in-law and say, "Please don't take Seth and Felix away. I'll do whatever it takes to make it work, but I don't . . . I don't want to lose them. I'll resign my post if necessary. I'll do whatever is the best for Seth and Felix."

Benbrook's eyes welled with tears. "I think . . . I think I might actually believe you."

Steele's throat grew thick with emotion. "I mean it. Every word. I love those boys with all my heart."

Benbrook's gaze drifted off, and slowly he sank into the chair. "I think . . . I think that it's time."

Steele tensed. "Time for what?"

Sighing, Benbrook rubbed his eyes. "I think it's time for me to stop being such a prig."

Steele felt his eyes widen.

"I don't know why I was making a fuss . . ." Benbrook grimaced. "Habit, I suppose." He sighed. "Deidre chose you, Steele, and she was right." His eyes grew shiny. "You seem to have a good head on your shoulders . . . and are a good sort. And the boys do adore Miss West." He licked his lips. "It's just . . . I'm not used to all this . . . *change*. It's difficult."

"It doesn't have to be. We can still be a family. Seth and Felix need more than just a father and mother. They need a grandfather, too."

Benbrook stared out the window. "By all accounts the boys are happy here . . . I suppose I could buy a house in London . . . to be close . . . I am getting on in years . . ."

Inhaling a deep breath, Benbrook squared his shoulders and then stood. "I'd best be on my way then and allow you to get on with it." He moved toward the door, but then stopped and turned. "Just so you know, I expect to be invited to the wedding."

Steele inclined his head. "Of course. You're family."

Benbrook's lips lifted into a small smile. "Well then." Nodding to himself, he strode from the room.

After he'd gone, Steele looked down at the woman he adored. "Will you marry me, Abigail, and make me the happiest man in the world?"

Sudden tears filled Abigail's eyes, and she looked so positively miserable, his heart ached for her. "What's wrong, darling?"

"I don't know that you'll want to marry me," Abigail's voice quaked as tears spilled down her cheeks. "When you hear what I have to tell you."

Shaking his head, he wiped her tears with his thumb. "I love you with all my heart. Whatever you have to tell me won't change my mind."

Squaring her shoulders, she swallowed. "I'm . . .

I'm . . . the woman in black . . . the one you know as the widow . . . from Charing Cross."

Steele felt his jaw drop and his eyes bulge.

Then the pieces fell into place like a flawlessly crafted puzzle. Reggie . . . The widow was searching for a man . . . who was involved with Lucifer Laverty. The widow's quick thinking and fighting skills . . . How Abigail had neatly handled Carlton, and then Devonshire last night. Steele's desperate hunger for the widow and the passion Abigail inspired in him.

Shaking his head, Steele chuckled.

Abigail sniffed. "What's so funny?"

"The bloody universe!" He hugged her close, inhaling the familiar scent of heather and woman he adored. He laughed out loud. "No matter which life I chose, no matter which way I turned, you were there for me. I had to be blind not to see it before!"

"See what?"

"You, my dear, are *meant* to be my wife."

She pulled back, her gaze searching his, her lovely face beset by doubt. "But I'm a wanton, improper—"

"You're my perfect match, in the day and the night. You're mine, and not a word you say will convince me otherwise."

"Truly?" Tears spilled down her cheeks, but she was smiling.

"Absolutely!"

Raising her palm to his cheek, she beamed through her tears. "I swear, I'll burn that widow's costume, the veil, the boots, all of it!"

"Please don't." His smile was wicked, his tone

filled with mischief. "At our wedding I want you to wear a white veil, but in the bedroom . . . the black might be nice, too."

Her eyes darkened with desire, igniting his hunger. Her breasts rose and fell with a breathy sigh. Arching her back, she leaned into him, pressing her soft body into his. She fit him perfectly. His body hardened.

Her lips lifted playfully. "I love you dearly, even though you are a *wicked*, *wicked* man."

Grinning, his lips claimed hers, making love to her mouth. Abigail was engulfed by a passion that demanded to be sated. He moved to her neck, nipping, teasing, tasting.

Closing her eyes, she sighed. "I do love you . . ."

"Jason," he murmured. "To you, it's Jason."

She smiled, feeling happy enough to float away on a cloud. "I love you, Jason. So very much."

"And I love the sound of my name on your lips, *Abigail*." His tongue traced the inside of her ear, and she quivered with yearning. "You are, by far, the most incredible woman I have ever known."

"I can get my veil . . ." Her voice was a husky purr.

He was on fire, his passion so great, his love so deep, he couldn't wait to claim her. He lifted her into his arms. "There's no need." Then he carried her into the bedchamber.

*Next month, don't miss these exciting new love stories only from* Avon Books

## How to Propose to a Prince by Kathryn Caskie
**An Avon Romantic Treasure**

Elizabeth Royle has dreamt she's going to marry a prince and now all she has to do is find him. The one thing Lizzie never counted on was that her prince might not actually be royalty. Lizzie knows there's something about Lord Whitevale and prince or no, she won't stop until they are where they belong—together forever.

## Making Over Mr. Right by Judi McCoy
**An Avon Contemporary Romance**

Zoë, the Muse of Beauty, has been banished from Mount Olympus and she's not going to let anyone stand in the way of her return, certainly not a reluctant businessman with a poor sense of style. But once she meets handsome Theodore Maragos, Zoë starts to wonder what's so bad about a life on Earth?

## The Return of the Rogue by Donna Fletcher
**An Avon Romance**

Cavan Sinclare returns home after being held captive by barbarians only to find himself married to a woman he once rejected. Frustrated with the fear he sees on his new bride's face, Cavan must find a way to gentle the harshness his difficult life has left him with. Will he and his new wife ever learn to trust . . . and to love?

## The Kiss by Sophia Nash
**An Avon Romance**

Georgiana Wilde has been in love with Quinn Fortesque for as long as she can remember. Unfortunately, he seems to harbor no feelings for her other than friendship. When Quinn is offered a second chance at enduring love, will he be ready to open his heart to the lady standing behind the veil of friendship . . . a true bride for all seasons?

REL 0208